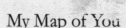

My Map of You

'Everything you want in a novel – warm, smart, moving, vivid and with so much heart to it, as well as fabulous, lovable characters. All in all, the perfect summer read' Stella Newman, author of *The Dish*

'A mysterious legacy, family secrets and slow-burning romance – *My Map of You*'s the next best thing to a one-way ticket to Zakynthos, the Greek island that makes a perfect setting' Fanny Blake, author and Books Editor of *Woman & Home*

'This gorgeous story has it all: a stunning setting, a secret that will break your heart and a romance that'll leave you weak at the knees. The perfect summer read' Lucy Robinson

'I've just finished reading *My Map of You*. I loved it. I'm an emotional wreck! Such an evocative book. An emotional rollercoaster of a ride with breathtaking scenery along the way. A real taste of Greece' Jo Thomas, author of *The Oyster Catcher*

'That's it – I'm moving to Zakynthos immediately! A perfect summer read of intrigue and escapism. I absolutely loved every minute' Lisa Dickenson, author of *The Twelve Dates of Christmas*

'An incredible debut novel, with a beautifully woven story about loss, hope, love, and finding where you belong. It is honestly one of the best books I have read in a long, long time – everything about it was captivating' Cressida McLaughlin, author of the *Primrose Terrace* novels

'A romantic and fulfilling story, beautifully told. Isabelle writes with a humorous eye, and the evocative poignancy of her writing brought Holly's story vividly to life. I was hooked from first word until final page and was left with tears on my face and an urgent need for a holiday!' Katie Marsh, author of *My Everything*

'I feel like I've had an ~~exciting~~ holiday on a Greek island with sun, sea, secrets and hot men. .... You'
Claire Frost, Boo.........

Isabelle Broom was born in Cambridge nine days before the 1980s began and studied Media Arts at the University of West London before starting a career first in local newspapers and then as a junior sub-editor at *heat* magazine. She travelled through Europe during her gap year and went to live on the Greek island of Zakynthos for an unforgettable and life-shaping six months after completing her degree. Since then, she has travelled to Canada, Sri Lanka, Sicily, New York, LA, the Canary Islands, Spain and lots more of Greece, but her wanderlust was reined in when she met Max, a fluffy little Bolognese puppy desperate for a home. When she's not writing novels set in far-flung locations, Isabelle spends her time being the Book Reviews Editor at *heat* magazine and walking her beloved dog round the parks of North London.

If you like pictures of dogs, chatter about books and very bad jokes, you can follow her on Twitter @Isabelle_Broom or find her on Facebook under Isabelle Broom Author.

My Map of You

ISABELLE BROOM

PENGUIN BOOKS

PENGUIN BOOKS

UK | USA | Canada | Ireland | Australia
India | New Zealand | South Africa

Penguin Books is part of the Penguin Random House group of companies
whose addresses can be found at global.penguinrandomhouse.com.

First published in Penguin Books 2016
001

Set in 12.5/14.75 pt Garamond MT Std
Typeset by Jouve (UK), Milton Keynes
Printed in Great Britain by Clays Ltd, St Ives plc

A CIP catalogue record for this book is available from the British Library

ISBN: 978–1–405–93303–2

www.greenpenguin.co.uk

MIX
Paper from
responsible sources
FSC® C018179

Penguin Random House is committed to a
sustainable future for our business, our readers
and our planet. This book is made from Forest
Stewardship Council® certified paper.

For Mum

If you shut up truth and bury it under the ground, it will but grow, and gather to itself such explosive power that the day it bursts through it will blow up everything in its way.

– Émile Zola

Prologue

The little girl brought her knees up to her chin and scrunched her bare toes into the damp sand. A wave scurried up the shore towards her, stopping just short of the bucket and spade that her mum and dad had bought her that morning. They were red to match her new swimming costume, which was decorated with white polka dots. Her sister had the same one, but hers was blue, which Jenny thought was silly – everyone knew that blue was a colour for boys, and boys were smelly. Red, on the other hand, was a colour worn by queens, a colour that could not be ignored. It made Jenny think of the postboxes back in Kent and the phone box on the corner of their road. It was her very favourite colour.

She stretched her legs out in front of her and giggled as the frothy edge of another determined wave tickled the soles of her feet. She could see her sister in the distance, her own yellow bucket clasped in one hand as she used the other to collect shells. It was a bit pointless, Jenny thought, because Mummy would never let those stinky things come back to England with them.

Thinking about home made Jenny feel a little sad. She didn't want to go back to where it rained every day and cows escaped from the back field and did big flat poos in the street – she wanted to stay here, on this island, where the sun sparkled like fairy dust on the surface of the sea and it was hot enough to eat ice cream for breakfast if you wanted to. As she stared across the ocean into the distance, Jenny realised that one of the islands rising up out of the water looked just like a turtle. A turtle island!

'Sandy!' she shouted, getting to her feet with excitement. 'Look over there!' By the time she reached her sister, Sandra had seen the island too, and was full of plans to get Mummy and Daddy to hire a boat and take them over there.

'I think this might be the best place in the whole world,' she told Jenny, who immediately gave her the very best strict face she could muster.

'Don't be so stupid,' she scolded.

A light breeze lifted all the strands of hair that had escaped Sandy's plait and blew them right across her face – Jenny laughed then, because her sister looked completely mad.

'This definitely is the best place in the world,' she told her, being sure to make her tone stern, like Mummy did when she was cross. 'When I grow up, I'm going to come and live here for ever.'

'Me too,' Sandy said, taking her hand. 'We can live here together.'

I

The letter arrived on a Wednesday.

It was May, and London was struggling to shrug off the stubborn remnants of a particularly wet April. Grey clouds lay scattered across the sky like shorn sheep's wool and tourists were forced to buy overpriced plastic ponchos from the gift shops littering the banks of the Thames. Everything pointed to it being an unremarkable day; one that would slip past unnoticed, like a blank page amidst an otherwise full notebook.

The letter, however, meant that this day was destined to stand triumphant right at the very top of the remarkable heap.

Holly waited while her eyes slowly adjusted to the darkness. She knew it was late, because the sound of the traffic on the road outside had lessened, with only the occasional bus or lorry causing the coat hangers in her wardrobe to tremble as it passed. Some would call this the witching hour – that time between 3 a.m. and 5 a.m., when the pure and unapologetic darkness swallowed its way across the cities, towns and villages, oozing into gaps and underneath doors.

But this was London, and the darkness was never total. As Holly lay silently against her pillows, she could see the dim light from the streetlamps snaking its pale fingers through the gap in the curtains and stretching across the duvet towards her. Rupert shifted next to her, causing the yellow pattern to bend and distort. He had turned his head towards her and she could see the outline of his full lips and the dark pattern of his hair where it was stuck haphazardly to his forehead.

He hadn't shown up at her flat until well past midnight, leaning on the buzzer and singing nonsense into the intercom. He'd been out drinking with his mates from the office again, but Holly didn't mind. In fact, she had been glad of the distraction as he staggered up the stairs and planted a clumsy wet kiss in the vicinity of her mouth. She had known since she got home from work that sleep was not something she was going to be able to do tonight.

Holly had suffered from insomnia on and off for years, ever since her late teens, and she'd come to think of it as a creature, a troll-like form that sat hunched over and cross-legged on her chest, dripping its icy fingers through her skin and gripping her heart. It was anxiety that caused the insomnia, and the insomnia that fed the anxiety – a seemingly never-ending pattern of misery. Throwing it off had been tough the first time around, and now the creature was well and truly back. Holly could feel herself stiffening with frustration, and the duvet suddenly felt heavy and suffocating against her skin.

Rupert had started to drool slightly and a bubble of spit was inflating and deflating in the corner of his open mouth. Holly could smell the telltale metallic scent of stale alcohol on his breath, and she turned to face away from him, to where her bag sat on the floor; the bag that contained the letter.

The metaphorical weight of that letter and what it contained was so great that Holly half expected it to crack the floorboards beneath the rug, creating a sinkhole in the middle of Hackney and dragging her and Rupert down into the sewers below. She could see the corner of the envelope poking out, a dull grey in the dark bedroom, and thought how innocuous it had looked when she had first come across it, nestled between a gas bill and a flyer advertising cheap pizzas. It was one of those envelopes with a clear plastic window in the front, the sort used by banks and hospitals, and her name and address had been clearly typed on the letter inside. She hadn't noticed the foreign postmark until after she'd opened it.

After reading the two letters and examining the photo inside, Holly had simply sat for a long time, staring at a hole that had started to form on the throw covering the old sofa. She'd knitted it herself a few years ago, but it had been a long time since she'd picked up her needles, or indeed any of her sewing equipment. But in that moment, she was struck with a sudden urge to find it all. Chucking the contents of the envelope down on the coffee table, she'd rooted through the boxes under her bed until she found the tools she needed to mend the hole.

'Just concentrate on this,' she told herself. 'Deal with the letter later.'

And it had worked, for a time. Holly was nothing if not resourceful when it came to distracting herself from the thoughts in her head. She'd managed to fill her entire evening with odd jobs, and had only just run out of ideas when Rupert arrived at the door. Relishing the idea of another few hours of blissful procrastination, Holly had welcomed him in a far more energetic manner than usual and a thrilled Rupert had been more than happy to comply – albeit with less finesse than usual – with her advances. Alas, her drunken and spent boyfriend was never going to stay awake very long, so now Holly found herself in bed, unable to sleep and positively itching with anxiety.

Taking a deep breath, she closed her eyes and tried to focus her thoughts on something else – anything else – but the letter immediately swam into view.

Dear Holly,

You won't remember me, but I think about you every day. I was there the day you were born . . .

'No,' she said aloud, the sound making her jump in the silent room. Rupert muttered something unintelligible, popping his bubble of drool as he stirred on the pillow. Holly held her breath, willing him not to wake up. He would want to know why she was awake, why her cheeks were wet with tears, and she wasn't ready to have any answers for him.

She waited for his breathing to return to an even rhythm before snaking an arm out from under the covers and picking up her mobile phone from the bedside table. It was 4.45 a.m. She would wait until 5.30 a.m., then get up and go for a run. Yes, a run would chase away the Insomnia Troll and focus her mind elsewhere. Comforted slightly by her plan, Holly relaxed enough to let her eyes droop and finally, miraculously, sleep snuck in and stole her away.

The dream always started the same way: with fear.

She knew that she had to open the door and cross the threshold, but she also knew that if she did then her old, familiar life would be over. She would never be able to forget the scene that lay beyond that door, yet she could never stop her dream-self from venturing forward. Just as her hand was on the handle, dread piled up like butts in an ashtray in the back of her throat, the scene swirled and dappled. All at once, the ocean was in front of her, and there was a distant shape on the horizon . . .

A few hours later, Holly stood at the window in her small front room and stared across to where an ominous dark cloud was creeping its way towards the centre of the city. The May sunshine was fighting a losing battle against a determinedly dreary spring, and everything looked tinged with grey. Her clammy fingers were starting to dismantle the envelope clutched in her hands. From somewhere behind her in the depths of the flat, she could hear Rupert belting out a rendition of a Springsteen song as he took a shower. Usually it would bring a smile to her face, but not this morning.

If you're reading this letter now, I'm sorry to say that I have passed away . . .

Holly shook her head. She'd only read the letter through once, but the words had apparently plunged deep roots into her subconscious. She closed her eyes, but they were still there, blazing away as if a child had taken a sparkler to a dark November night and written the words into the blackness.

The water stopped running in the bathroom and Holly heard Rupert blowing his nose. As if on cue, the heavens opened on the other side of the glass and rain pelted the window. She pressed her nose against it, watching in silence as her breath created a kidney-shaped crescent of condensation.

'Darling?' Rupert was standing in the hallway near the bedroom. 'You'd better get a wriggle on – it's almost eight.'

Why had she been sent this letter now, when it was too bloody late?

'Coming, babe,' she trilled, trying her best to sound normal. Slipping the envelope into her bag out of sight, she padded quickly into the bedroom and gave her boyfriend the most convincing smile she could muster.

'It's raining again,' she told him, slipping off her robe and reaching for a pencil skirt.

'We should get away – go somewhere sunny,' Rupert said, pausing as he passed to give her waist an affectionate squeeze. 'The boys were talking about Ibiza last night – the clubs there are supposed to be amazing.'

'Mmm-hmm,' she murmured, tucking in her blouse. Privately, she could think of nothing worse than a week of clubbing in the Balearics – she was twenty-nine, not nineteen.

'You look so sexy in that skirt,' Rupert told her now. He was watching her in the mirror as he applied wax to his floppy, dark blonde hair. Holly loved the effect she had on him. Even after a year, she only had to give him a slight look and he was tugging off her clothes. Their eyes met in the mirror and she smiled at him. When he looked at her like he was now, with his eyelids drooping and his lips parted, Holly still felt nervous. It was exciting that she could have this power over him, but the thought of really letting herself go and feeling what he was clearly feeling . . . Well, that scared her.

Rupert tossed his tie on the bed and strode across to her.

'Sod the nine a.m. breakfast meeting,' he grunted, burying his face in her neck. Gathering up her dark curls in one hand, he expertly undid her zip with the other. Holly stiffened for a second, then turned her head to kiss him, letting out an obedient yelp of pleasure as he bent her over the end of the bed. It was all over in minutes.

'Oh God, I really have to go,' he told her, buttoning up. He looked flushed and happy, and Holly rearranged his hair for him as he did up his blazer.

'See you tonight, sexy,' he told her, and then he was gone.

The flat rang with silence for a few minutes while Holly tried her best to gather her thoughts. Rupert's energetic display of passion had helped, but now the letter was once again looming on the edge of her consciousness, demanding attention like a stroppy toddler.

Slowly, reluctantly, Holly let herself be led back towards her bag and felt inside for the envelope. Ignoring the folded paper of the two letters, she took out the photograph and waited for her heart to lurch down into her stomach.

The photo was of a house, small and square and built from cream stone, with curved terracotta tiles on the roof and a balcony surrounded by a thick wooden trellis. But it wasn't the house that alarmed her; it was the fact that it looked exactly the same as a model that had belonged to her mother. Jenny Wright had never been a fan of holding on to stuff unless it was absolutely necessary, but she'd held on to the little model of that house right until the end. Looking at the photo of it now made Holly feel haunted, as if she'd walked through a ghost.

She was still gazing at the photo a few minutes later when her phone beeped. It was Aliana, informing her cheerfully that she was, as usual, running late for work, and could Holly cover for her?

As she tapped back a 'yes', Holly realised that she was probably going to be late herself if she didn't get a move on. Promising herself that she'd deal with the contents of the letter at lunchtime, she scurried around collecting her stuff, then headed out and slammed the front door behind her.

2

Like so many people carving out a life for themselves in the UK's capital, Holly had ended up in London rather than actually choosing to live there. It was the last place her mum had moved the two of them to, and the only real place that Holly could describe as home, given the years she'd been there. It had never felt like much of a home, however. Not in the way Holly took the word 'home' to mean, anyway. Sometimes she would just stop in her tracks as scores of people hurried past, wondering what the hell she was doing there. She hated hustle and bustle and rubbish and rudeness, yet here she was.

Holly worked in Camden at the head offices of a large online clothing retailer called Flash. Along with a team of around fifteen others, it was her job to write enticing product descriptions and then upload them to the website. While it wasn't quite as creative as Holly would have liked, she found the work undemanding and occasionally even enjoyable. The money was average and the benefits worse, but Holly still felt lucky to have the job, given her circumstances.

The worst thing about working at Flash was undoubtedly her line manager, Fiona, who was as humourless and dry as a box of stale cornflakes. She knew it was a total cliché to have a boss who was a bitch, but there it was.

As Holly slid into her seat just as the clock reached

9.30 a.m., an email pinged up from Fiona demanding that she redo all the copy for the latest line of palazzo pants. Great.

'What's with the face?' Aliana hissed ten minutes later, causing Holly to almost leap out of her chair in fright.

'Where the hell did you come from?' she shot back, mopping up the tea she'd just spilled all over the desk.

'The floor,' Aliana replied, laughing. 'I wasn't about to let the old dragon see that I was late, was I?'

Aliana felt the same way about Fiona as Holly did.

'Who was late?'

Fiona had popped up out of nowhere like a joyless jack-in-the-box.

'Nobody.' Aliana smiled sweetly.

'Why is your computer off?' countered Fiona, her nostrils flaring. She had her hair pulled back in a very severe bun today and there was a line around the edges of her face where she hadn't blended her foundation properly.

'It crashed.' Aliana was still smiling like something the Aardman animators would mould out of clay.

Fiona pulled a face. 'You can make up the extra fifteen minutes at lunchtime,' she snapped, before stalking away back to her office.

'I wish she'd find herself a boyfriend already,' Aliana groaned, sticking her tongue out at Fiona's departing back. 'I've never met someone so uptight in my whole life.'

Holly nodded. 'She is a bit . . . stiff. Maybe she just needs a good night out.'

'Well, I'm not taking her!' exclaimed Aliana, mistyping her login password for the third time in a row then swearing as the system promptly locked her out.

Holly stared at the trousers on her screen: they were a dark blue paisley print with a cinched waist and a flattering, wide-cut leg. Holly admired the tailoring, wondering for the millionth time since she'd started working at Flash why she no longer made her own clothes. It had been the one thing, during those terrible, dark years, to keep her sane. Nothing else had made her quite as happy since. Not even Ru—

'So, how's that sexy man of yours?' Aliana cut in. She was on hold to the IT service desk and had the patience of a wasp.

'He's great.' Holly thawed a little. 'He brought me a robe back from Japan. It's silk and embroidered with all these orchids and—'

'Did it cost a bomb?' Aliana interrupted. 'I bet it did.'

While Holly was fully aware that Rupert had a good job – he was a corporate accountant – and that he was very comfortably off, it still grated a bit when Aliana equated all his positive attributes as being to do with money. Having grown up with very little herself, and certainly no luxuries, Holly didn't ever take money for granted and found herself agonising over even the smallest purchase. Aliana would blithely burn a large hole in her credit card during a lunchtime visit to the clothing shops on Camden High Street, while Holly, by comparison, would take three weeks to decide if she really wanted those winter boots enough to shell out £40. It had taken her a while to get used to Rupert's wealth, and while she pretended to love it when he took her to expensive restaurants or presented her with an obscenely large bouquet of flowers, inside it made her itch with discomfort.

'I didn't ask,' she sniffed. 'I assume it was an early birth-day present.'

'Oh yeah,' Aliana looked at her sideways. 'The big three-o. How are you feeling about it? I'm bloody glad that I've still got five years to go. I mean, no offence, but I definitely want to be married by the time I'm thirty.'

'None taken,' lied Holly. 'And I'm not all that bothered, to be honest. It's only another birthday just like any other. I don't want a fuss made.'

'Oh, but Rupert will definitely want to make a big fuss,' said Aliana, failing to keep the envy out of her voice. 'He'll probably take you on a skiing trip to Verbier – or buy you a diamond ring.'

At this, Holly actually laughed.

'What? I bet he bloody does now and you'll have to eat your words,' Aliana continued, breaking off for a moment to sweet-talk the guy on the other end of the phone. Once logged in, she ignored her overflowing inbox and opened Facebook.

'Wow. I'm sorry, Hols, but your boyfriend is seri-ously fit.'

Holly looked across at the photos on Aliana's screen. They were of Rupert, taken while he was on his recent work trip to Japan. With his pale blue shirtsleeves rolled up and a lopsided, slightly tipsy smile on his face, he did look very handsome.

'Yeah, I know,' she smiled.

'If you ever, you know, get sick of him or anythi— OW!' The hole puncher that Holly had lobbed across the desk bounced off Aliana's arm and hit the carpet.

*

In the end, Holly had to abandon her plan to deal with the letter at lunchtime, because Aliana dragged her to the market to get a falafel wrap ('They are so good, babe. It's like having an orgasm in your mouth!') and then to the nail bar. Holly resisted the temptation to join her. She had made her lunch the night before and brought it to work with her. The falafel wraps might look delicious and smell divine, but why would you spend £4.50 on one when you could build your own tuna and mayonnaise sandwiches for a fraction of the price?

The morning's sheeting rain had blessedly passed, but the sky remained heavy with thick clouds the colour of paving slabs. Camden did its best to inject some colour into proceedings, boasting extravagantly decorated stalls and clusters of punks with neon-bright Mohicans. Holly wandered past them all as if in a daze, letting her friend fill the silence with an uninterrupted patter of excited babble.

Having conveniently forgotten that she had been told to make up the lost time from her tardiness that morning, Aliana was summoned into Fiona's office the minute they got back and rewarded with the mind-numbing task of deleting all the old stock off the website.

While she felt for her friend, Holly was glad of the peace and quiet. She always worked far better when she could really get into a zone and concentrate. Instead of homing in on fabrics and fastenings, however, she found herself thinking about her mother again.

Back in the days of Holly's early childhood, before Jenny Wright had started turning to the bottle to get her through each day, she used to make up bedtime stories for

15

Holly to help her fall asleep – clearly something she had always struggled with, even as a very young girl. One of these stories had been about a fairy called Hope, who her mum described as having blonde hair plaited into pigtails and a blue dress with red petticoats underneath. When Hope danced, her skirts would swirl together – and sometimes she spun so fast that her dress looked purple. Holly had always loved that idea, because her favourite colour was purple – she was even wearing it today.

Whenever Holly was having a particularly tough day, or when she found herself in a situation that frightened her, she still conjured up Hope. She would let her dance, just on the very edge of her mind, watching as she spun round, faster and faster. As Holly sat at her desk now, gazing at her screen but seeing only her past, she felt Hope's presence as keenly as she had all those years ago, back when she had no idea just how scary life could become.

'Your phone's ringing.' Aliana had wheeled across and actually nudged her. Flustered, Holly snatched up her mobile; dimly aware as she did so of Hope dissolving into a smudge of colour.

'Hi, darling!' It was Rupert. He always called her at around this time, when the sleep-inducing effects of his lunchtime drink had kicked in. She felt sorry for him, in a way, having to do so many meetings with clients that expected to be entertained. But then, he did seem to enjoy himself.

'You sound worn out,' Holly told him sympathetically, as she always did.

'Had a few at lunchtime,' he admitted. 'In fact, the boys

16

and I were just discussing having a few more after we're done here. Can we count you in?'

Drinking with the boys meant that Rupert would be drinking a lot, and staying out very late, which in turn meant that Holly would probably have to put off doing anything about the contents of that envelope for another whole day.

'Yes,' she told him, suddenly excited. 'Will you be at the usual place?'

'Oh, I should think so . . .' Someone on Rupert's end of the line was distracting him. 'I'll text you if we move. See you later, sexy.'

'You going out later, then?' Aliana didn't even pretend she hadn't been eavesdropping.

Holly nodded.

'I don't have any plans . . .'

'Oh, for God's sake, stop making that face,' Holly chided. 'You can come too.'

With Aliana on board, the chances of her making it home before midnight had now gone from slim to non-existent. A wave of relief flooded over her, taking with it the melancholy thoughts that had been dogging her all day. Refreshed and defiant, she turned back to her screen and found that inspiration had mercifully made a return.

3

It had taken Holly many years and a fair few failed attempts before she realised that the whole 'relationship' thing was just a big game. All you had to do was work out what the other person wanted, and then provide it for them. Simple.

She had decided that she wanted to provide Rupert with whatever he wanted about five minutes after they first met each other. He'd bumped into her in a bar – literally – and spilled red wine down her dress, prompting a mortified apology and a promise to take her shopping for a new dress the very next day to make up for it. When they met after lunch outside Bond Street station, Rupert had immediately whisked her into one designer boutique after another, urging her to try on dresses that cost hundreds of pounds.

For Holly, who had spent her teens and twenties making her own clothes from scraps of material and second-hand shop bargains, the afternoon had felt like a corny romcom where she was the star. She had never been materialistic, but letting this confident man lead her from rail to rail and wave aside her protests at how much everything cost felt utterly decadent, and totally unlike anything she had experienced before. Hours later, as they clinked their Champagne flutes and gazed out over London from the window of Paramount bar at the top of Centre Point,

Holly looked down at her brand-new dress boasting a Burberry label and felt, for the first time in a long while, like she was on a path that was heading in the right direction.

When Rupert had gently taken the glass from her hand and placed it on the table, running his fingers down the side of her face before leaning across to kiss her, Holly had told herself that she must not, under any circumstances, do anything to scare this man off. In that moment, the all-new Holly burst into bloom, baptised by Champagne bubbles and the taste of Rupert's kiss.

Making him happy was so straightforward at first: she simply listened. He enjoyed talking about himself and she enjoyed hearing all about his life. In time, he opened up about his upbringing (a sprawling house in the Kent countryside with two fairly conservative parents and one older brother), his job (an accountant in a large City firm) and even his past relationships (Franny, his university girlfriend and first love, who broke his heart when she went off travelling and fell in love with an Aussie surfer), followed by a series of girls he'd met through contacts at work. Rupert's disparaging descriptions of these past conquests included 'utterly daft', 'bottom-numbingly dull' and 'a total bloody stalker'.

It didn't take more than a few dates for Holly to realise that Rupert wasn't a fan of overly keen girls, so she'd made very sure that she could never fall under that label – even waiting an agonising three days to reply to text messages and pretending not to be free for half the dates she was invited on. For some reason, making herself unavailable and refusing to chase Rupert had made her utterly irresistible to him. She was vaguely aware that all the game-playing probably wasn't the healthiest approach, but from what she had read in magazines and online about relationships, everyone was at it. Pretending to be something she wasn't was a skill that Holly had perfected many years ago.

Of course, Rupert eventually did get around to asking her about her own upbringing (she told him her parents died in a car crash), job (she'd been honest about that), and her past relationships (she'd had a few boyfriends, but had never been in love). Holly was astute enough to realise that a man with an ego as endearingly transparent as Rupert's would adore the idea that he might be her first love. And it wasn't a complete fib, anyway, because she never had been in love before she met him. When he'd plucked up the courage to admit that he'd fallen for her about six months after they met, she'd had no qualms about saying those three little words back to him. Okay, so there hadn't been any fireworks or a eureka moment when she realised she was in love, but in that moment she believed that she must be. Rupert was as good a candidate as she was ever likely to find for the position of first love.

In the end they were twenty minutes late to meet everyone that evening because Aliana had insisted on taking off all her make-up and reapplying it from scratch – a task that proved tricky given the large acrylic nails she'd had attached during their lunch hour.

'Darling, there you are,' Rupert sprang off his stool as she and Aliana made their way through the crowded bar to where he and his four companions had managed to snag a table. Pulling her into a hug, he slid a casual hand across her rear and gave it a small squeeze. 'I've been thinking about this morning all day,' he whispered. 'I can't wait to get you home later . . .'

Holly gave him a quick kiss on the cheek in response. 'You remember Aliana,' she said, turning and putting her arm round her friend. Rupert smiled broadly and leaned forward to give her a kiss.

'Aliana, so good to see you! It's been ages, hasn't it? But then Holly does like to keep me all to herself.'

'Can't say I blame her.' Aliana returned his kiss enthusiastically, a flirty giggle escaping her painted pink lips. Holly did her best not to roll her eyes, instead stepping around the two of them to greet Rupert's friends.

Toby was the first to get up, dwarfing her with his vast, bear-like frame and yanking her against his chest for a hug, while at the same time burying her face in one of his rather sodden armpits. 'Holly! You're looking well. Love the purple – suits you.'

Running her hands across her skirt self-consciously, Holly smiled up at him. Despite the whiffy pits, she had a bit of a soft spot for Toby, who was sweet, friendly and unashamedly loud. His girlfriend, however, was a drier cracker to swallow.

'Penelope, how are you?'

Toby's girlfriend regarded her sternly over the top of her wine glass. The first time Holly had been introduced to Penelope, she was convinced that she'd managed to offend her in some way, but Rupert was quick to reassure her that it was fine, and that his best mate's girlfriend just had a 'funny way' about her.

'As well as can be expected, given that this bar seems to have turned into a zoo,' Penelope told her. She didn't bother to get out of her seat, but she did instruct Toby to get an empty glass from the bar so that Holly could share her bottle of Pinot Grigio.

The other couple at the table, Clemmie and Boris, didn't get up either, but both greeted her with warm smiles. Holly had struggled for years to feel accepted by strangers, and with this crowd she always found herself slipping into another version of herself – one that was more confident and boisterous than the real Holly.

'Round of shots?' suggested Rupert, who had finally disentangled himself from Aliana. This elicited a cheer from the table – and from Holly, who for once actually relished the idea of the oblivion that enough alcohol would bring.

'So, Holly, have you thought about what you're going to do for your birthday?' Clemmie asked. 'I mean, it is the big three-o, isn't it?'

'Oh God, don't remind me,' groaned Holly.

'I think we should all get really dressed up, you know, make a real effort, and go somewhere really nice,' Clemmie continued, gently elbowing Penelope into nodding along in agreement.

Clemmie – who was wearing a jazzy monochrome jumpsuit with bright orange stilettos – always looked dressed up as far as Holly was concerned. But it was nice that they obviously wanted to include her.

'You girls are the ones who know all the best places,' she told them, hoping the flattery would go down well. 'I don't have the first clue.'

'There's that new bar near Spitalfields Market,' Boris suggested. 'You need a secret password to get in, or some silly crap like that, but I take clients there all the time so I'm sure I can sort it out.'

'When is your birthday again?' asked Penelope. She didn't seem as excited as the others, but then nothing ever really seemed to excite her.

'It's the thirtieth of June,' said Rupert, arriving back with a tray of tequilas. Holly did a quick count and realised he'd bought them two each. She could almost hear her liver weeping in protest.

'Wow, you're good,' Penelope deadpanned. 'Toby never remembers mine, even after five years.'

'Nonsense!' Toby had turned an unflattering shade of puce.

'It's easy to remember, because it was the day we first met,' Rupert told them as he passed round the salt.

Holly flushed with pleasure and smiled across at him. She couldn't believe they'd been together for almost a year – a whole twelve months and she hadn't done anything to screw it up.

Clemmie sniffed at her first tequila and pulled a face. With her blonde hair set in curls around her face, she looked like an angry Cupid.

Boris put an arm around his girlfriend's shoulders and rubbed his nose against her cheek. Holly had never seen Clemmie be particularly affectionate towards Boris, but that didn't seem to deter him in the slightest. She and Rupert weren't really known for their PDAs either, but he did get touchy-feely after a few drinks.

Aliana hadn't waited for the others and was now

chewing on a slice of lemon, her eyes watering with the effort. Catching Rupert's eye across the table and winking, Holly lifted her glass. 'Cheers!'

After another three tequilas, two large glasses of white wine and just a handful of olives for dinner, Holly was somewhat bewildered to find herself sitting in a locked cubicle in the ladies' toilet with the two letters spread across her lap. This wasn't what was supposed to have happened: the alcohol was supposed to have distracted her, taken her mind off the unwelcome revelations. In reality, all it had done was strip away her remaining vestiges of self-control and propel her – via the edges of several tables on the way – in here away from the prying eyes of her friends.

She wasn't ready to absorb these letters herself, let alone try to explain them to Rupert. Leaving the personal one safely folded, Holly took out the typed letter for the second time and gave in to the need that had been burning a hole in her brain all day long.

Dear Miss Wright,

I am writing to you from the offices of Olympus Solicitors in Zakynthos. My client, a Miss Sandra Wright, instructed me to forward you the enclosed in the event of her death. I am sorry to inform you now that she has passed away.

Holly searched inside herself for an emotion, but there was nothing but numbness. This Sandra woman shared her name, had apparently been her relative – but she wasn't someone Holly had ever met. She continued reading.

Miss Wright assured us that everything you need to know is
included in her letter to you, but we are at liberty to inform you
that her house here in Zakynthos, along with its contents, now
belongs to you. If you have any further questions, please do not
hesitate to contact us.

We are sorry again for your loss.

Kind regards,
Takis Boulos

A house? Her own house? Presumably the one that was in the photo – the very same house that her mother had kept an ornament of her whole life, which Holly had seen so many times as she grew up. She'd just unfolded the other letter, the one from Sandra herself, when there was a loud bang on the door.

'Holly, are you in there?'

She could see the pointy toes of Aliana's patent heels under the bottom of the door.

'Won't be a minute,' she replied, grumbling to herself as she stuffed away the letters and needlessly yanked the flush.

'You've been gone ages.' Aliana's tone was accusatory as she watched Holly cross to the bank of basins.

'I just had a funny turn,' she lied. 'Probably the tequila.'

Aliana joined her and took out her lipstick.

'Clemmie is so sweet,' she said, trying to meet Holly's eyes in the mirror. 'She said I should come out with you all next month, you know, for your birthday.'

Holly was already sick of her birthday and it was over a month away. What she really wanted was a quiet night in with Rupert, or maybe dinner in the local pub. Just something simple. But she knew Rupert would use it as an excuse to throw a big party, and there wasn't much point trying to dissuade him once he'd got the bit between his teeth.

'You should,' she said simply, drowning out Aliana's reply by sticking her hands under the dryer. She was suddenly hit by a wave of exhaustion. When she had managed to fall asleep the previous night, it had only been for a few hours before the alarm went off. There were dark circles forming under her eyes and she'd long ago rubbed off her mascara.

'You look awful,' Aliana told her, apparently reading her mind.

Holly managed a sheepish smile. 'Thanks. Who needs enemies with friends like you?'

Both girls giggled and the tension eased. Aliana was clearly very drunk. There was a glazed look in her eyes and a spot of colour high on each cheek. Like Holly, she was olive-skinned and her hair was dark. But unlike Holly's natural curls, Aliana's hair was so straight that it looked like she ironed it every morning. It also hung much further down her back, and she'd boasted several times that she'd been able to sit on it as a child. Petite and with just the right amount of curves, Aliana had the sort of figure that turned the heads of both men and women, but she was endearingly unaware of the effect she could have. In the three years that Holly had known her, she'd only ever dated utterly vile men – a fact that everyone who knew her found baffling. Outwardly, she exuded the sort of natural confidence that Holly could only play-act, but she suspected that her friend wasn't quite as together as she liked to make out. Either that, or she simply had the worst taste in men ever.

Standing there in the bathroom, Holly found herself unexpectedly overcome with affection for Aliana, and uncharacteristically linked an arm through hers as they made their way back to the table. The clock on the wall was edging close to 11 p.m., but that wasn't enough to deter Rupert.

'Another bottle, ladies?' he asked, lifting the empty one out of the ice bucket. Holly sighed. 'Oh, go on then.'

4

'Darling, wake up.'

Holly groaned. The second bottle of wine had been a very bad idea.

'Come on, Hols, there's something we need to talk about.'

She opened her eyes to see the blurry outline of Rupert, bending over her with what she could smell was a cup of coffee in his hand. Her stomach lurched in protest.

'I'm up.' She forced out a smile and inched backwards into a sitting position. It was only then that she saw the look on his face. 'What's the matter?'

Looking slightly guilty, Rupert put his hand into the pocket of his dressing gown and produced the envelope that she'd last seen crumpled in the bottom of her bag.

There was a horrible silence.

'I was going to tell you about it,' she said, not meeting his eyes. 'I just didn't want everyone to know, that's all.'

Rupert pulled a face that made him resemble a wounded baby seal. Holly, feeling her irritation begin to prickle, took a deep breath. 'I really was going to tell you,' she repeated.

'So tell me.' Rupert was now sitting on the edge of the bed, his weight trapping her inside the duvet. Holly could feel agitation building inside her as he sipped his coffee and waited. She knew she was being ridiculous. After all, this was her dear, sweet Rupert – all he wanted was for her to be honest. It was just that when it came to her family history, she had spun such a tapestry of fantasy she was afraid that pulling at any of the threads would unravel the perfect image she'd created so carefully.

'It turns out that I had an aunt,' she managed. 'One that I had never met.' She assumed Rupert would interrupt her and ask why, but he didn't. She continued, 'This aunt, she lived in a place called Zakynthos, which is apparently a Greek island. And, well, she's left me her house there.'

Rupert raised an eyebrow.

'So, I guess I'm a home owner now.' She tried a laugh, but it came out more like a rasping cough. Rupert flinched and put down his mug.

'So, that's all it is? The big secret you couldn't tell the gang last night?'

Holly forced a smile to hide her irritation at his use of the word 'gang'. She really wanted to get up, but the uneasiness between them was making her feel uncomfortable at the idea of him seeing her naked. They'd had drunk, clumsy sex after getting back to his flat last night, and Holly could see her discarded knickers crumpled on the floor by the doorway.

'It was a bit of a shock, that's all,' she told him. 'I wasn't really ready to tell anyone except you.'

She'd meant this to sound like a compliment, and it seemed to do the trick. Rupert's expression thawed a little and he moved closer to her, taking one of her hands in both of his.

'I understand, Hols. It's no big deal that you didn't tell

me, but it is a big deal that you got a house. What a shame that the Greek economy has been so unstable lately. It might be ages before you can get a good price for it.'

Holly, who had been about to take a sip of her own, rapidly cooling coffee, almost choked. Not once had it even occurred to her that she might sell the house, the one thing she had left of her real family – even if that family had chosen not to make contact before it was too late.

'I thought I'd fly over there,' she told him now. She hadn't even realised that was her plan until she said it out loud, but there it was. 'I need to go over to Zakynthos, to take a look. I'd like to see the house.'

'I can't take any time off at the moment.' Rupert was frowning at her. 'I have a deal coming up that needs to be handled with a lot of sensitivity.'

'I could just go on my own?' It came out as an almost whisper. The thought of turning up to poke around her dead aunt's house with Rupert in tow made her feel even sicker than the idea of facing it alone. What if there was something incriminating in there about her mum? Or what if her aunt had been one of those weird hoarders and had lived underneath teetering stacks of decade-old newspapers and unmentionable filth? She pulled the duvet up to her chin.

'Well, only if you're sure . . .' Rupert squeezed her hand again. 'I really want to be there for you. Are you sure it can't wait a month or so?'

Holly shook her head.

'Well, okay then.' Rupert finally stood up. 'I'm off to hit the shower. You'd better get a wriggle on too. I left the paracetamol on the breakfast bar.'

She waited until the bathroom door was shut before scuttling over to the door, scooping up her knickers from the floor and shoving them into her bag. There was a pile of clean towels in the hallway, and Holly wrapped one around herself as she made her way into the kitchen.

Rupert was so perfect in some ways, she thought, helping herself to a couple of the painkillers that he'd so thoughtfully left out. But then he could be an idiot as well. Did he not see that the big news was not that an aunt had left her a house, but that she had an aunt at all?

She filled the kettle and opened the fridge door, then shut it again and sat down on one of Rupert's uncomfortable chrome bar stools. It took her a few minutes to realise that she was angry. She'd been so shocked to be confronted by Rupert that she hadn't taken time to consider the fact that he'd been snooping through her bag. To Holly, privacy was the most sacred thing in the world. She couldn't believe that Rupert had so openly abused her trust like this. Everything in her gut was telling her to march into the bathroom and yell at him, but that was what the old Holly would have done. She'd left that Holly behind a long time ago. If Rupert were to see the real her, she wouldn't have to worry about him looking in her bag any more, because he most likely wouldn't be in her life any more, simple as that. If he thought that rifling through her stuff was acceptable, then it was probably her own fault. She let him take charge in every other aspect of their relationship, so why would he think this was any different?

Filling a glass with water from the tap, Holly forced herself to gulp it down and take a series of long, deep breaths. The red mist cleared, and reason stepped in. He was probably just looking for painkillers and came across the envelope by accident. She'd been drunk when they got in – maybe she'd knocked the bag over and the letters fell out? He was just trying to be nice and put them back, when curiosity got the better of him.

She realised she was gritting her teeth when Rupert appeared behind her, his chest wet from the shower, and kissed her lightly on the cheek.

'I've got to have dinner with the folks tonight,' he said, all talk of her aunt and the house in Greece apparently forgotten. 'My brother's over from Dubai and they want to treat us.'

'That sounds nice.' Holly was amazed that it didn't come out as a growl. She was still only wearing a towel.

'I'd invite you,' he added, rubbing his legs dry then moving the towel up to his hair. 'But I think it's just a family thing.'

Holly had only been introduced to Mr and Mrs Farlington-Clark once in the year that she'd known Rupert and it hadn't gone well. They'd met for lunch at a French restaurant on the Strand and Holly had somehow managed to flick her snail entrée across the table and down the front of Rupert's mum's silk blouse. She wasn't surprised not to be invited out for round two.

'That's okay.' She stepped around him and headed towards the bathroom. 'I should book some flights anyway.'

'You want to go to Greece? In a week's time?'

Holly forced her legs not to tremble under the weight

of Fiona's scowl. She'd clearly been out drinking the night before as well, because she was in an even worse mood than usual.

'It's a family matter,' Holly told her. That's what people said in these situations, wasn't it?

Fiona glared at her for what felt like a full ten minutes, before finally nodding with irritation. 'Fine,' she snapped. 'Log your holiday request on the system and I'll approve it. But in future, do try to give me a bit more warning.'

Holly nodded as she inched backwards across the horrible beige carpet, promising to leave an extremely detailed list of dos and don'ts for her temporary replacement. Despite the frostiness she'd just created between herself and her boss, she felt elated. It felt good getting her own way, even on a small thing like this.

Aliana, who was still at the blessed stage of her mid-twenties where hangovers could be cured with a single pint of water and three hours' sleep, had bounced into work that morning like a chirpy little imp. She was predictably over the moon when Holly filled her in on the reason for her meeting with Fiona.

'A house in Greece? That's bloody amazing!'

Holly smiled. 'I suppose it is.'

'Which island did you say it was again?' Aliana was poised with her hands over her keyboard.

'Zakynthos,' Holly told her. 'I think it's an Ionian isla—'

'You mean Zante?' Aliana actually shrieked the last word. Dave with the hairy ears from the ads department, who happened to be passing at that moment, almost spilled his tea in fright. 'Zante is, like, one of *the* biggest

33

party islands in Greece,' she babbled. 'I went there the year I finished uni – it was absolutely crazy!'

'Are you sure?' Holly pulled a face. That didn't sound like a place where an old lady would choose to live. Perhaps her aunt had been a crazy party animal? She grinned at the thought of a doddery old dear in a floral smock throwing some shapes on the dance floor – but then who said she'd been old? Holly's smile drooped like a sad dandelion as she remembered that her mum had only been thirty-eight when she died. Her aunt could have been the younger sister.

As she waited for Aliana to look up photos of the resort she'd stayed in, Holly wondered for the first time how her aunt had died. There was no mention of that in the letter at all, although she'd clearly known it was going to happen.

'Here it is!' Aliana spun round in her chair. 'Laganas is the best resort. There's a road which is just bars, clubs and restaurants, then a beach at the bottom.'

Holly got up and peered at the photos on Aliana's screen. The beach looked narrow and dirty and she curled up her nose. 'I don't think that's where the house is,' she said. 'Hang on, I've got the address in my bag.'

'I wish I could come with you,' Aliana was saying now, as she dreamily flicked through snap after snap of unblemished skies and lush green mountains. 'But Fiona would never let us be off at the same time.'

Holly ignored her. 'Here it is – look up Lithakia.'

Aliana typed it in obediently, stumbling over the spelling, and both girls cooed as photos flicked up of a golden beach, clear blue water and a cloudless sky. That was more like it, Holly thought, as more images appeared showing whitewashed stone buildings with tiled terracotta roofs, pots overflowing with brightly coloured flowers and acres of olive groves. Aliana giggled as she came across a photo of an ancient-looking lady with wispy white hair. She was wearing a long black dress and clutching the halter of a decidedly dog-eared donkey.

'That could be you in a few years,' she told Holly, ducking out of the way to avoid the resulting indignant swipe.

'Oi!' Holly scolded. 'I'm going there for a fortnight, not forty-five years!'

'Do you tan well?' Aliana asked. 'I bet you do.'

'I'm not actually sure,' Holly told her honestly. 'I don't remember ever going on holiday abroad as a kid, and the only time I've been away with Rupert, we've either been skiing or on a city break. Plus, it's never sunny here, is it?'

'Tell me about it.' Aliana stretched out her slender arms and groaned. 'I'm paler than the moon in an old Western.'

'Poetic.' Holly grinned at her.

'What will Rupert do while you're gone?' Aliana asked now, her eyes on her screen. 'He won't know what to do with himself, the poor boy's so smitten.'

'He said he's going to be really busy at work.'

They both looked up as Holly's mobile started vibrating across the desk. A photo of Rupert, grinning and wearing ski goggles on the top of his head, filled the screen.

'Hi, babe,' she whispered, bending over in her chair as Fiona's office door opened. 'I can't really talk . . .'

'I won't keep you,' Rupert sounded a bit put out. 'I just

wanted to check everything was okay with us, you know, after this morning?'

'It's totally fine.' She forced herself to smile in the hope that he'd hear it in her voice. 'I've actually just booked some time off.'

'You know I'd come with you if I cou—' Holly waited as she heard him put his hand over the receiver and speak to someone else. 'Sorry, darling, I'm snowed under here. Can I call you back later?'

He hung up before Holly had a chance to reply.

'What's up?' Aliana had, of course, been listening in.

'Oh, nothing – Rupert just saying he'll call me later. He's having dinner with his parents tonight,' Holly added, feeling guilty at her failure to keep the resentment out of her voice.

'But that's so sweet!'

Holly stared at her blankly.

'I went out with this bloke called Mike once. He worked in sales, or something. I never really did find out. Anyway, we were together for over a year and I don't think he ever even told his parents that I existed. I bet Rupert talks about you non-stop.'

'Do you really think so?' Holly's guilt level was rising like an over-egged soufflé.

'Of course! Seriously, Holly, men can be really weird about the whole parents thing. The fact that he sees them at all is a very good sign.'

'That's true, I suppose,' she allowed.

Aliana opened her mouth to retort, but Fiona chose that moment to sweep across and hand them each a folder containing all the product information for the new summer clothing range. There was enough in there to keep them busy until the end of the year.

Thursday, 12 April 1984
Sandypants!

I can't believe you went to Zakynthos without me! That is OUR place. But I suppose it's only fair. I feel like I've been on holiday for ever. I'd like to say something deep about India helping me to find myself, but all it's really helped me realise is that you should never sniff at running water and a decent meal. If I eat any more rice, I swear I'll die of boredom halfway through eating it. Are you planning to stay on the island for a while? Are you working over there? What's happened to the house back in Kent? Sorry, I know, too many questions. Please write back and tell me EVERYTHING. Right now!

Love you loads,
Jenny Bear xxx

5

Holly wrapped her fingers around her paper cup of coffee and stared out across the tarmac. From her position in the main lounge of Gatwick Airport, she could see seven planes, situated at regular intervals along the length of the departure gates. The sky into which each of these huge metal beasts would soon soar was a deep blue, but a smattering of clouds lay across the west corner, as if someone had spilled a bag of flour and run their fingers through the mess. In just under two hours, Holly would be flying up, through those clouds, to begin her 1,400-mile journey to the Greek island of Zakynthos.

It was a Saturday morning and the terminal was fizzing with the excited hum of holidaymakers. Holly watched as a stag party trudged past her and headed into a bar. The groom was wearing a pink tutu and matching fairy wings, a plastic wand clutched in his hand.

Despite the fact that Aliana was constantly joking with her about a possible engagement, Holly didn't sense that Rupert was on the verge of proposing. On the contrary, he had quite a measured and sensible approach to big life decisions. And if there was one thing she really despised, it was surprises. You couldn't prepare for a surprise, or plan what to say, or how to react. She was terrified of being caught unawares and letting her guard down. If Rupert suddenly dropped down on one knee, she had no idea how she would react – whether she'd be thrilled or absolutely terrified.

The stag party had just been joined by a gang of girls on a hen do, the bride-to-be festooned in L-plates and sporting a headband with a large rubber willy hanging off the front of it. After a certain amount of encouragement from his mates, the groom stepped forward and put his mouth round the end of it, causing both parties to scream and bellow their approval.

Rupert had insisted on accompanying her as far as Victoria Station that morning to wave her off on the Gatwick Express, pressing a Greek phrase book into her hand as a little going-away gift. Her flight back to London wasn't for another two weeks, and this would be the longest they hadn't seen each other since they'd got together.

Despite his constant assurances that he was totally fine with her going alone, Holly could tell he was nervous about the prospect of letting her go. He'd been making a lot of half-hearted jokes about her running off with a Greek waiter recently, which was, of course, a ridiculous notion. She doubted that anyone in the whole of Greece, let alone just one small island, could offer her anything better than Rupert could.

In the week since she'd received the letter, Holly's nightmares had returned with aggressive regularity. When she'd finally shrugged off the Insomnia Troll last night, she had woken up a few hours later, shaking and drenched in sweat. Thankfully, she hadn't actually cried out during her sleep, so Rupert remained blissfully unaware of her recurring problem. She couldn't tell him about it anyway, because telling him would mean unscrewing the lid on the memory of the most traumatic thing that had ever happened to her. As her mind wandered back to it now, Holly shivered.

She realised that her coffee had turned cold and tossed it into a bin, then spent the next hour wandering aimlessly around the shops, picking up perfume testers in duty free and treating herself to a new pair of flip-flops. As her departure time crept nearer, Holly's hands started to turn clammy with nerves. She had no idea what she was going to find when she got to her aunt's house – well, it was her house now, she reminded herself – or how she was going to feel when she got there. For the millionth time, she felt a surge of relief at the fact that she was making the journey alone.

As soon as the plane was airborne, Holly ordered herself a large gin and tonic and tried to concentrate on her new book. When it came to picking a title, she always went for the darkest crime thrillers she could find – a fact that Aliana found hilarious. Holly had lost count of the times she'd come back from lunch to find a colourful romance on her desk and Aliana's hopeful face grinning up at her. She had delved into a few, but always found the central characters totally alien – she simply couldn't relate to them.

The man sitting next to her had dozed off and a string of drool was stretching from the corner of his mouth to the newspaper in his lap, which he'd folded open at page three. The grin of the dead-behind-the-eyes girl proudly displaying her assets was being slowly obliterated by saliva. Holly turned away and took a gulp of her drink. Most of the passengers seemed to be either families with very young children, retirement-age couples, or groups of twenty-something girls and boys. Blessedly, the stag and hen parties that she'd encountered in the airport had clearly headed somewhere else for their final days of freedom.

With a growing sense of unease, Holly realised that she'd read the same paragraph five times over and reluctantly abandoned her book. Taking out her aunt's letter, she decided to read it one last time.

Dear Holly,

You won't remember me, but I think about you every day. I was there the day you were born and saw you every day until you were five years old. If you're reading this letter now, I'm sorry to say that I have passed away. I don't know if your mum Jenny ever talked about me, but my name is Sandra and I'm her sister. Or I was, I guess. I know that she died when you were only eighteen, and I'm so very sorry for your loss. I was worried when I didn't hear from her, but I'm ashamed to say that a combination of cowardice and hope stopped me from finding out the truth until recently. I hoped that she had simply forgotten me, given up on me, perhaps. It was all I deserved, in the end.

I know you must have so many questions. Questions about me, about your mother, about why I never got to see you grow up – but I fear I have run out of time to answer those questions. I am hoping that if you come to Zakynthos, to the house where it all began, then you will find some truth in the wreckage that I have left behind.

I am so sorry that we never knew each other properly, Holly, and I hope you find whatever it is you're looking for.

All my love,
Sandra

PS The key is under the pot.

'Ladies and gentlemen, we will shortly begin our descent into Zakynthos. Please return your seats to the upright positions and fasten your seat belts.'

The man with the drool jerked awake as Holly stuffed the letter away, wiping her eyes and snapping open the plastic blind covering the window.

The sun was starting to sag sleepily in the sky, and the view of the island was nothing short of stunning. She gazed down at the light reflecting off the ocean, letting her eyes travel along the coastline and over the irregular shapes of the mountains rising up in the distance. As the plane turned to the west and headed for the runway, the surface of the water seemed to rise up towards her at an almost alarming rate. Looking across to her left, Holly saw the famous Turtle Island that she'd read so much about over the past week. Situated a few miles off the coast of the mainland, the mass of land really did look like a turtle emerging from the sea, and Holly could hear other passengers making appreciative noises as they also noticed it for the first time.

Squinting back down at what she could now see was a long, sandy beach, Holly thought she could make out the shapes of holidaymakers, making the most of the final few rays of the day. For the first time since a brief rush when she'd woken up that morning, Holly felt excited.

Zakynthos airport was eerily quiet after the mayhem of Gatwick, and Holly and her fellow travellers appeared to have been on the final flight of the day. Aside from two Greek immigration officers, one of whom gave her a small wink as he handed back her passport, everyone else seemed to have gone home for the day. There were only two luggage carousels, so Holly chose a spot close to the exit and waited for her case to trundle out.

Two girls, who looked about eighteen, wandered over and stood next to her.

'We've gotta, like, go straight out on the strip tonight,' the shorter of the two told her blonde friend. They were already dressed for the climate in microscopic denim hot pants and brightly coloured vests, plastic sunglasses nestled firmly in their hair.

'You better not shag that barman again like you did last year,' the blonde replied. 'You took the bloody key and I had to sleep on a sun lounger.'

'Chill, woman,' came the reply. 'I'm not shagging no barmen this time – that last one gave me crabs.'

This was met with a hoot of laughter, not just from the small brunette, but also from a group of boys standing within earshot.

'Whatever. You always say you'll never and then you always do,' her friend retorted.

Holly wondered what it must be like to be allowed away on holiday alone at their age. Her own teenage years had been hijacked by her mother's deteriorating health and eventual death. Plus, she'd never really had that many close friends, and certainly no spare cash. After losing her mum, Holly's priority had been scraping enough money together to feed herself and pay the bills; there wasn't anything left over for indulgent holidays.

She'd been staring into space and missed the first circuit of cases. The two girls had just dragged their vast, pink suitcases off next to her when she spotted her own small, nondescript case making its jaunty way round. She had tied a blue ribbon to the handle before checking in, and she was comforted to see that it had survived the journey. Snapping up the handle and gathering up her handbag, Holly headed outside into what felt like an actual blanket of heat.

She knew that Greece was a hell of a lot hotter than the UK, but she'd never felt as if she was being literally bathed in warmth before. She found herself smiling immediately; her shoulders relaxed and her senses opened up to drink in this strange new environment. Even the tarmac felt toasty through her shoes as she wheeled her case round to the boot of a taxi and she continued to smile as the driver stowed it for her.

He was a head shorter than her, with wiry grey hair, cracked skin the colour of builder's tea and tatty jeans. Jeans! How could anyone bear to wear denim in this weather?

Fishing the address of her aunt's house out of her bag, Holly handed it over and smiled apologetically as he squinted in confusion.

'Hotel?'

Holly shook her head. 'Just a house, I think. Sorry, this is my first time – I haven't been here before.'

'Ah!' This seemed to please him. 'First time Zakynthos? First time Greece?'

They were pulling out of the airport car park now and Holly's eyes widened as she took in the mountains, the fields of wild grass and the gnarled-looking trees that were flitting past the window. 'First time in Greece,' she confirmed.

'You are alone?' he asked, as if this was highly unusual.

'Yes,' she replied carefully. 'Just me.'

44

'No husband?' There was a cheeky edge to his tone and Holly found herself smiling again.

'Nope, just me.'

It occurred to Holly, as they drove past white-walled tavernas, half-finished buildings in various shades of dark gold and souvenir shops, that it might not be the wisest idea to tell a strange man in a foreign country that you're a girl travelling alone. You certainly wouldn't do it in London – she barely made eye contact with taxi drivers back home. But then, there weren't any alarm bells going off in her head. This man seemed genuinely friendly and legitimately interested. Holly had always trusted her instincts, and right now they were telling her that she had nothing at all to worry about.

As they navigated the narrow roads, passing banks of mopeds, goats and small groups of tourists as they went, the bubbles of excitement inside her began to pop with dread. She hadn't allowed herself to think too much about what she might find at her Aunt Sandra's house. Would anyone have been in and cleared anything out? Would there be mouldy food, dirty sheets and any other manner of horrors waiting for her? As the taxi took another turn and started up a steep hill, Holly realised that she hadn't even thought to pick up any food or water. She hoped this house didn't end up being too remote.

They rounded another corner and Holly saw a flash of what looked like a small supermarket next door to a bar. Her driver picked up the piece of paper she'd given him with the address and nodded to himself.

'Here,' he told her, pointing through the windscreen. 'The car cannot go.'

Peering through the glass, Holly saw a low wall ahead of them with an opening that led to a narrow stone path. About 100 metres further along, were what looked like two small houses, both of which had no lights on that she could see. Taking a deep breath, she opened the car door and met her driver by the path, her case already removed from the boot and balanced up against the wall.

'Thank you,' she said, handing over a twenty-euro note and refusing any change.

'In Greece, you say *efharisto*,' he told her, before giving her arm a friendly squeeze and returning to his car. Holly watched as he drove away, trying to ignore the drunken butterflies having a violent rave in her stomach. 'Come on, woman,' she scolded herself. 'Let's get this done.' Taking her case in one hand, she stepped off the road and made her way along the smooth, flat stone of the path.

There it was: the house that had always been in her life. The house that had meant so much to her mother that she had carried a keepsake of it with her until the day she died. Despite the warmth of the evening, Holly felt a shiver run through her and prickles of anxiety start to wrap around her guts, like barbed wire pulled tight.

It felt familiar, yet at the same time frightening, and as she stood looking up at the darkened windows, Holly found she was unable to move any closer. She'd spent the past week thinking about this moment and how it would play out. She knew that coming here would feel strange, but she hadn't been prepared for the weight of emotions that were now fighting their way to the surface. It was just a house, for God's sake – how scary could it really be?

Very.

Forcing her eyes down, she spotted a large pot lurking in the shadows under the front porch. This must be the pot from the letter – the one hiding the front-door key. Taking a tentative few steps forward, Holly forced down the bubbling waves of anxiety and pushed the pot to one side. The key was there, shining brightly against the stone tiles.

What if the place was filthy and full of cockroaches?

What if her aunt's clothes still smelled of her?

What if she was about to open the door into a past she wasn't ready to see?

Holly's hand shook as she watched it extend out towards the lock. There was a small click, and she was in.

Her first thought as she flicked on the light switch was relief that she could smell disinfectant rather than decay. And any fears she may have had about opening the door into a hoarder's paradise were immediately allayed, because the space she was looking into was largely clear of clutter.

Dropping her bag beside her, Holly took a very deep breath and stepped further into the house. She felt so much like an intruder. Her brain was telling her that this was *her* house now, and that she should feel at home here, but her heart was determinedly doing its best to hammer its way out through her chest. This had been someone's home – someone who knew her, but who was also a total stranger. Now that she was here, it seemed unbelievable that she should be. It was all too much to take in, and Holly's eyes began to speckle with black spots.

Glancing round in desperation for something to hold on to, her eyes grazed over the open-plan space, taking in a table and chairs, a sofa covered with a yellow blanket, a low coffee table and a large vase of pink flowers.

What the hell was a vase of flowers doing here?

Someone must have been here in the house. Someone must have put them there.

Holly lurched forward and gripped the back of the sofa, her breath coming in ragged pants and cold sweat dappling her back and arms. As she stood there, trying to concentrate her way out of the fog, she stared again at the flowers. They really were very beautiful, and as she looked at them she regained her composure. The feeling that she was intruding here itched at her skin like heat rash, but she focused her mind and made it as far as the back doors, which were glass-fronted and nestled behind thin red curtains.

The space directly behind the house was mostly paved in large, square, honey- and white-coloured stones, with a few terracotta pots forming a makeshift wall along the right-hand side. Past the end of the paved area was a low wall, similar to the one by the road outside, and beyond that a steep drop obscured by a tangle of lush green plants. Holly could see the tops of trees, which clearly had roots further down the slope. Wandering across the space and enjoying the freedom of being back outside, she mounted the wall and gasped – below her, spread out like an endless inky blue tapestry, was the ocean. It was breathtaking.

Holly stood on her spot on the wall for what felt like an age, taking comfort from the calming energy of the sea and the gentle hum of insects coming from the surrounding trees.

She knew she had to go back inside. Face whatever it was waiting for her in the cupboards and under the beds; confront the unmistakable feelings of déjà vu that had been prodding her since she arrived.

Had she been here before? It hadn't even occurred to her before now, but perhaps she had. There was definitely a feeling inside her, something unfamiliar but impossible to ignore – an insistent whispering from the very deepest and most forgotten parts of her mind.

'I saw you every day until you were five,' Sandra had written in her letter. Holly had presumed that her aunt had been referring to time spent in the UK, but perhaps it wasn't that simple. If her mum had kept the model of this place for so many years, it stood to reason that she'd been here – perhaps even lived here. Perhaps she, Holly, had lived here too.

Reluctantly stepping down from her viewing platform and sucking in one last lungful of warm evening air, Holly headed stoically back into the house and straight up the stone stairs.

There were two bedrooms on the first floor, one of which had very obviously been her aunt's. In here, unlike the rest of the house, clutter and trinkets covered every available surface and the bed was neatly made. The other room, by contrast, was stripped bare save for a small wardrobe and single bed. It reminded Holly of her own room in her rented flat back in London. That, too, was nondescript and sparsely decorated. Both bedrooms contained doors that led out on to a wide balcony and, peering through the dusty glass, Holly could make out a table and chairs.

She felt horribly uncomfortable in her aunt's old room. She could detect a faint hint of lavender under the more powerful smell of disinfectant coming from downstairs, but there was an awful sadness to the place. Abandoned heaps of jewellery nestled in clumps of dust on the dressing table and the silk scarves knotted to the framed mirror hung flat and defeated.

Holly thought about searching through the place there and then, but her uneasiness took over and she backed quickly out of the room, shutting the door firmly behind her. By the time she got back downstairs, the uneasiness had grown so much that the need to escape was over-whelming. Grabbing her bag from the floor and shoving the key in her pocket, she slammed the front door behind her and practically ran out to the path. What her dry mouth needed now was water – and maybe something a bit stronger, as well.

'*Kalispera.*' The Greek man behind the till in the super-market greeted Holly cheerfully as she walked up the stone steps into his shop. Already feeling better after put-ting a safe distance between herself and the house, Holly managed a smile and a 'hello'. She found water, bread, cheese, milk and toilet roll, and then tossed in a few yoghurts. It was a long time since she'd eaten breakfast and her stomach was growling.

'*Ti kanis?* How are you?' The Greek man smiled again as he bagged her goods. He looked around fifty, and had a large dark beard speckled with grey and an even larger belly, which he was resting gently on the edge of the counter.

Realising that she was getting a lesson in how to speak Greek, Holly tentatively repeated *'ti kanis'* back to him.

He laughed. 'I am Kostas,' he told her, reaching over to shake her hand.

'Holly,' she smiled.

'This is your first time Zakynthos?'

Clearly this was a common question. 'Yes.'

'Ah, you are a friend of Aidan,' he declared.

Holly's face must have registered confusion, because Kostas peered at her for a second and laughed again. 'You stay there?' This time he pointed over her shoulder, towards the road he'd presumably watched her walk down. She didn't quite know what to tell him. How do you explain to a Greek man you've never met before that you've inherited a house from a woman you never knew in a country you've never visited? She settled for nodding and handing over some money.

Kostas merely smiled when he gave her back the change, but she got the impression that he would have liked her to be more forthcoming. If he worked here all the time, then it stood to reason that he would have known her aunt; probably known her quite well. She would have to save that conversation for another day.

A drink: that was what she needed. Thankfully, the place next door was both open and serving a variety of beverages. Pulling out a stool at the bar, Holly dumped her shopping bags on the floor and ordered a large red wine, all the time trying to silence the relentless hammering of her heart inside her chest.

'Everything all right, love?' The barmaid leaned

towards her, her greying bun wobbling precariously on the top of her head. Holly recognised a Yorkshire accent.

'I'm fine, thanks,' she said, although it came out as more of a choking noise.

'You look like you've seen a ghost,' the woman informed her cheerily, and without a hint of irony. Holly agreed with the judgement wholeheartedly, but she merely shook her head.

'Just been a long day,' she explained, sipping her wine. 'This is lovely.'

'It's village wine,' the woman told her. 'It's made here on the island and it's far better than any of that crap they import from Italy or wherever.'

Holly nodded politely. 'It's very good.'

'I shouldn't tell you this,' the woman was whispering now, 'but you can get a whole litre of the stuff from Kostas next door for three euros.'

Holly thought back to the twenty-five-pound bottles of Pinot Grigio that Rupert had ordered in the bar the week before and gulped. This stuff tasted much nicer. She was fully aware that she would most definitely wake up the next day with the mother of all hangovers, but at the moment she couldn't care less.

'Thanks for the tip – but won't you get in trouble with the boss?'

This seemed to amuse her new friend. 'I *am* the boss, darling,' she giggled. 'My name's Annie.'

They shook hands, but when Holly told Annie her name the woman frowned.

'You're Sandra's Holly?' she asked, her crinkled eyes immediately full of pity.

'She was my aunt,' Holly admitted, taking another sip.

'Sandra was such a peach,' Annie smiled. 'It was such a shame what happened. She was younger than me, for God's sake.'

Holly still had no idea what had actually happened, but she wasn't about to admit it.

'Did you know her well?' the wine helped her ask.

'Of course I did.' Annie seemed surprised by the question. 'Did she never mention me?'

Holly was sure that her aunt Sandra would have, had they ever spoken. 'Yes, she did – I just forgot,' she lied, adding a 'Silly me!' for effect.

Annie was about to reply, but was interrupted by a group of three older couples who had just made their way to one of the tables at the front. Scooping up some laminated cocktail menus from the back bar, she scurried over to turn on the charm. Holly didn't mind; she was happy to sit and drink her wine, enjoying the feel of the warm night air on her bare legs.

She tried to imagine her aunt sitting here, gossiping with Annie and talking about her, the niece she had never met. But clearly Sandra hadn't told Annie the whole truth, either. Was this why Holly found it so hard to be honest with people? Perhaps it was genetic, and she was part of a family of natural-born liars. Her mother had certainly been an expert.

'Same again?' Annie was holding up her empty wine glass.

'Keep it coming.' Holly really was feeling rather merry now, and the panic she'd felt while nosing around the house had subsided. In the warmth of the bar, with the music playing and the relative normality of the situation, the whole thing seemed less of a big deal. Tomorrow she would go through all her aunt's stuff and find what she needed, simple as that. How hard could it really be?

'Have you met Aidan yet?' asked Annie, who had just returned from delivering a tray full of multi-coloured cocktails.

'No.' Holly raised a quizzical eyebrow. Who the hell was this Aidan?

'Oh, you will soon – he's your neighbour,' Annie told her, with what looked an awful lot like a wink. She picked up a glass from the draining board and started drying it with a cloth that was hanging off her apron. 'He's pretty dishy. Aidan, I mean.'

'Oh?' Holly was careful to keep her tone non-committal.

'He moved here with his girlfriend a few years back – gorgeous thing, she was, looked like a model – but they broke up,' she continued. 'I don't know who ended it, but it was her that left the island. Such a shame, nice-looking couple like that.'

Holly wondered what this Aidan person would think if he knew that the locals were gossiping about him with total strangers.

'I'm sure he'll meet someone else,' she replied, mostly because it sounded like the right thing to say. 'If he's as good-looking as you say, he'll have no trouble.'

'Ah, but Aidan's a fussy one, see?' Annie told her conspiratorially, topping up her glass. 'I've seen girls in here throw themselves at him plenty of times and he's never done anything more than politely turn them down. He must still be hung up on his ex, I reckon. She did look like a model, as I said.'

'Sounds too good to be true,' Holly said. She could already tell that Aidan was Annie's favourite subject. Her cheeks were glowing brighter than the neon 'cocktails' sign that was hanging up behind the bar.

'Are you, erm, spoken for?' Annie enquired, staring pointedly at Holly's left hand.

'I'm not married, if that's what you mean,' Holly replied. 'But I am with someone.'

Annie tried to hide her relief. 'Oh. Well, that's nice. Make sure you say hello to him while you're here, though. Aidan, I mean. He is only next door after all.'

Wow. This Aidan guy must need to carry around a fire extinguisher for his ears with Annie going on about him this much. Holly couldn't believe any man could be as perfect as Annie was making out. What she really wanted to do was ask the older woman to tell her stories about her aunt, but even three glasses of village wine hadn't given her enough courage. Her stomach rumbled again, loudly this time. 'I'd better be off,' she called to Annie, who was busy wiping down tables. 'Nice to meet you.'

'See you soon, darling,' came the reply. 'Pop in any time.'

It was only as she started walking back up the hill that Holly realised just how drunk she was. The carrier bag containing her now-tepid yoghurts banged against her bare shins as she half-trudged, half-stumbled back towards the house. There was now a jeep parked right next to the path, and Holly careered into it sideways as she attempted to leap over the low wall.

'Bugger,' she giggled, doing her best to put the wing mirror back in place. Opening the door a few minutes later, she realised she'd not only left all the lights on, but that the window in the kitchen was open too. Cursing herself for not unpacking earlier, she unzipped her case and rifled through her neatly rolled clothes until she found Rupert's old university T-shirt. He'd slipped it into her suitcase that morning and told her to sleep in it.

'It's the second-best thing to me being there with you.'

Rupert! 'Bugger,' she swore for the second time. She'd completely forgotten to text him to tell him she'd arrived. She was officially the worst girlfriend in the world. Fishing her phone out of her bag as she scrambled up the stairs, Holly found the screen black. With the wine sloshing about in her empty stomach, the prospect of digging around in her case for her phone charger was akin to tackling the trek to Everest base camp in nothing but a bikini – it would have to wait until the morning.

Ten minutes later, with a blissfully empty bladder and a scratchy but clean-looking blanket that she'd discovered in one of the cupboards on the landing, Holly clambered on to the sofa and closed her eyes. For a few bleary seconds, she was vaguely aware of a buzzing in her ears. Then she passed out.

6

Bang. Bang. Bang.

Oh God, someone was trying to break down the door and kill her.

Bang. Bang. Bang.

Okay, so maybe they were just knocking. Groaning, Holly stood up and promptly stubbed her toe on the leg of the coffee table.

'Shitting bastard!' she yelled.

The knocking stopped.

Scooping up the blanket to cover her bottom half, Holly stomped over to the front door and flung it open with a loud crash. Standing on the threshold, a set of keys dangling from one finger and a wry grin on his face, stood what could only be described as a tall, dark, handsome stranger.

'Were you talking to me?' he asked, his Irish accent immediately apparent.

'What? No!' Holly snapped, feeling indignant.

'So you don't think I'm a, what was it, "shitting bastard"?' He was clearly mocking her now, and Holly was horribly aware of her dry mouth and the fact that she hadn't removed yesterday's make-up before she'd passed out.

'I stubbed my toe,' she told him, rather begrudgingly. They both glanced down at the same time, but Holly's feet were obscured by the blanket.

'You must be Holly?' He was wearing a red T-shirt with a cluster of holes in the front, a pair of navy shorts and very beaten-up-looking flip-flops.

'That's right. Are you Aidan?'

If he was surprised that she knew his name, he didn't show it, just gave a brief nod. Holly shifted her weight from one foot to the other. She didn't like the way this man was looking at her – he was clearly amused by her bedraggled appearance. The fact that he was undeniably good-looking was beside the point.

'The man in the shop mentioned you,' she added, pulling the blanket tighter.

Aidan smiled. 'Kostas?'

It was Holly's turn to nod. She decided not to tell him what Annie had said.

'I came round last night,' he told her now. 'I thought you were here, given that all the lights were on.'

Holly brought her hand up to scratch her face, realising as she did so that a cluster of bites had appeared on her cheek.

'The mozzies are attracted to the light at night,' he continued, raising an eyebrow as she snatched her hand away. God, he was so infuriating. She couldn't help picturing how awful she must look, with last night's mascara crusted on her eyelids, mosquito bites all over her face and the slept-in hair of a Highland goat.

Aidan held out the keys. 'These are yours. Sandy liked me having a spare set, just in case, but now that you're here . . .' he trailed off. 'Are you running a bath?'

'What?' Holly gaped at him. 'No. Why?'

'Can't you hear that?' He stepped past her and headed

58

towards the stairs. Holly followed him, limping slightly on her still throbbing toe. They stood there in silence, and sure enough, there was a persistent dripping sound coming from somewhere upstairs. Aidan headed up without asking, leaving Holly to hobble indignantly after him.

'Ah . . .' his voice filtered out from inside the bathroom. 'Nobody warned you about the Greek plumbing system, did they?'

'What do you me— Oh.' Holly recoiled in horror as she took in the scene of devastation on the other side of the door. The toilet, which she'd only used twice since arriving, was full to the brim with the same murky water that was covering the floor, and there were a few sheets of disintegrating toilet paper floating about on the tide.

'You can't flush toilet paper over here,' Aidan told her. He managed to keep his voice very matter-of-fact, which was impressive given the circumstances.

Holly found that she had lost the power of speech, so when he told her that he was nipping back next door to get the tools necessary to unblock her U-bend, she merely nodded at him stupidly. As soon as she heard his feet on the stairs, Holly rushed into the spare bedroom and slammed the door behind her. The mirror on the wall confirmed her worst fears: she really did look like a mountain goat – one that had failed to find its way around the forty-five or so hedges in its path. Then again, Aidan would probably remember the bathroom floor more than he would the state of her face.

Rooted to the spot by the wet-cement effect of total and utter humiliation, Holly listened as Aidan made his way back into the bathroom, clanking a bit this time with what she assumed must be some sort of toolbox. He definitely had the look of a man that would have a proper toolbox – and one that he would actually use, rather than the smart-looking one wrapped in cellophane that Rupert kept in the cupboard under his kitchen sink.

'Holly?' Oh God, he was calling for her. With some effort, she unglued her bare feet from the tiled floor and tiptoed back to the bathroom doorway. She was still wearing Rupert's T-shirt and the blanket, which she snatched up away from the rancid water.

'Do you have a bucket?' he asked. He was down on all fours now, one gloved hand poised and ready to plunge.

'I . . . Um . . . I don't know,' Holly stuttered. Why was she behaving like such a moron? 'I'll go and check,' she added quickly, seeing a frown begin to form on his face. Once downstairs, she discovered a bucket, bleach and a whole heap of sponges and cloths stuffed into a cupboard in the kitchen. Pausing at her suitcase to pull on a pair of denim shorts, she took the whole lot up to the bathroom and gingerly placed them on the floor next to where Aidan was now rummaging about in the toilet. He didn't need any help, he told her, but a cup of tea would be nice.

Thank God she'd picked up some milk the night before, she thought, carefully decanting water from the large bottle in the fridge into the kettle and readying two mugs that she'd found on a low shelf beside the cooker. While the kettle chugged away, Holly ran a brush through her hair and cleaned her teeth over the sink. Her hands were still shaking when she poured out the boiling water.

As she waited for Aidan to reappear, Holly spotted her phone on the coffee table and realised with a pang that she still hadn't sent a message to Rupert. She wondered what would have happened if he had been here with her when the toilet decided to explode. The thought of Rupert down on his hands and knees, elbow-deep in sewage, was so absurd that Holly found herself laughing out loud.

'Glad you see the funny side.'

It was Aidan, coming down the stairs looking slightly more flustered and a lot damper than he had before.

'I wasn't laughing at . . . I was just . . . Here you go.' Holly held out his mug.

He took a sip, staring at her over the rim. 'This is a good cup of tea. It's the one thing the Greeks are terrible at, making tea. Their coffee is probably the best in the world, but their tea tastes like horse piss.'

'Thank you for fixing the, erm, problem in the bathroom.' Holly flushed crimson.

'No trouble,' he told her. He was drinking his tea very quickly. The poor man must be desperate to get away from her. Holly knew she should make small talk, ask him about himself or remark on the weather, but it was hard to concentrate on chit-chat with a man so blatantly good-looking. Even as the thought entered her head, she felt guilty. Plus, there was something about Aidan that made her feel on edge. When he looked at her, she felt like he could see right through all the body armour she'd painstakingly bolted around herself. That was ridiculous, though – he'd only just met her. She must simply be feeling vulnerable because he'd caught her looking so utterly hideous.

'So,' he said eventually. 'When was the last time you spoke to your Auntie Sandra?'

Holly gulped. Should she lie? Somehow she knew that Aidan wouldn't fall for it. 'I never met her,' she told him, taking an aggressive swig of tea and almost choking as the scalding liquid hit the back of her throat. 'I didn't even know she existed until about a week ago.'

For the first time since she'd opened the door to him, Aidan seemed to lose a layer of his unflappable cool. He was scrutinising her now with what felt like distrust. 'But you are her niece, right? You are Holly?'

'Apparently, I am,' she replied. He may have unblocked her loo, but there was no way she was ready to tell him all about her family history.

'She told me that she was leaving this place to you,' Aidan continued, placing his mug carefully on the table. 'As soon as she found out about the cancer, she knew exactly who was going to get the house: it was always going to be you.'

Holly fiddled with the frayed bottom of her shorts and fought the tears that had inexplicably welled up at his words. So it had been cancer that had taken away her aunt. Clearly Aidan assumed that she already knew all about it, but she was damned if she was going to let him know just how much his accidental bombshell had affected her. She'd spent years keeping her true emotions well hidden, even from those she felt closest to, and she'd only just met this man. Sniffing loudly and giving a shrug, she snapped, 'Listen, I'm just here to clear this place out and sell it. I don't know why Sandra left me her house – and I don't care, either.'

Aidan flinched as though he'd been slapped. 'Wow, you

don't mince your words, do you? I'm glad Sandy isn't here to see this.'

Ouch, that hurt. Holly glared at him for a moment while she tried to quell the ugly froth of anger that she could feel rising up inside her chest. The last thing she wanted was to give in to her horrible, irrational rage – the same rage that she'd been struggling to control since losing her mum.

'Listen, I don't care what you think of me,' she told him calmly. 'I don't even know who you are. You come round here at the crack of dawn, banging on the door like a madman, mocking me—'

'You swore at *me*!' he interrupted.

'I swore at the bloody table!' she argued.

'And I fixed your fecking toilet!' he said, his voice rising an octave.

Infuriatingly, he then seemed to steady himself and even smiled again, although not at Holly. Retrieving the keys from the pocket of his shorts, Aidan stared at her for a few seconds before throwing them down on to the table, where they slid along to the vase of flowers and stopped with a soft clunk. As the front door clicked shut behind him, Holly realised with dismay that it must have been him who put the flowers there in the first place – and now he thought she was a complete cow.

The tears were threatening to fall now, but that only hardened Holly's resolve not to care. It didn't matter what Aidan thought of her. In a matter of weeks, she'd be back in London, having sold this weird mausoleum, and she could forget all about Sandra *and* Aidan.

He had unnerved her, though, the way he'd made her anger almost come to the surface like that. She'd been with Rupert for almost a year and he'd never seen even a hint of her bad temper. Whenever Holly felt even a rumbling of that side of her start to appear, she always made an excuse to be by herself, whether it was an afternoon run, or a trip to the local shop. She was afraid of what would happen if she ever let herself ride the waves of that anger – and with Aidan, for the first time since she was a teenager, she'd almost lost control of herself.

Nope, he was definitely bad news. She would have to do everything in her power to avoid him for the rest of her trip.

7

'Darling! At last! I thought you'd been abducted.'

Holly cringed into the phone. 'I'm so sorry. I forgot to pack my charger and it's taken me this long to buy another one.' It was amazing how easily she could lie to Rupert sometimes.

'Oh, you poor thing. Has it been awful?'

Holly reflected that yes, given the toe stubbing, creepy dead person's belongings, toilet explosion and several dozen mosquito bites, it had been pretty awful so far – but she decided another lie would be far easier.

'It's been fine,' she told him. 'A bit weird, I suppose, but everyone is very nice.' Well, except for Aidan, she thought darkly. But there was no way she was mentioning him.

'What's the house like?' asked Rupert. His voice sounded different on the long-distance connection, like he was talking to her from the bottom of a very deep hole.

Holly considered his question, looking round at the downstairs area from her position on the sofa. 'It's nice,' she said at last. 'I haven't had a chance to look around the island yet, really – I'm going to do that today.'

There was the sound of chatter on the other end of the line. 'Darling, I'm so sorry, but I've got to go. A meeting.'

She caught her sigh just as it was about to escape her throat. 'That's fine.' She forced herself to smile as usual, in the hope that he'd hear it in her voice. 'I'll call you this evening instead.'

After he'd hung up, Holly sat for a while staring at the vase of flowers on the table. A few of the petals had dropped off and started to curl up at the edges. Aidan put them there; *he can't be that bad*, a voice whispered in her ear.

She couldn't help but feel a bit cross at her Aunt Sandra. Why had she chosen to reveal her existence now, when it was too late? Why had she left Holly this house, which had already disrupted her life so entirely? At this moment in time, bitten, hungover and humiliated, Holly wished that she'd never bothered to open that bloody letter.

But this wouldn't do. Holly hadn't got as far as she had in life by sitting around feeling sorry for herself. It was time she got up and faced her reality, starting with a little bit of exploring. The idea of venturing into her aunt's bedroom still made the hairs stand up on the back of her neck, but maybe a day out in the sunshine would give her a bit of courage. If she really had been on this island before, as she was beginning to suspect, then she wanted to have a look round and see if she could stir up any memories.

It was only 11 a.m., but already the sun was beating a relentless symphony against her bare shoulders. The pavement felt warm beneath her sandals, and as she headed down the hill a tiny lizard scuttled across her toes and disappeared into the sparse undergrowth.

Holly couldn't see any crickets, but she could hear their shrill chirping coming from the trees. The leather strap of her bag was slipping from her arm with sweat and more beads were starting to pool on her upper lip.

Kostas greeted her in his shop like an old friend.

'*Yassou, koukla – ti kanis?*'

She must have pulled a face, because he repeated it in English. 'Hello, doll – how are you?'

'Hot.' Holly smiled at him as she fanned her face with her free hand, the other already reaching into the fridge for a bottle of water.

'Yes, yes. Very hot today.' He seemed quite proud of the fact, and beamed at her as she handed over some coins.

'Is there . . . ?' she began, not really sure what she wanted to ask.

Kostas was still grinning. 'You want to go for swimming?' he asked. 'The beach?'

'Yes!' That would be as good a place as any to start.

'This way, twenty minutes.' He was pointing out of the shop to the left. 'There is a bus,' he added, patting her arm. 'One every hour. Outside.'

She'd gone about fifteen metres when she heard the flap-flapping of flip-flops coming up behind her.

'This for you,' Kostas said, pressing a tube of cream into her hand.

'What is it?'

'*Ti!*' He laughed. '*Ti* is "what".'

When she didn't reply, he pointed at her face. 'For bites.'

'Oh.' Holly immediately put her hand up to the cluster of pink lumps on her cheek. 'Thank you.'

'*Efharisto* is "thank you",' he told her with a grin. 'I like to teach Greek for you.'

'That's very kind of you.' Holly was genuinely touched. It wasn't often that she'd experienced random acts of kindness – especially not living in London, where you'd be more likely to run in the opposite direction if you heard anyone coming up behind you than stop for a nice chat. She obediently dabbed a few spots of the cream on to her face.

'Bravo!' Kostas nodded in approval. 'Tomorrow, no spots – all vanished.'

What the hell had he given her, miracle cream?

They were interrupted by a squealing of brakes, and a ramshackle bus groaned its way round the corner towards them. Holly, who had not quite reached the stop, went to start running, but Kostas was already standing in the road, his hairy forearm stretched out. The bus stopped. Mumbling her thanks in Greek, first to Kostas and then to the driver, Holly handed over a two-euro coin, then eased herself into one of the cracked leather seats and rested her head against the glass.

According to her guidebook, which she'd surreptitiously taken out of her bag to consult on the journey, Laganas was the first resort they would reach. She remembered what Aliana had told her about it being one of the biggest party places in the whole of Greece, and wondered just how touristy it would be. The limited bits of the island she'd seen so far had been beautiful, colourful and unspoilt, and it was with a certain amount of apprehension that she descended the steps of the bus after the driver yelled, 'Laganas!'

She was standing at the circular end of a very long road that stretched away from her inland. Immediately in front of her, beyond about six metres of sand, was the sea, and the accompanying beach lay in each direction, forming a 'T' shape with the main road.

Holly turned so she was facing the road, her back to the ocean. To her left was a series of bars and to her right a restaurant. She could see a few holidaymakers tucking into a late breakfast, and her stomach rumbled with envy. She really should start remembering to feed herself properly. There didn't appear to be much of interest on the street – all she could see were bars, souvenir shops and fast-food restaurants. Squinting into the distance, she spotted the telltale golden arches of the McDonald's sign and shuddered. Aliana had been right about it being touristy. It already felt so different from her secluded little house up on the hill, and Holly wondered what her Aunt Sandra had made of it, and whether or not she ever bothered to come down here.

According to the map in her book, if she turned left along the beach then she could walk all the way along the seafront to the next resort along, which was called Kalamaki. This place was, the guide assured her, much smaller and far less spoiled than its bigger, messier neighbour.

Laganas beach was in no way like the white sandy slices of paradise that came up on the internet when you searched for 'Greek beaches', thought Holly, as she averted her eyes from where two girls were lounging on plastic sunbeds, their exposed nipples roasting in the sun. For as far along as she could see, the beach housed a variety of bars and restaurants, all crammed next to one another and all with their own collection of sun loungers available to rent. Music was filtering down from each venue, and seemed to vary from traditional Greek to popular UK chart hits.

'Hello, pretty lady!' A Greek teen wearing cut-off jeans, a bum bag and a sun-faded baseball cap stepped into

Holly's path. He was smiling and looked friendly enough, but Holly could sense she was about to get the hard sell. 'Where are you going?' he asked, as she went to step around him.

'Kalamaki,' she told him, pointing along the beach.

'No? Kalamaki? Why? You stay in Kalamaki?'

'That's a lot of questions,' Holly told him. He couldn't be more than sixteen, she decided. The skin on his chest was smooth and the colour of a freshly popped conker.

'We have very nice sunbeds here for you,' he continued. 'Very good food. I make for you, cocktail on the house!'

'Maybe later,' she tried, but he wasn't about to give up yet.

'I am Sakis. I will look after you very good,' he insisted, taking her hand and shaking it. 'What is your name?'

Holly told him.

'Holly? Holly?' he repeated a few times before laughing. 'It is a very pretty name. A very pretty name for a very pretty girl.'

'That's very sweet of you, but I'm not stopping today.'

Sakis looked at her with a level of dismay that most people would reserve for news about fatal car accidents or terminal illness. 'Blue Sea is the best restaurant in the whole of Laganas,' he continued. 'This is your first time, Laganas?'

'First time in Zakynthos,' she confirmed, watching his face light up.

Reaching into his back pocket, Sakis pulled out a card and handed it to her. There was a photo of Blue Sea restaurant on the front and a crudely drawn map of its location on the back. 'Bring this when you come,' he squeezed her hand. 'And free cocktail – just for you. Special one.' He pronounced it 'speshall'.

Holly thanked him and took advantage of an approaching group of girls to make her escape. As she walked on, she heard Sakis doing the same spiel all over again. It turned out that every single one of the thirty or so beach bars and restaurants that Holly passed had their own version of Sakis, and twenty minutes later she had another ten cards, each with the promise of something free if she chose to return. How the hell did these places ever make any money? They had all been very friendly, though, and very complimentary, although Holly wasn't naive enough to believe their flattery was sincere – especially given how rank she looked today.

She'd had to tie up her dark curls because they'd been sticking to her neck with sweat, and she was very much regretting wearing her smallest, tightest shorts. No matter how much she ran and how many carbs she dodged, her thighs remained stubbornly fleshy. Then again, there were a lot of people on Laganas beach with far larger thighs than hers, none of whom appeared to care how they looked.

The sand, which had been as hard as concrete under her feet up to this point, started to become softer and cleaner. The gauntlet of bars had given way to a series of hotels, the gardens and pools of which were set much further back on the beach. Holly slipped off her flip-flops and relished the feeling of the sand between her toes. She'd tucked the straps of her vest into the back of her bikini top to avoid getting any tan lines, and she stopped to reapply some lotion. The sun was now at its highest point and she could feel the weight of it pressing down on her shoulders.

While Laganas beach was crowded and noisy, there was no denying the breathtaking view when you turned your back on it and faced out towards the sea. The turtle-shaped island was clearly visible in the north-east corner of the horizon, and Laganas bay curved round in front of it, the sand giving way to rocks in the distance. The sea was relatively calm here too, with just a gentle lapping sound as the waves curled into shore.

Now that there were fewer people around, Holly allowed herself to slow down and chose a path along the very edge of the water. She liked how her bare feet left prints in the wet sand, only to be washed away a second later as a wave scurried inland, smoothing down the canvas again and again, like a child shaking an Etch A Sketch. There were more shells on this part of the beach, and Holly was reminded of the time she'd been taken to Brighton beach by her mother.

She must have been about seven or eight at the time, and it was in the magical time of her life before Jenny had started to drink heavily. They'd got the train together from London, taking advantage of the first hot day of the school summer holiday. Her mum had always talked about how much she missed the ocean, and as Holly sat by the window, watching fields and houses flash by, she listened again as Jenny told her how wonderful it felt to stand on a beach and look out at the sea, how it would feel as if anything was possible.

'You used to love the seaside when you were a baby, Hols,' she told her, clasping her hands together in her lap. 'You've always been just like your mum, so I know you'll love it in Brighton just as much as I do.'

And Holly had loved it. She'd loved chasing waves and shrieking in delight when they chased her back, she'd loved building sandcastles and decorating them with pebbles, she'd loved the taste of the ice cream as it melted down the side of the cone – but most of all she'd loved how her mum had been that day: so happy, so carefree, so full of joy. It was one of the only really strong memories that Holly had of her mum. Well, one of the only ones that she enjoyed remembering. There were others, of course, but those had been banished into a part of her mind that she kept under strict lock and key.

She knew now that her mum had most probably been here, in Zakynthos – maybe even stood where Holly was standing right now. Was that why she'd had such an affinity with the sea? Had she stood on this beach, looking out at that endless expanse of blueness, and let herself believe that anything was possible? Had her Aunt Sandra done the same thing?

Holly forced herself to turn away from the view and continue down the beach. These dark thoughts weren't going to do her any favours, and neither would sending questions out into the universe that would never be answered. Her mum was dead, her aunt was dead, and she was alone. That was all there was to it.

Monday, 14 May 1984
My darling sister,

Thanks for writing back to me so fast. Your letter made me laugh A LOT! So, you've gone and fallen in love with a bloody local, have you? Well, that's sealed the deal — I'm going to have to come over there immediately and make sure he's good enough for you, which of course he won't be, because you're the best person on the planet . . . after me! Anyway, I'm only writing this to tell you that my flight is booked to Athens, so I'll get the boat from there and see you very soon. Be safe over there in the meantime — don't get pregnant or anything stupid like that. Ha ha!

Miss you SO MUCH. Heaps of love,
Jenny xxx

8

Kalamaki beach turned out to be a further twenty minutes' walk, but Holly was glad she'd made the journey. She'd read something in her book about this area being the main nesting ground for rare sea turtles, and as such it was protected, almost like a nature reserve. Despite having only one restaurant and just a handful of sunbeds scattered haphazardly across the sand, this beach had the benefit of being cleaner, wider and far more beautiful than the one in Laganas. Instead of hotels, the beach here backed straight into the rough edges of a cliff, the highest point of which looked to have some sort of viewing platform jutting out. Holly promised herself she would find a way up there to check out the view, but first she needed a drink. Her water had long since run out, and there hadn't been a single shop or bar for the last few hundred metres of her trek along the sand.

The beachside taverna was large and square, with tables stretching all the way to the back, where Holly could see a bank of fridges and a till sitting on a table. An extremely old woman was sitting there, a black shawl pulled across her hunched shoulders. There were a number of waiters zipping around between occupied tables, and Holly caught the eye of one who motioned for her to sit wherever she liked. Glancing around, she spied an empty table in the corner that offered an impressive view of the beach and sea beyond. There was a large wood and wicker umbrella above it, sheltering the chairs from the sun, and Holly slid thankfully into one of the light-dappled seats.

'*Yassou!*' came a voice at her ear, and she jumped as a menu was unceremoniously tossed down on to the table in front of her. She looked up to where a waiter was standing, his pen hovering over a tatty-looking notepad. Catching her eye, he smiled broadly, displaying a number of missing teeth and what looked like a large chunk of spinach jammed in between two of the remaining ones. Holly swallowed her giggle.

'*Yassou,*' she replied, smiling back. 'Can I have a water, please, and some coffee?'

The gap-toothed waiter pulled a face. 'It is too hot for coffee,' he informed her, swinging a random arm round at the beach. 'You like frappé? Coffee with ice?'

'Um,' Holly hesitated. The waiter grinned at her again, nodding his head. 'Okay,' she said, smiling up at him before turning to examine the menu. She wondered what Rupert would have made of that little exchange, of being told what to order. After a frugal breakfast of yoghurt and a few lumps of cheese, she was starving, and her mouth watered as she read the list of ingredients in a Greek salad.

'Frappé!' The waiter was back, and placed her drink on the table top with an exaggerated flourish. Holly ordered her salad and even managed an '*efharisto*' at the end, which made the waiter show off even more gaps in his lower set of teeth. He might have a mouth like a graveyard, decided Holly, but he was still totally adorable. The more Greek people she met, the more she liked them. They all seemed to have such a relaxed outlook and a cheeky sense of humour. Holly couldn't remember the last time she'd been anywhere close to crying with laughter, but she could sense that the Greeks made that a daily priority. Perhaps when you lived in such a beautiful place, with such gorgeous weather, it was much easier to feel happy.

Even on its sunniest days, London felt oppressive, crowded and restless. Relaxing was more of a carefully selected activity than an everyday part of life, something people seemed to schedule in between their hair appointment and the weekly shop. As she slipped off her flip-flops, stretched her bare toes into a patch of sunlight and took a sip of her delicious frappé, Holly realised that she was feeling more relaxed than she had in months – perhaps even years. For the next half an hour, she decided to just let herself enjoy that feeling and shut out everything that threatened it.

Banishing thoughts of her mum, Sandra, Rupert and especially Aidan to a small compartment in the back of her brain, Holly tucked into her salad, relishing the sweetness of the tomatoes, the saltiness of the olives and the tangy flavour of the feta cheese as it crumbled over her tongue. As she ate, she took in her surroundings, watching as holidaymakers applied more sun cream to leathery brown limbs and children took their buckets and spades to the shoreline, immersed in their own made-up games. A middle-aged German couple were laughing together over something the wife had just read in her magazine, and further down the beach a boy in his late teens had the back of his shorts pulled down by his girlfriend, who seconds before he'd been attempting to drag into the sea by her feet.

It was a few moments before she realised that the waiter had returned to take away her empty plate. Rather than heading back into the kitchen, however, he stood for a moment at her elbow, taking in the scene spread out below them.

'It's so beautiful here,' Holly blurted.

This seemed to please him, and he smiled without looking at her, nodding his head in agreement.

'I am very tired,' he said.

'Oh?' Holly wasn't sure how to respond, and looked up at him with what she hoped was concern.

'I work here, very early, then I work at the hotel, very late.' As he said the last part, he waved a hand in the direction of Laganas.

'You work in a hotel in Laganas?' guessed Holly, earning herself another nod of the head.

'Yes. It's very good, but I finish at two thirty in the morning. Then here at six thirty in the morning.' He was still smiling, so Holly assumed he must be content with the arrangements, even if they did mean that he got about three hours' sleep a night.

'You're a very good waiter,' she told him now. 'Are you a waiter at the hotel, as well?'

'I work on the bar. I am barman,' came the reply. He told her this with a certain amount of pride. 'I am Nikos,' he added, putting down her empty plate and shaking her hand as she told him her name in return. He repeated it back to her several times, before telling her it was 'very nice'.

Then came the inevitable, 'This your first time Zakynthos?'

'First time in Greece,' she said, waiting for the eruption of excitement she'd come to expect from all Greeks.

Nikos looked at her. 'You like? How many days come?'

'Yes, very much. And just two da—'

'You stay in Kalamaki?' he interrupted. For some reason, Holly found being interrupted by a Greek was more endearing than irritating, and she laughed.

'No, Lithakia,' she told him, smiling as he crinkled his forehead in surprise.

'Lithakia is very good,' he went on, nodding to himself and reaching across to pick up her plate again. 'Close to Porto Koukla. Very good. *Poli kala*. You should make a visit to there.'

'Porto Koukla?' Holly repeated.

'Yes. It is very nice beach. Not like Laganas.' As he said the word, he threw his arm up again, and Holly ducked to avoid being hit with the empty frappé glass.

She was starting to like Nikos more and more. It was such a long time since she'd spoken to anyone she didn't already know. Chatting to Nikos was so easy, and so much fun. If she started jabbering away to a waiter like this back home, they'd probably call the men in white coats to come and cart her off.

She ordered a second frappé and opened her guidebook at the map page. Sure enough, just down the hill from Lithakia there was a beach area marked as Porto Koukla. If the map was correct, the beach there would be nestled in the bay directly opposite the famous Turtle Island, which Holly now discovered was actually called Marathonissi. Running her finger around the coastline on the map, she mouthed the unfamiliar Greek names one by one. They all sounded so magical: Agios Sostis, Marathia, Vassilikos, Argassi. If only she'd taken the time to learn to drive, she could have rented a car and gone exploring. It had never seemed necessary, though, not when she lived in London. Plus, driving lessons weren't cheap. On the rare occasions that she and Rupert ever left the city, he would do the driving or, more often than not, book them both a first-class train ticket.

Holly gazed longingly at the map and wondered vaguely if she could see the island by bus. No, that was silly. She was here to pack up her aunt's house and move on, simple as that. Maybe she would come back one day and see much more, but for now she had to focus on her real reason for being here.

Despite her resolve to exercise self-restraint, Holly continued to read her guidebook as the sun slipped lazily across the sky. After settling her bill and leaving a very generous tip for Nikos, she relocated to her towel down on the beach and sat watching the gently shifting ocean, her toes scrunching through the sand. One hour soon turned into two and she lay back and closed her eyes, letting the sound of the sea and the tickling fingers of warm breeze lull her into a doze.

Something was wrong. Holly closed the front door behind her and dropped her bag on the floor.

There was a cloying smell in the air, and she instinctively brought her hand up to shield her nose, noticing as she did so that the red nail varnish she'd applied during that afternoon's English lesson had already begun to chip.

'Mum?'

The voice that came out of her mouth sounded strangled – muffled by a fear that until now Holly hadn't realised she was feeling. Taking a timid step towards the front room, she peered through the crack where the door hinges met the wooden frame. The TV was on, as it always was, but the volume had been muted. On the screen, a blonde woman with impeccably neat hair was holding up an ugly ornament of a bird sitting on a branch. The price underneath read £34.99, and Holly let out a startled laugh. In the suffocating silence of the hallway, it sounded like a gun had been fired.

'Mum?' she tried again, knowing even as she spoke that it was hopeless. She knew what she'd find when she walked into that room, and over to that chair. The large, squashy armchair, upholstered in tatty brown corduroy; the place her mum always retreated to after she'd got far enough through that day's bottle of vodka to render her legs unreliable.

Holly stood balanced on the tips of her toes, staring down at the carpet, which was littered with leaflets about local cleaning services, takeaways and taxi companies. As she gazed, the colours began to run into one another, until all that swam before her was blackness . . .

'What are you doing? Geddoff!'

Holly sat bolt upright and slapped away the hand that had shaken her awake. After the darkness of her dream, the sunlight on the beach felt blinding.

Nikos crouched down beside her, his bare feet half-obscured by the sand. 'You were . . . moving,' he told her, not unkindly. 'I . . . I think you would want to wake up.'

Holly failed to hold in the groan as she remembered what she'd just been dreaming about. It was haunting her, even here, in this beautiful place. She must have been asleep for a while, because the beach around her was practically empty. A small, elderly man wearing a shocking pink visor was busy stacking up sun loungers, while a much younger boy raked the sand flat behind him. The Insomnia Troll had picked a bloody inconvenient time to stage a disappearing act.

'It is seven o'clock,' Nikos informed her.

Holly rubbed her eyes, then swore as she transferred sand straight into one of them. Before she could do anything, Nikos had unscrewed the lid of his water bottle and unceremoniously lobbed the contents into her face.

Now she was awake. Grabbing her discarded vest top from her open bag, Holly swung it round to wallop him, causing Nikos to leap back on his haunches with a bellow of laughter.

'You . . . You . . .' Holly grinned at him as she attempted to dry her straggly wet hair. Her towel had been on the sand, though, so all she managed to get was a headful of grit.

'You go to Lithakia?'

Nikos really was the master of coming straight to the point.

'Yes,' she nodded, pointing a vague arm down the beach.

'You get a bike.' It wasn't a question.

'No, no,' she tried, but he shook his head.

'I am not madman,' he assured her. 'We go on my bike.'

He probably wasn't going to kill her, Holly reasoned. She was just shaken up because of the dream. He didn't look like the murdering sort. If he tried anything funny, she'd just knock the rest of his teeth out.

Gathering up her bag and giving her towel a firm shake, Holly waited by the path and watched Nikos disappear behind the back of the restaurant. Shortly afterwards, there was a loud spluttering noise and he re-emerged in a cloud of dust and black smoke, his gangly legs sticking out from either side of his moped in the manner of a drunk daddy-long-legs.

Dumping her bag in between his bare feet on the foot-well, Nikos shuffled forward on the seat and nodded for her to climb on. It was hard to tell what colour the saddle was, because it was covered with a criss-crossing array of thick parcel tape in various states of disintegration. Foam was escaping from cracks where the seat joined the metal frame and there was a large hole in the framework of the bike, just behind where Holly was about to put her bottom.

Nikos revved the engine impatiently, and no sooner had Holly swung her leg across the seat than he zoomed off up the road. Realising that she was not wearing a helmet and, rather alarmingly, hadn't located the footrests in time, Holly forgot to be reserved and wound her arms tightly around Nikos' skinny waist, clinging tightly to his slightly damp T-shirt as they rounded the first corner.

The noise from the engine was a deafening mix of pneumatic drill and demented wasp, but Holly quickly started to relish the feeling of the wind rushing through her hair. Opening her mouth in a wide grin as her crazy Greek chauffeur pulled back the throttle even further, she almost choked as a fly hit the back of her throat. Beneath her hands, she felt Nikos start to laugh.

She was enjoying the sensation of being on the bike too

much to really take in the passing scenery, but she did notice a gaggle of horses tethered together under the shade of a large tree and a group of girls traipsing back from the beach, their lilos tucked under one arm and carrier bags full of booze and crisps bouncing against their bare legs.

The dipping sun had cast a marmalade glow across the rooftops, and Holly braved another smile as she breathed in the warm evening air. Again, she marvelled at how relaxed she felt. It was ridiculous: here she was, limbs wrapped around a man she'd met only hours before, hurtling along narrow roads on an island that, just ten days ago, she never even knew existed. She barely recognised herself.

Holly saw a sign for Laganas and a few seconds later Nikos turned into the forecourt of what looked to be a moped hire company and turned off the engine, leaving her to flail clumsily on the seat as he disappeared into a small, glass-fronted office. Soon after, she heard the loud babble of several male Greek voices and just a few minutes later, Nikos re-emerged and asked her for thirty euros.

'For the bike,' he explained, grinning at her.

Mystified, she handed over the last of the cash in her purse, watching as he vanished again, this time into a garage at the back of the open yard. There was the sound of an engine spluttering into life, and a thin buzzing as Nikos drove towards her on another moped, only marginally less battered than his own.

'This, your bike!' he beamed, slithering off and beckoning for her to take the handles.

'But I can't drive!'

'*Ela*, it is easy.' Nikos laughed again, pointing at the handles and levers. 'This one, go. This one, stop.'

One of the men from inside the office was walking towards them now, a bored expression on his face and three helmets in his hands. Holly sat still as he tried each of them on her head in turn, nodding when he was satisfied before trudging off again.

'My cousin,' Nikos told her. 'He make this bike for you. Two weeks.'

Holly thought she might finally understand what was happening. It appeared she now had the use of her very own moped for the next fortnight.

'*Efharisto!*' she exclaimed, grinning at Nikos from the depths of her helmet.

He laughed out loud at this, then spent the next few minutes showing her how to stow things under the seat and how to balance the bike on its little metal parking rod. After a shaky start that almost saw her plough straight into the wall of a restaurant, Holly discovered that driving a moped wasn't actually all that difficult. By the time she and Nikos had reached the base of the hill in Lithakia that led up to the house, she was positively bursting with pleasure.

'I see you, tomorrow, at the beach?' asked Nikos, using his feet to turn his bike round the right way.

Holly pictured her aunt's bedroom, packed full of clutter and still-unopened drawers.

'I'll try,' she promised. 'If not, then the next day.'

This seemed to be good enough, and Nikos nodded briefly before buzzing off back down the road, showering her with an arsenal of grit as he went.

9

There was no sign of life from next door as Holly let herself into the house, but she still kept her eyes firmly on the ground just in case. She was reluctant to admit even to herself how much that morning's encounter with Aidan had affected her. In the very short time that they'd spent together, he'd somehow managed to lure the real Holly to the surface – the side that she'd worked so hard to keep under wraps for as long as she could remember – and that made her nervous.

Instead of heading straight upstairs to her aunt's bedroom, Holly kicked off her flip-flops, dumped her bag on the table and opened the back doors. Stepping up on to the low wall, she could see the ocean spread out below her, vast and a deep midnight blue in the approaching dusk. It was stunning, and for a long time she simply stood still, drinking it all in. No wonder her aunt had loved it here. It had only been two days, and already the thought of London's grey landscape was a depressing prospect in comparison to such raw and natural beauty.

Aidan's back garden, which was separated from her own by a long, knee-height hedge, was equally bare of decoration, but he had at least taken the trouble to arrange a wrought-iron table and chairs in the shade of a fig tree. Holly could smell its intoxicatingly sweet scent from where she was standing. There was also a rusty-looking bicycle propped up against the back wall of his house, and she was surprised to see that it was unlocked. Then again, she supposed this little island wasn't really a place where people would steal from one another.

The sun had dropped even further now, and as Holly gazed out across the water, she could see the faint white pebble of the moon on the horizon as it began its fruitless chase of the sun. The sky, which had been a stunning shade of azure blue all day, had now transformed into a mix of pinks, creams and dusty greys. The intense heat of the day had given way to a calm and comfortable evening temperature, and Holly shook her hair back with pleasure and drank in the view.

She was roused from her blissful trance a few minutes later by the sound of a car door slamming and an Irish accent yelling, 'Wait there, you little bugger,' to an unknown entity. Lurching round in horror, Holly gazelle-hopped across the garden and slammed the back doors just as Aidan stomped around the corner. If he'd seen her, he didn't comment, and a few seconds later she heard the sound of his own door banging shut.

She really needed to get a grip. He was only some bloke – it wasn't like she'd ever see him again after these two weeks. And so what if he'd had his hand down her U-bend? The memory of that was enough to send Holly scuttling up the stairs, as if Aidan would be able to see her through the walls. Distracted by the gut-wrenching humiliation, she found herself once again in her Aunt Sandra's bedroom.

Okay, so it was a little bit creepy in here, but she was a grown woman. As she looked around, wondering whether to just give up and bolt down the hill for some more village wine, Holly's eyes fell on an ancient-looking radio that was sitting on a small table next to the bed. Dropping to her hands and knees, she found the plug socket and switched it on, smiling with relief as music flooded into her ears.

After knob-fiddling her way through several Greek stations, all of which seemed to feature the same wailing old man plucking at a guitar, Holly found a channel playing English songs, and Tears For Fears were soon chasing away the last vestiges of creepiness.

Humming and warbling along out of tune, she yanked open a drawer and spluttered noisily as a cloud of dust wafted out. Her Aunt Sandra had been a big fan of floral, she decided, peering with distaste at the fifteen or so patterned shirts. She found an empty brown suitcase on the top of the wardrobe and started packing most of her aunt's clothes inside. She'd decided to head down to the bar a bit later and ask Annie if there was a way of donating stuff to charity. It seemed like an enormous waste to simply throw it all away, and actually, on closer inspection, some of the things she was pulling out weren't all that bad.

Aside from the frumpier stuff, Holly had also unearthed some gems: a white blouse embroidered with delicate lace, a cashmere shawl and a beautiful pale pink silk kimono. These things she folded carefully and set on the bed. Everything smelled faintly of lavender and, as she worked, Holly began to relax and take her time.

When the chest of drawers was empty, she began examining the little ornaments that were clustered about the room. There were tiny china birds, porcelain ponies and a large number of turtles, some made from shells, others from clay and one from bright green and brown glass. As she bent forward to get a better look, one small turtle caught the light and seemed to glow from within. Holly had never really been a fan of trinkets, but for some reason this particular turtle had seized her attention. Picking it up carefully with both hands, she used the bottom of her vest to smear away the layer of settled dust. She had the strangest feeling that it wasn't the first time she'd held it. Perhaps she'd had something similar as a child.

'You're coming home with me,' she whispered to the turtle, immediately feeling stupid. As she laughed out loud at herself, the radio coughed out a burst of static and, in a flash, Holly was transported back to her mum's grotty living room.

In the weeks leading up to her death, Jenny Wright had been slipping further and further away from anything resembling normality. Drinking heavily on a daily basis, she spent all of her time either slouched in an armchair staring at the TV, or slumped at the kitchen table smoking. It reached a point where Holly couldn't remember the last time she'd seen her mum in clean clothes or with brushed hair. She'd tried to help her, of course, but Jenny only became increasingly upset.

'I don't have any reason to be alive any more,' she'd wail, sucking on her roll-up and blowing acrid smoke into her daughter's face.

'That's a nice thing to say to me, your daughter,' Holly would reply, stepping around her mum's scrawny frame and reaching for the tin opener. That particular day, she'd swiped a couple of tins of baked beans from the corner shop on her way home from college. It wasn't like her mum was going to give her any money, not when she was pouring it all down her throat.

'I never wanted all this to happen,' Jenny continued, throwing a limp arm around the room and sniffing in disgust. 'I should have let someone else take you in – we'd have all been better off.'

Holly sighed. Once upon a time, those sorts of comments would have sent her running up the stairs in tears, but it had been years now since she'd allowed what her mum said to hurt her feelings. Jenny was always muttering about what a bad mother she was when she was drunk, but then a few seconds after an outpouring of remorse she would go on the attack, mumbling nonsense about the life she was owed and that it wasn't her fault she had ended up like this. Holly had been sympathetic once upon a time, back in the days before Jenny had relapsed into her alcoholism for the fifth or sixth time. To Holly, it seemed as if her mum was choosing the easy option. She knew that she could fight harder to get off the booze, but she didn't want it enough, and Holly found that very difficult to forgive.

'Try and eat some dinner, Mum,' she said, pointing at the beans on toast she'd just put on the table in front of her.

Jenny wrinkled her nose and reached for her coffee mug. Why she even bothered trying to disguise the fact she was drinking baffled Holly – it wasn't as if either of them were deluded when it came to the cold, hard facts. It had been a very long time since Holly had bothered emptying any of Jenny's bottles down the sink. It only caused a row, and she simply didn't have the energy any more.

It would always surprise her that she'd been so upset

when her mum had died a few weeks later. She hadn't thought herself capable of feeling anything any more, let alone sadness at losing such a malevolent presence. But the weight with which the death had hit her had felt like a wrecking ball smashing into a glass wall. She'd fallen apart completely, and had been painstakingly trying to piece herself back together ever since.

Holly could only remember snatches of what happened on the day her mum died. After making the discovery, she had run back out into the hallway where she assumed she must have passed out. When she came round, she stayed on the floor for what felt like hours, telling herself over and over to get up and call the police. She couldn't, though – she was as rooted to the spot as the old apple tree in the back field of the college. Some of the kids still climbed it, thinking that the twisty branches would disguise their illicit cigarettes. Holly never joined them, preferring to watch from a distance. She hated herself for envying them, with their Topshop shoes, highlighted hair and easy lives – they had no idea how good they had it. Holly would listen to them, bemoaning their latest break-up or whingeing about not having the latest mobile phone, and wish she could scream in their faces.

She had no memory of the 999 call she eventually must have made, but at around eight in the evening an ambulance arrived, followed closely by a police car. While the paramedics rustled past her in their neon-striped jackets, a female police officer crouched down next to her on the hall floor and took her hands.

'You need to come with us now, Holly. It's going to be okay.'

But it never was okay. It never had been, ever since.

Suddenly spooked by the glass turtle in her now clammy hands, Holly tossed it down on to the bed, where it bounced lightly and slid off the edge.

'Shit!' She dived to her knees. Thankfully, the tatty rug had prevented any breakage, and as Holly leaned forward to retrieve it, she noticed a beige case poking out from under the bed beside a very dog-eared and dust-covered shoebox.

'Oh, you little legend,' she breathed, pulling out the case and ignoring the box. Yanking off the lid, she gasped out loud as a polished and gleaming sewing machine greeted her. It was a genuine thing of beauty, and Holly felt a wave of real affection for her late aunt. If Sandra had liked sewing, then they clearly had a lot more in common than Holly had first thought.

It had been years now since she'd used one of these but, as she ran her fingers over the spool, she was overwhelmed by an urge to rip up the clothes she'd just packed and then refashion them all. What had begun as a necessity after her mum died, when she was buying all her clothes from markets and second-hand shops, had quickly become Holly's favourite thing to do. She adored the whole process: collecting the material, planning new garments on paper, then creating her very own pieces from scratch. She'd loved building something new and beautiful out of other people's discarded items – there was a sort of magic to it.

Although she'd stopped making her own clothes after securing her first decently paid job, Holly still had a box of her stuff that she'd hidden away in the back of her wardrobe. Rupert was never likely to venture in there, after all, and knowing the box was there gave her a bizarre sort of comfort.

As she knelt there now, her feet slowly going numb on the hard tiles that lay beneath the rug, Holly wondered why she'd given up her hobby. She didn't need to make clothes any more, obviously, but why had she felt the need to give up something she loved so much? Thinking about it now, she realised that she'd stopped sewing at around the same time she first met Rupert. She tried to picture herself sitting at the breakfast bar in her boyfriend's swanky east-London apartment, rattling away on her sewing machine while he watched TV. Nope, it would never happen. He wouldn't see the point. He'd laugh and offer to take her shopping, tell her that it was weird to wear other people's cast-offs. Still, there was nothing to stop her doing some sewing while she was here, all by herself, with nobody around to make judgments. Gathering up a pile of clothes from the suitcase and heaving the machine up under one arm, Holly switched off the radio, headed downstairs and prepared to settle in for the night.

She'd decided to start with something fairly simple – a patchwork tapestry that she could hang up on the empty wall by the back door. She remembered seeing some decent-looking scissors in one of the kitchen drawers, so she collected these and started on the heap of old blouses and skirts she'd brought down.

Using two old mugs to pin the material flat, she marked out rough square shapes with a pencil then set about cutting them out. It was fiddly work, but Holly immediately felt soothed by the monotonous action. Before long, she had enough patches ready to start sewing, and she spent a good ten minutes arranging them on the floor to work out the order. Sandra had certainly liked her patterns and her embellishments, and Holly smiled to herself as she pictured how beautiful the finished creation would look when the early morning light sneaked in through the glass back door.

It felt so right to be back sitting at a sewing machine again, her nimble fingers sliding the thread on to the bobbin and pulling the material taut as the tip of the needle dived up and down. In that moment, she almost forgot that she was in a strange house and a strange country – all that mattered was what her hands were doing, what her eyes were seeing and what her heart was telling her. This was where she was happy.

The pastel sky outside bled slowly into an inky blackness and the eager moon raced up to join the stars. As the light of the day vanished, the crickets ceased their incessant chorus, until the only sound came from the gentle lapping of the ocean.

Far below where Holly sat, her brow furrowed in concentration and her bare toes resting lightly on the foot pedal of the sewing machine, an egg cracked open beneath the damp sand and a baby turtle wriggled free. He was all alone, but not frightened. He knew what he had to do. Discarding the sticky pieces of his first home, he made his way to the surface and paused to bathe for a moment in the comforting light of the moon. Leaving barely a mark on the sand as he went, the tiny, soft-shelled creature slithered clumsily down to the water and plunged fearlessly into his future.

Tuesday, 6 November 1984
Hello Sandy.

I wasn't sure whether or not to send this, but I thought you'd probably want to know that I was still alive at the very least. You always have been the sensible one, the sweeter one, the better one. I was planning to head to Australia, but I haven't made it quite that far yet. I met a man – he's called Nic – and I'm just staying with him at the moment. Are you still cross with me? I miss you so much that I swear I can feel it burning inside my chest. You're the only person in my life that I care about – I just wanted you to know that. I hope the storms haven't been too bad on the island. I keep picturing us running down the beach in the rain. I wish we still were. Please write back and tell me your news. My address is below. I love you.

Jen Bear xxx

10

Holly's mobile phone was ringing. Propping herself up on one elbow, she cursed herself for leaving it right next to the bed. Peering at the screen as she wiped the sleep out of her eyes, she took a deep breath and forced herself to smile.

'Hi, darling!'

'Hello, poppet – I didn't wake you, did I?' Poppet? That was a new one. Holly gritted her teeth.

'Not at all,' she told him. 'I was just about to get in the shower.'

In reality, she'd only put her head down three hours ago after sitting up sewing until the early hours. The last thing she wanted to do was be awake, especially as she'd been finding it increasingly easy to sleep since she'd been here on the island. Zakynthos: one, Insomnia Troll: nil. Rupert was rabbiting on about some work deal he'd done and Holly felt her mind glazing over.

'Did you hear that, darling?'

'Sorry, sweetie – it's not the best connection this end.' It was a lie, of course; she could hear him perfectly well.

'This new client I've secured – he's worth over ten million for the business. I'm getting a nice bonus out of it.'

'Wow! Babe, that's great news. Well done you.' Holly wondered if she sounded as bored as she felt. Poor Rupert. Here he was calling her to share his exciting news, and she couldn't even be bothered to listen. She must be more tired than she thought. She was always grumpy when she got overtired.

'Are you okay?' Rupert sounded concerned. 'You don't sound like your normal happy self.'

Her normal *happy* self?

'I'm fine,' she replied automatically. 'It's just been a bit weird, you know, all this.'

'You poor thing,' he said. There was genuine concern in his voice, which made Holly feel even worse. 'I miss you,' he added, and she felt her bad mood retreating.

'I miss you too,' she whispered, realising as she said it that she actually did. She knew who to be when Rupert was with her. Out here, it felt dangerously like another version of herself was on the verge of making a reappearance. 'I really do miss you,' she added. 'Very much.'

'I know what you mean,' he admitted. 'It's only been a few days, but you feel so far away from me.'

Given that he spent a lot of time abroad with work, this revelation came as quite a surprise to Holly. He'd never talked about missing her so much before. Perhaps it was coming back to his flat alone every night that was getting to him.

'It's only two weeks,' she told him now. 'Less than two weeks! And I'll be nice and tanned for you when I get back.'

'I don't care about a tan; I just want you back. And you didn't call me last night.' He was beginning to sound a bit like a grumpy toddler now.

'You should go, before you're late for work,' she said, abandoning all hopes of a lie-in and swinging her legs out from under the sheet.

'Okay, darling.' He still sounded sulky. 'Will you remember to call me later?'

She promised that she would, obediently returning his 'I love you' before ending the call.

Holly sat in silence staring at the phone in her hand. Why was she being such a cow to poor Rupert? She'd only been away from London for a few days, but she already felt as if her life had changed. Being here in Zakynthos had awakened something in her – she couldn't quite put her finger on what it was yet, but there had definitely been a shift. She was in an environment that should, by all accounts, feel completely alien to her, but instead she found herself feeling more relaxed here than she could ever remember feeling back in England. She shook her head at the ridiculousness of it all. She must have sun-stroke or something – the heat was sending her doolally.

Stretching her arms up over her head and groaning as her muscles creaked into life, Holly let her eyes roam the room. The spare bedroom had little in the way of clutter, but as her gaze reached the wardrobe nestled in the far corner, Holly spotted what looked like a folded piece of paper on the top of it. Intrigued, she fetched the stool from her aunt's bedroom next door and stood on it to take a closer look. Age had curled the corners of the paper and turned them yellow, but when she unfolded it, she almost fell off the stool in surprise.

'Jenny and Sandy's Secret Map' was written across the top in red biro, and underneath was a very clumsily drawn map of Zakynthos. Whoever had drawn it had labelled a lot of silly landmarks along the scribbled coastline, including 'field that always smells of poo', 'rock that looks like dog face' and 'sexy barman'. Some village names had also been added in black pen, clearly by someone else, and next to a place called Porto Limnionas, someone had drawn a large heart. At the northern tip of the drawing, with a big star helpfully drawn next to it, was a place simply labelled 'our secret beach'.

Holly stepped down from the stool, the map in her hand and her heart racing. Had her aunt left this map here for her to find? She didn't care, but she did know that she wanted to visit every single place that Jenny and Sandra had marked on it. She wanted to go everywhere – she wanted to swim in the same sea, lay her towel on the same sand and gaze out at the same views. Racing down the stairs, she snatched up her guidebook and flicked through it until she found the map, then ran her finger around the outline of the island, picking out the names that matched those on the drawing.

As far as she could tell, her mum and Sandra's 'secret beach' was close to a place called Korithi, which was a very long way indeed from Lithakia. On her moped and with very limited local knowledge, Holly guessed it would take her hours to get all the way up there. Plus, who was to say that she'd even be able to find this beach when she got there?

For a reason she couldn't quite put her finger on yet, that was the one place marked on the map that she wanted to see the most, but she would really need a car to get there. Correction, she would need someone who could drive a car. Maybe Annie would run her up there. She decided that she would pop down to the bar later and ask, but for now, it was time to have some breakfast while she took a better look at this new treasure.

*

99

By the time Holly opened the back door, a chair awkwardly hooked over one arm and a plate of breakfast and the map in the other hand, it was almost 10 a.m. The patio stones were already beginning to warm beneath her feet, and in the distance she could see the sunlight dancing wildly on the surface of the sea.

Arranging the chair so she was sitting with her back to the house, Holly balanced her plate across her lap and started to devour the slices of tomato that she'd just cut up. They were so much sweeter and juicier here, like an entirely different species to the chalky ones she bought in the supermarkets back home, and Holly had drizzled some honey over the top and seasoned them with black pepper. If anyone could see her, they'd probably think she was disgusting and quite possibly mad, but she loved the way the oozy honey lifted the sweetness of the plump fruit and the sharp pepper kept the whole combination from becoming too much.

Once she'd finished, she put the plate on the floor and tore the lid off her yoghurt. There was a light breeze this morning, which was lifting the ends of her just-washed hair and gently rustling the trees. Lost in her own sleepy thoughts, she didn't hear Aidan's back door open, but a few seconds later she was almost knocked sideways by something very hairy and *very* slobbery.

'PHELAN! I said WAIT!'

It only took Aidan a few seconds to leap over the small hedge and reach Holly, but he wasn't in time to save her yoghurt. Phelan, his apparently deaf red setter, was now happily licking it up from where it had exploded down Holly's leg.

'I am so sorry,' he said, hooking his fingers through Phelan's collar and giving it a determined yank.

Holly, who had spent the past few moments running a full gauntlet of emotions from intense shock to extreme amusement, could only look down at her yoghurt-splattered shins and laugh.

'It's okay,' she finally managed. 'It wasn't that nice anyway.'

'Wait there a sec, will you?' Aidan had galloped back to his own house, leaving Holly to stare after him in bemusement. Phelan, finding himself released once again, shuffled forward to pinch the upturned yoghurt pot, which he held neatly between his paws and started to lick.

'Well, aren't you something?' Holly told him.

Phelan stopped licking and flashed her a wet, yoghurty grin, his tongue lolling out of his mouth in the manner of a friendly lunatic.

By the time Holly had been into the kitchen to sponge her sticky shins, Aidan had returned – and he'd brought her a gift.

'It's just an orange,' he said, handing it over.

'Thanks.' Holly sneaked a look at him. 'But I know what an orange is.'

'Smart-arse.' Aidan squinted at her through his mess of black hair. He was wearing a pale blue shirt today and faded yellow shorts. There were freckles on his lower arms and across his nose, and one of his toenails was black.

'I'm sorry I was such a bitch to you yesterday,' Holly was amazed to hear herself tell him. 'I had no right to bite your head off like that.'

'You are a bit prickly, I'll give you that,' he grinned. 'Is that how you got your name, like?'

'Now who's being a smart-arse?'

They both looked over to where Phelan, yoghurt completely devoured, was rolling around on his back in the dust.

'He's brilliant,' Holly smiled. 'How long have you had him?'

'He's a naughty little fecker, but I do love the little shite.' Aidan crouched down so he could rub the dog's exposed tummy. 'I found him wandering the streets down in the town about two years ago now. He was in a right old state. It happens here a lot, unfortunately. The Greeks are a bit funny about giving their pets the snip, so they always end up with a load of puppies nobody wants.'

Holly looked over at the floppy, beaming, ridiculous dog. 'Well, he looks a lot happier than any animal I've ever seen – you must be doing a good job.'

'Nah, he's just a soppy eejit.'

'So, you've lived here for a while, then?' Holly asked. She was finding it hard to meet his eyes. There was something deeply unnerving about the way he seemed to look right into her head. If she caught his eye, she was irrationally afraid that he'd be able to read her mind. Instead she let her eyes rest on his lips, which were light pink and smattered with a trace of his characteristic freckles.

'Oh, a few years, on and off,' he told her, fiddling with his tatty flip-flop. 'I used to come here as a teenager too. My mum always loved it over here, so when she moved away I took over the house.'

'Where did she go? Back home to Ireland?' Holly asked,

before adding, 'Sorry ... I mean, it's none of my business.'

'Don't worry,' he looked at her sideways. 'She moved over to Kefalonia, actually. It's the closest island to this one.' There was a hint of something cold in his tone, but Holly didn't feel as if it was directed at her. Clearly the topic of his mum was a sore subject for Aidan.

'Have you managed to see much of the island yet?' he asked, neatly changing the subject.

Glad to have an easy question to answer, Holly told him all about her walk down to Kalamaki Beach the previous day, and how she'd befriended Nikos and secured her moped. Aidan laughed as she explained about Nikos' rickety bike that belched black smoke and was held together with bits of tape.

'Sounds exactly like one I had,' he said, smiling at some personal memory. 'Mum hated me going out on that thing, but it was the best way to pick up chicks down in Laganas.'

Holly pulled a face.

'Hey! Don't give me that look – it didn't take you long to clamber behind that Nikos fella, now did it?'

Holly was about to retort that she already had a boyfriend, thank you very much, but something stopped her. She was aware of a slight charge developing in the air between them and hurriedly crossed her legs in the opposite direction.

'I'd love to see more of the island,' she said, shyly unfolding the map she'd found and laying it across her legs so he could see. 'Although I'm not sure I'd ever get to half these places on that thing parked out front.'

Aidan openly laughed as he read some of the descriptions. It was a lovely, warm sound – and very infectious.

'Listen,' he paused for a second. 'If you can keep the day after tomorrow and the next few days after that free, then I can help you find a few of these places.'

'Oh, I didn't mean to hint.' Holly was mortified. 'I wouldn't want to eat into your free time.'

'Nonsense!' Aidan held up a freckled hand. 'Shut your trap, woman. I insist.'

Holly ignored the miniature version of herself that had popped up on her shoulder and was wagging a wary finger at her. 'Don't be a fool,' it whispered. 'What about Rupert? What would he think?'

'In that case, I'd love to,' she grinned, sticking a metaphorical finger up at her tiny sensible side.

'I'd wager that I'm a better driver than Nikos, anyway,' Aidan said, standing up and clicking his fingers at Phelan. The dog twitched slightly at the sound, and Holly thought she heard him actually sigh, but eventually he clambered up and trotted over, resting his head affectionately on his master's thigh. Holly was still clutching the orange he'd brought her, and he pointed to it as he turned to leave. 'Make sure you eat that – I grew it myself.'

'What are you, a farmer?' she asked his departing back, digging a thumb through the glossy peel.

'No,' he stopped at the corner of her house and grinned at her. 'I'm a vet. See you the day after tomorrow.'

Holly stayed in her sunny spot on the chair long after he'd gone, chewing chunks of orange and trying to make sense of the peculiar sensation bubbling in her stomach. She felt guilty, that much was undeniable, but there was something far stronger and more alluring that was tugging at her insides. Rupert was her boyfriend, he was the one she loved, the man she wanted to be with, but Aidan was just so . . . She swallowed the last piece of orange as she searched for the word. He was just so unapologetic, that was it. She liked the fact that he poked fun at her and swore like a sailor and dressed in clothes peppered with holes. He didn't pretend to be anything other than who he was, and for some reason it was making her feel far more at ease with herself than she normally did. With Rupert, she was always on her best behaviour, terrified that if she said the wrong thing or reacted in the wrong way then he would leave her, but she didn't feel that way with Aidan. Perhaps it was the security of knowing that she'd only ever spend a couple of weeks with him, and that Rupert was waiting patiently for her back in London. It didn't matter what Aidan thought of her, in the end, because she wouldn't be around long enough to disappoint him.

At around three that afternoon, Holly abandoned the clearing out of her aunt's bedroom and set out in search of Porto Koukla, the little beach that Nikos had recommended. It had taken the majority of the morning to pack up the rest of Sandra's clothes and wrap all the many thousands – or so it felt – of ornaments in newspaper. Sandra had been a big fan of the local Greek paper, Holly discovered, but she had also been rather fond of a certain British tabloid.

'Greek economy in tatters!' one particularly histrionic headline screamed. Holly had scanned the article briefly, before tearing the page out and wrapping it around a china plate decorated with painted flowers. She hadn't seen any evidence of these so-called 'tatters' since arriving on the island. Perhaps it was a different story on the mainland of Greece, but everyone she'd encountered here seemed happy enough.

Much as she enjoyed her life in London, Holly could easily imagine herself living a more simple existence. She couldn't see anyone here obsessing about what someone posted on Facebook, or who was doing the dirty with whom in *EastEnders*. Not that she cared about such things much, either, but a lot of the people she knew did. Aliana, for example, spent more time on Facebook, Twitter, Vine, Snapchat, Tinder and God knows what else than she did actually working – and to Holly it all seemed to be a load of nonsense. Her own online profile contained just a few photos of herself and Rupert and details of where she worked – there was nothing about where she'd gone to school or anything.

On the rare occasion that Holly had received a message or a friend request from someone she'd known from her schooldays, she'd deleted them without a second glance. Those times were done, and she had no intention of ever allowing herself or anyone else to stir up those miserable memories. She had been a very different person back then; a person she didn't like to even think about. In fact, she was mildly surprised that anyone from those awful days would even think to contact her.

Hugely sociable and friendly as a child, Holly had become increasingly withdrawn as her mum had slipped down the slope of alcoholism. The girls with whom she had once been so close had stopped inviting her round to their houses to play after school. She could remember with heartbreaking clarity the day that her best friend, Daisy Davies, had awkwardly told her that they couldn't be friends any more.

They had been standing in the corner of the playground, not far from where a group of boys were kicking a ball around, and Daisy, her thumb firmly wedged into the corner of her mouth, had said to Holly, 'My mum says your mum is dirty; she says that she's a bad person. She said that I might get dirty if I'm friends with you.'

Holly, who had only just turned nine, gawped at her in horror. She knew there was something weird going on with her mum. She no longer walked the fifteen minutes from their flat down to the school gates every afternoon, and she didn't always make nice dinners like she used to, but she wasn't 'dirty'.

'My mum's not dirty,' she'd mumbled. 'Your mum is probably just confused or something.'

Daisy had shaken her head sadly. She had been wearing a T-shirt with a pink Care Bear on the front, the irony of which would only occur to Holly years later. 'She said I'm not allowed to talk to you, and if she finds out that I did then she'll give Bambi away.'

Bambi was the tortoiseshell kitten that the two girls had found wandering in the street outside Daisy's house, and that Daisy's mum had wrinkled her nose at in disgust as soon as it was carried into her kitchen. Holly had known then that she was fighting a losing battle. Daisy was obsessed with that kitten. She drew pictures of her all over the back of her hands when they were supposed to be practising their spellings in Miss Patterson's class.

'It's okay,' she'd told her friend. 'Bambi needs you. I'll be fine by myself.'

And that was that. Daisy had shuffled off to join the rest of the girls from their class and Holly had kept her distance. From that moment on, right through to when she left the education system for good at eighteen, Holly was always on her own. Making friends was more effort than it was worth – especially when her mum's fondness for the odd G&T evolved into something more dangerous. Nobody wanted to be associated with a smelly drunk, not even Holly herself, but then she hadn't had a choice.

'*Yassou, koukla!*' The sound of Kostas' cheerful bellow pulled Holly abruptly out of her miserable meander down crap-memory lane.

'*Yassou*, Kostas,' she replied, waving as she headed past his shop and onwards down the hill. She had thought about taking the moped, but it was too hot to face wearing the helmet. And, in the end, it only took ten minutes of walking and one encounter with a rather grizzly-looking goat for Holly to find the place she was looking for.

Unlike the beaches at Laganas and Kalamaki, Porto Koukla's coastline was narrow, with only three or so metres of sand between the steps of the rustic beach bar and the lapping water. The wind was slightly brisker than it had been that morning and Holly could hear the Greek flag flapping wildly at the top of its beachside pole as she threw down her towel and slipped out of her purple sundress.

There were far fewer people here than there had been in the busier resorts of Laganas and Kalamaki, and Holly could feel the residue of tension easing away as she wriggled into a comfortable position and opened her book. Spending too much time in the house had been making her feel edgy – she couldn't shake the feeling that she was being watched – so she was determined to spend the next few hours experiencing pure escapism.

She'd just read the first sentence of chapter two when a shadow passed across the page.

'It's Holly, isn't it?'

Annie from the bar at the bottom of the hill was standing next to her. Holly stared at the chipped pink varnish on Annie's toenails for a few seconds and took a deep breath before closing her book.

'That's right. How are you, Annie?'

'Ooh, I'm just peachy, my darling. Lovely afternoon, isn't it? Do you mind if I pitch my towel here?'

She was pointing to the empty patch of sand right next to Holly.

'Of course I don't mind.' Holly smiled as Annie stripped off to reveal a rather worn-looking black bikini encasing a rather worn-looking bottom and boobs. Her skin was so dark it looked like she'd treated it with wood stain.

'So,' she turned to face Holly, 'have you bumped into Aidan yet?'

Clearly, it wasn't just the Greeks who got straight to the point around here.

'Yes, and he's very nice.' Holly contemplated telling her about the bathroom incident, then thought better of it.

'Nice-looking too, eh?' Annie cackled. She'd brought a large bottle of water down from the bar, and offered some to Holly.

'No thanks, I'm good.'

'So, you didn't think Aidan was good-looking, then?'

She clearly wasn't going to let this subject go. Holly allowed herself to picture her scruffy Irish neighbour for a second, her mind lingering on the broad freckled forearms, messy dark hair and slightly mocking half-smile.

'He's quite attractive,' she admitted. 'Not really my type, but I can see the appeal.'

'Tall, dark and handsome is everybody's type, surely?' giggled Annie, pulling a face as Holly shook her head. 'Well, each to their own, I suppose. I tell you what, though,' she added with a wink. 'If I was living right next door to him, I'd probably have become a Peeping Tom by now.'

'Annie!' Holly was laughing now. She'd never met such an unashamed pervert. Well, not a female one, anyway.

Annie merely cackled in response, unscrewing the lid of her water bottle and taking another big swig. 'Bleedin' hell, it's hot today.'

Holly reached for her sun lotion and squirted a fresh coat across her stomach.

'You're so lucky,' Annie told her now. 'Having olive skin. I bet you never burn.'

Holly glanced down at her rapidly bronzing body and shrugged. 'I never really thought about it,' she admitted. 'I'm not even sure why I have this skin type – my mum was pure English rose.'

'Sandra was too,' Annie informed her. 'She wasn't a big fan of the sun, either. I always used to say to her, "Sandy, why have you chosen to live in a place like this if it means scuttling from one patch of shade to the next all summer long?"'

'What was her answer?' Holly was genuinely intrigued.

'She always said the same thing: that this was her home and always would be. Her parents loved it here too, of course – but I suppose you knew that?'

Holly bit her lip. Jenny had talked about her parents – Holly's grandparents – quite a lot before she'd started to drink on a daily basis. She'd been particularly close to her mother, Jenny had said, her eyes always misting up at the thought of her. They had died in an accident when Jenny was only nineteen and had left her their house, but Holly had never seen it. Apparently Jenny had sold it in the end to start up a new business with a friend, but it had failed and she'd lost everything. Her family was cursed.

Looking up at Annie, she noticed a sadness in her eyes.

'Do you miss her?' she asked. 'Sandra, I mean.'

'I do, yes,' Annie sniffed. 'She was such a lovely woman, as you know.'

'Well, I . . .' Holly stopped as she remembered that she'd lied to Annie on the first night about how well she knew her aunt. 'I didn't meet her that many times,' she finished lamely.

'She and Aidan were pretty good friends too,' Annie went on, her tone brightening considerably as she went back to her favourite subject. 'They used to come down to the bar some nights and have a few whiskies. I don't mind telling you that I think Sandy had a bit of a crush on him.'

'Pardon?' Holly was struggling for a suitable response, what with all the metaphorical pots and kettles banging together.

'Oh yeah, it was quite sweet, really. She even knitted

him a jumper one Christmas. It had a turtle on the front of it and he wore it pretty much every day in the winter.'

Holly couldn't help but smile at the vivid image this conjured up.

'He helped her out a lot when she got really sick, you know, found a new home for Caretta—'

'Caretta?' interrupted Holly.

'Her cat. Did you never meet him? He was quite a character – huge bloody thing, almost as big as a sea turtle.'

'What happened to him?'

'Aidan found him a new home on the other side of the island after Sandy went,' Annie told her. 'He wanted to keep him, but Caretta didn't take kindly to having his back end sniffed by the dog on a daily basis.'

Despite the scorching sun and the lively Greek music floating down from the bar, Holly felt a sudden chill.

'Was it very bad, in the end?' she forced herself to ask.

Annie considered this for a moment before answering, planting her eyes firmly on the horizon. 'She was very brave,' she said eventually. 'Cancer is an evil disease, I'll tell you that – but she seemed positive enough.'

Holly felt an overwhelming pang of sadness for Sandra, who had clearly suffered so much. At least her mum had been completely out of it when she died – the only person in any pain over that particular death was Holly herself.

'I wish I'd known her better,' Holly said now, really meaning it.

'Would you like me to tell you some stories about her?' Annie turned back and smiled at her. 'She was very funny after a few cheeky bevvies, your auntie.'

'I'd like that very much,' Holly beamed.

Annie clapped her hands together with glee, delighted to have been given permission to natter away uninterrupted.

'Tell you what, darling – you pop up to the bar and get us a couple of cold beers, and I'll tell you every story I've got.'

She didn't have to say anything else. Holly was already on her feet.

Three beers and two hours later, Holly had decided that she would have liked her Aunt Sandra very much. Annie had no idea how many gaps she was filling with her anecdotes, but Holly was positively lapping them all up. She discovered that Sandra spent a large part of the year making all the traditional costumes for the annual island carnival, which took place over two weeks in late February and early March. 'If anyone wanted anything making, they'd always go to Sandy,' Annie told her, in between hearty swigs of Mythos. 'She did hundreds of costumes on that tiny machine of hers. She worked until her fingers had blisters, but she never complained.'

'I like to make clothes too,' Holly admitted, the beer loosening her tongue.

'Well, that's just lovely,' Annie smiled sideways at her. 'You must get that from her – after all, your mum *was* her twin sister.'

Twin sister? Holly almost spat her mouthful of beer out across the sand. She'd had no idea that her mum had been a twin. Just why and how could Jenny have allowed her own twin sister to become a virtual stranger? Why the hell would she have cut Sandra out of their lives for so long?

'Do you still see your dad?' Annie's question crashed through Holly's racing thoughts like a sledgehammer on a frozen lake.

'Oh no, he . . . er,' she spluttered, caught off guard. She had grown up thinking that her dad was a freedom fighter that her mum had met while she was travelling the world. According to Jenny, he was a bit of a renegade and had ended up in a foreign jail, which was why he couldn't come and visit them. She'd heard the story so often over the years that she'd never thought to question it, and a father wasn't anything she'd ever really craved, in any case. Before Jenny started drinking, she had been a wonderful mother, and the two of them together had always felt to Holly like a little team.

'I still see my stepdad sometimes,' she said, stumbling slightly on the white lie. 'He's called Simon. My mum dumped him when I was about eight, but he still comes to see me from time to time.'

Annie was looking at her a little oddly now. Holly got the impression that she had been about to say something but had stopped herself.

'He lives in Canada now,' she added. 'We write to each other.'

Simon had flown back to the UK when he heard about Jenny's death, and he and Holly had been the only two people in the crematorium on the day of her sad, lonely funeral. Holly hadn't known how to contact any other remaining family, because Jenny had always said she was the only one left, and Simon was none the wiser, either. He'd tried awkwardly to reach across and hold her hand during the short reading, his glasses balanced right on the end of his thin nose and his hair curling around his ears.

Holly had wanted nothing more than to throw herself on to the cheap laminate floor by his feet and wail, but she'd found herself paralysed. Simon had waited a week to see if she would thaw, but eventually he had to fly back and get on with life with his new family. Holly never resented him for that, but she did miss him. She wondered now if he had ever known about Sandra, and if so, why he would have kept it from her.

Holly was distracted from her thoughts as Annie chattered on, oblivious to the effect her words were having. As well as being the seamstress of the island, it seemed that Sandra had also volunteered at the local veterinary clinic – Aidan's clinic – and had become foster mum to a number of dogs and cats while new owners were found. Caretta had been a stray, Annie told her, but for some reason Sandra fell much harder for the enormous black and white cat than she had for any of the others. 'He would follow her up and down the hill, like a dog,' Annie recalled. 'Sometimes she'd sit at one of my tables, watching the sun set, you know, and he'd perch up on her shoulder.'

No wonder Sandra and Aidan had been such good friends, Holly thought. It sounded like her aunt had been a bona fide Mother Teresa when it came to animals.

After the third empty beer bottle was nestling in the sand by her bare toes, Holly plucked up the courage to ask the question she'd been wanting to ask all afternoon.

'Did you ever meet my mum?'

Annie looked surprised. 'Oh no, I didn't arrive on the island until 'ninety-two.' She must have seen the shadow of disappointment cross Holly's face, because she quickly added, 'But I have heard some tall tales about what her and Sandra used to get up to.'

'Oh?' Holly tried her best to remain nonchalant.

'They were a right pair of tearaways, is how I heard it. Skinny-dipping down at Porto Limnionas and drinking all night in town. There was no mum and dad around to keep them in check, I suppose, so they just had a few wild months.'

Holly was smiling at the thought of her mum being happy and free. By the end of her life she'd turned so grey and immobile – like a caged bird, trapped behind the bars of her own destructive habit. Then again, it was her own fault, Holly told herself sternly. Jenny Wright only really had herself to blame for what happened to her.

'So, are you a bit of a wild one, like your mum was?' Annie pressed.

Holly considered the question and thought back into her past. She'd certainly gone off the rails for a while after her mum died, staying out as late as possible on her own in bars and clubs. Anything to avoid going back to the place where it had happened. For a few months, Holly had been on a mission not to think about anything, not her mum, not her future and certainly not herself. She'd told herself that all the drinking and all the men was her right – something she deserved after years of struggling to look after her mother, but of course it had only left her feeling more empty in the end. It wasn't a time that she was proud of, and she had no intention of telling Annie anything about it.

'I've never been too crazy,' she gave Annie a half-wink. 'I'm afraid that I'm very sensible and boring these days.'

They both looked down at the stack of empty bottles by their feet and started to giggle.

'Okay, okay!' Holly held up her hands. 'Maybe I still have the odd moment.'

The two of them sat there chatting until the sun started to slip towards the water and long shadows crept along the sand. Holly was at last starting to feel like she had a better idea of who her aunt had been, but she'd also been left with so many other questions: why had Jenny and Sandra fallen out so badly? Why had her mum left Zakynthos if she had been so happy here? And why did Sandra wait until after it was too late to get in contact?

And if she was honest with herself, Holly realised, as she made her way slowly back up the hill, she was also now seriously questioning the identity of her father for the very first time.

Thursday, 22 September 1987
Sandy!

Are you surprised? I saw this in Kostas' shop the other day and it made me laugh so much that I had to buy it, but then I remembered that I had no one to send it to! Idiot!! I used to love writing you postcards when I was away travelling, so I thought, why not? Holly has drawn you a turtle as well. Well, she told me it was a turtle, but it looks more like a green scribble to me. I still find it hilarious that 'turtle' was her first word, but then she never puts that little glass one down, does she? Oh God, I love her so much. I love you all so much. I'm so glad we made Zakynthos our home. Now put the kettle on, will you?

Love Mummy Bear xxx

11

Holly opened her suitcase and rummaged through the jumble of clothes until she found the straps of her mum's rucksack. Along with the little ornament of the house and a creased photo of Holly's grandparents on their wedding day, this rucksack had been the only personal possession Jenny Wright had left when she died. Holly had only thrown it in her case at the last minute and couldn't quite remember now why she had, but here it was – battered yellow canvas with badges sewn all across the front. One of them, Holly realised with a start, was a Greek flag.

Jenny had travelled the world after losing her parents, she'd said as much, so Holly had always known that this rucksack and its contents meant a lot to her mum. Inside there was a rolled-up map of the world with holes where the younger Jenny had once planted pins. One day she'd sat on the sofa with Holly by her side, retracing her own steps with a finger and teaching Holly the names of all the places she'd visited: China, Sri Lanka, Thailand, Indonesia, Bali – the list seemed to go on for ever, and Holly, wide-eyed and naive on the cushion next to her, had begged in earnest for the two of them to go back to all these places together. It was in the days before Jenny's blue eyes had lost their sparkle, and she'd smiled down at her daughter and promised that yes, of course they would go on an adventure together.

It was the morning after her chat on the beach with Annie, and Holly was in the process of rereading the letter from Sandra for at least the twentieth time.

. . . I'm ashamed to say that a combination of cowardice and hope stopped me from finding out the truth until recently. I hoped that she had simply forgotten me, given up on me, perhaps. It was all I deserved, in the end.

Why? Why was it all she deserved?

. . . I know you must have so many questions. Questions about me, about your mother, about why I never got to see you grow up – but I fear I have run out of time to answer those questions. I am hoping that if you come to Zakynthos, to the house where it all began, then you will find some truth in the wreckage that I have left behind.

But where? Where was this truth and these answers? Holly had been through every drawer in Sandra's bedroom and turned out every cupboard in the house, but her search had turned up nothing.

She sat now on the hard tiled floor with her back against the bed, Jenny's world map unfurled across her bare knees. Running a finger down through Europe, she snaked her way south until the tip of her nail found the hole where Zakynthos was marked. She could probably go to all the places on this map bearing pinholes and not find any answers – it was here, on this island, that she knew the truth was waiting. And she didn't want to wait another day to find it.

What was the name of that place Annie had mentioned yesterday, where her mum and Sandra had gone skinny-dipping? Porto something? Rolling the map back up and stowing it carefully inside Jenny's old rucksack, Holly went downstairs and retrieved their hand-drawn map from underneath a heap of discarded scraps of material on the kitchen table. Opening it up, she scoured the scribbled names along the coastline: Porto Koukla, Porto Roxi, Porto Limnionas ... That was it! It was the very same place where either her mum or her aunt had taken the trouble to draw a big heart, so it must be important.

Holly opened her guidebook to the map page and compared the two. She was no expert in map reading, but Porto Limnionas didn't look like it was that far away, perhaps a few miles further than Kalamaki, but on the south-west side of the island rather than the southeast. According to the instructions in the book, all you had to do was follow the signs heading north to a place called Kiliomenos, and Limnionas would be signposted from there. How hard could it really be?

Buoyed by her plan and eager to get out into the sunshine, Holly threw a few essentials into a bag, scribbled the place names on her hand in biro and grabbed her moped helmet from the back of the sofa. If her mum could go gallivanting off on adventures, then Holly could damn well do it too.

Porto Limnionas turned out to be a natural inlet situated at the base of a very long asphalt road. Holly had to trust her instincts as she navigated the twists and turns slowly, because the cove itself wasn't visible until she was right on top of it. According to the guidebook, the place had been kept secret from visiting tourists for many years and as such had remained largely unspoiled, the raw, rugged beauty of the landscape and the ocean beneath exactly as nature intended.

At the top of the cliff edge, looking out over the sea and the flat, polished rocks below, was a smallish taverna with painted white walls and faded gold tiles on the roof. As Holly pulled up outside rather unsteadily and removed her helmet and sunglasses, she could see that a number of the outside tables were occupied, and waiters were dashing in and out of the main building. The stones beneath her trainers were a clean, bleached white and there was an incessant humming chorus coming from all the crickets that had set up home in the surrounding trees.

Walking past the taverna entrance, Holly peered down the side of the cliff and gasped. Below her was a boot-shaped cove with rocks either side and the most brilliantly turquoise water she had ever seen. Even from up here, she could tell that the sea below her was beautifully clear. There were darker patches where the water became deeper, and it was into these Prussian blue pools that a group of young Greek boys were taking it in turns to jump from the neighbouring side of the cliff.

While her head was urging her to nip into the taverna and quench the thirst she'd built up on the forty-minute drive over, her heart would not allow her to resist that water. Slinging her bag across one shoulder, she picked her way down the sloping stony path until she reached some steps that had been crudely cut into the side of the cliff. She was glad that she'd chosen her trainers over her flip-flops, because with every step a new shoal of pebbles went scuttling down ahead of her. It was hard to focus on your feet when there was such beauty to take in, and Holly took her time making her way right down to the bottom.

The sun had just reached its highest point and most of the visitors had headed up to the taverna for lunch in the shade. She was glad of the relative quiet, save for the odd yelp from the group of cliff-jumpers, and wasted no time in slipping out of her clothes and stretching out on a flat rock in her bikini. In just the past few days, her skin had turned a darker shade than Holly even knew was possible. She wondered idly what Rupert would think of her tan, then thought about Aidan, his freckly skin burned light pink.

She tried to picture her mum here, naked and giggling as she leapt into the water. Who had Sandra and Jenny been skinny-dipping with? Or had they simply dared each other to strip off? Holly felt a pang of jealousy as she pictured the scene – she'd never had a brother or sister, of course, and barely anyone close to resembling a best friend. If she had, she wouldn't have been as careless with them as her mum and aunt had been. How could twins allow themselves to become so distant?

She hadn't really thought about what she'd discover by coming here, distracted as she had been by everything she saw on the drive over. Fields of goats, acres of forest and villages that seemed to erupt from the landscape out of nowhere and disappear just as quickly as she passed through. But she had hoped that she'd feel something when she arrived – a renewed closeness to her mum, perhaps. Holly was loath to admit it, even to herself, but she could still feel a lingering and deep-rooted hatred towards her mother. Both the adults she'd spoken to about it – namely Simon and a grief counsellor named, rather ironically, Joy – had urged her to let all those feelings go. She had nodded and smiled and told them that she would, but she never did.

'*Yassou!*'

A menu was plonked down in front of her and she smiled up at the young male waiter. She had stayed down in the glorious cool water until she could see that the taverna was emptying, and then made her way back up the stone steps – which turned out to be far easier than the descent had been.

She gave the list a cursory glance, but she already knew what she wanted: water, frappé and a Greek salad. There were a number of other items that almost tempted her into breaking what had become a serious tomato and feta cheese habit: fresh grilled sardines, octopus in vinegar, village sausage and hearty meatballs, but she resisted for now. There would be plenty of time to try all those things over the next ten days. As she sipped her sweet, cold coffee and waited for the food to arrive, Holly dragged her eyes away from the view and watched the hive of activity going on inside the restaurant.

Having a very old lady in charge of the till seemed to be a commonplace in Zakynthos, but Holly observed that all the people ferrying around food and drinks here were male. There were Greek children of various ages running around and getting under the feet of the waiters, most of whom merely laughed and pretended to scold them.

One little girl of about five, her dark hair in two plaits and with a scrape on one knee, was sitting up on one of the tables eating an enormous chocolate ice cream, an adorable look of utter concentration on her face. Holly smiled. As she watched, an older Greek man with a neatly trimmed beard and a grey shirt stepped across to the little girl and wiped a napkin under her chin. Holly could hear him muttering what sounded like endearments. As he turned to go back into the kitchen, he noticed Holly staring over at them and she looked away quickly, embarrassed to have been caught gawping. When she sneaked a glance back a few seconds later, he was still staring – in fact, he seemed unable to tear his eyes away.

'Blatant, much?' she giggled to herself, pulling her vest on over her bikini top and turning her head back to look out across the ocean once again. A wide veranda containing more tables, each one with four wicker-seated chairs and a small vase of wild flowers, ringed the outside of the restaurant. There were vibrant patches of bougainvillea hanging down over the edge of the roof, the pink petals contrasting deliciously with the white painted walls and the light-dappled expanse of sapphire ocean below. Holly's ears had grown accustomed to the symphony of the crickets, and she could now hear the faint sound of waves pitching up against the rocks.

The Greek salad arrived and she continued to watch the view as she ate, letting her senses savour their own individual moment.

'Yassou.'

The little Greek girl with the ice cream had sauntered over to Holly's table and was peering at her shyly. One of her plaits was starting to come loose and she was clutching a pink plastic straw in one hand.

'*Yassou.*' Holly's limited Greek vocabulary didn't let her say much more, so the two of them just smiled at one another in companionable silence for a few minutes.

'England?' the little girl asked eventually. It came out as barely a whisper.

'Yes!' Holly beamed at her. 'My name is Holly.' As she said it, she gestured to herself, feeling a bit ridiculous.

'Holly,' the girl repeated. She furrowed her brow for a few seconds, chewing on the end of her straw, before touching her own chest and whispering, 'Maria.'

'Maria is a beautiful name,' Holly told her, hoping that at least the sentiment of what she was saying would be understood.

The little girl squirmed a little, still gazing at her, then very carefully placed her chewed straw on the table and skipped off in the direction of the kitchen.

Holly stared after her for a few seconds and then continued to fork up some red onion. What an amazing place to grow up, she thought, looking around at all the other boisterous and contented children who were skipping around. She often found herself feeling sorry for the morose-looking kids she saw trudging around London, the unknown dangers of the city ensuring they were never allowed more than a few feet away from their parents. The children here must have so much more freedom and spend so much more time playing outside, as opposed to being stuck in high-rise blocks of flats or those grotty after-school clubs.

Holly didn't have much contact with children back in London. None of her and Rupert's friends had kids yet and, aside from the odd perso[n] [...] new baby in for a visit, Holly rarely [...] wasn't that she disliked children – in tr[uth] they were adorable – she'd just never had a[...] have any of her own. She wondered now whethe[r] Rupert had thought about the two of them having a b[...]. They'd never discussed it, and thankfully none of his friends had mentioned it yet. They were all having far too much fun going out socialising most nights to think about kids.

Holly had always thought having a baby would be a bad idea, after what had happened to her mum. Could it have been that the stress of having Holly was what drove her to start drinking in the first place? She'd told Holly many times in those last few dark months that she hated herself, that she was a bad mother, that she'd failed both of them. There was no way that Holly was ever going to risk that happening to another child.

She knew that her mum had got pregnant with her at the age of twenty, which seemed ludicrously young by today's standards. She was about to turn thirty and she still didn't feel like an adult. Perhaps it was because she'd been forced to look after herself from such a young age. Now that she finally had a bit of security again, she was at last beginning to enjoy life.

But are you really *happy?* a small voice whispered. *Is your life in London with Rupert what you really want?* For some reason, as soon as she started to think about Rupert, Aidan popped into her head. Aidan, with his tatty clothes, messy hair and singsong Irish accent. Holly wondered what he was doing here. Why had he chosen Zakynthos as his

...ee mentioned that his mum used to live here, but there must be a deeper reason. Holly vowed to find out on their trip the next day.

The thought of spending so much time with him was starting to make her feel nervous, but it was a nice feeling at the same time. She and Rupert had got into such a routine, and she'd found herself cherishing the predictability of their relationship. Now, however, she was being reminded what it felt like to have that buzz you get when you first meet someone. All the uncertainty and excitement bubbling away whenever you know you're going to see them. There was something about Aidan that made her feel excited, but it was almost more to do with who she was when she was near him than the man himself. She didn't feel as if she had to be anything other than herself, and it had been a very long time since she'd allowed that side of her to take over from the cautious, more guarded Holly Wright.

A waiter scurried over and swept up her empty plate, and as she headed to the till to settle the bill, Holly reached into the freezer and grabbed herself a chocolate ice cream. Little Maria wasn't the only girl in this place with a sweet tooth. Tearing off the wrapper and stepping back out into the sun, Holly headed back down the stone steps towards the sea below. She was in paradise; it was a fact. Whatever had happened to make her mum leave this place behind, it must have been pretty bad.

12

Choosing what to wear for her first day out with Aidan was proving to be far more difficult than it should, Holly decided, as she hurled a dress across the room in frustration.

She was also already feeling irrationally annoyed at the man himself for not telling her what time they were setting off, so she had no idea if he was about to bang on the door and find her standing uselessly in the middle of a heap of clothes.

It was 7.30 a.m., and the sun was still low in the sky. A pleasant morning light was snaking its way slowly across the tiled floor, and Holly forced herself to take three deep breaths as she watched it. During her sessions with Joy the counsellor, she'd been taught about the calming benefits of slow and measured breathing. Apparently most human beings never breathed properly, only taking the air in as far as the level of their shoulders before exhaling, when you were actually supposed to take it right down into your stomach. That was all well and good, the grief-stricken and grumpy Holly had rudely pointed out at the time, but who the hell had time for that?

She remembered her first date with Rupert all those months ago, how nervous she'd been and how many dresses, trousers, blouses, skirts and different sets of underwear she'd tried on in preparation. Of course, it hadn't mattered what she wore in the end, because he'd taken her straight out to buy a new dress and then insisted she put it on right away. It had been such a perfect day.

Cheered slightly by the reminder that she already had a lovely man in her life and so shouldn't be worrying this much about a new one, Holly pulled out her cut-off jeans and fed one of Sandra's old patterned scarves through the belt loops. She fished a plain white vest out of the heap on the bed and pulled it on over her bikini top. That would have to do, she told herself stubbornly. It wasn't like she was trying to impress Aidan, anyway.

The sound of barking came just before a knock at the front door.

'Ready to go exploring?' Aidan said as she opened the door. Today he was wearing black shorts, frayed espadrilles, a navy blue T-shirt and a grin almost as large as Phelan's, who was sitting panting by his feet.

'Sure,' she flashed him a shy smile. 'I'll just get my bag.'

Aidan peered over the threshold as she gathered her stuff from the table. Away from her ordered London life, Holly had slipped back into her old untidy ways, and there were ripped up bits of material littering the floor.

'Been busy?' Aidan held up the remains of a particularly garish sarong.

Holly flushed an even darker shade of red than the tatters in his hand. 'I like sewing,' she told him, wondering why she'd suddenly started speaking like an inarticulate moron.

'Right.' He dropped it back on the floor. Phelan had been sniffing around underneath the table and was now happily chewing on the underwire of a very large flesh-coloured bra.

'Phelan! Drop it! Leave it!'

'Oh, don't worry,' Holly was whooping with laughter now like a mad hen. 'It's not mine.'

Aidan's eyes flickered straight to her own, far less ample chest, and she folded her arms self-consciously. Was she imagining it, or was he the one blushing now?

'I like what you've done with the place,' he told her, motioning to the new tablecloth. Holly had created it from the remains of Sandra's cotton dressing gown and some lace doilies she'd found in a kitchen cupboard. She'd also finished the patchwork wall hanging the previous evening and hung it up by the back doors where it did, as she had predicted, look stunning in the daylight.

'I just thought it would help the place to look more like a home,' she said. 'I'm selling it, so I need it to look nice for potential buyers.'

Aidan raised his eyebrows at this, but didn't comment. Instead, he asked if he could nip to the loo before they set off. 'Don't worry,' he joked as he headed up the stairs. 'I won't flush any paper!'

'Oh, ha ha,' retorted Holly, but she was smiling.

Phelan leapt around their legs in excitement as they headed out along the path to where Aidan's jeep was parked. It was covered in a thick coating of dust on the outside, but Holly discovered that it was impressively clean on the inside. A faint smell of antiseptic greeted her as she opened the door, and there was a tartan blanket covered in red-gold dog hair spread across the back seat. Phelan clambered in happily and stuck his glossy head out of the window, dribbling a trail of saliva through the grime on the door.

Holly buckled up and dumped her bag on the floor. She had already switched her phone over to silent in case Rupert called. She'd played the perfect girlfriend yesterday evening and spoken to him for a full hour after she got back from Porto Limnionas. He was missing her like mad, he'd told her. She was never to go away without him again, apparently. He'd actually sounded genuinely interested when she'd told him about what she'd seen on the island, obviously omitting all the stories Annie had told her about her aunt. Talking about Sandra would inevitably lead to the subject of her mum, and Rupert had no idea what had really happened to Jenny Wright. But thankfully, he hadn't mentioned Sandra at all. She wondered if it was because he could sense that she didn't want to talk about it, or because he just wasn't that interested.

'Have you eaten breakfast?' Aidan was staring at her, his hands on the steering wheel.

'Yes. I mean no. I mean yes.' Holly gave up. Talking coherently was clearly something she was unable to do around this man.

'Righto,' he replied cheerfully. 'I think I know where I'll take you first, then. We'll grab a bite and then try to track down a few of those places on Sandy's map. What was it again, field that smells of shite?'

Holly giggled and wound down the window as he started the engine, breathing in the sweet aroma from the surrounding fig trees. As Aidan wrestled with the gear stick and turned the jeep round to face downhill, his bare knee brushed against Holly's and she felt a bolt of electricity shoot into her chest. She really needed to get a grip.

They set off in a northerly direction, and for the first

ten minutes neither of them spoke. Holly was content just to sit and take in the view and Aidan didn't seem to be bothered by the silence. Phelan eventually curled up on the back seat and put his silky head on his paws, looking up at each of them in turn from under his eyelashes.

There were a few more clouds around today, but they simply served to make the skyline look all the more dramatic. After following a coastal road for a few miles, Aidan turned the jeep inland and soon the roads started to get steeper. Holly took advantage of his concentration to study him surreptitiously. She liked the way his hands looked as they gripped the wheel and the way the muscles in his forearms rippled as they rounded a corner. Despite the wind rushing in through the open windows, she felt an overwhelming need to start fanning herself with the folded map.

'So, Holly,' he finally turned briefly to face her. 'What is it that you do, back in . . . Where are you from?'

'Well, I live in London,' she told him. She wasn't really 'from' anywhere. 'In Dalston, which isn't far from Hackney – do you know it?'

'Nah, sorry,' Aidan grinned at her. 'I've never really fancied London. I grew up in the countryside and then spent years on the go. I think a big city would scare me.'

Holly thought privately that nothing much could possibly scare a man as big and confident as Aidan, but instead she said, 'I work for a website that sells clothes. It's called Flash.'

'Flash?' Aidan failed to hold in his laugh. 'Are you for real?'

'I know,' she laughed too. 'It is probably the most naff name in the world, but there are worse places to work.'

'I always wanted to be a vet, right from when I was a little boy,' he continued. There was a stooped, ancient-looking man up ahead herding a load of goats across the road, and Aidan stopped to let them pass. 'I found a lamb once, when I was about six or seven. The poor little thing was tangled up in this barbed wire fence and I couldn't get him out. He was struggling and bleeding and it was miles from anywhere.'

Aidan paused to shout something cheerful in Greek to the man with the goats, before putting the jeep into gear and looking again at Holly.

'What happened to the lamb?' she asked, a certain amount of trepidation in her voice.

'He died,' Aidan told her simply, smiling at Holly's gasp of horror. 'I ran the three miles back to the farm and all the old bastard farmer did was drive out there with his rifle and shoot the poor bugger.'

'That must have been a bit traumatic,' Holly said.

'Well, I never forgot it,' he admitted. 'I thought to myself that day, "I'm going to learn how to look after animals so that next time this happens, I'll be able to help".'

'I still don't really know what I want to do,' Holly told him, not realising what she was saying until the words had left her mouth.

'Well, that's easy.' He rested an elbow on the jeep door. 'What are you passionate about?'

'I like sewing,' she told him in a small voice.

'So do that.'

'It's not that easy, though, is it?' she said. 'I can't just sew stuff.'

'Why not?'

God, he was so infuriating.

'Because London is an expensive place to live.'

'Surely all those top designers, you know, Dulchy and Gaffney or whoever, surely they all need people to sew for them. Or better still – why don't you become one of them and design the stuff as well?' He was actually being serious, Holly realised.

'I should just become Dolce and Gabbana?' she enquired. 'Start speaking Italian and charge thousands of pounds for socks?'

'Would have to be some socks,' Aidan laughed. 'But seriously, you should do what makes you happy.'

Absurdly, Holly felt tears gathering in her eyes. Turning away from him, she wound the window back up and surreptitiously wiped her eyes on her bare arm. If Aidan noticed anything, he didn't comment, instead smoothly changing the subject by pointing to a tiny, dilapidated church that was on the left up ahead.

'My mam got married there,' he said as they passed.

'Oh?' Holly made an interested sound.

'It didn't last. The marriage, I mean.' He shrugged at Holly's expression. 'Only a matter of months. My mam never was very good at the whole relationship thing. I'm actually amazed that she seems to be making the latest one last. If I was a betting man I'd have given it no more than a few months.'

Holly didn't know what to say; she was suddenly uncomfortable with how much Aidan was telling her.

'Sorry,' he turned to her. 'I didn't mean to kill the mood, like. As you can probably tell, my mam and I aren't the closest.'

'Don't be sorry,' Holly was mortified. 'It's not like I can say anything about not having the best relationship with your mother.'

'What about your Auntie Sandra?'

It was an innocent enough question, but Holly felt herself start to clam up.

'I'm sad that I didn't know her better,' she said carefully. 'I get the impression that we're quite similar – I mean, that she would have been like me.'

'Well, she did like to sew,' Aidan agreed. 'And you do look like her sometimes, just the way you hold yourself. It reminds me of her.'

Had he been studying her that closely?

'I didn't even know that my mum and her were twins until this week,' she blurted. 'I haven't even seen a photo of Sandra yet, either.'

'Really?' He sounded shocked at that. 'There must be some in the house, aren't there?'

'Not that I've found,' Holly told him. 'I was expecting there to be more, you know, letters and stuff, but I haven't found anything.'

Aidan was quiet for a few seconds as he concentrated on steering them round a particularly narrow bend. The stone walls on either side of the jeep were only a foot or so away, and Holly reflexively squeezed her shoulders together as they passed through the lane.

'We're not far now,' he told her. Ahead Holly could see what looked like a small village. There were windmills visible on the hillside above them and what appeared to be a circular stone tower nestled between low white houses.

'This is Volimes,' he said, slowing right down as they

passed a cluster of squat buildings. 'I'm not sure if it's marked on your map there, but it's somewhere I like to come, so I thought I'd show it to you.'

They drove into a small square and Aidan parked in the shade of a large tree. Phelan whined with excitement and pawed at the door as he waited to be let out, then promptly lifted his leg on a nearby patch of grass. The square was deserted save for one old man who was standing by some makeshift stalls. From where they were parked, Holly could see a variety of pots in all shapes, sizes and colours, plus a heap of rugs and some neatly packaged bags of wild herbs.

'The tour buses come through here sometimes,' Aidan explained. 'It's a good way for the locals to make a bit of extra cash.'

She started to follow him across the square, but found herself drawn to the last stall along. The wooden top was adorned with spools of lace, and Holly ran her fingers across each of them in turn.

'That's all made locally.' Aidan had appeared at her shoulder. The old man had shuffled down to greet them and was now smiling at Holly, showing off a row of gnarly teeth. Aidan said something to him in Greek and then turned to Holly. 'It's usually ten euros per metre, but he says for you it's a special price.' He winked at her. The Greek man gabbled something else at Aidan, pointing across the table as he did so.

'He will make you a special deal,' Aidan translated. 'Eight metres for forty euros.'

'Is that good?' Holly was thinking about all the beautiful things she could make with the lace.

Aidan shrugged. 'Things are only worth what you're willing to pay for them.'

Ten minutes later, her stash of Greek lace safely stowed in the jeep, Aidan and Holly finally sat down in a café. They were the only customers, but the middle-aged woman looking after the place still took her time taking their order. Aidan grinned widely at her departing back.

'You have to love the Greeks,' he said. 'You could drop ten million euros out of the sky and they'd still finish their coffee before they bothered to pick any up.'

'I can't say I blame them,' Holly said, thinking of how manic and pushy everybody was in London. 'Everyone here just seems so relaxed.'

'Too relaxed, sometimes,' he replied. 'Trying to tell a Greek that their sick animal needs to be seen to today, rather than next week, can be a trial. When I first opened my practice down in the town, I thought everyone would bring their pets to me. I was sadly mistaken on that score.'

The woman was back with their frappés and she smiled shyly at Holly as she set down the napkins.

'She probably recognises you,' Aidan said when they were alone again. 'Sandy used to drive up here all the time to buy her lace.'

Holly looked at him. 'Is that why you brought me here?'

'Partly.' He didn't look at all contrite. 'But it was mostly because I wanted you to see what the real Zakynthos is like, away from the more touristy areas. The way people live here, in this village, is how they've lived for centuries.'

'It's so quiet,' marvelled Holly. It was beautiful too, she thought. The café in which they were sitting had white walls and a trellis covering the outside seating area. When

Holly looked up, she could see grapes dangling down through the gaps, their plump little bodies basking happily in the sunshine.

'I thought we could go up to the viewing point above the Shipwreck,' Aidan said, sipping his frappé. 'It's a bit of a tourist haunt, but it's also the most famous landmark on the island and, if I'm not mistaken, your ma and Sandra thought it was worth a look.'

Holly had seen photos of the famous Shipwreck beach, with its white sand and paintbox-blue sea. Jenny and Sandra had drawn a half-sunk boat on their own map and scribbled the words 'photo opp' next to it.

'That sounds perfect,' she smiled at him. 'Thanks for this – for taking me out, I mean. I know you must be busy.'

'Nonsense,' Aidan held up his hand. 'I'm never too busy to spend the day with a pretty girl.'

A flush of warmth crept across Holly's chest at this and she started to laugh it off.

'I'm sure you could have your pick of the girls on this island,' she told him. 'Annie told me that you're not short of admirers.'

'Oh, did she now?' Aidan laughed. 'She needs to wind in her gob, that one.'

'Do you not get lonely?' Holly asked, immediately regretting it. Her mouth seemed to have a mind of its own today.

'It's impossible to get lonely on this island,' he said, stirring the ice around in his glass. 'Once you're friends with the Greeks, they become more like family, you know? Everywhere I go I'm welcomed with open arms.'

As if to reinforce the point, he suddenly wrapped his arms around her shoulders and gave her a squeeze. Holly, caught completely by surprise, became uncomfortably aware of how broad and firm his chest was, and how much her knees were now trembling.

'Just like that, you see!' Aidan pulled away as if nothing had happened, leaving Holly to hyperventilate quietly into her glass of water. 'But anyway, what was I saying? Oh yeah, um, no, I don't really get lonely. And I always have Phelan here, don't forget.'

At the sound of his name, Phelan lifted his head and wagged his tail through the dust. He'd been sitting so quietly by their feet that Holly had forgotten he was there at all. The waitress arrived back with their breakfast – an omelette for Aidan and cheese pies for Holly. She had been tempted to order a tomato salad and ask for extra honey, but she didn't want Aidan to think she was mad. The pies were more than a worthy contender in the taste stakes anyway. Holly almost let out a groan of pleasure as she bit through the flaky warm pastry and encountered the salty, oozy cheese inside.

'So, you said your mum lived here?' she asked once she'd finished her first pie. She was keen to steer the conversation away from anything that might lead to talking about relationships. If Aidan did have a secret girlfriend squirrelled away somewhere, she didn't want to know – and she wasn't ready to tell him about Rupert, either.

'That's right.' Aidan had finished his water and started picking at the label on the bottle.

'Did she work here too?'

'She used to be an artist.' He turned but didn't quite

meet her eyes. 'She had a lot of success when I was growing up, but it tailed off as she got older. She didn't cope with that very well.'

'That's understandable,' Holly said.

'Well, not really.' Something in Aidan's manner had hardened. 'Not when it means you have to cut yourself off from your family and everyone who cares about you.'

There was an uncomfortable silence.

'Was she depressed?' Holly asked quietly.

'Yeah, the silly old mare. Nobody was buying any of her paintings any more and she took it *way* too personally. It was actually Sandra who helped her get back on her feet, you know.'

Holly nodded and took another bite of her pie. It really was very tasty.

'I think that's why we became such good friends, you know, your aunt and me – I think she felt like she had a duty to look after me too, because my mam wasn't really in a position to do it herself.'

He was saying all this to her so matter-of-factly, and seemed so strong about it all, that Holly couldn't help but feel a wave of affection towards him.

'I'm sorry,' she finally muttered, unsure what else she could say. She understood exactly what it was like to have a person there who wasn't really there at all. But at least Aidan's mum was still alive – at least she had friends and family to help her. Holly thought helplessly of her own mum sitting in that chair, her head lolling to one side, her skin tinged blue.

'I still get on great with my dad, mind,' Aidan went on, mercifully yanking Holly's attention back to the present day. 'He lives over in Ireland, though, so visits are a rare thing these days.'

Holly thought about mentioning her own dad, but what would she say? That he might be a freedom fighter in jail somewhere, or that, more likely, he was a random drifter that her mum had shacked up with for a few weeks then forgotten all about. Holly had been thinking a lot about who her father might have been over the past few days. He'd always been an unknown entity before; she'd accepted long ago that she'd never meet him. But getting the letter from Sandra had made her question everything her mum had ever told her. If Jenny had omitted to tell Holly about the existence of an aunt, then it made sense that she would have fabricated the whole story about her dad too. The problem was, she didn't even know where to begin looking for him.

She looked over at Aidan, who seemed to be lost in melancholy thoughts of his own. Astounded at her own bravery, Holly slid a timid hand across and squeezed his arm.

As they sat together, each lost in their own memories but comforted by the support of the other, the bells in the village church began to ring.

Monday, 25 June 1990
Dearest Sandra,

Well now, that sounds all wrong. I never call you Sandra, do I? I wish I could sit here and tell you that I'm sorry it ever happened, but I can't. I can't tell you what you really want to hear. We reached Indonesia two days ago. Sandy, you would love it here – the sea is like bath water and the people are so open with their hearts. I'm sitting here now on the sand, writing to you, and a local boy is plaiting Holly's hair. It's so adorable. I think we may stay here for a few months. Well, unless you tell me to come home. You know we would be on the next flight. I miss you, Sandy, and Holly misses you too. All my love, now and for ever, your twinny,

Jen Bear xxx

13

It was only a short drive from Volimes to Navagio, which was home to the lookout point above the Shipwreck Beach. Despite the fact that it had become a major tourist attraction, the Greeks hadn't cashed in with buildings on the picturesque cliff edge. In fact, the only things there other than a large car park filled with coaches, quad bikes and hire cars was a small mobile food stall and a few dubious toilets housed inside small huts.

They arrived at the same time as a coach full of German tourists, so Aidan suggested they wait in the jeep until the coast was clear. It was nearing 11 a.m. now and the morning clouds had long since been brushed away by the sweeping power of the sun. Holly rested her bare arm on the jeep door and fanned herself with the map. The air was deliciously fragrant thanks to the surrounding pine trees and she could still taste the cheesy remnants of her breakfast. Aidan, meanwhile, was thoughtfully picking at a bit of spinach that had become lodged in his teeth – a leftover from his own morning meal.

'Will you take a look at her,' he exclaimed, tapping Holly on the arm as a young woman strutted past the jeep wearing high-heeled wedges and a thong bikini. Her bottom was so round and so brown that it looked like a freshly dropped conker.

'Bloody hell!' Holly slapped a hand over her mouth so

the woman wouldn't hear her yelp of laughter. 'She's brave.'

'You say brave, I say bleeding ridiculous,' Aidan replied, not bothering to hide his own bellow of mirth. The young woman inclined her head slightly in their direction, but she looked to Holly to be more delighted than embarrassed.

'I mean,' Aidan went on, 'I'm all for ladies getting their bottoms out and all, but there's a time and a place for such stuff. A more private place, perhaps?'

The idea of bare bottoms in private places with Aidan made Holly blush from her throat to her hairline, so she quickly changed the subject.

'Come on then, Mr Tour Guide, tell me what I'm about to see. What is this shipwreck place?'

Aidan put on an authoritative voice as he replied, which made them both giggle. 'Known locally as Smugglers' Cove, this beach is home to the wreck of a cigarette smuggler's boat, which crashed here in the late 1970s,' he announced. 'Thanks to the limestone cliffs in this area of the island, the sea around the cove is crystal clear.'

'You're very knowledgeable,' Holly told him, still grinning at the stupid voice.

'I haven't been up here in ages, actually,' he said, turning to look at her. 'My ex used to like bringing a picnic up here sometimes, in the spring when there weren't as many tourists around. I guess since she left I haven't really bothered.'

Holly wanted to ask him what had happened to break them up, but she couldn't quite pluck up the courage. Instead she turned away from him and reached over to the back seat to stroke Phelan, who was gently snoring with one eye open.

'Ridiculous creature,' Aidan said, taking his hand off the steering wheel and ruffling Phelan's silky head. As his fingers brushed against hers, Holly felt a trickle of delight spread through her hand and into her bare arm, and quickly moved out of reach.

'Come on,' Aidan said, defusing whatever it was that had just fizzled up between them. 'Thong lady's back on her bus – I reckon the coast is clear.'

Holly had looked at endless photos of the Shipwreck Beach before she arrived on the island, but none of them prepared her for how stunning it was when you were standing looking down at it. From their position on a narrow viewing platform, which Aidan cheerily informed her was 'at least one hundred metres' above the sea below, the shipwreck itself looked small enough to pick up. It sat half-buried in a bay of clean white sand, which was surrounded by a semicircle of sheer limestone cliffs. The brilliant bright-blue water lapping up against the shoreline was dotted with tiny boats and even tinier people.

'Is there any way down?' she asked Aidan. He was standing close enough behind her that she could feel the soft warmth of his breath on the back of her neck, and despite the heat of the late morning, the hair on her arms was standing fully to attention.

'Not from here.' He shook his head. 'You can only get on to the beach by boat, and even then it's only really possible on a day when the sea is calm. As you can see, everyone is taking advantage of that fact today.'

'It's stunning,' Holly breathed. 'The water doesn't even look real – it's as if someone's poured turquoise paint over the side of one of those boats.'

'My mum used to say the same thing,' Aidan smiled. 'She painted up here, of course. It was her who first brought me to this very spot.'

Picnics with his ex-girlfriend, painting trips with his mum – Aidan clearly had a lot of memories associated with this place. And now she did too, thanks to him. Well, she corrected herself, it was actually more to do with Jenny and Sandra. They'd marked this place on their own map, after all. Sandra must have meant for her to spot it and find her way up here. Knowing that she was staring down at a view that her mum must have gazed at made Holly's eyes suddenly fill up with tears. The fact that it was so beautiful here only seemed to make the whole situation more tragic. She wished she'd been able to come here with Jenny, perhaps on one of the adventures that her mum had always promised her they would go on together. She was very glad that she'd come here today, but she was also overwhelmed with a pang of loneliness. She wondered if Aidan, who had fallen silent behind her as he too gazed down at the spellbinding vista below, was thinking the same thing.

Without fully realising what she was doing, Holly leaned back a fraction so that the back of her head was resting against his chest. She needed the comfort from him as much as she could sense he craved it from her, and for a few minutes they stood without moving. Holly could just about make out the sound of the distant sea and a light murmur of chatter filtering over from the car park.

She could have happily stayed there all day, but before long another group of sweaty-looking tourists filed over, and Aidan slowly led her away.

Phelan, who had been waiting patiently in a nearby patch of shade, greeted them with a shower of drool and promptly rolled over on to his back so that Holly could tickle his belly.

'I think you've made a friend there,' Aidan laughed, borrowing Holly's phone to take a photo. He had slipped back into his easy, jokey manner, their shared moment on the platform now seemingly forgotten, and Holly was grateful to him. There was a feeling starting to bubble in the pit of her own belly that she definitely didn't feel ready to deal with. If only she could roll over on to her back like Phelan and get someone to rub it away.

After leaving Navagio, Aidan drove Holly east across the island to an area called Mikro Nissi. The tiny coastal village boasted a beautiful pebbled beach and a handful of bars, all of which looked out across the water. Jenny and Sandra had illustrated this particular area with a series of wonky drawings of what looked like pints of beer, alongside some very unseaworthy-looking boats.

Holly, who was dusty from the long drive and keen to put a bit of safe distance between herself and Aidan, took her towel straight across the stones and made her way into the clear, calm water. Phelan sat guarding her bag, while Aidan crossed the pebbles and started chatting to a man who was unravelling a mess of fishing nets by the shore. His boat, Holly could see, was called *Maria*.

She felt like she was beginning to understand Sandra

more with every hour that she spent on this island, but this was only serving to make her more upset about the fact that they'd never met. It had crossed her mind to ask Aidan if he knew what had caused the rift between Sandra and her mum, but surely he would have told her already if he did? He'd shown himself to be pretty direct up until now, so she didn't think he'd be the sort to keep anything hidden.

It had shaken her up to hear him talk about his difficult relationship with his mum so openly. In a way she was envious that he could be so matter-of-fact about it all, but in another way that level of openness frightened her. She'd spent so many years hiding behind the alternative past she'd created for herself that to pull those walls down now seemed like the most unnatural – not to mention downright terrifying – idea in the world. Despite this, though, she had found herself on the verge of telling Aidan how she felt about her mother several times already. What was it about him that made her so keen to share? *And it wouldn't be very fair on Rupert if you did*, whispered a voice inside her. Surely he should be the one she opened up to, but would she ever be able to be honest with him about who she really was? As she pondered this, Holly stared down at her toes beneath the water. A tiny fish had swum over to investigate and was now nibbling at the hard skin on her heel. People would pay a fortune for a fish pedicure in London, she thought. *And here I am, in this beautiful, tranquil place, getting one absolutely free.*

She distracted herself by looking at all the little boats bobbing gently in the harbour next to the beach. They were a mixture of shapes, sizes, colours and stages of disrepair, and Holly wondered if her mum and Sandra had ever been out on one. There had to be a reason why they'd drawn boats all over this part of the map. Perhaps Aidan knew someone who could take them out on the water. Holly had never been on a boat before, not a proper one, anyway. She was pretty sure that the punting trip she and Rupert had taken down the river on a day trip to Cambridge didn't count – it certainly wasn't as exciting as being out on the ocean.

Rolling over on to her stomach in the shallows, she watched Phelan pad over to where the nearest fishing boat was providing an arc of shade. Aidan was still chatting to the fisherman, who had his back to Holly, but every so often the two men would glance over in her direction. The man was bearded and looked faintly familiar, but that was probably just because every Greek man of a certain age seemed to have the same facial hair. This man had a tatty bum bag strapped around his waist and was wearing a shirt that had definitely seen better days. Fashion certainly wasn't something the folk here seemed to worry about much, Holly thought, and, despite her job at Flash, she kind of admired it. Other things were presumably more important over here, such as work and family and simply enjoying life. And it would be hard not to enjoy life here, after all.

'Holly!'

It was Aidan. She looked up and watched as he made his way down the beach, guiltily aware that she was enjoying the way the light breeze was making his T-shirt ripple across his chest. He picked up her towel and held it up politely as she stumbled out across the stones. It was impossible to look ladylike when your feet were being bruised with every step.

'Ready for a cold beer yet?' he asked, not bothering to avert his eyes at all as she started to dry herself.

'Yes, please,' she said, thinking again of the scribbled pint glasses on the map. She smiled at him, squinting slightly as the sun slipped out from behind his ear.

Taking her hand as if it was the most natural thing in the world, Aidan led her up the beach and straight across the road into a bar. Holly had put her cropped jeans and vest back on, but her wet bikini had left a big stain on her bottom and on the front of each boob.

'Just take it off?' suggested Aidan, eyeing her chest with a knowing look that could only be described as decidedly suggestive. There it was again, that electricity fizzing between them. Holly slapped his arm in mock outrage. The sun had dried the salt water on her face and she could feel her skin tightening as she sipped her Mythos. She'd slipped off her shoes so that her bare feet could dangle down from the bar stools where they sat. She felt clean and free and delicious.

'Are you really going to sell the house?'

Aidan had failed to keep the pleading tone from his voice and Holly let out a deep sigh before she replied.

'I think it's for the best,' she said, refusing to meet his eyes. 'I feel weird having it at all, to be honest. Like I said to you before, I never even met Sandra.'

'But she clearly wanted *you* to have it,' he insisted. 'And she *was* your auntie, regardless of whether you met her or not.'

He was right, of course, but before she came out here

Holly had made a promise to herself – and to Rupert – that she would pack the house up and sell it. She had spent her whole life trying to move forward, and being here felt a bit like she was being dragged back into the past by the ankles. At this stage, she still wasn't sure whether to grab hold of something sturdy until whatever it was went away, or whether to just let herself be taken.

'It's complicated,' she said, trying to convey in two words all the things she couldn't explain. 'My life is in London – I don't need a house in Greece.'

'That's the maddest thing I've ever heard!' Aidan actually slapped his thigh. 'Anyone else in the world would be overjoyed to be given a house in a place like this.'

'I'm not like everyone else.'

The electricity that had been crackling between them was still there, but it had rapidly gone from flirty to twitchy. Aidan seemed to sense the change in mood and paused for a moment, taking a sip of his beer and glaring at her in bemusement.

'Listen, I'm sorry,' he said eventually. 'It's really none of my business what you do with your own house.'

'Thank you.' Holly was relieved.

'I just know how much Sandra wanted you to have it,' he continued.

Exasperated, Holly took an aggressive slug of beer and ended up pouring most of it down the front of her top. Why was Aidan trying to make her feel guilty? Did he not realise how difficult it already was for her?

'What did she say to you about me?' If Aidan was going to play this game, then she may as well make him squirm a bit too.

'Not a lot, you know, just that you were all she had left and stuff.' He was definitely looking a bit shifty now, Holly decided.

'She must have said more than that,' she pushed. 'Come on . . .'

'Another beer?' Aidan raised a hand in the direction of the bar.

'Oi, stop changing the subject.' Holly was starting to feel indignant now and had to take a deep breath to curb the slight swell of anger that had risen up in her chest. Aidan responded by giving her such a lazy smile that she found she couldn't help but smile back. Bloody hell, he really was *so* infuriating.

The waiter who brought over their drinks – another beer for Holly and a bottle of water for Aidan – looked at least eighty. His gnarled hands were trembling with the effort of holding the tray and there were large liver spots on his cheeks. He was wearing a worn black vest, the neckline of which was decorated with a mass of wiry grey chest hair, and his feet were bare.

Aidan thanked him for the drinks and then motioned to Holly. 'This is Yiorgos,' he told her. 'He knew your Aunt Sandra.'

Yiorgos lifted his stooped neck and peered at Holly like a friendly vulture, his eyes brightening slightly. They were a brilliant, clear blue, and she was reminded of the sea down at Porto Limnionas. Turning back to Aidan, he began gabbling away in Greek, pausing every now and then to let him translate.

'He says that your aunt was very beautiful, but that you are even more beautiful,' Aidan told her. 'She made a wedding dress for his granddaughter, ten years ago, and it was the happiest day of her life.'

Holly felt a swell of pride and beamed across at Yiorgos.

'He wants to know if you're married,' Aidan added. Holly shook her head.

The old man then said something to Aidan and both men laughed, but whatever it was apparently didn't warrant translation. They sat for a further ten minutes, while Yiorgos told them stories about Sandra. He had known her since she first came to the island with her parents, and they became friends again when she moved back after they died. He remembered Holly's mum too, and was keen to point out how nice but naughty she had been. When Holly told Aidan to tell him that her mum had died, he looked genuinely upset, and reached across the table to grasp her hand.

'Your mum must have been some woman,' Aidan said, after Yiorgos had kissed them both on the cheek and shuffled back inside the bar.

'Oh, she was certainly that,' Holly replied, not bothering to keep the disdain from her voice.

'You never told me how she died,' Aidan said carefully.

'Car crash,' Holly replied immediately. It was such a well-weathered lie now, and anyway, the truth was just too depressing.

Aidan remained silent for a few seconds, then pointed at her empty beer bottle. 'One for the road?'

Holly knew that he had her pegged. He could tell that

she was lying just as clearly as he could see that the sky was blue, but she was grateful that he had chosen not to push her on the subject. She couldn't help but feel a little bit guilty. After all, he'd been totally honest about his own mother, but she just wasn't ready.

For years now the truth had remained buried. She didn't even know how she'd begin to say the words, let alone what her emotional reaction would be. Aidan already thought she was crazy, *and*, the pernicious voice whispered in her ear, *you don't want to risk scaring him away, do you?*

Aidan was quiet as they drove back towards Lithakia. He seemed lost in his own thoughts and Holly never had been one for small talk. Instead, she watched as the landscape swept by, her eyes drawn again and again to the rich blue of the ocean. She'd only been away from home for a few days, but in some ways it felt as though she'd always been here. Perhaps it was because a part of her always *had* been here – her aunt. Was that why she had wanted Holly to come and see the island so much? Was she afraid that by dying she would be leaving the place unattended?

It had been a long day and the thoughts swirling around in Holly's head were beginning to become exhausting. She was relieved when they finally rounded the corner and drove up the hill towards their respective homes. For the first time in as long as she could remember, she was actually looking forward to getting into bed and closing her eyes – and for once she knew that it wouldn't be long before sleep stole in and whisked her away.

Aidan opened the door for Phelan before he reached Holly, and for a second their eyes met through the jeep window.

'I have to put in a morning at the clinic tomorrow,' he told her as she clambered out on to the path. 'But I thought we could maybe drive over to Keri in the afternoon?'

Holly consulted the map. Keri didn't look like it was very far away at all, and someone – she suspected this time it had been her mum – had written the words 'yummy barman at Ocean View' in large, enthusiastic letters.

Aidan looked down and grinned. 'I can't promise you a yummy barman, but Ocean View is still there. We could have some late lunch there, if you like?'

Holly nodded. 'I'd like that very much.'

They walked up the path in silence with Phelan padding along next to them and Holly let the comforting scent from the lemon and fig trees swim happily across her senses. In that moment, everything felt right.

'Sleep well, Holly,' Aidan said gently, and then he was gone.

Friday, 4 January 1991
Dearest Sandbags,

As you can see from the other side of this postcard, we've arrived back in England. It feels very strange to be back after so many years – and it's cold enough to freeze your bits off. But there is some good news – I've met someone, and I really think this one could be different. He's called Simon and he has beautiful black

*and white hair. I've taken to calling him Badger, which Holly
thinks is just the funniest thing. He's great with her, as well. We
met just before Christmas in Sri Lanka and he's invited Holly
and me to live with him. Imagine! Me all settled down. I never
thought I'd see the day. I've put my new address in the corner, so
please do write back and tell me your news. I miss you every day.*

Jen Bear xxx

14

As she had predicted, Holly fell asleep almost as soon as her head hit the pillow in the spare room and when she woke up, over ten hours later, it wasn't with the shaking fear and nightmare sweating that she'd grown accustomed to. She felt absolutely amazing, and even sang loudly through the open bathroom window as she took a morning shower.

Swinging aside the soggy curtain with a flourish ten minutes later, Holly flipped open the glass door of the cabinet to retrieve her toothpaste and froze – there was a photograph tucked up on the shelf above, part-obscured by a dusty bottle of lavender perfume. How the hell had she missed that?

Jenny Wright was instantly recognisable, her brown hair pulled back into an untidy ponytail and a silly, lopsided grin on her face. She was wearing a bright yellow sundress with a red ribbon sash and had her arm casually draped around two young men with dark hair and lazy smiles. Given the depth of their tans and the fact that the photo had clearly been taken on a beach, Holly guessed that they were most likely Greeks. On the other side of them was another brunette girl. She was smiling too, albeit with less obvious confidence, and was wearing a white broderie anglaise blouse tucked into pale blue shorts. Her hand was clasped firmly in that of the Greek man closest to her.

There was no denying the similarity between this girl and Jenny, and as Holly stared at them she sank down to sit on the edge of the bath. So, this must be her Aunt Sandra. Wow, they really had been twins. Holly felt her eyes widen as she scoured the faded photo for details. It had been years since she'd let herself look at a photo of her mum, and seeing her there so suddenly, looking so happy, so young and so clearly carefree, was like taking a hard punch to the chest. She could hear her heart hammering and forced herself to take a deep breath.

Flipping the photo over, she saw that someone had scrawled 'Zakynthos, 1984' on the back. That meant Jenny and Sandra must have been around nineteen when it was taken, a whole ten years younger than Holly was now. It was such a lovely photo, full of colour, vitality and smiles, and Holly felt a pang of genuine regret for the sisters. They must have been so close when this was taken, having just lost their parents and come over to Zakynthos together. At least, that's what Holly was starting to assume must have happened. Perhaps there had been too many memories back home in the UK, too many painful reminders of what they'd both lost, lurking in the shadows.

Jenny had told Holly when she was younger that she'd grown up in Kent, in a small village with only a few shops, acres of farmland and cowpats dotted all down the high street. When Holly had asked why they never went there for a visit, her mum had simply shrugged and told her that there was nothing there for them any more. 'There's nothing to be gained from living in the past,' she'd told her, waggling her finger as she said it and making Holly laugh. 'The only way to keep going is to keep moving forward, not looking backward.'

As she sat here now, the photo of happy Jenny from the past clutched in her hand, Holly thought that perhaps her mum had been wrong. Whatever had happened to make this beaming-with-joy girl turn her back on this part of her past must have been something that she really couldn't take back – something worse than the future she'd ended up in. Holly waited for a beat or two and sure enough, there it was, the enormous punch of guilt that always came. She hadn't been enough to make her mum happy. Jenny had stared into a future with only Holly and decided that it wasn't worth the effort.

She was still sitting there ten minutes later when a loud knock at the door almost made her scream out loud in fright.

'Oh sorry, love – I didn't mean to disturb you.'

Holly wound her towel tighter around her front and stepped aside to let Annie in. She looked so cheerful – and slightly mad with her lopsided bun and shiny cheeks – that Holly found herself immediately comforted.

'Tea?' she asked, retreating into the kitchen.

'Always,' came the reply. Annie had dumped her bag on the table and was poking through all the scraps of Sandra's old clothes.

'You've been busy,' she remarked, and Holly flushed.

'Oh no,' Annie held up her hands. 'I didn't mean that in a bad way. Sandra would have loved this. I mean, she was always on this thing,' she added, gesturing to the sewing machine. Holly had already found herself wondering how the hell she was going to get it back to London.

'Do you really think so?' Holly asked, pouring boiling water into two mugs.

'Oh, definitely.' Annie beamed at her. 'You're so much like her, you know? People must tell you that all the time.'

'No.' Holly thought it was better not to lie on this occasion.

Annie shrugged and took her tea, blowing on the top as Holly darted upstairs to throw on some clothes. The photograph was still on the edge of the basin in the bathroom, but something stopped her from taking it down to show Annie. She was still feeling far too wobbly to get into a conversation about her mum.

'This is gorgeous!' Annie was standing by the back doors looking up at the patchwork tapestry.

'I thought it would look nice with a bit of colour in here,' Holly replied. She had never been comfortable with praise, and squirmed as Annie raved about how clever she was to create something so beautiful from a load of old clothes.

'I see you've been buying up the local lace supplies too,' Annie said now, running the hand that wasn't holding the mug of tea over the treasured swathes of material Holly had picked up the previous day.

'I'm going to use it to make myself some clothes,' she told her, deciding in that moment that it was exactly what she was going to do.

'Where did you get it?' Annie asked now. 'Don't tell me you drove up into the mountains on that heap of crap parked outside?'

For a second Holly was confused, but then she laughed as she remembered the moped.

'Aidan drove me up to Volimes,' she said, immediately regretting it. Annie's bun wobbled a bit as she absorbed this new bit of information.

'That was going to be my next question,' she said, looking at Holly with a gleam in her eye. 'I guessed you might have run into each other a few more times by now.'

Holly had started to squirm again.

'You could do a lot worse, you know?' Annie stared into her half-empty cup. 'Aidan is a good catch.'

'You make him sound like a fish.' Holly knew it was a lame joke, and Annie's expression confirmed it.

'You know, if I was ten years younger . . .' she went on, raising an eyebrow.

'Why let age stop you?' Holly quipped. 'If you like him that much, then go for it.'

Annie waved her arms in front of her face as if a wasp had just flown into the room. 'You flatter me, Holly love – but he'd no more look at me than he would at old Kostas down the hill.'

'I'm not interested in Aidan like that,' Holly reassured her. 'He's just been showing me around. Taking me to some of the places that my aunt used to go.'

'That's why I popped round,' Annie said, taking her mug over to the sink and pouring away the dregs. 'I thought I could take you up to the market where Sandy used to have her stall sometimes, on the other side of town. I'm going over there this afternoon anyway, and I thought you might like to meet some of her other friends.'

Holly was incredibly touched and was about to agree, but then she remembered Aidan, and the late lunch they had planned in Keri.

'I actually have plans,' she admitted sheepishly. 'Aidan is taking me to Keri.'

'Oh?' Annie's eyebrows were practically dusting the ceiling now.

Bugger. This was not making her claim about Aidan just being a friend look very convincing.

'I can probably rearrange,' she finished lamely, realising as she said it that she had no way of actually contacting Aidan, even if she wanted to.

'No, no, no!' Annie was already heading towards the door. 'I would never want to get in the way of a burgeoning, ahem, friendship between the two of you.'

If she hadn't been smiling quite so cheekily, Holly would have thought Annie was having a sly dig.

'Could we go another day, maybe?' she pleaded at the door. 'I'd really like to see the market.'

'Of course.' Annie hesitated for a moment and then stepped forward and put her arms round Holly's shoulders, pulling her into a hug.

'What's this for?' Holly asked, her voice muffled by Annie's nest of hair.

'You just looked like you needed it, darling,' Annie said, releasing her and giving her shoulders a quick squeeze before making her way back out to the path.

She was right, thought Holly, blinking away the tears: she really had needed it.

Aidan arrived just as Holly was putting the finishing touches to a new blouse she had created using a cream camisole she'd brought with her from London and some of the most delicate of the Greek lace. She'd discovered a little velvet bag of buttons in one of the drawers in Sandra's bedroom, and it was the last of these that she was sewing on by hand when he appeared at the open back doors.

'I can wait,' he said straight away, holding up his hand as she made to leap up from her chair. As she bent back over her work, Holly could sense rather than see his eyes on her, and it took every ounce of her self-control to finish the stitch without stabbing herself in the finger with nerves.

'No Phelan today?' she asked, slipping the finished garment on a hanger and transferring it to the back of another chair.

'Nah.' Aidan stepped forward and picked up a sleeve of her creation, letting the material slip slowly back through his fingers. 'Silly idiot's scared of boats, and I thought we might go out on one after lunch. This is beautiful, by the way.'

'Really?' Holly blushed with delight. 'I mean, it's not a big deal, I just had a few hours to kill.'

'You'd think I'd be good at sewing, being a vet,' he added. 'But I'm terrible. There are a lot of poor animals on this island sporting hideous wonky scars thanks to my sausage fingers.'

Holly giggled, looking down at her own petite hands. Her mum's had been the same. As Holly was growing up, Jenny would always hold her palm out and Holly would place her own on top so they could compare sizes. She hadn't thought about that for a long time, and picturing it now made her smile.

'You okay?' Aidan was peering at her.

'Yes.' Holly shook herself out of the memory. 'Let's get out of here.'

The small coastal village of Keri was situated on a hillside in the south of the island, around four miles from Lithakia. It took Aidan less than fifteen minutes to drive them there, and before parking the jeep he gave Holly a quick tour, pointing out the clusters of stone houses high up above them on the cliffs and the thin strip of beach separating the main road from the sea. The famous turtle-shaped island of Marathonissi sat large and proud in the ocean opposite the harbour, which was dotted with fishing boats, sailing vessels and even the odd yacht.

'It's so beautiful here,' Holly said, as Aidan swung the jeep into a dusty parking space next to the narrow beach.

'The best thing about Keri is the sunset,' he informed her. 'I'm happy to hang around for it, if you are?'

Holly nodded, trying to ignore the bubbles of excitement popping up in her chest. As if on cue, her phone started to vibrate inside her bag. Rupert had messaged earlier saying that he'd call her after his lunch meeting, so it must be him. She ignored it and swung the bag round on her hip. It wasn't very nice of her, she knew that, but she couldn't very well talk to him now, not when Aidan still didn't have any idea that he even existed.

'Ocean View's up there,' Aidan was pointing at the sheer cliff face that curved round the bay. There was what looked like a restaurant close to the top, which had an outdoor balcony area dotted with tables and chairs. Knowing that her mum and Sandra must have spent lots of time there gave Holly goosebumps.

They wandered along the seafront in companionable

silence, Holly taking in the bars, restaurants and souvenir shops and Aidan staring out across the water. The little patch of sand was bustling with families, and Aidan explained that there were a lot of holiday villas in this part of the island.

'You wouldn't really want to take little Billy and little Lizzie down Laganas' main road, now, would you?' he joked.

'I haven't been down there at night,' Holly confessed. 'Is it mental?'

'Well, that depends,' he looked at her sideways. The light breeze that was coming in across the sea had blown some of his curls up in the air. 'If stepping over puddles of puke is your thing, then you'd love it.'

She pulled a face which made it very clear that no, that was definitely not her thing, and Aidan laughed. They'd reached the end of the main road now and arrived at the harbour. Considering she'd never actually been on a proper boat, Holly was surprised at how much she was drawn to them now. She loved the fact that they all had names, and asked Aidan what he'd call a boat if he ever bought one.

'Probably something predictably Irish, like the *Shamrock*,' he shrugged. 'I've never really thought about it. What about you?'

'It would be something Greek,' Holly said. 'But I haven't learnt enough words yet to pick a good one. Did it take you long to learn?'

Aidan picked up a flat stone and threw it sideways into the water, jumping up and cheering as it skimmed the surface and bounced three times before sinking.

'Less time than it took me to learn that trick,' he grinned. 'And I'm a lot better at speaking Greek than I am at skimming stones.'

'I wouldn't have the first clue how to do either,' she said, squinting up at him through her sunglasses and noticing for the first time that he only had a dimple on one side of his lopsided grin.

'Come on – I'll teach you!'

It turned out that skimming stones was nowhere near as easy as it looked, and after ten minutes of Holly only managing what Aidan quickly coined 'drop and plops', she was just deliberately lobbing stones right to the bottom with frustration.

'I'm sensing that prickly side of you is back,' Aidan taunted as she squinted with concentration and flung out her arm, only for another pebble to sink.

'This is a stupid game,' she told him. The sun was beating down on her shoulders and she absent-mindedly slipped her vest straps down. For a brief second, so brief that Holly couldn't be sure if she'd imagined it, Aidan's eyes skimmed over the bare flesh.

'Come on, Missy,' he said, selecting a new stone from the pile he'd made around their feet. Moving right behind her, he picked up her right hand and slotted the warm rock into it.

'You have to hold it like this, see?' he instructed, turning her hand to the side with his own and gently pushing her index finger up so it hooked over the top of the stone.

'If you throw it flat, like this, then it should skim,' he added. Despite the heat, Holly felt the hairs on the back of her neck stand on end. Aidan had slipped his other hand round her waist, and was explaining how she must lean into the throw. She bit her lip and forced herself to concentrate, imagining her stone hitting the water and flinging back up again through the surface.

Aidan's breath was in her hair and caressing the dip between her collarbones. As he leaned against her and pulled her arm back ready to throw, Holly felt a stirring somewhere deep inside herself that made her hands turn instantly clammy, and just as she was about to release the stone it slipped, hitting the concrete edge of the harbour wall and vanishing beneath the water.

'I don't think I'm cut out for skimming,' she said, determinedly defusing the strange atmosphere with a laugh.

Aidan stepped back and let go of her hand. There was something in his eyes that made Holly shiver, a sort of animal hunger, but he quickly pulled himself together.

'Like I said, it takes bloody years to learn. Come on, let's go and get you fed.'

15

When Holly was a child, her mum had always encouraged her to try new things. Whether it was scaling the biggest tree in the park, knitting herself a teddy bear or hurtling down a hill in roller skates, Jenny had always been enthusiastic (though perhaps less so about the roller skates after the tenth or so bloody knee). This translated into their meals too. Holly could remember eating Stilton omelettes with tinned anchovies and banana and lettuce sandwiches. Anything she had wanted to try, Jenny would let her have it, even if it must have turned her stomach to prepare it.

When her drinking started, however, Jenny lost the lust she'd always had for life, and for Holly's life, and they'd increasingly end up with oven chips and beans or cheap microwaveable pizzas. Jenny would plonk whatever it was down on the table and tell her to 'eat up, now, before it gets cold', but then push her own food around on the plate before scraping a good two thirds of it into the bin. It was as if for all those earlier years, Jenny had been wearing a mask – a 'perfect mother' disguise. After years of watching her mum fall further into addiction and darkness, Holly found it impossible to believe that the warm, loving person she'd grown up with had ever been the real Jenny at all. She'd just been playing at being the mum she had never really wanted to be.

It was only when she started seeing Rupert that Holly rediscovered her appetite for varied cuisine. He liked to eat out as much as possible, and all his working lunches meant that he was an expert when it came to the best new restaurants and hidden gems. After a few months of gentle persuasion from her boyfriend, Holly started devouring things like sushi, Indian tapas and curries that made her sweat. It was one of the things they did together that she enjoyed the most.

Being here in Zakynthos, however, Holly had developed a real taste for more simple food. It was all so fresh and delicious that it didn't need much in the way of accompaniment, and she thought she could live quite happily just eating the same things here for the rest of her life.

Aidan was more of a typical man, and glanced at the menu for only a few seconds before ordering himself a steak.

'What?' He held his hands up as Holly pulled a face at him. 'I never get to go out – this is a treat for me.'

'I wasn't judging, honest,' she grinned, choosing a tomato salad and grilled sardines for herself. The waitress at Ocean View was young and British, and Holly felt a mild stab of jealousy. How wonderful to be living and working in a place like this in your early twenties. When she shared her thoughts with Aidan, however, he laughed and said that the poor girl was probably working seven days a week and getting paid less than minimum wage. For this view, Holly thought privately, gazing out across the sun-dappled water, I'd happily work for free. They had chosen a table out on the terrace by the outer wall, and everything below them was green, blue and golden. It was stunning.

They chatted while they waited for the food to arrive, mostly about Aidan's work and the characters he encountered, but also about Holly's passion for sewing. She was astonished to find herself admitting to Aidan that she actually hadn't done any for over a year. Well, not until coming here.

'There just never seems to be enough time to do anything in London,' she explained. 'Everything seems so rushed and hectic all the time.'

Aidan nodded. 'I'd hate it,' he told her. 'That's what I love so much about this place; everyone takes their time and there's none of this pressure coming in from all sides.'

'I love that too,' she agreed, even though she'd never really considered it properly before. She slept better here and ate better and generally felt less stressed. It was hard to feel anxious when it was so warm and everything around you was so beautiful. Since arriving on the island, she felt almost as if some of the air had been let out of her. It was ridiculous, though, given the circumstances and the fact that she'd never been here before.

'Are you sure this is your first time on the island?' Aidan asked suddenly. Was he actually a mind reader?

'It's weird.' Holly took a sip of her water. 'I keep getting these waves of déjà vu, like my body sort of recognises where I am. Does that make me sound mad?'

'Yes.' Aidan laughed. 'But perhaps it just means that you feel at home here. I mean, you do own a home here, after all. Do you have a place back in London too?'

'God, no!' Holly exclaimed. 'I couldn't even begin to afford to buy somewhere. I've always rented.'

'Does London feel like home to you?' he asked.

It was a difficult question and Holly fell silent as she considered her answer.

'I guess it does,' she said eventually. 'My job is there, my friends, my . . .' She stopped just before saying 'my boyfriend'.

Aidan didn't seem to notice, thankfully, instead telling her that Zakynthos had felt like home to him from the first moment he set foot on her, and that he couldn't really explain why, but that it was just a fact.

'It came as quite a shock to the ex,' he added, sucking on his frappé straw and tapping his fingers on the table. It was the first time he'd mentioned her since they'd been at Smugglers' Cove, and Holly felt a little bit of colour drain from her cheeks.

'What happened?' she asked. 'You don't have to tell me, sorry.'

'It's fine.' Aidan looked up and met her eyes. 'I came over here to see my mum and brought her with me, but the two of them didn't hit it off, so to speak.'

'Oh?' Holly thought about the snail she'd flicked down the front of Rupert's mum's blouse and grimaced.

'We were so good together back in Ireland. I loved the bones of that girl and I thought we were strong enough to take on anything together. I never had any doubt in my mind that she was the girl for me, but I did have doubt in my mind about where I wanted us to live. She had trained as a teacher and wanted to do that back home, and I wanted to try and make a life here. My mum hating her guts for no reason just exacerbated things.'

'What happened?' Holly asked, watching the muscle

that had started to throb in his cheek. Clearly this was still a sensitive subject for him.

'She left me,' he said simply, his fingers still tapping away. 'She kept threatening to do it, but I never believed she would. I thought that love was enough . . .' He trailed off.

Holly reached across instinctively to touch his hand, but stopped herself at the last second.

'I think she assumed I would follow her,' he went on. 'And I did think about it, but in the end it wasn't what I wanted. I would have been settling for a life that wasn't my first choice, and I wasn't prepared to do that. I guess she wasn't either, and that's fair enough.'

'Do you still speak to her?' Holly asked, wondering why she felt so sick at the thought of it.

'Only very occasionally,' he shrugged. 'Learning how not to love someone any more is the hardest thing I think a person can do. It feels wrong in such an inherent way, and I struggled with that for a long time.'

'When did you break up?' Holly asked again, her need for facts overwhelming the discomfort at hearing them.

'Ages ago now.' That shrug again. 'More than three years.'

'And there hasn't been anyone else since her?'

Aidan glanced at her and grinned. 'What is this, woman? Are you gonna shine a light in my eyes next?'

'Sorry,' Holly said, realising what an enormous hypocrite she was being. She wondered if he hadn't asked about her love life because he didn't want to know, or just didn't care. Neither reason was particularly nice to swallow.

'*Yassou!*'

The food had arrived, and with it a cheery, red-cheeked Greek man wearing a tight white shirt and even tighter jeans. He looked to be in his forties, Holly guessed, and he was the first Greek man of that age that she'd met who wasn't sporting elaborate facial hair.

Aidan stood up to shake the man's hand, as they clearly knew one another, and then they both turned towards Holly.

'Holly, this is Alix. He owns this place and knew your aunt well.'

'Who is she?' Alix interrupted, beaming at Holly as he placed the plates of food in front of them.

'My aunt was Sandra,' she said carefully.

'Ah, yes. Sandy!' he announced, still grinning at her. 'I know her from a very long time ago. Maybe twenty years or more.'

A little spark ignited in Holly's head.

'So you knew her when she was young?' she asked.

'Yes!' he clapped his hands. 'Who is your mother?'

Clearly Alix was one of the more direct Greeks. He reminded her of Nikos and she smiled up at him.

'My mother was Jenny and—'

'Jennifer?' Alix interrupted again, his smile fading for the first time.

'Yes. She died ten years ago, but—'

'No!' Alix looked so genuinely devastated to hear this news that Aidan stood up again and pulled out a chair for him.

'What happened?' he asked Holly, making her prickle with discomfort. This man seemed so sweet and she hated having to lie to him, but she had no choice. Not when she'd told Aidan her standard fabricated version of events.

'A car crash,' she said quietly, watching Alix's eyes fill up with tears.

'I cannot believe it,' he said, shaking his head in dismay. 'I have not seen her for many years, but I still think about her. She was so full of life.'

Holly simply nodded, unsure of what to say. The grilled sardines that had smelled so delicious just a few seconds ago were now making her insides grumble with revulsion.

'Me and your mother, we were . . .' Alix paused for a second and looked at Aidan, who nodded. 'We were close, at one time.'

Holly thought back to the photo she'd discovered. Could Alix be one of the men in that photo? She didn't think he was, but it had been taken a very long time ago.

'You look like her,' he said now, wiping the back of his hairy hand across his eyes. 'But you also look a little bit Greek too, eh?'

'I do?' Now it was Holly's turn to look at Aidan. He didn't say anything, just smiled helplessly and picked up his knife and fork.

'You have the Greek eyes and the Greek hair,' Alix told her. 'Who is your father?'

Aidan choked on a piece of steak, causing Alix to leap up and thump him hard in the back. Much coughing and spluttering followed, and Holly took deep breaths to regain her composure.

'I am sorry to ask all these questions.' Alix did a little bow in Holly's direction. 'I must leave you to enjoy your lunch now, but later we can have a drink for your mother, yes?'

Holly managed to smile. 'That would be nice.'

She was still shaken up an hour later when he returned with a bottle of red wine and three glasses, and as they sat and toasted Jenny Wright, she examined Alix's face in detail. He had been close to her mum, he was Greek . . . Could he be her father? Could this jolly, lithe man be the one who had been missing from her life all these years?

But surely she would know if he was. Surely some sort of deep-rooted biological phenomenon would occur and her brain would somehow just know that they were related. Nothing like that happened, but Alix did keep gazing at her over the top of his glass, his eyes misty as he told them both stories about the younger Sandra and Jenny.

'Your mother, she like a drink,' he said at one point, making Holly wince. 'She could drink me, how you say, under the table?' He roared with laughter at the memory and Holly politely joined in. Again and again she was struck with the same question: why had her mum left Zakynthos if she had been so happy here?

Another hour passed and another bottle was summoned over. Aidan had stopped after just one glass, but Alix had easily drunk over a bottle to himself. Holly, meanwhile, was starting to feel a bit fuzzy around the edges. The intense heat of the day, combined with the wine and the tiny amount of food she'd managed to consume, was assailing her senses.

She kept feeling Aidan's eyes on her, and at one point his bare knee brushed against her own under the table, sending a glorious tickle of anticipation up her spine. In her bag on the back of her chair, her phone continued to buzz with unanswered calls from Rupert. Holly knew she was straying into dangerous territory, but she didn't want to burst this bubble. She wanted to sit here and listen to stories about her mum and aunt and gaze at the view and feel the sun on her skin. She wanted to shut out the rest of her life and pretend, just for now, that she could stay here in this spot for ever.

Friday, 3 July 1992
Dear Sandy,

It was Holly's seventh birthday last week. Can you believe how fast time has gone? We had a little party for her in the back garden at Simon's – jelly, ice cream, the works. It reminded me so much of the parties we had as kids that I half expected you to come strolling through the back gate at any second. I'm sure Holly would have loved to see you. I won't let her forget her Auntie Sandra, I promise. I'm going to take her to the beach in Brighton soon so she can see the ocean again. She seems to have forgotten that she used to play by one every single day. Do you remember how we used to play? I think about those days all the time. I miss you so much. Please tell us to come and we will.

All my love,
Jen xxx

16

They left Alix just as the light was beginning to fade, his dark head resting on his arms and his gentle snores providing a backing track to the sounds of the waiting staff setting up the restaurant for the evening. Over the past few hours, Holly had come to like him very much, and had decided that he definitely couldn't be her real father. Yes, they might have similar colouring, and yes, he might have been Jenny's ex-boyfriend, but she just refused to believe that it would be that simple – that she would walk into a restaurant on a Greek island and find her dad after twenty-nine years. Life just didn't work that way.

'Fancy a quick skim before we get on board?' Aidan joked, as they climbed out of the jeep by the harbour.

'No, I do not,' she grinned up at him. His cheeks were slightly pink from the sun and she was reminded of Rupert. He'd got seriously sunburnt after a day on the slopes when they'd been skiing and his cheeks had looked the same, only worse. Holly had enjoyed nursing him back to health with aftersun and sympathy. Poor Rupert, she must call him soon before he got really worried.

Oblivious to her tussle with her conscience, Aidan had bounded ahead and was busy grappling with a rope which was attached to a small fishing boat at one end and a metal stump at the other. The vessel was sitting low in the clear water and bobbing from side to side. Once upon a time this boat must have been blue, but the paint had all but peeled off, with just a few cracked shards remaining along one side. There was only room for about four people to sit comfortably on board, and Holly felt her earlier excitement dissolve into nerves.

'Come on, you'll be totally safe with me,' said Aidan, holding out his hand and then grabbing her under the arms and lifting her clean off the ground and into the boat. Horribly flustered, Holly staggered away from him and almost went over the side.

Aidan narrowed his eyes at her in mock anger and passed her a life jacket. She was sure she looked like a complete idiot in it, but she wasn't willing to risk going without. She got the impression that Aidan was only wearing his for show, and he quickly got the motor going and steered them away from the shore like a true pro.

After the initial sensation of being in something incredibly fast-moving and close to the surface of the water passed, Holly relaxed and trailed her fingers in the sea. Aidan pointed the boat east and they headed straight for Marathonissi, which seemed to look even more like a giant turtle from this side of the bay.

Like the beach in Kalamaki, this island was a hotspot for turtle nests, and much of it was roped off from the public. Tour boats came over here every day from Laganas, Aidan told her, but there was a strict limit on how long people could linger on the sand. He'd done a lot of work with the local conservation group that looked after the turtles – or Caretta carettas, as they were referred to locally – and it was something the inhabitants of Zakynthos took very seriously. Out of all the Greek islands in this area, this was the one the turtles had chosen to return to year after year – and to Holly, as well as everyone else here, that made the place all the more special.

It took them around twenty minutes to reach the island. When they arrived, Aidan curled up his nose in disgust at a cluster of tourist boats that had formed a circle not far from the sandy shore.

'They've spotted a turtle,' he explained. 'The Caretta caretta turtle has to come up to the surface to breathe air every five minutes or so, which means everyone gets to take their photo.'

'Do you think it upsets them?' Holly asked, taking in the frown on his face as they passed the boats at a distance.

'I don't know,' he shrugged. 'I just think it's a bit much when there's a gang of boats like that. If the turtles become disorientated, then they'll be distressed. But I suppose if it means people will donate money and not stick their beach umbrellas into the nests, then it's a good thing.'

Holly nodded in agreement. She'd always felt the same way about zoos – that they were a bit cruel but also necessary. It was far harder to care about something you'd never seen, than an animal you'd been a few inches away from. She was going to make the point to Aidan, but she sensed he'd be against the entire concept of an animal in a cage. Holly had often thought that her mum had turned into a sort of caged animal in the end – unable to leave the house, her wings clipped by years of alcohol abuse. Looking up, she saw a flock of birds soaring high above the island and wondered if there was any way Jenny could be one of them. If you could choose to come back as any-thing, Jenny would definitely have picked a bird, and it comforted Holly to think of her that way, taking flight and seeking out new adventures.

'If we head out to sea a bit, we can watch the sun go down,' Aidan shouted over the roar of the engine. Mara-thonissi was vanishing rapidly behind them now and all that lay ahead was vast, blue ocean. Holly's phone had finally stopped vibrating, either from lack of signal or lack of battery, and she tried in vain to shove the guilt away and throw it overboard. She hadn't done anything wrong, she reassured herself. Yes, she was out in a boat about to watch the sun set with a man she barely knew, but she hadn't yet crossed that line. Everything would be okay if she could just stay on her side of the fence.

Aidan seemed to know exactly where to go and after a time he killed the engine and dropped the anchor. Two large rocks stood some distance ahead of them in the water, each poking its nose through the surface like an inquisitive mole. The fiery red ball of the sun sat fatly in the sky just above them, dropping a fraction closer to the horizon with the lap of each gentle wave against the side of the boat.

'I used to bring Sandra out here sometimes,' Aidan said, removing his life jacket and propping it behind his back like a cushion. 'She was a very good listener, your aunt, and very patient with me when I was going through all my break-up nonsense.'

'I'm sure it wasn't nonsense,' Holly said. The words that Aidan had used to describe how he felt earlier had really stayed with her. The idea of having to learn not to love somebody was heartbreaking, but hadn't she been doing the exact same thing ever since Jenny died?

'I think she'd been through some heartbreak of her own,' he said carefully. 'She understood how wretched I was feeling and she never lied.'

'Lied about what?' Holly was intrigued.

'You know how some people will always just tell you what they think you need to hear, like, "Don't worry, old chap, plenty more fish in the sea," and all that crap?'

'I don't think anyone has used the words "old chap" since Dickensian times,' Holly giggled. 'But yes, I get what you mean. I think people get fed up of other people's grief and misery. After a while it's just easier to pretend that you're all right, so as not to bear the weight of their guilt on top of your own sadness.'

Aidan was looking at her intently now, and his face was so close that she could have counted his eyelashes if she'd wanted to.

'Is that what you do, Holly?' he asked. 'Do you pretend that everything is okay?'

'Sometimes,' she shrugged, amazed at how easily she was admitting all this. 'For a time it's all I did. It helped me to survive after I lost my mum. I just played a part of someone who was coping, but inside I was . . .'

She had to stop there before her voice betrayed her, and Aidan fell silent too. The sun was almost down and the sky was transforming into a riot of gold, red and amber. The surface of the water looked like a rippling sheet of bronze, freshly baked and ready to be twisted and shaped into something else, something beautiful.

'You can't put a time frame on these sorts of things,' he

said gently. 'Heartbreak, grief, sadness – they all cut their own shape into you. Wanting to feel better is just the beginning – it can take a lifetime to recover. In fact, I think some people never do. I don't think Sandra ever did.'

Holly thought about the letter, about what her aunt had said about not being deserving. Had Sandra done something so awful to Jenny that it had severed the bond between them for good? Surely that was the answer. But what? She opened her mouth to ask Aidan, but quickly shut it again. If he knew what had happened, then he would have told her already – of that she was sure. Despite not knowing him very well, she trusted him. Her instincts were telling her that he was a good guy, and for now she was happy to listen to them.

'I hope I do,' she said, not taking her eyes off the sun. It was half-obscured by the ocean now and burning a bright, angry red.

Aidan sat up and put a big, warm hand on her shoulder. 'For ever is a long time,' he said, squeezing her muscle with his fingers. 'You have to want to be happy, though. I get the impression that you're far too hard on yourself. You don't give yourself enough credit.'

There he went again, looking right through her and seeing the bits she'd hidden the deepest.

'What happened with your mum, it wasn't your fault. You have to know that.'

But it *had* been her fault, to a certain extent. If she had been less of a disappointment, less of a burden, then maybe her mum would have found the strength to get better. If she hadn't gone to college on that day, if she'd been there to clear her mum's airway before it was too late. If, if, if . . . The word stabbed at Holly like a knife, making her double over. She took her eyes off the sun and stared down at her feet in the bottom of the boat. Aidan said nothing, just kept scrunching his fingers against her shoulder until she felt herself start to relax. By the time she looked up again at the horizon, it was pitch black.

'That sunset was amazing,' she said, turning to Aidan and finding the whites of his eyes in the darkness.

'Some people prefer the sunrise,' he said, his voice barely a whisper. 'But I prefer this. The darkness that follows is so absolute out here.'

'On that note . . .' Holly forced a shred of humour into her voice. 'You are going to be able to get us back to shore, aren't you?'

Aidan laughed. 'Yes. Don't worry. This boat does have a light and there's probably even a compass, somewhere on this wreck.'

'Whose boat is this, anyway?' Holly asked, shifting slightly against the weight of his hand, which was still resting on her back.

'Just a guy I know, a Greek bloke,' he muttered. 'He's got a few boats, I think, but this is the worst of them.'

'I feel so flattered,' Holly giggled. She was keen to get the atmosphere back from serious to jovial, and she was enjoying the sensation of being this close to Aidan – more than was safe.

'I'll take us back to Keri in a minute,' he told her, 'but first I want you to shut your eyes and lie down.'

'You want me to *what*?' Holly spluttered.

Aidan laughed. 'Don't worry, I'm not trying to have my wicked way with you, woman – just trust me.'

Holly shut her eyes and let Aidan guide her down on to her back. The boat was still rocking against the waves and she felt horribly vulnerable not being able to see what was going on. After arranging his life jacket under her head, he lay down next to her and brushed a stray finger against the back of her hand.

'Okay, you can open them now.'

Holly opened her eyes and gasped. The sky was absolutely littered with stars, hundreds of them. It was as if someone had sprinkled glitter, and each one sparkled with such magical beauty that Holly felt a lump form in her throat. She'd read about things taking your breath away, but she realised in this moment that she'd never experienced it herself. There were no words to describe what she was seeing, just feelings. She could feel her heart hammering away in her chest and she could feel Aidan's too. He must have seen these stars so many times before, but even he had been hushed into reverent silence by the sheer majesty of this night sky.

'It never gets old, this view,' he whispered, reading her mind as he always seemed to do. 'The first time I came out here, I knew I could never leave this place. I'm not afraid to admit that these stars made me cry. I wasn't sad, I was just moved, and I'm still moved by them now.'

That was it, that was what she was feeling. It was impossible not to feel small and insignificant down here, so many thousands of miles beneath those stars, but at the same time she also sensed that this moment was huge, that it was one that she would never forget, and she wanted to wrap it up and take it with her.

'Are you okay?' Aidan turned to her at the same time as

she turned to him, and for a second she thought he was going to kiss her. His eyes flicked to her lips then back to her eyes, and she felt her body start to throb with energy. He brought his hand up and gently stroked a curl off her cheek, letting his fingers rest for a second in the soft part where her jaw met her throat. She knew she should move, but she couldn't, so instead she forced her eyes away from his and back up towards the glittering canopy above. There was a pause and Aidan took a deep breath, pushing himself back up into a sitting position and reaching for his bag.

'Is it time to go?' Holly asked, still unable to tear her eyes away.

Aidan sighed and stole one last glance at the sky.

'Yes, Holly – it's time to go home.'

17

'Holly! Where the hell have you been?'

Rupert was not happy.

After Aidan had dropped her off the previous evening, Holly had unearthed her phone to find seventeen missed calls and a flurry of increasingly agitated text messages. Unable to face talking to him so soon after her and Aidan's almost-kiss on the boat, she'd done the cowardly thing and switched off her phone, before heading down the hill for a nightcap at Annie's bar.

'I'm so sorry!' Holly pleaded. 'I was out all day and forgot my phone. They don't really have payphones here, either.'

She really should stop telling so many lies.

'I was so worried,' Rupert said, clearly angry. 'I thought you'd bloody drowned or something.'

'I'm sorry,' she said again, sighing under the weight of her guilt. 'I don't know what to say. I promise it won't happen again.'

She heard him mutter something to someone in the background and tried to flatten her heckles. He was always distracted when she spoke to him on the phone. She knew it shouldn't matter and she knew he had a busy job, but it still wound her up when she was cut off mid-sentence.

'Is the house on the market yet?' he asked now, making

her even angrier. She'd been on the island less than a week, for heaven's sake.

'Not yet, no — I haven't been able to get an appointment with the estate agent until next week.' That at least was the truth, but what she didn't tell Rupert was that she was secretly dreading it. The more time she spent in this house, the more she loved it. Was it really worth selling it, when she'd still not even be able to afford a bedsit in a grotty area of London?

'I really miss you,' Rupert said now, making her feel like the worst girlfriend in the entire world. She had plans with Aidan again this afternoon, and she knew deep down that her feelings for him weren't as innocent as she had been trying to convince herself they were. What that meant for her and Rupert, she didn't know, but it was something she was starting to realise she had little control over. The sensible thing would be to stop spending time with him, of course, but the stubborn part of her refused to play along. Perhaps she was more like her mum than she'd thought.

'I miss you too,' she told him. She couldn't believe that she'd been away from London for such a short time yet had changed such a lot. Would Rupert even recognise her when she got back?

'Do you really need to stay there another week?' he asked now. 'I miss my girlfriend. I miss kissing you and . . . Sorry, just one second.'

There were more sounds of background chatter and Holly used the time to cut up some tomatoes for her breakfast. She was feeling mildly guilty about the fact that she hadn't been back to Kalamaki to see Nikos, and wondered if she had time for a quick drive before Aidan

188

came to pick her up. Today they were aiming to cross off two more locations from Jenny and Sandra's map, one dubbed 'nosebleed point' and the other simply 'blue caves'. After that it was only the secret beach to go.

'Where was I?' Rupert was back. 'Oh yeah, I was saying how much I miss kissing you – and I don't just mean on your mouth, I mean in that other place . . . What? Oh crikey.'

Holly sighed.

'Sorry, darling. Toby needs me for something. Promise me you'll call again tomorrow morning?'

'I promise.'

'Okay. Bye, darling. I love you.'

'I love you too.'

As she pressed the red button and stowed her phone back in her bag, Holly thought again about what Aidan had said about learning not to love. She had the opposite problem with Rupert – she was still trying to learn *how* to love him. There were so many things about him that were lovable: his kindness, his intelligence, his loyalty, his politeness, his good looks, his ambition. She ticked them off on her fingers, waiting to feel something.

Perhaps these things just took time? Perhaps love was something that grew as you were together, something that you needed to nurture and spend time working on. It had stung Holly when Aidan had spoken so openly about the love he felt for his ex-girlfriend. It had made her relationship with Rupert seem silly and childish by comparison, and telling him she loved him just now had made her feel like a fraud.

The truth was, she wanted to love Rupert. She wanted

to love him very much, but she'd always assumed that it was her that was the problem. It was her fear and insecurity holding her back from feeling anything too deeply, and nothing to do with how she really felt. Rupert told her that he loved her all the time, but she never really felt it. She wanted to know for sure, and she didn't.

Taking her phone back out of her bag, Holly flicked through her photos. There were a few of the house here, the beach at Kalamaki and an assortment from her two trips out with Aidan, but after that they were mostly of herself and Rupert. She wasn't a big fan of having her photo taken as a rule, but Rupert was the opposite, and most of these pictures were ones that he'd taken of the two of them. She peered at her face, trying to detect something in her own eyes. She looked happy, she was smiling, there was even a hint of laughter in some – but in none of the photos was she smiling at Rupert. Wouldn't she be looking at him if she felt love for him? And if she hadn't been, shouldn't she start trying harder?

As she sat pondering these questions in the back garden, Holly realised she'd left it too late to go to Kalamaki. She'd have to go tomorrow. She was already aware of a mild tug of panic over the fact that a week had almost passed. Today was Friday, which meant she only had eight days left. It didn't feel like long enough – not even close.

Nosebleed point turned out to be a simple patch of dry earth at the highest point of the island. They had to drive off-road to get there, and Holly was very glad that Aidan's vehicle of choice was a jeep. Even in that they were thrown around all over the place and Phelan, who had climbed from the back seat right across Holly's lap and into the footwell below, whined as they bounced off every bump.

'You wouldn't want to come up here on a moped,' Holly shouted over the roaring of the engine.

'You couldn't!' Aidan yelled back, his knuckles white on the steering wheel.

Whatever awkwardness had been there between the two of them the night before, after the boat, there was no trace of it from Aidan today. He'd shown up at the door looking his usual scruffy self in a faded green polo shirt and beige cargo trousers, and presented her with another of his oranges. Holly had eaten it on the way over and Phelan, much to her surprise, had eaten the skin.

'Daft mutt would eat plastic bottles if I let him,' Aidan had said affectionately, as Phelan choked down the rind.

There were more clouds in the sky today, but it was still brilliantly sunny. Holly had pulled on a white dress at the last minute and left her trusty denim shorts on the bedroom floor – a decision she was already regretting due to the amount of dust pouring in through the open windows. When they finally left the dirt track and rolled on to the smooth concrete of the proper road, she was sure she heard Phelan actually sigh with relief.

'You see that island?' Aidan was standing next to her pointing north. Holly looked out across the ocean and squinted. Sure enough, she could make out a mass of land, its edges blurred with distance.

'That's Kefalonia,' he told her. 'And that,' he added, swinging his arm round to the west, 'is the mainland of Greece.'

'How long would it take to get there?' she asked, still squinting.

'Kilini on the mainland is about an hour away by ferry,' he said. 'And Kefalonia is around the same, I think, although I haven't been there for a while.'

'Isn't that where . . . ?'

'Yeah, my mum lives there. She met a guy here and moved there with him. But, like I said, I haven't been to see her in quite a while now. We sort of lost touch.'

She didn't say it to Aidan, but all Holly could think was how nice it must be to have a mum just an hour away. It was none of her business and she could tell by his tone that he didn't want to elaborate, but she felt frustrated all the same. Hadn't the time he spent with Sandra taught him that grudges are pointless and self-destructive? Then again, she'd been holding a grudge against her own mother for as long as she could remember.

'You're very quiet today,' Aidan said. He'd walked to the edge of the flat area of ground and was peering down over the side of the cliff. It seemed bizarre to Holly that there were no fences up to prevent people from falling, but apparently nobody ever had. She'd asked Aidan about it as soon as they'd arrived.

'Not quiet,' she smiled across at him. 'Just enjoying the view.'

'You know, on a clear day you can see Big Ben from here,' he told her.

'Really?' Holly stood on tiptoes for a second and stared again at the middle distance.

'Yeah, really,' Aidan said, then he started roaring with laughter.

'Oi!' Holly picked up a nearby pebble and hurled it at him. 'You cheeky arse.'

'Too easy,' he chuckled again. 'And here was me thinking you were a smart cookie. I was wrong about that . . .'

She hurled another pebble.

'Incoming!' yelled Aidan, ducking to avoid a third and laughing again as Phelan leapt between them, barking with excitement at this new game he didn't understand.

Holly was laughing now too, and for a few minutes she continued to make half-hearted attempts to hit him with stones and old twigs.

'Did Sandra ever come up here?' she asked him eventually, pausing in her pursuit of him to take a gulp of water from the bottle in her bag.

'Not that I know of,' he frowned. 'Certainly not with me. She only had this little car that was practically held together with bits of string – if she'd brought that thing up here she'd have had to carry it back down in pieces.'

'What happened to it?' Holly asked.

'She got it scrapped before . . . You know. She wanted everything to be organised so that nobody else would be left with any burden.'

Holly nodded. Sandra may have taken care of her car and her cat, but she hadn't provided Holly with any of the answers she really craved. And then there was the house. Why had she been so adamant that Holly should have it if she'd never met her?

'You've gone quiet again,' Aidan nudged her with his tatty trainer. 'Shall we get going to the Blue Caves?'

Holly agreed and followed him back to the jeep, but she didn't really feel ready to leave this place yet. It was so desolate up here, with the wind blowing the dust around her ankles and the undergrowth peppered with the crunchy corpses of long-dead plants. What had her mum and Sandra liked about this place enough for it to warrant a mention on their map? It certainly afforded a good view, she supposed, but there must be more to it than that.

'It's really nice of you to do this,' she said when they'd cleared the dirt track for the second time and were back on the relatively smooth roads. Phelan was still sitting in the footwell and every now and again he would bring his head up and rest it on Holly's knee.

'It's no bother,' Aidan replied.

'I feel bad eating into so much of your time,' she went on. 'I mean, what about all the sick animals?'

'Before this week, I haven't had a day off in about six months,' he told her. 'I do have someone else at the clinic, a lady who works for me, so the animals are just fine.'

'Oh right,' Holly said, mentally conjuring up a sexy young Greek woman wearing a tiny vet's uniform and a coy grin.

'Yes, Paloma,' Aidan went on. 'She's married and has a daughter.'

'Oh.'

She was doing that thing again where she lost the ability to speak properly around him.

'Our busiest time tends to be towards the end of the season,' he explained, slowing down as they drove through a rustic little village. Two old women sitting on wooden chairs outside one of the houses gave them a friendly wave.

'The seasonal workers, you know, the kids that work down in Laganas for the summer, they often take in stray puppies and kittens that they come across in the street or down at the beach.'

'Isn't that a good thing?' she asked.

'You would think so, right, because they get fed and looked after. But the problem is that they get too domesticated. There are plenty of cats and dogs that live in the wild here and look after themselves pretty well, but if they're taken in by us humans too young then they never learn those vital survival skills.'

'I see,' Holly said, giving Phelan's head a pat. It was horrible to think of dogs and cats living on their own – especially dogs, who always seemed to Holly to be so helpless without their owners.

'Come October, the workers all go home and turf their pets back out on to the street, then they become my problem. We have so many brought in that are close to death. It can be quite harrowing.'

'What happens to them after that?' Holly asked, dreading the answer.

'Well, me and Paloma try to rehome as many as we can, but if the injuries or malnutrition are too severe then we have to put them to sleep.'

'That's sad,' she said, feeling lame.

'There is a charity here that goes round and gives a lot of the strays the jabs they need and treats them for any ticks or worms they might have picked up,' he added. 'Sandra used to help by taking a few of the poorly kittens in while they recovered. That was how she came to have Caretta.'

Holly liked this side of her aunt. Nobody who cared that much about animals could be a bad person, no matter what mistakes they may have made. She had never had a pet in her life, but thought if she ever lived here then she'd probably end up with a houseful.

When she said as much to Aidan, he laughed uproariously and told her to keep that nugget of information under her hat before he moved half the clinic into her spare room. The mood between them was different to that of the previous day, when Holly felt Aidan had been in a more serious frame of mind. Today he was definitely feeling playful, and proceeded to tease and taunt her all the way up the island.

The Blue Caves were situated in Cape Skinari, which was the northernmost cape on Zakynthos, and were only accessible by boat. This meant that Phelan had to stay behind, and Holly and Aidan were forced to share the local shuttle boat with a handful of British tourists who had just rocked up on a convoy of quad bikes.

After parking the jeep under the shade of a tree and leaving Phelan tethered to a low branch with a chewy treat and a big bowl of water, Aidan took hold of Holly's hand and led her down a long and winding set of stone steps to a narrow wooden jetty. He then insisted on paying the seven euros each for both of them before lifting her gently into the boat.

The group of tourists who'd arrived on the bikes were all quite young and very chatty, and Holly found herself wincing with embarrassment as one of the girls asked their captain a series of ridiculous questions. Her boyfriend seemed to be completely mute by comparison, although Holly did wonder if the extreme sunburn on his face had rendered him unable to open his mouth.

A slightly older couple sat opposite Holly and Aidan on the thin wooden bench, their fingers entwined and a look of contented bliss on their faces. They caught Holly looking and smiled at her.

'Have you been to the caves before?' the woman asked them as the boat left the jetty and headed eastward.

'He has, I haven't,' Holly told her. She had no idea if that was right or not, but Aidan nodded in agreement.

'Well, you're in for a treat,' she went on. 'Is this your first holiday together, then? You look like a new couple to me, I hope you don't mind me saying.'

Aidan laughed behind his hand and Holly felt herself turn red.

'We're not a couple,' she said, gritting her teeth into a smile. 'Just friends.'

The woman looked momentarily confused and her husband leaned across. 'Don't mind her,' he said. 'She always has been a hopeless romantic. She sees love in every face, I always say.'

'I think that's marvellous,' Aidan announced, giving Holly a tiny dig in the ribs.

'Me too!' she trilled obediently.

This seemed to appease the woman, and when Aidan turned his head to look out across the water, she gave Holly a very obvious wink.

It only took ten minutes to reach the caves, and as soon as they came into view there was a chorus of oohs and aahs from the boat. Similarly to the cove where the shipwreck sat, the rocks here were limestone and so provided a brilliant white surface to reflect the turquoise sea. The water was so clear that you could see just how deep it was, and Holly felt her legs tingle with a mixture of nerves and excitement. The captain steered the little boat through the arches and deeper into the caves, where the turquoise turned to bright, bottle green and the walls were wet with seaweed and condensation.

Before long, the engine was turned off and the younger holidaymakers were diving into the water, eliciting shrieks as their sun-warmed flesh hit the cold waves.

'Coming in?'

Holly turned to find Aidan had already taken off his shirt and cargo trousers and was only wearing a pair of rather alarmingly floral shorts. Her face must have registered what her brain was thinking, because he laughed and slapped two hands down to cover them.

'My other pair were in the wash, okay? Now are you coming in or not?'

Holly nodded and Aidan dived straight over the side, his big body barely leaving a ripple as he cut expertly through the water. Holly unpeeled her white dress and immediately felt self-conscious in just her purple bikini. As she climbed awkwardly down the metal ladder on the side of the boat and into the water, she prayed that Aidan wasn't staring directly at her bum.

Swimming had been one thing that Jenny had insisted on Holly learning from a young age, and she said a silent thank you to her mum for that now, because Aidan had already swum back out through the limestone arches and was beckoning for her to follow.

As she neared, he put a finger to his lips. 'Don't say anything, but I think there's a turtle underneath us,' he whispered. 'I don't want the others to know or they'll all start screaming their heads off, and I reckon the acoustics in these caves are pretty good.'

There was a big droplet of water on the end of his nose and his curls were flat against the top of his head. Holly sent up another thanks to herself for not bothering to apply mascara that morning. It was bad enough that her hair must make her look like a drowned rat – or worse.

'Shhhh,' Aidan whispered. 'I think he's coming up. Just there, look.'

Holly turned to where he was pointing just as a little speckled head poked up through the water. The turtle was a lot bigger than she'd imagined, a good metre or so in length, and it had a beautiful brown, white and yellow shell. After gulping in a good lungful of air, the turtle appeared to look at them for a second, before blinking its large, wise brown eyes and slipping back below the surface.

'Wow,' Holly breathed, turning back to Aidan. The droplet had gone from his nose and he was beaming at her.

'I'm so glad you got to see one so close,' he said, his foot colliding with hers as they trod water. 'And you didn't even have to go on one of those horrible glass-bottomed boats.'

'Result!' she agreed, her teeth chattering slightly from the cold.

'Come on,' Aidan was all at once concerned. 'Let's keep moving before you freeze to death.'

They stayed in the water for another fifteen minutes or so, and when it came to clambering back on the boat, Holly made sure Aidan went before her. Feeling very naughty, she watched as he strode quickly up the ladder and admired the shape of his bottom through his ridiculous trunks. When she joined him a few moments later, he was wrapped in his own towel and holding hers out. If only she'd bothered to go to the gym more before she came out here. There was no way that he wouldn't have seen her untoned stomach and wobbly thighs, but then it was probably for the best that he didn't fancy her.

The caves were stunning and she fully understood why they'd earned themselves a spot on the map, but she hadn't felt anything coming here. She wasn't even sure what it was she needed to feel. A closeness, perhaps, or just an inkling that this place had been special to Jenny or to Sandra. She'd felt it a bit at Porto Limnionas and Ocean View, but nowhere else since except the house.

Aidan was quiet as they drove back towards Lithakia. His earlier playful mood had gone back into hibernation and he seemed lost in his own thoughts. Instead of bothering with small talk, she wound down the window and breathed in the sweet, cloying scent of pine trees and wild lavender. Everything here seemed to smell so much stronger and so much fresher, and she could almost feel her senses opening up to drink it all in.

It had been a long day and the thoughts swirling around in Holly's head about her mum, the map, Rupert and even Aidan were beginning to become exhausting. The prospect of going back to sit alone in the house wasn't something she was particularly relishing, and she'd half-decided to take herself out to dinner somewhere when Aidan piped up.

'There's a bottle of village wine at mine,' he said, not taking his eyes off the road. 'Do you fancy sharing it? I might even stretch to dinner if you ask nicely.'

For a brief, fleeting second, Holly pictured Rupert, his floppy dark-blond fringe and his big soppy grin.

'That would be lovely,' she said.

They pulled up outside their houses and Holly muttered something about getting changed before scuttling off up the path. She wanted to brush her salty hair and clean her teeth at least – and her bikini was still a little bit soggy from her swim in the caves. Heading into the bathroom to find her toothbrush, she noticed the photo of Jenny, Sandra and their mystery men propped up on the basin and snatched it up.

'Any idea who these men might be?' she asked Aidan ten minutes later. She'd strolled straight in through his open back door to find him in the process of opening the wine, and he paused to look at the photo she was holding up under his nose.

'Nope, sorry.' He pulled an apologetic face. 'Do you know when it was taken?'

'In 1984,' she told him, flipping it over to show him.

'Three years after I was born.' He pulled out the cork. 'Way before my time on this island.'

'It looks like this bloke here and Sandra were a couple,' Holly persisted. 'Did she ever have a boyfriend or anything when you knew her?'

Aidan turned his back to fetch some wine glasses from next to the sink. 'Not that I knew of,' he said. 'She sometimes hinted that there was someone a long time ago, but she never told me who he was.'

'I wonder if Kostas might know who they are?' Holly had managed to convince herself on the short walk over here that if she found out who these men were, then she would be bound to find out what had caused the rift between the sisters. And if not, they would at least have some great stories to share.

'Sorry the place is such a mess,' Aidan swung an arm round. 'I'm hardly ever at home to tidy up.'

Holly put the photo down and glanced around. The lay-out of Aidan's house was similar to her own next door, but his kitchen area was on the other side. Someone had added a low wall, which ran along by the stairs, and there were pictures on every available wall space. Getting up from her chair by the open back doors, Holly walked across to the largest painting. It was a landscape, painted with busy strokes. Holly was reminded of Renoir as she ran her eyes across the waves breaking on the shore and the tiny child figures building sandcastles on the beach. Everything had been dappled in beautiful light, and looking at it made Holly feel as though she could hear the sound of the ocean.

'It's beautiful,' she told him. 'I feel almost as if it's coming alive before my eyes.'

The signature in the bottom corner read 'S Flynn'.

'What's your mother's name?' she asked.

'Savannah. Savannah Flynn.' Aidan had appeared behind her with two glasses of wine.

'Is that your surname too? Flynn?'

'Yep. She didn't want me to take my dad's. And you're Wright, right?'

Holly nodded. Rupert always joked about her name, calling her his 'Miss Wright' and 'The Wright One'.

She mustn't think about Rupert.

The painting was starting to swim before Holly's eyes so she turned, bumping straight into Aidan as she did so. A slop of wine left her glass and dribbled down the front of his polo shirt. Unlike Holly, he hadn't bothered to get changed after they got back.

'I'm so sorry.' She rubbed her hand unthinkingly against the stain and blushed as her fingers encountered solid muscle.

Aidan stepped back and laughed as he looked down at himself. 'Not to worry – as you can probably tell, this shirt cost about two euros.'

Before she had time to catch her breath, he'd whipped it off and flung it over the back of a nearby chair. Holly saw a flash of the soft black chest hair and smattering of freckles that she'd glimpsed in the caves, and then he was gone, bounding up the stairs to get a clean shirt.

She forced herself to sit back down and ignore the feelings that were pulsing through her body. It was just the sun, she told herself. And the wine on an empty stomach.

'Hungry?' Aidan had reappeared in a clean grey T-shirt.

Holly wondered if she'd be able to eat, given that her stomach had ridden all the way down to her feet on waves of guilty lust, but she nodded anyway. They made polite chit-chat as Aidan crashed about in the kitchen, frying onions and tomatoes and boiling water for fresh pasta. Holly asked him more about his mother's work and he asked her to tell him about her friends in London. When she got to Aliana, he stopped stirring and raised a curious eyebrow.

'I like the sound of this Aliana girl,' he teased. 'I think

you should bring her over for a visit. She can always stay with me, you know, if there's no room over at yours.'

Holly knew he was winding her up, but it didn't stop her feeling a pang of unwarranted jealousy towards her absent friend. Thank God Aliana hadn't managed to talk Fiona the Dragon into letting her take time off too.

By the time dinner was finished, the first bottle of wine was long empty and they took a second out into Aidan's back garden. The rusted metal chair screeched in protest as he pulled it out over the tiles, causing Phelan to leap sideways in alarm.

'Daft mutt,' said Aidan, giving the dog an affectionate rub and carefully pulling out his own chair from under the table. The night sky was clear and the stars seemed to be everywhere Holly looked. There weren't as many as there had been out on the water, but they were still a sight to behold. There was a faint smell of figs and lemons and she could hear the gentle lapping of the sea from below. How would she ever bear to go back to the noise and dirt of London?

'Have you got any music?'

Aidan went back inside, and a few minutes later the mournful voice of Johnny Cash filtered out to join them.

'I hope this is okay?' Aidan said, topping up her glass before he sat down. 'I've always loved Johnny.'

'He sounds so haunted,' Holly mused. 'Like he's being tortured or something.'

'Yeah.' Aidan listened for a few beats. 'But I think that's what I like about his music, the rawness of it.'

He was right, the words of the songs and his voice were raw, and as she listened, Holly felt fat, stupid tears welling up in her eyes.

'She forgave him in the end, you know,' Aidan said. 'His wife, June Carter. She forgave all the hurt because he was the love of her life.'

Holly sniffed.

'It took me a long time to forgive my ex for walking out on me,' he went on. 'I listened to a lot of this fella while I was trying to come to terms with it all.'

'I can't imagine how hard it must have been,' croaked Holly.

'Losing someone you love is never going to be easy.' He turned to her. 'But I don't have to tell you that, do I?'

She shook her head. It was becoming very difficult not to cry. Damn the wine.

'But, you know, life goes on.' He seemed to be trying to persuade her as much as himself. 'If you hold on to all those feelings of anger and resentment, you'll never be able to move on with your own life.'

'I should go.' Holly stood up abruptly, her wine glass wobbling precariously as her legs banged against the table.

'Hey, I didn't mean to get all maudlin on you.' Aidan was following her across the garden. 'Stay and help me finish the wine at least, woman.'

'I can't, I'm sorry.' The tears really were falling now, and Holly broke into a jog as she reached the low hedge separating their gardens. As she was about to step over it, Aidan grabbed her wrist.

'Hey, what's the matter?' he said, his voice softening as the moonlight illuminated her tears. Without waiting for an answer, he pulled her face against his chest and wrapped his arms around her, his fingers tracing a firm circle in the small of her back. Holly stiffened for a few seconds, then let herself melt against him. How was he to know that he'd hit the nail on the head with all that talk of forgiveness? How was he to know that she had been trying to forgive her own mum for years, but couldn't ever seem to do it?

She cried a puddle on to his clean T-shirt, finally giving in to the emotions she'd been keeping a tight lid on since she'd arrived. She cried for her mum, for the aunt she'd never meet and for herself, and the mess she was making of everything. Eventually, the sobs subsided. Aidan had moved his hand up and was running it through her hair, all the while whispering that everything would be all right. She closed her eyes briefly and lifted her face up towards his, opening them again to find him staring down at her. For a moment they just looked at each other, then, very slowly, Aidan bent his head down towards her, and when their lips met Holly felt it everywhere. Even the very tips of her fingers tingled. She resisted for a split second, and then parted her own lips to let his tongue slide between them, bringing her own across to meet it. It was tentative and quiet, the only sound the frantic crashing of her heart – then suddenly it was urgent. Aidan scrunched his hand into her hair and kissed her harder, pressing his body against her. Holly heard herself groan and arched her back. She could feel how much he wanted her, and she wanted him. Wanted him like she'd never wanted anyone before.

But when his hand came up to burrow under her vest, Holly knew she had to stop. Closing her mouth and slipping her face away from his, she took a step backwards and slowly but firmly pushed his hands away.

'What's the matter?' He was almost panting as he stood there, the light from his open back door turning his face darker in the fading light.

'I've got a boyfriend,' she said. 'I'm sorry. I should have told you. I just . . .'

They stared at each other, both full of a separate regret. Aidan looked genuinely shocked and Holly felt in that moment that things would probably never be the same between them again.

She wanted so much to explain why she hadn't told him, but she didn't have any words. Aidan, too, seemed bewildered into silence, and he simply stood and watched as she stepped slowly over the hedge and returned to the house, closing the doors quietly behind her.

18

When Holly finally forced herself to crawl out of bed the next morning, Aidan's jeep was nowhere to be seen. After wrestling with her old friend the Insomnia Troll until 5 a.m., she'd given up on sleep, switched the lamp on and spent hours just staring at the photo of her mum, aunt and their mystery Greek friends. Her eyes felt dry and her skin was sore from yesterday's afternoon out in the sun. Every time she thought about kissing Aidan, she felt sick.

Guilt hadn't allowed her to contact Rupert yet, but that didn't stop him from calling her at 9 a.m. to see how she was. By some miracle, Holly managed to assure him that all was well. As he chatted away about work and what he'd been up to in London, Holly could only think about how much her life had changed. How could he not tell that she was a totally different person?

The sky was thick with clouds and when she popped down to the shop to get some fresh bread, Kostas informed her cheerily that they might even get a spot of rain. 'It is not a good day for swimming,' he laughed. That suited Holly just fine, because she had vowed to spend the entire day packing up the rest of the house. She needed to keep her mind distracted somehow.

She started in the bathroom, chasing away any thoughts of Aidan by crashing perfume bottles and shampoo dregs into a rubbish sack. A thorough search of the bathroom cabinet elicited no further photos, but she couldn't shake off the inkling that she would find some more if she just kept looking. By midday, the downstairs of the house and the bathroom were sparkling, with every non-essential item either in a bin liner or a box waiting to be collected.

In an attempt to get the place looking as good as possible for potential buyers, Holly also hung more pictures on the bare walls upstairs and refreshed the vase of flowers on the table. Throwing away the ones Aidan had left for her caused a slight pang, but she told herself not to be so stupid. She had half-hoped last night that he would follow her into the house, and had stood trembling by the closed curtains for a full ten minutes after she left him standing by the hedge. She pictured him yanking open the door and taking her in his arms, ignoring her protests and carrying her straight up the stairs. Aidan was no cave man, though, and Holly had eventually given up and headed to bed, where she had lain for hours, twitching with a mixture of longing and self-loathing.

After rifling through every cupboard and drawer and even pulling them out to look down in the gaps behind, Holly had given up on the idea that there were any more secret photos hidden away. Collapsing on to the sofa downstairs with a frustrated groan, she reached for her bag and took out the hand-drawn map.

As far as she could tell, her mum and Sandra's 'secret beach' was close to a place called Korithi, which wasn't far from where she and Aidan had drunk their beers by the beach a few days before. As she realised this, Holly let out another groan – it had taken a good two hours for her and Aidan to get all the way up there, and they'd been in the jeep. On her rickety old moped and with very limited local knowledge, Holly guessed it would take a lot longer. Plus, who was to say that she'd even be able to find this beach when she got there? She needed a full day now that using the jeep was out of the equation. If she set off at first light, she might just make it there in time to explore a bit.

The realisation that she wasn't going to spend any more time driving around with Aidan made her feel suddenly deflated. The energy that she'd pumped into herself that morning promptly whooshed out of her like air out of a sad balloon. She was done with tidying. Perhaps a visit to Kalamaki would cheer her up – one of those amazing Greek salads and a chat with Nikos. Yes, that was what she would do.

As she sped off down the hill twenty minutes later, her hair twisting in the wind beneath her helmet, Holly immediately felt better. Unfortunately, there was no sign of Nikos when she reached the beach bar, and none of the other waiters could tell her where he was. Frustrated after driving all this way, she decided against lunch and instead took her bag a little way down the beach, past all the other holidaymakers, and settled down to read her book. The wind had dropped, and the sun was slipping lazily in and out of the drifting clouds, playing a game of hide and seek with the tan-hungry tourists down on the sand. Holly had positioned herself behind some shrubbery and from the beach she was completely hidden. It only took a few chapters in the soft sand and she was asleep, her head resting lightly on the crook of her arm.

*

'Mum. Mum, you have to wake up now.'

Holly had finally made her way from the hallway into the living room and was standing a few feet in front of the chair where Jenny Wright was slumped.

'Mum, I mean it – this isn't funny.'

But Jenny Wright wasn't trying to be funny; Jenny wasn't trying to be anything. Jenny was dead.

An empty bottle of vodka was on the carpet by her feet and Holly could smell stale vomit mixed with something like defrosting meat. Jenny's hair was covering her face, but Holly could see that the skin around her bony chest was grey.

She swallowed and took a step closer. She knew she should reach out and check her mum's pulse, stick her fingers into her throat and clear her airway, but her hands seemed all of a sudden too heavy to move.

There was a crash as the wind blew against one of the open kitchen windows, and Holly jumped as a sob escaped from her mouth. She fell slowly to her knees and started to weep.

'Please, Mum – don't leave me on my own. Don't you leave me.'

Holly woke with a start just as the first Greek storm of the summer crashed into life overhead. The thunder that had roused her from her nightmare hammered across the sky, providing a rumbling percussion to the fat raindrops that were pelting down on the top of her head.

Thoroughly bewildered, she staggered to her feet just as a jagged stripe of lightning hurtled across the sky. Holly had never seen anything like it, and she gasped in fright. The beach was deserted now save for a few abandoned sun loungers, and the rain was coming down in what felt like solid waves. Her towel was already saturated, and

Holly held it out at arm's length as she scurried along the sand towards the restaurant. Her moped, which she'd parked in the middle of the car park, refused to start.

'Shit!' she swore, removing her helmet and trying not to hurl it across the stony surface in a rage. Looking in desperation in the direction of the taverna, Holly was greeted by bolted doors and closed shutters. Why the hell would they stay open in this weather? she scolded herself. Her thin vest and shorts were turning translucent under the relentless deluge and her feet slipped precariously around in her sodden flip-flops as she pushed the useless bike under the shelter of a nearby tree.

She had two choices: stay here getting steadily soaked until the rain stopped, then try to get the moped working and drive back to the house, or leave the bike behind and walk back. As she deliberated, there was another clap of thunder that was so loud she felt her teeth rattling inside her head. This could go on for hours – she didn't really have much choice.

Hooking her flip-flops under two fingers and stowing her wet towel under the seat of her bike, Holly hung her helmet across the handlebars and then set off at a jog along the beach towards Laganas. The sea, which was ordinarily as calm as bath water, crashed angrily around her ankles. The shoreline was framed with white foam, as if someone had poured a generous dollop of bubble bath into the waves.

Dodging clumps of driftwood and the sharp edges of pebbles as she ran, Holly panted with the effort of dragging her bare feet through the wet sand. Her hair was plastered to her face and her boobs ached as they bounced around beneath the flimsy support of her bikini top. She was acutely aware that she must look utterly ridiculous, but there was no one around to see her anyway. It was eerily quiet, in fact, as even the livelier bars at the Laganas end of the beach had pulled down their shutters against the storm.

As Holly's legs and lungs began to tire, her determination to get home started to wane. But she'd come this far – it would only take her twenty minutes or so to get back up the hill and into her hot shower. She couldn't believe how fast the weather had turned – or how aggressively. She thought about her poor, sodden moped, abandoned all the way back in Kalamaki. She would have to walk all the way back tomorrow to retrieve it – that's if she could get the poor old dear to start again.

The rain wasn't showing any sign of relenting, but Holly's weary legs had started to burn with the effort of running, so she slowed to a halt and bent forward, her hands gripping her slippery bare knees as she gulped in lungfuls of air. She had almost reached the mid-point of Laganas beach, where the road came down and joined the sand. She debated the idea of trying to locate a taxi, but she could already see there were none in the usual place by the corner restaurant, and the idea of padding barefoot up the main road was hugely unappealing. She'd been lucky not to bump into anyone this far, but she doubted that would be the case by the time she reached McDonald's.

The canvas beach bag she'd brought with her was no match for the rain, either, and Holly thought forlornly of her mobile phone, which she knew had completely run out of battery. Then again, who could she call to come and rescue her? Certainly not Aidan – not after she'd made such a fool of herself in front of him. And anyway, she hated the idea of having to be rescued by a man. She'd managed almost thirty years without a knight in shining armour, so she was damned if she was going to plead for one now, just because of a little bit of rain.

Another sky-shattering clap of thunder rang out, as if it was mocking her. 'A little bit of rain?' she imagined the heavens yelling. 'I'll show you, Missy!'

Holly had reached the road part of her journey now, but her wet flip-flops had slowed her progress quite considerably. The sheeting downpour made it difficult to see more than a few feet ahead, and she kept stumbling from the edge of the tarmac into the grassy verge. When she was about ten minutes away from home, a car came hurtling round the corner at speed, narrowly missing Holly as she threw herself headfirst into the undergrowth with an indignant yelp.

'*Malaka!*' she screamed, putting to good use the Greek word she'd been taught for 'idiot'. Her knee stung where she'd cut it open on some stones and a stream of blood was running down her leg. Just as she was scrambling back on to her feet, Holly became aware that there was something hidden in the grass beside her. Something small and wet, which was shivering uncontrollably.

Forgetting about her wound, Holly knelt back down and slid her hands gently under the tiny, terrified body of a puppy. It was scrawny and dirty and its little ribs poked out all along its back, but as Holly lifted it closer towards her chest, it slipped out a tiny pink tongue and gave her a very determined lick on the nose.

'Well then,' she told it, smiling despite the horrendous situation they were both in. 'I think we'd better take you home, hadn't we?' In answer, the puppy snuggled closer to her and ceased shaking a fraction.

Having never had a dog or known anyone who did until a few days ago, Holly had no idea what sort of state this little creature was in. As the rain flew into her eyes and she felt the puppy's tiny heart bashing away against her own, she realised gloomily that there was only one person who would be able to help.

'Jesus, Mary and Joseph!' Aidan had opened the door on the first knock, almost as if he'd been standing right behind it. His eyes widened as he took in her bedraggled appearance, bloody knee and, last of all, the quivering ball of wet fluff clutched in her arms.

'Please help it,' Holly thrust the puppy at him. 'I found it in the bushes down the road. A car. I fell.' She tailed off. It was the first time since she'd met him that he wasn't looking at her in amusement – he looked deadly serious.

Aidan pushed open the door and beckoned her inside, taking the puppy in one of his big hands and putting the other one in the small of her back.

'Here,' he produced a towel as if from nowhere and handed it to her. 'Get your wet clothes off and dry yourself. I'll, um, I'll find you something to put on.'

'I'm fine, really.' The idea of stripping naked in Aidan's house was making her feel uncomfortable for all the wrong sorts of reasons.

As if to show how resolute she was, Holly started

rubbing herself dry through her clothes, defiantly flicking her head over and shaking her wet hair from side to side.

'Suit yourself.' Aidan glared at her.

Phelan had padded over and chose that moment to stick his nose right into Holly's crotch, earning himself a gentle kick from Aidan.

'Come on,' Aidan swallowed his laugh. 'Let's get this little one sorted out.'

Holly followed him into the kitchen area, watching as he spread some newspaper on the table and placed the still-shaking puppy on top. Holly could see now that it was predominantly white, but with one black floppy ear and one brown. Its black nose was upturned and it had big brown eyes, which were now following Aidan's every move as he crashed around from drawer to cupboard, eventually producing a small black holdall and placing it on the table beside the puppy.

From her half-obscured position beneath the towel, Holly was able to watch in undisturbed detail as he efficiently checked the puppy's eyes, mouth and paws, before using a small stethoscope to listen to its heart. After a few minutes of prodding and peering – all of which prompted no complaints from the patient – Aidan found another small towel and lifted the puppy into his arms, slowly rubbing it dry while making soothing noises into its mismatching ears. Holly sat down on the arm of the sofa. For some reason her legs were refusing to stop shaking.

'She'll be fine,' he said eventually. 'Just a bit shaken up. She's far too young to have been separated from her mammy.'

'She's a she?' Holly had found her voice at last.

'Well, you know, I'm no expert . . .' Aidan smiled for the first time since he'd opened the door. 'Oh no, I am. That's right, silly me.'

'Sorry for bringing it – I mean her – here,' Holly stuttered. 'I didn't know what else to do – I know you said they shouldn't be domesticated and all that, but I couldn't just leave her there.'

'You did the right thing.' Aidan smiled again, and this time it reached his eyes.

There was a silence as they both stared across at each other. Holly tried not to think about how awful she must look – she was determined not to be the first to look away, as she always seemed to be. She didn't want Aidan to think she was weak, even though being around him made her feel exactly that. And wasn't it true, anyway? The first sign of trouble and she'd run here, to him. The thought made blood rush to her cheeks again, and she was glad when he lowered his eyes first to whisper more silly nonsense to the puppy.

'This happens a lot,' he said, breaking the tense silence and motioning to the tiny dog with a nod of his head. 'She was lucky you found her – I don't think she would have lasted more than a few days on her own.'

Holly nodded. 'What will you do with her?' she asked.

Aidan gave her a rather grim smile. 'Well, I'll ask around the island, of course, see if anyone's missing her. But it's likely she'll end up with me.'

'Really?' Holly's voice came out a few octaves higher than she would have liked.

'At least for a little while, until she's stronger.' Aidan had lifted the little mutt up now and Holly tried her best not to melt into a puddle of warm goo as he kissed and nuzzled its face.

Phelan, sensing that his master's attention was firmly elsewhere, sauntered over to Holly and writhed himself happily against her bare legs, leaving a trail of drool as he went. He really was the most ridiculous dog, she thought fondly, stretching out a hand and stroking his shiny head.

'He likes you,' remarked Aidan, pulling a face when Holly looked up. 'Okay, so he likes most people, but he definitely has a thing for you.'

'Well, I have a thing for him too.' The meaning lingering behind their words was not lost on either of them, and Holly very determinedly kept her eyes firmly on the dog.

Aidan took a deep breath. The puppy had now curled up in the warm space under his chin and closed her eyes. 'What is your story, Holly?'

The abrupt change in subject shocked her.

'What do you mean?'

'I mean, who are you? What are you really doing here? What's your story?'

'One question at a time!' She tried to laugh him away, but his gaze was unrelenting.

'The thing is,' he went on, moving from behind the table and making his way over to where she was still sitting on the arm of the sofa, 'Sandra told me she had a niece, but she couldn't tell me much about you. Then you show up, all stroppy and defensive – what?'

She was glaring at him.

'Come on, you *are* both those things. In the beginning you were, anyway, but then I've seen your softer side too.

Like this here, tonight, bringing this little lost puppy to me. It's . . . Well, it's confusing, that's all.'

'Maybe I'm just a confusing girl.' Holly's voice had become very small. She didn't like how much attention he'd been paying to the way she behaved, but then a little voice in her head was also whispering to her that she might just be a tiny bit thrilled about it at the same time.

'You intrigue me,' Aidan told her. 'It feels as if you're keeping part of yourself locked away out of sight. Like this business of you having a fella back home. Why didn't you mention him before?' He had sat down now at the opposite end of the sofa to her, and was still stroking the sleeping puppy with one thumb. Holly watched as he rotated it first one way, then the other. Not for the first time, she felt as if he was peeling back that protective shell she'd built around herself – and this time she was finding it harder to resist him. So what if he got a few fingers underneath? So what if he had a sense of the real her? She had been feeling more and more like the person she thought she'd always been ever since she arrived here. Zakynthos was drawing out something that she'd never been comfortable with before, and it was beginning to dawn on her that the something in question was herself.

'The truth is,' she said finally, daring herself to look at him. 'The truth is that I have no idea what I'm doing here, either. Until a few weeks ago, I didn't even know this place existed. I didn't know that Sandra existed. I thought that I was all that I had left.' She had to stop before her voice dissolved into a sob, and Aidan waited while she took a few deep breaths and stared hard at the opposite wall.

'It's hard to explain,' she ploughed on. 'But I feel as if there are answers in this place, on this island. Things that I need to know.'

Aidan shifted slightly at her words. 'What sort of things?'

'That's just it!' Holly threw her hands up in exasperation. 'I don't know. I just have this feeling – a sense that something is waiting for me.' Now that she was saying all this out loud, Holly realised that it had been on her mind for days, creeping into her subconscious like one of the bougainvilleas that ran up the side of the house.

'I'd like to help you find it, if you'll let me.'

Holly turned her gaze from the wall to find that Aidan had moved along the sofa. He was so close to her now that she could almost feel the hairs on his thigh brushing against her lower leg. Her still soaking wet top clung to her back, but she had stopped shivering. Outside, the rain continued to pelt against the ground – she could hear it in the trees and smell it in the air between them.

'I've got a boyfriend.' She hadn't planned to say it, and it was in no way an answer to Aidan's question, but it felt important to bring Rupert into the room with them. The image of him was becoming increasingly faded the more time she spent with Aidan, and she hated herself for being so disloyal.

'You said that already.' Very slowly, Aidan pulled a blanket down from the back of the sofa and wrapped it around the puppy, setting her aside on the cushion in a contented, sleepy ball. Holly only had to let herself slide down and she would be on his lap, in his arms.

'He's a good person,' she added. It was barely a whisper.

'I'm sure he is.'

They both jumped as another clap of thunder rang out, and Holly laughed gratefully, using the opportunity to stand up and reach for her bag on the floor.

'I should go,' she looked at him. 'I really do need to dry off.'

'Holly, Holly, Holly.' He sat forward and rested his elbows on his knees. 'Why do I feel like you're always trying to run away from me?'

She opened her mouth to reply, but there was nothing she could say. They both knew why she was going.

'Are you scared what will happen if you stay?' His voice was soft, but the meaning was clear.

She nodded, unable to speak.

'This boyfriend of yours,' said Aidan, standing up and taking a step towards her. 'Does he make you do this?' As he said it, he brushed a casual finger down the side of her face, and Holly quivered with pleasure.

'No.' It was a whisper.

She thought he was going to kiss her again, but instead he ran a hand into her wet hair, gathering it up and squeezing out the excess water. The droplets slid down her back and along his bare arm. Aidan stared at her exposed neck as if transfixed, his hand still clenched in her hair. Holly wanted desperately to touch him, but she was frozen. Her breath caught in her throat as he ran another finger behind her ear and down along her collarbone. This was the moment she must stop, pull away and tell him she wasn't interested – but she didn't.

She started to shake, not with cold but with the desire that was now flooding through her. There was a burning feeling coming from below her belly button, and she felt her tongue come out and moisten her lips. Aidan saw it too, and finally, deliciously, dipped his face towards hers. There was a moment before their lips touched, when just for a second Holly pictured the two of them as a stranger would, locked on to one another. She wondered briefly if the sparks she could feel would be visible, like a match being struck in a darkened room. And then Aidan's lips were on hers, and she didn't think about anything but him.

Thursday, 24 December 1992
Darling sister,

As you can see from the front of this card, we're up in Edinburgh for Christmas and I can't even tell you how cold it is. Imagine a bath full of ice, on the top of Everest, with a chilly breeze. Holly loves it here because there is real snow and it never seems to snow in London. Do you remember the time it snowed on the island and we ran starkers down the beach to Porto Koukla? It was the year before we lost Mum and Dad, and I thought we would die laughing. I think about you all the time, S. Will you forgive me? It is Christmas, after all. At least write back to me and tell me that you're okay. Please. I hope you have something nice planned for Christmas. Mine is just to get as drunk as I possibly can. Ha ha ha!

Jenny Bear xxx

19

She wasn't sure when it had stopped raining, but when Holly woke up the next morning there was a thin, bright trail of sunshine thrown across the tangled sheets.

Aidan's sheets.

Oh dear God, she was in Aidan's bed.

Mercifully, given the mild panic she was feeling and the way her hair appeared to have dried in the shape of a bashed-in beehive, Aidan himself was nowhere to be seen. Feeling like a total idiot, Holly bent her head to sniff his pillow and allowed herself a small smile. She lay there for a few seconds, straining to hear the waves hitting the shore and waiting for the guilt to crash over her. Oddly, though, she didn't feel very guilty at all. What had happened last night had felt inevitable, but more than that: it had felt right. She quelled a sudden ridiculous urge to get up and jump up and down on the bed – she wanted to throw open the windows and yell across the mountains, 'I had sex with an amazing man last night!'

'The heat must be sending me mad,' she said out loud, and then laughed at herself. It was clear that Aidan was not in the vicinity, so eventually she gave up waiting and, pulling on a discarded T-shirt that smelled deliciously of tall, dark, Irish vet, she headed downstairs.

There was a handwritten note propped up against the kettle. 'Gone to get some stuff for the puppy. You're beautiful.' The puppy! She had almost forgotten all about her, the little lucky charm she'd rescued from the roadside. Had fate reached out a mischievous hand and placed her there for Holly to find? At this moment in time, it felt like a genuine possibility. Would this ever have happened had it not been for the puppy? The idea alarmed her, but she swept it aside just as quickly as it had occurred to her. No, this would always have happened, one way or another. There was something about Aidan, an extra layer to him that she'd never come across in another human being before – and whatever it was, it had worked its way under her skin.

You trust him, whispered the voice inside her head. *You've never trusted anyone before in your life, but you trust him.*

With this realisation, Holly also became urgently aware that she wanted to tell Aidan everything: all about her mum, her past, the things she'd discovered since she'd arrived in Zakynthos – all of it. What had seemed so terrifying just a day ago now felt like the most natural thing in the world, and she was impatient to get started now. The minutes clicked by like hours, and just as she was contemplating climbing an actual wall in frustration, Holly heard the sound of the jeep engine and felt her heart start to rattle with excitement. Ignoring the urge to run down the path and leap into Aidan's arms like a wild monkey – she wasn't entirely insane – Holly busied herself making tea in the kitchen and only turned round when she could sense that he was a few feet behind her.

'Morning,' he breathed, burying his head under her hair and kissing her behind the ear.

Holly squirmed and giggled as the teaspoon clattered against the mugs.

'This T-shirt looks a lot better on you than it does on me,' he added, looking her up and down appreciatively, before hooking an investigatory finger under the hem. 'No pants? Are you trying to kill me, woman?'

He moved to kiss her and Holly let herself melt against him for a second, pulling gently away as she felt a wet little nose against her foot. The puppy was looking up at them with wide brown eyes, her tiny stump of a tail wagging with delight.

'She remembers you,' Aidan told her, scooping the puppy up and placing her in Holly's arms. 'She's a smart little cookie, this one.'

Holly wondered how Rupert would react if she turned up one day with a puppy, then pushed the thought angrily from her head. Now was not the time to be thinking about Rupert. That was a mess to be sorted out another day.

As if sensing her sudden disquiet, Aidan stepped to one side and finished making the tea.

'Are you busy today?' Holly asked. Her voice sounded horribly polite, and she pulled an apologetic face as he looked round at her. 'I mean, do you . . . Are you?'

Aidan chucked the spoon into the sink and laughed, taking both her and the puppy in his arms again. 'Yes, I'd love to spend the day with you, Miss Wright. What would you like to do? I hear the water park is fun . . .'

'Water park?' Holly was aghast. 'As if! I was actually thinking . . . Well, I had this one idea.' Putting the puppy gently down on the tiled floor, she retrieved her shorts from the floor near the sofa and yanked them on.

'Do you think we can find the beach?' Holly asked him. 'The secret beach from the map? It's the last place to visit.'

Aidan stared into her eyes. There were golden flecks in his, and his lashes were the colour of cinnamon. 'We can certainly try.'

As she got dressed into clean clothes next door, Holly found herself absurdly missing him. It was ridiculous – she'd been away from him for all of ten minutes, but there was an ache of longing inside her. She could hear him outside through the open bedroom window, explaining to Phelan that he would have to stay at the house today to look after the little puppy.

'Don't look at me like that, you daft mutt,' he was chiding. 'This is important, okay?'

Could it really be true that she, Holly, was important to this man? As she looked at herself in the mirror, a brush half-dragged through her haystack-like hair, Holly couldn't help but smile – this was what it must feel like to jump out of a plane: terrifying, but exhilarating.

When she slithered across the front seat of the jeep a few minutes later, Aidan promptly put one of his big hands on her thigh and leaned over to give her a lingering kiss. It was bizarre how she'd gone from being so on edge around him to feeling as if they'd been together for years. Neither of them had mentioned the subject of her absent boyfriend since last night.

'I can't believe there aren't even any puddles,' Holly said as they drove down the hill and turned left, away from the coast. It was true. Despite the torrential downpour of the previous evening, there didn't appear to be even a droplet of water remaining. The sun, which was already high above them, had sponged up every last raindrop. There was a flavour to the air, however, that hinted at a difference. The plants seemed more fragrant than ever and the mugginess had been washed away, giving the landscape a renewed clarity. Holly felt as if her eyes were fully open for the first time that week, and wondered if it was just the effects of the storm, or something else.

'Penny for them?' Aidan joked. He had balanced the hand-drawn map on the dashboard and was glancing at it as he drove, a frown creasing lines across his smooth forehead.

'I was just thinking how beautiful this place is,' she replied, telling him a half-truth.

'Gets under your skin, doesn't it?' He was watching the road, but increased the pressure on her thigh by a fraction.

'It's going to be horrible going back to London,' she blurted, realising too late that this also meant being separated from him. They hadn't yet discussed what would happen next, and now she wished she could catch her words before they reached him, like butterflies with a net.

Aidan was silent for a few miles, apparently choosing to let the awkward moment pass. Holly sat squirming next to him, trying to quell the surge of panic that had risen up in her chest. What if she'd just scared him off? What if he thought she'd just been using him? But then, what the hell was she doing?

'This beach is definitely near the north-west tip of the island,' Aidan said, looking once again at the scribbled map. 'It would make sense – there are a lot of small coves in that area that I've never been to before. I think it will be in the same area as the Blue Caves.'

'Great. Whatever you think.' She knew she was being

lacklustre, but Holly couldn't help but feel responsible for sticking a big London pin in their idyllic Greek bubble. Just when she was deliberating whether or not to leap out of the jeep and leg it, Aidan took one of her clasped hands in his and squeezed it tight.

'Stop fretting, woman,' he told her gently. 'Let's find this beach. We can talk about all the other crap later, okay?'

It took them another hour to reach Korithi, by which time they'd passed at least fifteen separate fields that definitely smelled of poo. Aidan chatted to her as he drove, pointing out houses up on the mountainsides and telling her all about the people who lived there. It turned out that since moving to the island, Aidan had become quite the expert on goats and chickens – the predominant animals on Zakynthos.

'Why do you think my clothes are all full of bloody holes?' he laughed. 'Goats will eat anything, the little buggers. Never turn your back on a goat, I can tell you that for free.'

'Why are they so popular?' Holly asked. She was struggling to find anything very appealing about the grubby, toothy faces that kept peering at her from over low stone walls.

'Well, they're used for milk and cheese,' Aidan shifted slightly. 'And meat.'

'They eat them?' Holly felt suddenly guilty that she ever thought of them as ugly.

'Of course they do,' Aidan was amused now. 'They're not pets, are they? Not like cats and dogs.'

'It just seems such a shame,' she pouted. 'They're all so sweet.'

'Far better that they spend their days in the fields, roaming about freely with their goat mates,' Aidan argued. 'In Britain, they'd probably spend their life in a grotty old barn – or worse.'

He was right, of course, and clearly quite passionate about it.

'You're very sexy when you get angry,' she told him, immediately turning red.

Aidan didn't reply; he merely gave her a sly grin and carried on driving. Holly tried not to think about how much she wanted him to pull over and drag her into the nearest field. It would be totally worth losing her bikini bottoms to a hungry goat.

Aidan parked on the edge of a small square. The idea was that they'd explore on foot and try to find the rock that apparently looked like a dog's face. If the map was correct, then the path that led to the secret beach wasn't far from there.

Korithi was a beautiful place, and Holly paused for a few seconds to absorb the landscape as she clambered out of the jeep. The sky was so blue today that she could almost feel the weight of it. It was strange, there barely ever being a single cloud in the sky. Save for yesterday's freak storm, Holly had only seen a few since she arrived. It made the space around her feel larger, somehow, as if her eyes could search for ever and never find an end. London, by contrast, had already started to shrink in her mind. Silly, really, given that it was far larger than Zakynthos.

'Are you ready?' Aidan had walked round from the

driver's side and was standing beside her. She couldn't see his eyes through his sunglasses, but he was smiling. It was such an easy smile, just a slight lift in each corner of his wide mouth. His top lip was thinner than his bottom, but his Cupid's bow was invitingly pronounced. It took every ounce of strength she had not to reach upwards and kiss him again. She had to stop letting herself be distracted – they had a mission to accomplish.

They strolled hand in hand through the small village area, past window boxes overflowing with a riot of colourful flowers and a small bakery emitting a delicious smell of warm dough and cheese. Aidan explained that the place was one of the best on the island for spanakopita, a Greek type of pasty stuffed with feta cheese and spinach. He laughed as Holly clutched her rumbling stomach and groaned with pleasure, eventually turning back to nip in and buy them some to feast on when they reached the beach.

They left the tarmac of the main road after 100 metres or so and Holly followed Aidan along a stony path towards the top of a cliff. She could see the top sails of a windmill above the trees, and as they rounded the corner she let out a little gasp of pleasure. The windmill was nestled close to the edge of the cliff, a small, wood-panelled taverna propped up at its base. It was no longer in working order, but it was the first time Holly had seen one this close up.

'It's so cool,' she blurted, running her hand across the light grey stone.

'Yeah, it's, like, so rad.' Aidan laughed at her furious expression, pulling her against him and kissing the top of her head.

'Look.' They had moved around the windmill to the very

edge of the cliff, a decidedly rickety-looking fence the only thing separating them from a sheer drop into the sea below. 'You can see all along the coastline from here,' Aidan pointed. 'I thought we could see if there are any beaches.'

They both leaned over the fence as far as they dared, with Aidan's height giving him the advantage.

'I think I can see something,' he said. 'It might be nothing, but I say it's worth a look.'

'Let's do it.' Holly was happy to let him lead the way – especially when he chose a rubble-strewn path right along the cliff edge. This time there was no fence, so Holly concentrated very hard on where she placed each foot.

The heat was becoming all the more intense as they walked, mostly in silence, along the track. Her stomach rumbled loudly and she thought longingly of the spanako-pita Aidan was carrying.

'Here, drink some of this.' Aidan had conjured a huge bottle of water out of his rucksack and handed it to her.

'Thank you,' she gulped gratefully. 'How much further do you think we have to go?'

'It's hard to say.' Aidan pushed his sunglasses up on to his head and squinted at her. 'I can't see along the coast from here. But don't worry – I won't let us get lost.'

A lizard darted out from the undergrowth across Holly's feet and she jumped, clinging to Aidan as a waterfall of stones slithered over the edge.

'Steady now,' he put a firm hand on her back. 'You go in front, so I have more chance of catching you next time you wimp out over a tiny lizard . . .'

'Oi!' Holly shrugged him off. 'Less of your lip, Mister.'

Another ten minutes passed as they made their slow,

cautious way down the path. The plants on either side were scratching her bare ankles and the water had long since run out. Just as she was beginning to wonder if she'd still be alive to sample spanakopita, Holly rounded a narrow bend and froze, her heart in her throat.

Aidan, who had presumably been looking the other way, collided into her back. 'Whoa there! What's the hold-up?'

Holly stared at the large object by the path ahead of them.

'Does that look like a dog's head to you?' she whispered.

The rock was much smaller than she'd pictured when she'd first read the absurd description on the map, just about coming up to her knees. There was a pronounced nose-shaped lump on the front and grooves in the top that looked a bit like ears.

'That has to be it,' Aidan sounded excited behind her. 'I've never seen a rock that looked more like a dog's head in my life.'

Holly slipped the map out of her back pocket and peered at the crude drawing that her mum or Sandra had done. It did, indeed, seem to be a similar shape.

'Come on!' Aidan had stepped around her and was heading downwards through a tangle of trees. 'It's got to be down here.'

Holly followed him carefully, but she found that her legs had started to shake. If this was the beach, what would she find there? Would she feel anything? What if she broke down and started crying in front of Aidan again? However, the fact was, she wanted to see this place, she *needed* to see it. She couldn't explain it, not even to herself, but the need was all of a sudden like no other she'd ever experienced. Over the past few days, an image of her mother had begun to form in her mind, one that was happy and tanned and carefree – a world away from the stringy, matted, dirty heap that Holly had discovered slumped in the armchair that day. This new Jenny Wright was full of life and laughter. Holly found she could picture her very clearly in that way, and the image had become so vivid now that she was almost surprised not to find her mother peering out from behind one of the trees she and Aidan passed as they made their way downhill.

Aidan, perhaps sensing the change in mood, kept quiet, pausing only to hold branches out of Holly's way. She felt a wave of gratitude towards him for knowing not to interrupt her thoughts.

They were nearing the sea now. Holly knew because she could hear, rather than see it. There was salt in the air around them and a light breeze rustled the dry grass. Aidan parted an extra-thick tangle of leaves and suddenly there it was. For a few seconds, Holly just stared, taking in the perfect white stones of the curved beach, the intense blueness of the sea, the gentle lapping of the water on the shoreline . . .

'Do you think this is it?' Aidan laid a gentle hand on her arm.

For a moment, Holly didn't dare reply. She was so convinced that she was about to burst into tears.

'I know it is,' she managed at last. 'Don't ask me how, but I know.'

20

The spanakopita turned out to taste even better than it had smelled in the bakery, and Holly smiled with pleasure as the sharp, bitter spinach brought the salty feta to life on her tongue. Aidan had swallowed his in two bites, and was now wiping flakes of pastry out of his stubble.

'I need to tell you something,' Holly said eventually, folding the paper bag from the bakery into smaller and smaller squares.

'Whatever it is, you can tell me,' Aidan said, putting his hand over hers.

'My mum didn't die in a car crash.'

'Oh.' There was a crunching sound as Aidan shifted on the stones.

'She was an alcoholic, had been for years. She drank herself to death one day when I was at college, and I came home and found her.'

'Oh Jesus,' Aidan ran an agitated hand through his hair. 'You poor girl.'

'Afterwards, I was sent to see a grief counsellor,' she went on, staring very hard at the horizon. 'She told me that I had to forgive my mum for dying, and that I had to forgive myself for not being there to stop it, but I never really did. I don't think I wanted to forgive her at first, and then the hatred just became part of who I was. What I really wanted was to forget she had ever existed at all.

Thinking about her just hurt too much. I wanted the pain gone.' She shook her head at her own stupid teenage self, so full of self-loathing and fear.

'I really wanted to start my life again all by myself,' she told Aidan. 'And I was doing a great job of it, until the letter from Sandra turned up. Now it feels like my life is not only back to front, but upside down too.'

Aidan had been sitting very quietly since she began talking. Now, however, he reached across and stroked her cheek. She had managed not to cry throughout the entire confession, but now she felt herself begin to crack.

'Don't cry,' he whispered, as if reading her mind. 'You're so brave, coming here after everything that you've been through. I knew that you were tough – but I had no idea just how tough.'

'I'm not tough,' Holly argued. 'I'm scared of everything.'

'Are you scared of me?'

She looked into his eyes. 'Yes,' she admitted. 'I'm scared of who I am with you. I don't even recognise myself – does that make me sound crazy?'

'Yes.' Aidan braved a grin. 'But your craziness is part of what makes you so damn irresistible.'

'I think my mum was a bit crazy.' Holly pulled a face. 'In fact, who am I kidding? She was completely mental.'

'I know you have some very bad memories of your mam,' Aidan said carefully. 'But from what I've heard over the past few days, she was liked by a lot of people. She must have been a good person, at least in the beginning.'

'She was.' Holly turned away from him and stared out across the deserted beach. She knew that her mum had been here, probably sat in this very spot and looked out across the very same ocean. She tried to picture that version of her mum now, young and fearless, wringing every last drop of fun from life. Why was it so hard to admit that Jenny had been a good person?

'She was the greatest mum in the world when I was a child,' she told Aidan now. 'She was my best friend. We did everything together.'

'My mam used to let me sit on her knee sometimes when she was painting,' Aidan said. He was focusing very hard on a spot somewhere on the horizon, but Holly thought she could detect a slight wobble in his voice. 'I was too young at the time to really appreciate it, but later, when I was older and hopefully a bit wiser, she taught me that there is beauty everywhere – in every face, on every hillside, even in the blackest of dark skies. Despite everything that's happened between me and her over the past few years, I've never forgotten that lesson.'

'I think I understand a bit more about beauty since coming here,' Holly said, stretching her arms out to either side for effect. 'All this – it's just so beautiful. Even with everything that's happened, I can't feel miserable here.'

'Why do you think I moved here?' He gave her a sideways look. 'I only have to see the view from our hillside every morning and I feel refreshed and able to take on the world. But more than that, I feel like I want each one of my days to count, and for what I do to mean something. Does that make sense?'

Holly, who for the past ten years had simply existed in a weird, miserable limbo, knew exactly what he meant. Aidan was staring out again towards the point where sea met sky, an intermingling mess of blues. Just as Holly went to jump up, he grabbed her hand.

'Holly, there's something . . .' he began, but then caught sight of her grin. 'What?'

'Let's go for a swim!'

Aidan laughed as she pulled off her shorts and kicked her trainers across the stones, but his eyes widened as she flung her bikini after them.

'Miss Wright, are you suggesting that we go skinny dipping?'

'Not suggesting,' she quipped. 'Telling!'

It took him less than a minute to follow suit, and the two of them ran giggling down to the water, hand in hand.

What would you say if you could see me now, Mum? thought Holly, throwing herself into the surf. *Is this something you would have done?*

After the heat of the beach, the shock of the cold water made her gasp. It felt wonderfully liberating, though, to know that they could be caught out at any second. She let her hair down and shivered as the water stole up the strands and tickled at her scalp. Looking down, she could see her breasts beneath the surface, a pair of white pebbles on her toffee-coloured torso. Aidan had clearly spotted them too, and he swam across and took one in each of his big, freckled hands.

'Cold?' he asked, his thumbs finding her nipples.

In response, she lifted her legs up and around his waist, knotting her ankles together and pulling him towards her. 'Yes,' she whispered into his ear. 'But I have a feeling I'll be warmed up soon.'

*

Afterwards they lay on their backs, looking up at the cloudless sky and letting the natural buoyancy of the salt water keep them afloat in the shallows. Aidan closed his eyes, a contented smile on his face, and Holly watched him. She still couldn't quite believe that this was happening to her – and she certainly wasn't ready to think about what it meant for her life back home, for her future with Rupert.

'Do you think you can make it to that cave?' Aidan asked now, snapping her back to the present. The cave in question looked to be at least 200 metres away, but Holly was feeling invincible. Letting Aidan lead the way, she followed at a leisurely pace, enjoying the feel of the sea against her bare skin and the heat from the sun on her back.

The water in the cave was a clear, brilliant blue, and the rocks inside were bleached white, just as they were in the more famous caves a few miles along the coast. It looked like something out of a fairy tale, and Holly gazed up into the nooks and crannies, wondering if a little hobbit creature was about to peer down at her through the gloom. Then, as her eyes scanned a ledge a few feet ahead of them, she spotted something else.

'Do you see that?' she asked Aidan, lifting an arm out of the water to point. 'It looks like someone's engraved something up there.'

They paddled forward for a better look, with Aidan eventually clambering up the slippery side of a nearby rock to get closer. Holly admired his bottom from below, and was just about to shout up something cheeky when he turned, a look of pure incredulity on his face.

'I think you'd better see this,' he told her, reaching

down to steady her as she stumbled and slipped up beside him. There on the cave wall, as clear as if it had been carved there that morning, was a star. And inside it, very clearly, the names 'Jenny Bear' and 'Sandy Pants'.

'Do you think,' began Aidan, but quickly stopped because he had to reach out and catch Holly before she fell.

Being here in this cave, on the very same ledge where she now knew that her mum and her aunt would have stood together, giggling as they made their mark on the island that they loved so much, took Holly's breath away. Not since her childhood had she felt so close to her mum, so connected. Reaching out, she ran an unsteady finger over the inscription and around the jagged edges of the star. She knew she was shivering, but she couldn't feel the cold. Even Aidan, standing right behind her, his hands resting firmly on her shoulders, felt miles away from her. It was as if time had spun out into a long, thin tunnel and she, Holly, was the only thing in the pinprick of light at the very end. Holly and Jenny and Sandra – the three of them, united at last.

'Holly, you're shaking.'

Aidan was turning her around to face him, but she was finding it hard to tear her eyes away. She blinked, turned and suddenly remembered that she was completely naked.

Oh. Dear. God.

'You're right,' she said, blushing furiously. 'We should go back to the beach.' Without waiting for an answer, she moved away from him and slithered back into the water, landing with a splash that echoed around the walls of the cave.

By the time she reached the shoreline ten minutes later,

Holly's limbs were aching with the effort of swimming, but she still sprinted across the pebbles to retrieve her bikini. Aidan, looking thoroughly nonplussed, strolled nonchalantly after her, making no attempt whatsoever to put his own trunks back on.

'Don't you be going all shy on me now,' he remarked, but there was an edge to his voice.

Holly did her best to smile at him. He'd gone from feeling like the closest person in the world to a total stranger in the past few minutes, and she had no idea why. She hated herself for freezing up like this, but she couldn't seem to shrug it off. She'd brought her knees up under her chin and was now rocking backward and forward on her towel like a mad person.

'Are you okay?' Aidan crouched down as close to her as he dared. 'You've gone very pale, like.'

'I'm fine.' It came out automatically, and a lot more sharply than she'd intended. Aidan flinched.

'Sorry. I think I'm in shock.' Holly stared down at the stones between her toes. 'I'm a mess,' she added. 'I'm a total bitch.'

'Now, now,' he scolded. 'You're not a bitch, Holly. You're . . . well, I think you're pretty amazing, to be honest.'

'Don't.' She held up a hand. 'Please don't be so nice to me. I don't deserve it.'

'The thing is, Holly, you really do.' Aidan was finally pulling his tatty trunks back on. 'Probably more than anyone else I've ever met. You shouldn't give yourself such a hard time.'

Holly knew he was trying to be kind, but it felt as

though Aidan was telling her off. Of course she didn't want to be miserable – couldn't he see that? Frustrated, she picked up the largest stone she could find and lobbed it down the beach.

'Whoa there!' Aidan whistled, infuriating her even more when he started to laugh, and then hold up his towel as a makeshift shield. 'Watch out, people of Zakynthos,' he bellowed. 'The girl's lost it – she's throwing fecking rocks around now!'

Holly stood up, stuffing her things into her bag as Aidan danced around her, poking her in the ribs and giggling.

'And you say *I'm* mad!' she stormed, giving him a shove as he placed a large, bare foot on the edge of her towel. 'Get off!'

'Not until you smile.'

He really was infuriating.

'Sod off!'

'I can tell you want to . . .'

He was right, of course, and eventually she did smile, but not until he'd stepped across and taken her in his arms again. All he needed to do was kiss her, and her anger and distrust seemed to melt away. Holly had never let herself go like this, but she was so far down this path now, that it seemed to be her only choice. And it was a very enjoyable path, after all.

By the time they pulled up outside their houses later that afternoon, Holly was starting to feel more relaxed. Finding the beach and the inscription inside the cave had shaken her up, but as the shock settled she found that a comforting sort of warmth was taking its place. She felt as though her mum was turning back into the person she had once loved, and the anger that she'd held on to for so many years was beginning to ebb away. Sandra, too, was so much more real than she had been before, which was making Holly feel both happy and like her heart might shatter into pieces. If only she knew what had happened to drive such a permanent wedge between the two sisters.

'I know you've been stuck with me all day,' Aidan said, turning off the engine and reaching for her hand, 'but I know a great Italian place over in Keri . . .'

'I'd love to,' Holly returned the pressure with her own hand. 'And thank you, for today. I never would have found that place without you.'

'There you go again,' he chided. 'Doubting yourself. You would have found it just fine – although you may well have fallen off that path and plummeted headfirst into the sea.'

'Well then, thanks for saving my life too.'

They both laughed, but there was a slight uneasiness behind the chuckles. Holly knew she should be thinking about Rupert, just as she knew that Aidan must be thinking about him as well, but she was selfishly enjoying herself too much to bring the subject up. It was so much easier just to carry on and pretend that there was no elephant swinging its trunk around, trying to get their attention. She wanted to sit and have dinner with this man and talk about his life here on the island; she wanted the table overlooking the sunset and his hand in her own. The subject of her boyfriend didn't sit too comfortably in that scenario and, despite the fact that she knew in her heart that it was wrong, she resolutely decided to put the issue into one of her many internal boxes and lock it up until morning.

Aidan must have sensed her silent struggle, because he let go of her hand. 'Meet you back at mine in half an hour?' he asked.

'Deal!' Holly shrugged off her conscience and closed the jeep door before heading up the path and reaching forward to get the key from under the pot. The house was in darkness, but as she closed the door Holly could see her mobile phone illuminated on the table – she hadn't even realised that she'd left it behind.

Swinging her bag on to the sofa and flicking on the light, Holly took a few steps forward and all of a sudden found herself paralysed with a sense of impending doom. She took a deep breath and forced herself as far as the table, before gingerly picking up her phone.

The message on the screen confirmed her worst fears.

'AIDAN!' Holly was actually hammering on the door. She could hear Phelan skittering around inside and the distant sound of water running.

'AIDAN!' she tried again, close to tears now. Phelan started barking and eventually the door opened. Aidan was wet from the shower and wearing just a towel and a bemused expression.

'What's this?' he grinned. 'Couldn't stay away from me for all of ten minutes, eh?'

Holly said nothing, just handed him her phone, Rupert's text message still filling the screen.

'Oh.'

'I know.' It came out as barely a whisper. 'What the hell am I going to do?'

Aidan was silent for a few beats, and Holly watched as droplets of water fell from his fringe on to his bare chest.

'How much time do we have?' he asked, suddenly urgent.

'This was sent four hours ago,' Holly told him, her heart sinking down into her knees.

'His flight landed ten minutes ago . . .'

Tuesday, 12 October 1993
Dearest S,

Do you know what day it is? It's ten years to the day since Mum and Dad died in that stupid accident. I thought I should mark it somehow, and writing to you seemed like a better idea than opening a bottle of vodka, although neither one makes me feel any better. They would have hated this, you know? Us fighting like this. I so wish they hadn't gone on that trip. I wish they'd been here to meet Holly – they would have loved her so much. And I think they would still have loved me, despite it all. That might have helped you to forgive me. Will you forgive me? For Mum and Dad? Do it for them, not for me. I still miss you.

Jen x

21

'Holly!'

Rupert's shout of greeting was so loud in the cavernous arrivals lounge that Holly ducked, half-expecting the glass walls to splinter and fall in on top of her.

'Ru . . .' was all she managed, before he sprinted over and picked her up in his arms, spinning her round and round and kissing her neck with delight.

'It's so good to see you!' he blabbered. 'I almost didn't recognise you with that tan. I mean, wow. I can't wait to see the white bits.'

He didn't bother to lower his voice as he said the last part, earning himself a guffaw of approval from a group of passing lads who were no doubt heading to Laganas.

'What are you doing here?' Holly asked him, being careful to keep her tone light.

'I was starting to think you'd run off and left me for a Greek waiter,' he laughed. 'I thought I'd better pop over here to woo you back.'

Holly forced her mouth into the shape of a smile.

'I might have had a few on the flight over,' Rupert added, letting out a discreet belch behind his hand.

Holly, who hadn't even had time to shower off the remnants of her day at the beach with Aidan or run a brush through her salty, matted hair, felt horribly exposed under the bright lights in the terminal. She had convinced herself that the moment Rupert saw her he would be able to see her deceit. He would recognise her as the horrible lying cheat that she was. Mercifully, though, he seemed completely oblivious, although he did pull a face when he tried to run his hands through her hair.

'Did you crawl here through some bushes?' he asked, removing his fingers from her straggly locks.

'I came straight from the beach,' Holly stuttered, staring at her feet. 'I left my phone charging back at the house,' she added. 'That's why I was late to meet you – I'm so sorry.'

'Not to worry, sweetie,' he kissed the tip of her nose. 'You're here now, that's all that matters. I bought a nice bottle of white in duty free, but it's gone warm now. I hope this place of yours has some ice?'

Holly could only nod and smile. There was what felt like a heap of wet spaghetti busily whirring round on a fast spin cycle in her stomach.

Rupert hadn't let go of her hand since she got there, and insisted she sit in the back of the taxi with him even though the driver wasn't sure where they were going. As a result, she spent most of the journey with her head between the two front seats like a dog, one hand clasped tightly in Rupert's lap and his sharp-edged man-bag jabbing her in the ribs. Rupert stared out of the window as they drove, shouting out random descriptions of the things they were passing, such as, 'goat', 'shop', 'tree' and 'moped', all accompanied with snorts of laughter in varying volumes. He'd clearly had more than a few on the flight over. In contrast to her first taxi ride from the airport, this time the driver said barely a word.

As Rupert remarked that they'd just driven past a pack of stray dogs, Holly thought agonisingly of Phelan and the puppy. Would she ever see them again? She'd left Aidan standing mute and aghast in his doorway, promising that she'd do something to sort out the mess she'd made. But now, confronted with the reality of Rupert being here, in Zakynthos, just to see her, she found that it wasn't going to be that simple. Even if she wanted to, she couldn't tell Rupert about Aidan here, when he was so far from home – that wouldn't be fair. It was only today that the prospect of actually breaking up with her boyfriend had become a real consideration, and whatever thought she'd given to it as it niggled in the back of her mind, it never involved a scenario where he turned up here on the island. She had pictured the two of them sitting in a bar back in London or in his flat, her taking his hand and telling him it was over, that they wanted different things. This was literally the worst thing that could have happened. What the hell was she going to do?

Holly held her breath as the taxi began to climb the hill, but thankfully Aidan was nowhere to be seen. His doors and windows were shut and the jeep missing from its place by the wall. She dared not even imagine how he must be feeling, but then he had known about Rupert. She'd been honest about that, at least. In fact, she'd been more honest with Aidan than she ever had with anyone – a fact that made her feel all the more guilty towards Rupert, who was currently behaving like the sweetest, most caring boyfriend in the world.

'What a beautiful house!' he proclaimed, as they rounded the corner. 'Can you see the ocean from up here?'

Holly nodded. 'The view is amazing from the back garden. I'm glad you approve.'

Rupert crossed straight to the fridge after she'd let them inside. 'Is there any ice for this wine, darling?'

'Sorry, no.' Holly did her best to look apologetic. 'I can pop down to the shop?'

'I'll come with you!' Rupert was by her side faster than a bungee cord.

If Kostas was surprised to see that Holly suddenly had a strange male companion in tow, he didn't show it. He smiled as he always did and shook Rupert's hand as they paid for two bags of ice, three packs of beer and several bags of crisps, but he didn't chat to Holly as much as normal. The light was just starting to fade, and the undergrowth buzzed with the hum of crickets as they made their way back up the hill. Rupert chatted away to her about work and admitted that he'd managed to wangle a few days off by pretending an aunt had died.

'My aunt really did die,' Holly blurted, immediately going red.

'Oh . . .' Rupert looked crestfallen. 'I'm sorry, darling. I didn't mean to upset you. But I thought you didn't know her?'

'I didn't,' she admitted, trying to hide the hurt in her voice. 'I just . . . Well, she left me her house.'

There was an awkward silence as Rupert tried to work out why he'd suddenly ended up in the doghouse. As they reached the front door, he stopped and pulled Holly gently across the path.

'I've really missed you,' he whispered, pressing his body against hers. He felt like a stranger.

'I've missed you too,' she told him, kissing him lightly on the lips then stepping slowly away. 'Come on, I want to try this amazing wine you won't stop going on about.'

Holly survived the next few hours by doing a lot of needless tidying and even more drinking. Unable to face the idea of sharing the very small bed in the spare room with Rupert, she moved her own belongings out and reluctantly showed him into Sandra's former room. She'd unearthed some more blankets from the back of a cupboard, and she noticed Rupert wrinkle his nose as she shook them out.

'I would have bought some new stuff if I knew you were coming,' she told him, thinking longingly of the dinner she should be having with Aidan.

'It's fine,' Rupert smiled as he sat down. For the first time since she'd met him, he seemed a bit unsure of where to put himself. Despite her growing indifference, Holly felt a twinge of pity for him. After all, she told herself sternly, she was the bad person here, not him.

'You seem different,' he began, chewing nervously at a bit of loose skin on his thumb. 'Are you angry with me?'

Holly took a deep breath.

'No. Of course I'm not angry with you. It's just been a funny few days.'

'You haven't even kissed me properly,' he pouted. 'All I've wanted to do since I got here is kiss you.'

Holly thought of Aidan: his big hands in the small of her back, the scratch of his stubble in the cleft of her throat.

'Well, kiss me then.'

There was a tremble of silence as Rupert raised his eyes

to meet hers, then he stood and clasped each side of her face, kissing her with more passion and determination than he ever had before. Caught by surprise, Holly felt her knees weaken and a stirring in the pit of her belly. This wasn't supposed to happen. It was Aidan she wanted, not Rupert.

As he pulled back a few seconds later, Rupert beamed at her, his confidence restored.

'Shall we go out somewhere? To a club or something?' he asked, his hands still on her hot cheeks.

'Yeah, sure, of course,' she said, trying to slow the frantic hammering inside her chest. What in the hell was happening to her?

It was still relatively early in the summer season, but Laganas' main strip was very much awake. Bars and clubs jostled for attention next to one another, the bass from their competitive speaker systems making the street outside throb. Holly had only ever crossed the very bottom of the road, down by the beach, so she had no idea where to take Rupert. She needn't have worried, however, because there was a plethora of young British and Greek PRs doing their level best to talk them over the thresholds.

'Free fishbowl!' yelled a blonde girl with several tongue piercings.

'Free shot with every drink!' screamed a Geordie lad with a sunburnt forehead.

'Best bar in Laganas. Happy hour all night!' shouted a skinny Greek boy in cut-off jeans.

'This place is crazy,' enthused Rupert, laughing as a girl, her dress falling off both shoulders, staggered into the street and promptly threw up bright pink vomit into the gutter.

'We could go to Kalamaki instead?' Holly suggested. 'It's the next resort along, but it's much quieter and much more, erm, traditionally Greek.'

'This place seems fun,' Rupert said, not quite managing to avert his eyes as a group of girls shimmied past wearing matching micro hot pants and 'I ♥ Zante' vest tops.

Holly rolled her eyes as her tipsy boyfriend started giggling.

'Maybe we should go to Kalamaki?' she persisted. Looking around, she realised they could quite easily be standing in the middle of London's Soho. There was none of the Greek charm and character that she'd grown to love so much – it was utterly soulless.

'We can go there tomorrow.' Rupert grabbed her arm. 'I've already drunk too much to worry about dinner, anyway. Let's just enjoy ourselves.'

'Whatever you think,' Holly said, taking a deep breath to disguise her sigh. The girl with the pink sick had staggered back into the nearest bar and was happily lining up her next shot.

They carried on walking until Rupert suggested that a tacky-looking bar dubiously named Pulse looked like fun. The music was so loud inside that Holly could barely hear what he was saying.

Sent to the bar with an order of white wine, an apologetic Rupert returned a few minutes later with a tray laden with various multi-coloured cocktails and two plastic shot glasses of something that smelled like aniseed.

'They don't do wine,' he shrugged. 'I went for Sex on the Beach and something called the Zante Hammer – hope that's okay?'

'Here's hoping, eh?' she quipped, doing her best to look grateful. She couldn't believe that this noisy, smelly place was part of the tranquil, magical and stunningly beautiful island that she'd fallen so in love with over the past week. But then it was only one road out of so very many – the rest of the island appeared to have remained mercifully unscathed.

'I feel old,' Rupert moaned, pointing as yet another group of what looked like teenagers bustled into the bar demanding free shots. For Holly, who'd spent her teens and early twenties in a state of perpetual misery, the idea of being young again made her feel ill. Growing older wasn't exactly solving all her problems, but it had provided her with the self-sufficient security that she'd craved for so many years.

Just as they were taking tentative sips of their first cocktails, a Greek guy approached their table with a half-full bottle of something bright red. 'Free shots for the lady?' he cried, jumping up on to their low table and thrusting the neck end of his bottle towards Holly.

'Me next!' said Rupert, giving Holly a wink and opening his mouth. The Greek guy looked momentarily put out, but quickly recovered and poured a healthy slug of the red concoction straight down Rupert's throat and, not altogether accidentally, Holly suspected, down the front of his white shirt too.

Holly couldn't help but laugh, and Rupert was quick to join in. It occurred to her then that if they got drunk enough, her eager boyfriend might well pass out before making a move on her. The kiss they'd shared back at the house had unnerved her, and she didn't want to think about what would happen once she and Rupert were in a bed alone together.

'Come on then,' she announced, picking up her cocktail and downing it in three gulps. 'Let's go on a bar crawl!'

There is no such thing as last orders in Laganas – a fact that Holly soon discovered as they hurried, then later staggered, from bar to bar along the length of the strip. Everywhere they went, free shots were thrust into their hands, and it wasn't long before Rupert had reached the point of actual slurring.

Holly was drinking steadily, on a mission to eradicate the reality of what was happening, while Rupert was happy just to keep up, growing ever more tactile as the hours passed. Most of the places they went seemed to employ a mixture of both Greek and English staff, and Holly also heard a few Australian accents as she was handed her change. Many of the barmen were emulating Tom Cruise in the film *Cocktail*, throwing bottles around, while others went as far as swigging a mouthful of lamp oil and turning themselves into a human flame thrower. It was all quite impressive, in a way, but Holly saw none of the heart of Zakynthos that she loved so much. She found herself yearning for Annie's cute little cocktail bar and the slightly warm village wine from Kostas' shop.

At 5 a.m., they found themselves dancing in a club right back at the end of the strip, the shuttered windows of which faced out across Laganas bay. The DJ played cheesy 80s tunes from his booth inside a speed boat, and girls dressed in little more than dental floss clambered up to twerk on the bar. Holly had never been anywhere like this in her entire life, but it was impossible not to get caught up in the slightly wild atmosphere.

'I love you!' bellowed Rupert through the fog of dry ice and dancing limbs.

Holly blew him a kiss in return, spinning round to dance with a man wearing a bright green mankini.

'I mean it,' he slurred again, snatching thin air as he reached out for her hands and missed. 'Come and live with me!'

Holly laughed at him. 'You're so drunk,' she yelled over the music. 'You don't know what you're saying.'

Rupert laughed then too, more at himself than Holly, and went back to pirouetting around a nearby pillar. By the time the music was turned off and the shutters came up, the sun was starting to rise over the sea.

'I'm going to find some water,' Rupert muttered, leaving Holly on the beach and stumbling drunkenly off around the corner. She slipped off her shoes and sat down, pulling her knees together and digging her toes through the damp sand. The sun was still half-obscured by the sea, but she could already feel the powerful heat of it as dapples of amber light skittered across the water.

As she breathed in the dawn air and relished the feel of the cool sand on her hot feet, Holly realised for the first time just how lucky she was to be here. It was the most beautiful place she'd ever seen and she, scrappy little Holly Wright, who spent her teenage years on a grubby estate in South London, owned her very own slice of it.

She knew she loved the place, but what about the people? Or, to put it more accurately, the person. How the hell was she meant to have known what would happen when she came over here? All she'd wanted was some answers about her aunt, not to fall head over heels for a scruffy Irish vet. She felt as if her last vestiges of control were ebbing away like dry sand into the waves. How could she have let things get to this stage?

She thought about her friends back in London and the friends she'd made in the brief time she'd spent on the island. She counted Rupert, of course, and she had Aliana, but her younger friend was skittish, immature and probably never going to be someone that Holly trusted with her secrets. She didn't really consider Rupert's group of pals as true friends, either, but that was probably her own fault. Hadn't she been putting on a mask for years, only ever presenting to the outside world a careful, manufactured version of herself? Friendships didn't come naturally to Holly, but being here on the island had taught her how good it felt to be a bit more open with people, and that if you could only find it within yourself to share a little bit, the rewards from others would be enormous. Aidan had taught her that. But so had Kostas and Annie and Nikos – people here just exuded a warmth that was absent back in London.

Thinking about Aidan again made her grimace with discomfort. She wondered if he'd even bothered to come back that night, or whether he was hiding out somewhere until the Rupert-shaped storm had passed. Holly was torn between her longing to see him and the gut-bubbling fear of what would happen if she did.

'Darling, I come bearing gifts!'

It was Rupert, back from his trek to the shop and brandishing bottles of water and ice lollies.

'Is that our breakfast?' she asked, forcing her black mood back into its box. 'I bet there's somewhere open on the strip already if you fancied a fry-up?'

If she stalled for another few hours, with any luck Aidan would have left for work before they made it back to the house.

Lost in her own thoughts, feelings and fears, Holly failed to notice the jeep parked at the far end of the beach. As they passed by the driver's window and made their clumsy way back into the heart of Laganas, Rupert swung a lazy arm around Holly's shoulders and pulled her close to him for a kiss.

22

The soft hum of the sewing machine was almost soothing after the thumping music of the Laganas nightclubs. Holly had tried to sleep when they'd got back to the house, but the combination of her still-ringing ears and still-unsettled heart meant that slumber was impossible. The Insomnia Troll had sat up on her chest as he always did, waggling his finger as if to say, 'Ignore me all you like, I'm not going anywhere.' After a few hours of tossing and turning in the small corner of bed that Rupert wasn't sprawled across, she had given up and retreated downstairs to her beloved new toy.

As she worked on an intricate dress that she'd started making with more of the lace that she and Aidan had picked up on their first day out together, Holly felt her anxiety start to lessen. It was so much easier to listen to her thoughts when her hands were busy, and the monotonous action of running the beautiful, delicate material under the needle was proving extremely therapeutic. If only she'd known this years ago. She'd never have shelved her hobby so ruthlessly if she had understood just how much it helped her to relax.

Despite this revelation, she was still stubbornly refusing to dwell on the subject of Aidan. Instead, she thought about her mother and Sandra, suddenly remembering the photo she'd discovered in the bathroom. It already felt like ages ago – so much had happened in such a small space of time.

Holly waited until her work reached a natural stopping point before switching off the sewing machine and gathering her things. It was about time she found out more about the other people in that photograph – and she had a feeling that Kostas would be able to help. He seemed to know everyone around here, and her short time on the island had already taught her that the Greeks were nosier than even the most intrepid of tabloid journalists.

'Do you know who these men are?'

Kostas rubbed his eyes and peered at the photo, squinting as a shaft of sunlight filtered in under the shop blinds.

'Yes!' he exclaimed, looking very pleased with himself.

Holly waited.

'This is Dennis!' he told her, pointing at the man next to Sandra.

'This,' the same finger hovered uncertainly for a few seconds. 'I think this is Socrates. Maybe he was a policeman.'

'Sorry,' Holly gave the photo back to him. 'Do they live here, in Zakynthos?'

Kostas pulled a face. There was a coffee stain on his grey beard.

'No,' he said eventually, crossing his arms as if to end the subject.

'Do you know where they are?'

'Ah, Dennis go to Kefalonia.' He swung an arm back up in the direction of the house. 'He move there many years ago.' He shrugged again. 'I do not know Socrates, but I have not seen him for many years. Very many.'

'This is my mother,' she told him, pointing at Jenny.

At her words, Kostas' big Greek eyes suddenly filled with tears and he came out from behind the till to envelop her in a whiskery hug.

'I am very sorry for you,' he growled softly into her ear. 'I remember your mother. She was – how you say it – crazy, but very good in her heart.'

Holly took a gentle step backwards. 'And this man, Dennis?' she said again, pointing at the photo. 'Was he with . . . ?'

Kostas' eyes widened as he realised her meaning. 'No,' he interrupted, crossing his arms again and shaking his head. 'Dennis, he was with Sandy. Yes, Sandra. I think maybe he marry her.'

Sandra had been married? This was news to Holly. Before she could ask what had happened to split them up, however, Kostas reached across and took her arm. He looked at her very sheepishly, then said, 'Your mother . . . She was with many men. Greek men, English men, German men, Swedish men. I think this man also,' he pointed at Socrates the policeman and shook his head sadly. 'I am sorry.'

So it was as Holly had suspected – it was looking increasingly likely that her father had been one of many men that her mum picked up when she was living here, which meant he could still be alive somewhere and not locked up abroad as Jenny had claimed – although how would Holly ever find him? Chances were, he didn't even know that she existed.

'It's okay,' she told Kostas, who was still looking downcast. 'My mother was no angel.'

'No,' he agreed, but he was smiling again now. 'No angel, but a very good heart.'

Holly left him and walked slowly back up the hill towards the house. Kefalonia was the closest island to Zakynthos, so perhaps it wasn't beyond the realms of possibility that she might be able to locate Sandra's ex, Dennis. Perhaps Annie would know more about him and Socrates? Dennis might not even know that Sandra had passed away, and whatever the circumstances of the presumed break-up, he had still been with her for a time. He should be told about what had happened.

She was just about to turn off on to the path when the sound of an approaching car engine made her freeze. Aidan's jeep scattered dust as it pulled up next to her, and she took a deep breath, daring herself to turn round and face him. Aidan, however, was not alone.

The passenger door opened and Phelan leapt out, burying his nose straight in Holly's crotch.

'Phelan!' she cried, at exactly the same time as the occupant of the passenger seat. Holly's eyes widened in horror as two very long, very slim, tanned legs appeared, followed closely by a tiny waist, flat stomach, blindingly white smile and a mass of dark red curls.

'Hi,' said the girl, holding out her hand to Holly.

Holly shook it, but could only gape at her while trying to pry Phelan's snout off her nether regions.

'Phelan, off!' Aidan slammed the jeep door and stalked round to join them. The buttons of his shirt were done up wrong, Holly noticed, and he looked worn out.

The red-haired beauty giggled and hooked her arm through his.

'Did you leave Lexi in the jeep?' he asked, prompting the girl to yelp with alarm. Turning her back on them, she quickly opened the door and scooped up the puppy that Holly had rescued during the storm.

'Isn't she just the cutest?' she asked Holly now, holding the little mutt against one of her flawless cheeks.

'Yes,' was all she could force out. She sneaked a look at Aidan, but he was staring resolutely at the ground.

'I'm Clara,' the redhead said, as it became apparent that Aidan wasn't going to make the introductions. She had a very faint Irish accent.

'Holly.'

There was an awful, drawn-out silence, during which Clara looked from Aidan to Holly with increased confusion. He seemed unable to move, and Holly could see a muscle moving in his cheek.

'Right. Anyway, we should get going then, Aidan? It was nice to meet you, Holly,' she said over her shoulder as they walked round the corner. Holly tried not to burst into tears as she watched Aidan snake a casual arm round Clara's shoulders. Whoever this goddess-like creature was, she certainly knew Aidan very well – and he seemed very comfortable with her too. Holly remembered what Annie had told her about Aidan's ex looking like a model, and what Aidan himself had told her about how much the break-up had affected him. Was this her? Had Clara seen sense and come back to claim her man? Holly had no idea, but she did know one thing: she was very, very angry.

'Rupert! Rupert, wake up!'

'Whaaaa?' he mumbled. He'd fallen diagonally across

the bed when they'd got in at 8 a.m. that morning and hadn't moved since.

She stopped nudging him and lifted his arm instead, inching her way underneath it until her face was right next to his.

'Babe . . .' she breathed. 'Make some room for me, would you? I need a cuddle.'

This had the desired effect. Rupert opened a lazy eye and looked at her, a small grin starting to spread across his face. Snuggling a bit closer, Holly discovered that even a whole night spent devouring wine, beer, cocktails and all the free shots that Laganas had to offer apparently had no effect on this man's libido. He had propped himself up on one elbow now and was impatiently tugging down her shorts.

Holly closed her eyes and sighed. This wasn't what she'd wanted at all, but how could she reject him again? She pictured Aidan doing the same thing to the stunning Clara – lifting her up so she could wrap those insanely long legs of hers around his waist, running his hands through her hair and kissing the soft part of her neck – and her reluctance started to crumble. Perhaps this was exactly what she needed, to reconnect with her boyfriend. Rupert had flown all the way over here because he missed her, while bloody Aidan had led her to believe he had real feelings for her and then flaunted his gorgeous ex-girlfriend in her face. She couldn't believe she'd been so stupid – trusting a man she'd known for a few days over her sweet and devoted boyfriend. Forcing herself to concentrate on Rupert and what he was now doing to her, Holly buried her face in the pillow and let the sheets catch her tears.

*

It was long past lunchtime when Holly and Rupert finally made their way downstairs. Excited by the sunshine streaming in through the windows, Rupert took his beach towel straight out into the back garden and arranged himself on the sparse grass.

'Do you want a drink?' Holly asked, hovering nervously by the open doors.

'Beer, ta!' Rupert beamed at her.

'I meant water or juice,' she muttered, but went back inside to fetch one for him anyway. She felt wretched. After their sweaty and hurried session in the bedroom that morning, Rupert had promptly fallen back to sleep, leaving Holly to toss and turn with a mixture of hopelessness and frustration. She couldn't stop picturing Aidan with Clara, and she hated him for making her feel so horrible, despite the fact that she knew it made her the biggest hypocrite in the whole of Greece – possibly the world. She looked around now at her little house, at the curtains she'd sewn and hung in the small windows, at the flowers she'd arranged on the table by the sofa and the pictures she'd dusted down and put up on the bare walls – the place really looked like a home, which meant that someone would definitely want to buy it. The realisation of what she had to do next burst into her mind with deafening clarity: she needed to stop living in this silly bubble – it was time to sell this place and go back to London. And the sooner she could get it done, the better.

With a renewed sense of determination, Holly marched back outside with a beer only to find Aidan and Clara standing there, chatting away to Rupert like it was the most normal thing in the world. Rupert was staring unashamedly up at Clara, but she could hardly blame him — Aidan's ex was now wearing a microscopic red bikini top and white denim hot pants. Aidan himself was standing slightly to one side, but Phelan — the traitor, Holly thought with a stab — had his shaggy head firmly against Clara's bare thigh.

'Oh, there you are, Holly,' she said now, turning as the door clanged shut.

Why the hell was she acting like they were best friends all of a sudden?

'Here I am,' Holly replied, not managing to keep the disdain from her voice. Rupert, who'd shifted to a sitting position, raised his eyebrows a fraction at the exchange.

Clara, however, seemed oblivious to the frostiness, even though Holly was pretty sure that if anyone came within three metres of her at that moment then they'd probably be turned to stone by the ferociousness of her loathing. She didn't dare look at Aidan, mostly because she feared what she would do if he flashed that mocking grin of his. Why was he torturing her like this?

'We're heading over to Porto Limnionas for a spot of lunch,' Clara was now telling them. 'You guys are welcome to come, if you like? I'm sure we can make room in the jeep, right, Aidy?'

Aidy? AIDY?

'We've got our own plans,' Holly cut across just as Rupert was about to open his mouth. 'But thanks.' The last part was said with such insincerity that even Phelan pulled a face at her. She had better be more careful.

Clara looked a bit crestfallen, so Holly hurriedly explained that she'd left her moped in Kalamaki and was

264

taking Rupert with her to collect it. It hadn't been her plan at all, but it sounded convincing enough. Plus, she did want to get her bike – she needed it to ride into Zakynthos Town for her appointment with the estate agent.

'Have a great time,' Rupert called out slightly wistfully, as Aidan and Clara disappeared round the side of the house.

'He wasn't very friendly,' Rupert said after they'd gone, making Holly think back to the first day she and Aidan had met and the stupid argument they'd got into.

'I hardly know him,' she lied. 'And I only met her this morning.'

He was staring intently at her now, and Holly started to shift around uncomfortably in the dust.

'Come on,' she told him, taking hold of Rupert's hand and giving it a squeeze. 'Let's get the hell out of here.'

In the end, it took them over an hour to walk down the beach from Laganas to Kalamaki, mostly because Rupert kept stopping to reapply sun cream on his reddening shoulders. He held her hand until the heat of the afternoon made their palms too sweaty, but he never strayed far from her side. He'd always been fairly tactile, but Holly had never known him to be quite like this. Could he sense that she'd slipped away from him?

Holly was still doing her level best to force down a lid on the burgeoning rage she was feeling towards Aidan. She didn't trust herself to speak for fear that it would come out as a roar, so instead she said nothing, merely smiling and nodding along to Rupert's chatter about work and what he thought of the island so far.

When they got to the quiet part of the beach where the sand had been left soft and undisturbed for the nesting loggerhead turtles, Rupert kept stopping to pick up shells and present them to her. He was trying his best to jolly her out of her preoccupied mood, and she wished she could just chill out. If only she could find it in herself to run around on the sand with him and join in with his game, but she couldn't. Even the sight of the ocean, which she usually found so soothing, was having no effect. She would feel much better once she'd spoken to an estate agent and got the ball rolling – that was what she must prioritise now.

Nikos was waiting on the steps of the taverna in Kalamaki as if he'd been watching them walk down the beach for ages. As soon as Holly was within range, he grabbed her arm and marched her inside.

'Where have you been? I fix your bike. I thought you dead in the rain.'

Rupert, who'd been right behind Holly, muscled between them indignantly. 'Excuse me,' he said. 'Why are you shouting at *my* girlfriend? Leave her alone.'

Holly rolled her eyes as Nikos took a step back in surprise.

'It's okay,' she told him. 'This is Nikos – he's my friend.'

Rupert eyed the Greek suspiciously. Today he was wearing a bright red baseball cap with the word 'Athens' sewn across the front.

'You've only been here a few days,' Rupert argued. 'How can he be your friend already?'

'He just is.' Holly was starting to lose her temper. She took a deep breath and forced herself to smile. 'I'm sorry, but I told you about Nikos. He set me up with the moped, remember?'

'The moped that broke down?' Rupert grunted, but he looked less hostile.

Nikos beamed at them in turn, showing off his few remaining teeth.

'I fix your bike!' he said proudly, motioning to the car park. Holly peered through the bank of tables and saw her little moped, sheltering in the shade of a tree.

'*Efharisto.*' She took Nikos' hand and shook it. 'You are a very good man.'

'*Poli kala!*' Nikos told her. '*Poli kala* is meaning very good.'

'Well then, erm, that then,' she grinned.

Nikos bustled off to fetch them some menus and Rupert and Holly sat down at one of the outdoor tables. Rupert ordered a beer for himself, while she opted for water. She found that she didn't have any appetite – not even for her beloved Greek salad – but Rupert chose a burger and chips.

'Do you not want to try something Greek?' she asked in surprise, as Nikos hesitated next to them, the end of his already desecrated biro wedged between two of his stumpy teeth.

'Nah.' Rupert gave the menu another cursory glance. 'I need something with plenty of salt and carbs after all the booze we sank last night.'

It was fair enough, she reasoned. He should be able to order and eat whatever the hell he pleased, so why did she find it so aggravating? She made herself reach under the table and put her hand on his thigh, and Rupert turned to her and smiled. It was a real smile too, full of warmth and

267

love and contentment. She was being so unfair to him. This was her Rupert, her boyfriend, the man who had made her perfectly happy for the past year – why did she think that Aidan was any better for her? He clearly wasn't as good a person as Rupert, not if he was willing to run straight back to his ex after all these years and then rub her nose in it. She knew it must be weird for him to see her with Rupert, but she hadn't had a say in that – and she would never have rubbed his nose in anything.

'Will you come into town with me after this?' she asked him now. She had been planning to leave him at the beach and visit the estate agent on her own, but that seemed unfair somehow. And anyway, Rupert was better at all this official stuff than her, even if he didn't speak a word of Greek. She'd feel better equipped with him by her side, and he could take over if things became tricky.

'Of course I'll come with you,' he said.

'Oh no. I mean bugger.' Holly held a hand up. 'You can't. I don't have a spare helmet for the bike.'

'We can get a taxi then.'

'I have helmet,' Nikos interrupted, crashing Rupert's burger and chips down on the table so hard that a handful of fries toppled overboard.

'Really?' Holly smiled up at him.

'Yes. Of course. Every Greek man has helmet.'

Rupert snorted with laughter at the same time as taking his first bite of the burger, giving Nikos the perfect excuse to thump him across the back.

'I bring,' he said, retreating towards the kitchen. 'You can use it.'

And that was that.

Tuesday, 2 January 1996
Sandy,

I don't even know why I still write to you. I have no idea if you're even there. Are you there? I know I should be brave and just book a flight over to the island, but I never seem to have the money these days. Everything I got from the sale of Mum and Dad's house has gone. Simon used to look after all the money, but now he's gone too. Holly is all I have left, and sometimes I feel like I'm losing her too. She would have been better off staying with you. You would have been a better mother than me. I'm useless and worthless, and I know you know it's true. Happy New Year anyway, twin. I know you won't write back, but I still wish you would.

Jenny x

23

Holly carried her bag and the helmets across to a tiny wooden jetty. It was nestled along one side of a small harbour surrounded by stone walls, and a faded fishing boat bobbed gently in the water below her feet, the blue and white paint cracking in the sunshine.

It was nearing five, and the shadows were starting to lengthen in the fading light.

After spending an awkward hour in one of the island's estate agencies, with herself and Rupert doing their best to communicate everything they needed to about the house with their limited Greek vocabulary and the brief glossary in the back of the guidebook, Holly felt that they deserved a breather. Rupert had suggested he grab them both a coffee and the temptation to sit at the water's edge in the town was too great – especially given the stunning view.

She picked absent-mindedly at a small scab on her knee, the skin underneath pink and fresh, quite unlike the rest of her. In just a week, she'd turned a deep brown colour, and while she knew the sun was unhealthy, she couldn't help but luxuriate in the feel of it against her shoulders. She hadn't burnt at all, despite being irresponsibly sparing with her application of sun cream. Her natural colouring was in stark contrast to both Rupert and Aidan, whose fair complexions didn't stand a chance against the Greek summer sun.

Aidan. There he was again, strolling into her subconscious, boldly daring her to ignore him. She longed to give in and picture him: his freckled forearms, his lopsided smile, his broad chest beneath those tatty T-shirts . . . But she mustn't. What was the point? As she'd told the estate agent just now, what she wanted was to sell the house and cut all ties to the island as soon as possible. Her mum may have spent years here – and her aunt too – but that didn't mean she had to follow the same path. On the contrary, she had been trying to build a life for herself in London for years; why would she give that up now? Then again, if she was being completely honest with herself, she definitely had thought about moving over here. She loved this place, she knew that, and there had even been a few secret occasions when she'd imagined creating a life for herself here. A life with Aidan.

But that was before. Today, Aidan had made his feelings perfectly clear. Whatever he'd led her to believe, she now suspected that he must have made exactly the same promises to Clara as soon as she came running back. He probably hooked up with girls all year round on the island. She was nothing special, as she'd always believed. But maybe she really *was* something special to Rupert. Why the hell was she so fixated on Aidan when she had Rupert? Holly sighed as a flash of pain clenched at her heart. She knew why, of course – it was because Aidan was the only man she'd ever truly been herself with, the only man she'd ever really trusted – and that had meant everything to her.

She took a deep breath and stared down into the clear water. She knew what she must do. If she was ever going

271

to stand a chance of making things work with Rupert, then he had to know the truth.

'Coffee for the lady.' Rupert was back, looking slightly sweaty and pink-cheeked, but very happy. Holly suspected it was more to do with the visit to the estate agent than the view of the mountains across the water.

He sat down next to her and smiled.

'I'm going all pink,' he said, using his chin to point at his bare shoulders. His T-shirt was riding up and Holly stared for a second at the wiry blond hair around his belly button. 'Now you know why I've always preferred the slopes to the beach,' he told her with a laugh.

The end of his nose was starting to peel, and Holly felt her resolve weakening.

'You're very quiet today,' he said now, fixing her with one of his Rupert-Farlington-Clark-misses-nothing looks.

She nodded, biting her lip and covering her face with the Styrofoam cup.

While he wasn't as broad and tall as Aidan, Rupert's penchant for running, skiing and playing the occasional game of weekend rugby meant that he was in good shape. His fondness for a drink was to blame for the beginnings of a tiny paunch, but as Holly looked sideways at him now, she found that more endearing than anything else. Men that looked too perfect weren't attractive, as far as she was concerned – she preferred a few flaws.

As if sensing her thoughts, Rupert reached for Holly and held her against him. He was very quiet suddenly and seemed almost nervous. She'd never seen him like this before – it wasn't a version of Rupert that she recognised, which did little to ease the feelings of dread that were coursing through her.

'I've got something I need to tell you,' she began, immediately feeling him tense up next to her. Over his shoulder, she could see the distant shapes of two boys kicking a ball to one another on a patch of grass by the water and a child throwing pebbles into the waves.

'Listen, Hols,' he interrupted. 'I'm sorry for turning up here unannounced. That was stupid of me. I just missed you so much and I thought . . . Well, I thought it would be romantic.'

'It was!' Holly pulled away from him and used her fingers to gently lift his chin. 'It was so sweet of you – it really was. I'm the one who should be saying sorry.'

'No,' he squinted at her as the sunlight bounced off the surface of the water below their feet. 'I ambushed you. I really am sorry if I've annoyed you.'

'I'm sorry that I've been acting like a total cow,' Holly said, pushing a few stray tendrils of hair off her cheeks. 'The past week has been so weird. I feel . . . I feel different.'

'You feel differently about me?'

'No,' she lied, biting her lip. 'I mean me. I've found out things that have made me feel differently about myself, things about my past.'

'But I thought you never knew your aunt?' Rupert looked confused now, and Holly took a sip of her coffee before she continued.

'I didn't.' She took a deep breath. 'The thing is, I lied to you about my parents.'

He didn't say anything to this, merely watched as she struggled to find the words to continue.

'My mum didn't die in a car crash. She died from choking on her own vomit after drinking an entire bottle of vodka. That was something she did most days, because she was an alcoholic.'

This was it. He was going to look at her in disgust and tell her he couldn't be with someone like her, someone with a mother like the one she'd had.

'You poor thing.' Rupert took her in his arms again, his hand immediately coming up to stroke her hair. 'When was this? When did it happen?'

'When I was eighteen,' she choked out. She couldn't believe how sweet he was being. This wasn't what she'd prepared herself for.

'You were just a child, really.' He stared at her in wonder. 'What about your—'

'Father?'

He nodded.

'I have no idea who he is,' she shrugged. 'He could be alive still, but chances are he has no idea that I exist.'

She'd expected shock, a barrage of questions and demands about why she'd lied to him, but Rupert merely held her as tightly as he could. She felt a swell of emotion rise up in her chest. All this time she'd doubted his ability to deal with the truth of who she was, but she couldn't have been more wrong about him.

'I found her,' she told him now. 'My mum. I came home from college one day and she was dead in a chair. Just sitting there, like she always did, but this time she wasn't there any more. I don't even remember calling the police, but I must have.'

'You poor little mouse,' he said into her ear, his voice

cracking a bit. 'I can't bear the thought of you going through it. I wish I'd been there for you.'

'You're here for me now,' she smiled against his chest. There were fine hairs standing up on his arms and his sweaty fringe had dried into jagged points against his forehead. She thought about Aidan, how he'd simply sat next to her and listened as she'd told him the truth. Perhaps he thought her stronger than Rupert did, or perhaps he just didn't care as much.

'Why are you telling me all this now?' Rupert asked. There was a slight edge of suspicion to his voice, as if he was scared to hear her reply.

'My mum used to live here on the island.' She smiled. 'I think she was probably very happy here too, because, well, how could you not be?'

'Well, I dunno,' Rupert grinned at her. 'You know I'm more of a snowy mountains boy.'

'Something happened,' she continued. 'Something that made my mum and my Aunt Sandra, the one who left me the house, not speak to each other any more. My aunt hinted at it in her letter and I've been trying to work out what it was.'

'Do the locals not remember?' Rupert was frowning now as he took it all in.

'Oh, they remember my mum all right,' she grimaced. 'But either they don't know what the fight was about, or they're keeping it from me for some reason.' She told him about the photo of her aunt and her mum with Socrates the policeman and Dennis, the man Sandra had apparently been married to, but carefully left out the story of how she'd met Alix up at Ocean View.

'Well, there you go then,' Rupert told her. 'This Socrates man is the one you need to find. If he was with your mum back then, I bet he knows exactly what happened.'

'You're probably right,' she agreed. 'But apparently he's left Zakynthos now. I don't even know his last name.'

They sat in silence for a few minutes, listening to the waves lap gently against the wooden poles of the jetty. 'You might hate me for saying this . . .' Rupert took a deep breath. 'But do you *really* need to know what happened? I mean, it all happened so many years ago – and knowing will probably only upset you even more. Isn't it best to just, you know, leave the past in the past?'

Holly considered this for a moment. It was a very good point. Why was she so desperate to find out what had happened? Perhaps Rupert was right, and it was only bound to lead to more heartbreak. She'd really found herself beginning to forgive her mum over the past few days. Hell, she even had moments where she'd felt as if she might be able to love her again. Would finding out something terrible undo all the happiness she'd managed to stitch around herself?

'You're probably right,' she agreed at last. 'Maybe it is unwise to pull at that thread.'

'Speaking of threads,' Rupert took each side of her face in his hands. 'What's all this about you being some sort of secret sewing genius?'

She pulled a face at him.

'Oi! Don't make that face. I saw the sewing machine at the house and all the things you've been making. They're really good, Hols. Why don't you do that stuff in London?'

'I just thought it was a bit lame,' she mumbled, realising

as she said it how misguided she had been for denying herself the indulgence all this time.

'Listen.' He waited for her to stop staring at her toes and look at him. 'I've always known that you hold things back from me, Holly.'

He had?

'I just assumed that over time you'd start to thaw a bit and begin to trust me. I'm not an ogre, you know.'

'I know.' Her voice had become very small.

'God, I want you to be yourself and be happy – that's what I do. I would never pretend to be someone that I wasn't, not for anyone.'

She nodded, not trusting herself to speak.

'If you want to sit around in your pants sewing all day long, then you should,' he declared. 'In fact, I'd very much like to come home to find you sitting there in just your pants.'

'Cheeky!' She gave him a half-hearted pinch.

'I'm serious, Holly. I meant what I said to you last night. We spend pretty much every night together anyway. Why don't we just make it official?'

'You were drunk out of your skull when you said that,' she protested. 'You can't really have meant that you wanted us to live together?'

'Yes, I did.' He looked at her and laughed. 'Dear God, I'm not that scary a prospect, am I? I promise to try and put the toilet seat down and not leave wet towels on the bed.'

'It's not that.' Holly shook her head. How could she tell him that the real reason she was reluctant was because she'd been doing all sorts of intimate and forbidden things with another man? That she'd thought barely anything of cheating on him and lying to him?

'But how would we? Where?' she stammered.

'Well, you know my parents lent me a load of money to buy my place?'

Holly shook her head slowly.

'Okay, well, they did. I'm a spoilt little rich boy, blah blah. But it means that you can come and live with me for free. I mean it, just do your sewing and take some time out until you feel better. I can look after us, after you. I want to look after you.'

Holly's feelings of confusion, shock, love and guilt tangled up inside her belly like a big, knotted pile of fluffy wool and strips of Velcro. She was afraid to open her mouth in case Rupert heard the ripping sounds as it all came apart.

He looked so earnest and full of affection, so hopeful that she would say yes and let him look after her. And didn't she deserve to be looked after a bit? She'd spent years looking after herself – ever since she was about ten years old and her mum gave up on her. She tried to picture it: leaving her job at Flash to start a business making clothes from the comfort of Rupert's spacious flat while he was out at work all day; preparing dinner for when he came home each night and ironing his shirts. Wasn't it the thing she'd wanted all along, that sort of stability? Hadn't he just offered her exactly what she'd been secretly hoping he would since they met? It was a bit of a shock, sure, but what was the alternative?

Holly turned away from Rupert and stared across the bay, to where the mountains rose up like majestic warriors from the ocean. The sun was slowly making its way down the sky and they were edged in a warm golden light.

She allowed herself once again to picture herself and Aidan, side by side on the stony beach where Jenny and Sandra had hidden away in their own private little world. In her head it all looked so tantalising, but the reality was that Aidan wasn't the man she'd thought he was. Hadn't her mum made the same mistake? Picked the wrong man – or the wrong men – over and over again? Hadn't Jenny Wright always picked adventure and excitement over stability and security?

Simon had been the closest thing to a stepdad that Holly ever had, but her mum had torn apart the patch-work squares of love and commitment that he had so painstakingly tried to stitch together in their lives. Jenny had made a lot of mistakes with men, and Holly didn't want to do the same thing. If being here in Zakynthos had taught her anything, it was that there was such a thing as having too much of a good thing. She'd allowed herself to believe in the bubble she had floated around in over the past week, but it wasn't real. Rupert was real. He was sitting here next to her now, holding her hand and asking her to live with him, to be there when he went to sleep every night and when he woke up every morning. What was Aidan offering her? Nothing.

As the first spots of coloured light started to glow from the harbour bars and the pale moon crept up from its resting place down behind the navy curtain of ocean, Holly let herself take Rupert's hand in her own.

'Okay then, you crazy, sweet man – let's do it.'

24

The sun rose the next morning as it always did, wide and bright and unapologetically strong, but Holly felt as if she was looking at it through different eyes. She had woken early and slipped out from under the covers, leaving Rupert looking crumpled but content on the pillow. They'd had dinner on the beach in Laganas the night before, still in their casual clothes from the daytime, the warm evening breeze blowing tendrils of salt-mangled hair off their necks.

She stood now with her back to the house, staring out across the ocean below, and thought about her mother. Jenny Wright had been such a black spot in her mind for so many years, but this morning she was full of colour and ferocious vitality, refusing to stay hidden in the deep recesses of Holly's mind. Now that she'd been to so many of the places her mum had loved, gazed at the same stunning views, eaten off the same tables and scrunched her toes through the sand on the same beaches where Jenny had once been so happy, she felt as if she understood her better. But there was still a gaping hole there, a chasm of emptiness inside her, where the last few years' worth of memories festered. What had happened to turn her bright, beautiful mother into a bitter and sick individual?

I should have let someone else take you in.

Even knowing that her mother's addiction was a sickness didn't stop the recollection of those words stinging

Holly like the lash of a whip. Just thinking about it made her wince, all these years later. She had a real chance now to put her past behind her and embark on a future with Rupert, but yet here she was, lurking out here all alone having sneaked away from him.

She heard the sound of Aidan's back door opening too late to move, so instead she remained rooted to the spot, stubbornly refusing to turn her head. Phelan, presumably let out to have a morning wee, seemed to sense that even he wasn't welcome, and shuffled to an uneasy standstill just a few feet behind her. There was a palpable silence, and she knew that Aidan must be standing there. She could feel the force of his glare burning a smouldering hole into her back, but still she didn't move. Aidan was just one complication too much for her at the moment.

Eventually, as the sun rose higher in the sky and the surface of the water started to sparkle like discarded Christmas tinsel, Holly heard the sound of his door closing gently behind him.

'I can't believe I have to fly home today.'

Rupert was gazing up at her, his blue eyes ringed with sleep and a mosquito bite rising on his cheek. She'd managed to slip back under the covers next to him undetected, and now she reached across and stroked his hair.

'I know. I wish you could stay too,' she told him, meaning it. 'But I'll be back myself in a few days. I have to stay and deal with this estate agent that's coming round later.'

'Are you sure you want to sell?' Rupert asked. It was the first time he'd questioned the decision since reading the original letter.

'Yes.' She nodded at him. 'It's beautiful here, but I want to put the past in the past, like you said. And anyway, I'll need some money to start this business of mine, won't I?'

'You're an amazing person, you know that?' He had started to kiss her neck, and Holly felt a stab of guilt amidst the familiar flutterings of lust.

'I'm really not,' she argued, but he silenced her with a kiss.

Sex with Rupert, she realised afterwards, was rather like eating a huge custard doughnut: it felt amazing at the time, but didn't really provide you with any lasting goodness. Still, she scolded herself, being able to do something that felt amazing whenever you wanted could never be called a bad thing. In fact, after the intensity of Aidan, being with Rupert was like slipping into her comfiest clothes. She knew how to be and how to make him happy and, as she watched him skip off for a shower, she didn't see why she wouldn't just be able to keep doing it for the rest of her life.

In the end, Rupert rode to the airport on the back of Holly's moped with his gym bag strapped across his back. Popping into Kostas' shop first to pick up some snacks for his flight, Holly bumped into Annie at the till and promised to stop in for a drink later that evening. She felt a bit guilty for neglecting her new friend, but she hadn't wanted her to meet Rupert and have to do all the introductions. Annie knew that she'd spent a few days driving around the island with Aidan, even if she had no idea what had happened after that, and Holly didn't relish the idea of having to talk about it to Annie in front of her boyfriend.

'Promise to call me later,' Rupert said, hugging her extra tight as they waited for the check-in desk to open.

'I promise.' Holly smiled.

'I can't believe I've only been here a few days and so much has happened,' he added. He looked so relaxed and happy in his unbuttoned white shirt, his hair uncharacteristically free of any product and the beginnings of a tan across his cheeks. Holly hugged him again, but inside she was agreeing wholeheartedly with what he'd just said. Thank God he didn't realise just how on the money he was.

Rupert collected his boarding card and then proceeded to tell her over and over that he was going to miss her, that he'd call her the minute he got back to London, and that he couldn't wait for her to move in with him. It felt like a scene from a cheesy movie, but she couldn't feel anything close to the unbridled joy that he was radiating. The huge, dark secret of her betrayal was sitting up on her shoulders like a giant squid – sticky and clinging and dangerous.

She drove back to the house slowly, taking in the scenery as she went. She couldn't believe that in just a matter of days she'd be back in London, and all these brilliant blues and greens would be replaced with greys, and the scent of pine and lemons tingling her nose would instead be petrol fumes and commuters' stale sweat. The agent was coming round at 4 p.m. to view and value the house, which meant she had around an hour to get the place looking respectable. She'd put all the bedding into the rickety old washing machine before they left, so this was where she headed first.

'What the—?'

Holly gasped in horror as she pulled out the once-white sheets and covers. They were soaking wet and streaked with – she leaned forward and sniffed – mud. Thank goodness it was only mud. There must have been some already in the machine. She hadn't checked it, but then why would she?

'Bloody hell!' she swore, dumping the sodden bedding on the kitchen floor and switching the machine on to a short rinse to clear out the drum. There was no way she'd have these done in time now, and the uncovered mattresses upstairs were dotted with age-old stains from God only knew what.

Standing up in a temper, Holly smacked the top of her head on the bottom of a cupboard door and swore again, this time with feeling. What the hell was it doing open? The door creaked resentfully, earning itself a violent slamming shut from Holly. Her feeling of satisfaction was short-lived, however, because a split second later there was a cracking sound and the door actually fell off its hinges and clattered on to the floor by her feet.

What the hell was going on? Was the house fighting back?

She forced herself to take a few deep breaths and calm down. What was it Joy the counsellor had told her about negativity? It attracts more negativity. Let yourself become enraged by a broken cupboard door and you're more likely to stub your toe. Or something.

As she stood there, doing her best to quell the rage, her phone beeped.

When are you coming back? the message read. *This place is even worse without you here :(xx.* Aliana was clearly missing her. Holly realised with yet another stab of guilt that she hadn't even bothered to text her friend once since she arrived. She was going to have a fit when she found out about Holly moving in with Rupert.

I miss you too, she typed back, before adding, *Have LOTS to tell! C U soon xx.* If she really was going to make a go of this new life with Rupert, then she would have to make more effort with her female friends too. Aliana was probably the closest thing she had to a best one, even if they did have a way to go, and perhaps she should ask Penelope and Clemmie if they wanted to go shopping or out to lunch. The thought made her pull a face.

Her phone beeped again. This time Aliana had just written the word 'tease' followed by about fifty exclamation marks. Holly giggled at that and headed upstairs, only to find that two of the pictures she'd hung up along the landing had fallen off the wall, taking a heap of dust and plaster with them.

'Great. Thanks,' she told them, heading back the way she'd come to fetch a dustpan and brush. She'd only just shoved the last of the cleaning fluids back under the sink when there was a knock at the door.

'Co-ming!' she yelled, pausing to straighten the table-cloth and release her hair from its messy ponytail. Grabbing the handle, she swung the door open and tried her best to arrange her face into a welcoming expression. It wasn't the estate agent.

Aidan looked dreadful. His hair was sticking up at all angles and his face was pinched and drawn. There was an untidy mess of days-old stubble across his jaw that was speckled with grey and ginger hairs and a large smear of mud on his faded blue T-shirt.

'You look awful,' she blurted without thinking.

He had the grace to smile slightly at this, but it didn't quite reach his eyes.

'Can I come in?'

He had a bloody nerve.

'I'm expecting someone,' she told him.

'Oh?' He raised a quizzical eyebrow. It irritated Holly that he felt able to ask, as if he had any right to know her business after what had happened over the past few days. He'd reeled her in and then spat her out, rubbing Clara in her face without so much as a word of explanation. She could feel her hands starting to shake and clenched her fists.

'I'm having the place valued.' She looked at the floor. 'I need to sell it.'

'You know that's not what Sandy wanted,' Aidan said stiffly. She could feel his glare but refused to look up.

'Sandy's not here to make that decision,' she told him, deliberately making her tone cold and stern. 'She left me this house, therefore it's up to me what I do with it.'

'What's happened to you?' Aidan reached across to take her hand, but she snatched it away.

'I got my head out of the clouds,' she sighed. 'I realised that I'd been living in a fantasy world and that I needed to wise up.'

'You mean, your boyfriend told you to wise up?' He added an unpleasant emphasis to the word 'boyfriend', and Holly felt her hackles rise.

'No,' she finally looked at him. 'My *boyfriend* didn't tell me to do anything – but if he had, then he has a lot more right to than you, and more than some aunt I never knew, either.'

'Did what happened between us not mean anything to you?' he asked now. His eyes were shining, but Holly couldn't tell if he was upset or just very angry.

'What does it matter?' she said. She suddenly felt very weary with it all: the house, him, Rupert, this whole place. 'I have Rupert and you clearly have Clara back in your life again. What?'

He had actually started to laugh at her. The bastard was *laughing* at her.

'I'm glad you find it so funny,' she snarled. Aidan opened his mouth to reply, but at that moment the estate agent walked along the path, holding his hand up in greeting. Pushing Aidan firmly to one side, Holly beckoned the Greek man inside and slammed the front door shut behind her.

She was still seething with anger and frustration an hour later, despite being told by the agent that the house was 'very nice, yes' and that he couldn't foresee any problems selling it, although, given the current 'crisis', it may well take some time. The stained mattresses, broken cupboard door and holes in the upstairs walls had elicited nothing more than a sniff from him, so the house's plan to fight back hadn't paid off. When the man joked that maybe a 'ghost' was to blame, Holly felt a tickle of discomfort creep all the way along her spine.

She didn't want to risk Aidan coming over again or give in to the annoying need she had to go to him, so she left at the same time as the agent, locking the doors behind her and clambering quickly on to her moped. She had no idea where she was heading, instead just feeling the need to drive until the bubbles of unease subsided. She headed towards Kalamaki, but instead of turning left at the crossroads and driving into town, Holly aimed right and followed the coastal road around past the beaches of Porto Zoro and Porto Roma and down into Vasilikos. She'd never been to this part of the island before and felt safe that nobody would think to look for her here. Nobody being Aidan.

The beach here was much wider than those in Laganas and Kalamaki, and every sun lounger was occupied. Couples played bat and ball along the seafront and kids filled their plastic buckets with soggy sand. Holly was happy to stroll anonymously among them, stopping only to pick up the occasional pebble and turn it over in her hand. She knew that selling the house was the right decision – it was the only decision that made any sense – but if that was really the case, then why did it feel so wrong? Aidan had stung her with his comment about Sandra, but that just made her all the more determined to go through with it. She wanted to hurt his feelings so that he understood what it felt like. When she thought about him with Clara it still caused her so much pain that she felt almost winded by it.

Being in Zakynthos had opened her eyes to what it felt like to belong. It had felt like a home, this place, even though she'd only been here for eleven days. Whether it was the weather or the Greek people, or the fact that her mother had spent so much time here, Holly didn't know – but she did know that she'd never felt like this before. Although perhaps she was being sentimental and it was simply that it just happened to be the place where she'd finally found a way to be honest about who she really was. Opening up to Aidan, even if it had turned out to be a mistake, had altered something inside her. It had made her able to be herself in front of Rupert for the first time ever – and it had given her the confidence to admit what her real passion was in life. Try as she might – and she really did – Holly couldn't quite bring herself to hate her Irish nemesis.

Despite the afternoon turning to evening and the air growing cooler as the light faded into the mountains, she waited until it was almost dark before she headed back to Lithakia. The roads were twisty and peppered by blind corners, so she eased off on the throttle and enjoyed the feel of the air as it tangled her hair around her bare shoulders.

Parking the moped outside the front of Kostas' shop, which was shut for the night, she headed straight into Annie's bar. It was busier than usual tonight, and almost every table was overflowing with a variety of brightly coloured cocktails. Scuttling up to the bar, Holly slid on to a stool and promptly jumped off it again in fright as a wobbly-bunned head popped up from behind the till.

'Holly! Darling! I'm so sorry. I didn't mean to scare you.'

Holly managed to laugh. In fact, it actually felt really good to laugh after the day she'd just had, and Annie was quick to join in.

'It's so busy,' she said, gratefully accepting the glass of wine that Annie had hurriedly poured for her.

'A big group arrived at the huge villa on the hill over in Keri today, and they're all keen to get on the sauce. Can't say I blame them.'

Holly nodded. Annie's bar was the first place she'd headed on her first day here, too. There was something nice and homely about the place, with its rather worn-looking wicker chairs and flickering neon signs. Annie had covered the entire wall behind the bar with photos, and Holly squinted over her head at one in particular.

'Is that . . . ?' she asked, standing up in her stool to lean across and get a better look.

Annie frowned and turned to look in the direction that Holly was pointing, before throwing up her hands with a squeal. 'Yes! Of course! I can't believe I didn't show you this the other night.' Reaching across, she plucked the photo out from beneath its pin and placed it on the bar.

Holly had done the maths already and deduced that Sandra would have been around fifty when she died – no age at all – but this photo must have been taken a few years ago, because her aunt didn't look the slightest bit ill. With her glossy brown hair pulled back in a ponytail, a bronze glow on her smiling face and a bottle of beer clutched in a hand adorned with rings, she looked about the same age as Holly. Next to Sandra in the photo, also smiling broadly and also clutching a bottle of beer, was Aidan.

'I told you those two were close,' Annie said, as Holly blinked back the tears. Aidan looked like he'd just been laughing when the camera was brought out. His eyes were focused on something or someone out of sight, and his hair was all over the place as usual. Holly dragged her eyes off his face and looked again at Sandra, realising with a further stab of sadness that this was just how Jenny Wright would have looked, had she made it past her fortieth birthday.

'Are you okay, sweetheart?' Annie had appeared next to her and placed a comforting hand on her arm. Holly nodded, not trusting herself to speak. She loved the photo, but it actually hurt her to look at it. So much had changed since it had been taken; so many people had been hurt and lied to. It broke Holly's heart.

'How did you know that Zakynthos was where you belonged?' she asked Annie now, putting the photo face down on the bar and picking up her drink.

'I didn't, not at first.' Annie sighed as she pulled up a stool, yelling something in Greek to the two youngsters who were running drinks from the bar to the tables. 'I came over with my ex-husband – it was his idea to open this place, then of course he ran off with someone else. He cheated on me the whole time we were married.'

'What a rotter,' Holly said, trying not to choke on her own hypocrisy.

'Indeed.' Annie paused for a moment as she reminisced. 'When he finally did the decent thing and actually buggered off back to Leeds, I was all ready to sell this place. I thought all the memories would be too painful to deal with.'

'What changed your mind?' Holly tried to picture a younger Annie, beaten down and broken by betrayal, trying to make sense of everything on her own in a foreign country. She seemed so strong and content now that it was a tough image to conjure up.

'I took myself down to the beach one day. I had someone coming to look at the bar in the afternoon, and I just sat and watched the water for hours. It was so beautiful, I simply realised I couldn't leave it behind. And do you know what? I've never regretted it, not once.'

She was so lucky, thought Holly. If only she could have a eureka moment and know in her gut that she was in the right place, with the right person. She was her mother's daughter all right – Jenny had been flaky and indecisive until the day she died, and apparently she'd passed those traits on to Holly.

'What's all this about?' Annie asked. 'You look like you're carrying the weight of the world on your shoulders, if you don't mind me saying so.'

Holly shook her head. 'I don't mind at all. I guess I'm just looking for answers. I wish someone could make all my decisions for me.' As she said it, she was reminded of Rupert, ordering for her in restaurants, choosing her a dress, taking over in the estate agent's when she was struggling to make herself understood, telling her exactly how their life would be together. It should feel like a comfort, to have someone that cared enough to take the reins.

'Nobody can do that,' Annie laughed, patting her on the knee. 'My Derek used to try, and in the end it was the undoing of us. Well, that and all those other women he was ban— What?'

One of the young Greek waitresses had scurried up to them in a panic because a drink order had gone out wrong, and Annie made her apologies and went to smooth things over. Holly admired the way she got the complaining man laughing within a few seconds.

Downing the last of her wine and slipping the photo of Sandra and Aidan into her bag, Holly heaved herself off the stool and headed for home. It wasn't until she was safely in bed that she switched on her phone and let the light from the screen cast a dull glow across the room.

Huddled under the only clean and dry sheet that she had left in the house, she clutched her mum and aunt's secret map in her hands and traced a finger over their words. If only someone could draw her a map that would guide her to happiness. If only she could take out a compass and follow a route that would lead her to where she was supposed to be. Was it really her path to turn her back on this place and make a life in London with Rupert? And if so, then why did it feel as if something here, on this island, was holding her back?

25

'Are you sure you want to get rid of all of these?'

Annie was standing by the open back doors, a cardboard box full of ornaments balanced in her arms.

Holly had so far chickened out of telling her about the plans to sell. Why upset Annie now, when she'd be gone in a few days anyway?

'I'm not really one for ornaments,' she smiled, choosing to ignore the fact that she'd already stashed the little glass turtle in her suitcase. 'I'd like a charity to make some money from them, if they could. Better that they go to someone who will appreciate them.'

'But won't the place look a bit bare?' Annie persisted. She'd made a big show of nosing around every single room as soon as she'd arrived that morning, but if she was surprised by the changes Holly had made, she didn't mention it.

'Thank you for helping me out like this,' Holly told her, carefully sidestepping Annie's original question.

'Oh, it's no bother. No bother at all,' Annie beamed at her. There was a patch of angry-looking red skin on her chest where she'd clearly spent too long in the sun. She'd driven her rickety old car up the hill so she could fill the boot with boxes, and Holly was amazed when the entire chassis didn't buckle under the weight. As she eased a box of particularly chintzy crockery on to the back seat, she saw that the gearstick was held together by reams of Sellotape.

'Is this thing safe to drive?' Holly asked, earning herself a shout of mirth from Annie as she clambered behind the wheel.

'I assumed you wanted to keep that last box of stuff in the bedroom,' she said, fiddling with the rear-view mirror.

'Which box?' Holly was confused. She'd been sure that her aunt's room was clear.

'It was under the bed,' Annie said, doing up her seat belt. 'If you don't want it, just bring it on down to the bar later, yeah?'

'I will.' Holly waved her off, trying not to wince as Annie performed a five-point turn, narrowly missing the wall, the moped and a cat that was sunning itself on the kerb. Aidan's jeep was mercifully missing, which had elicited a groan of disappointment from Annie when she'd arrived earlier that morning. 'It would have taken half the time with some extra muscle,' she'd proclaimed. Probably true, but Holly would rather pack boxes with her teeth than ask Aidan for any help.

Filling a glass with cold water from the fridge, she headed back upstairs to investigate this mysterious box. She was hoping that it would contain some more sewing stuff. She'd long since plundered the original supplies.

No wonder she hadn't seen it before; the box was jammed into the furthest corner and was surrounded by a tangled heap of dust and hair. Yanking it out across the rug made Holly cough, and she brushed irritably at the fresh dirt on her clean shorts. The shoebox looked old and battered and the lid was held in place by several elastic bands. The thick layer of dust covering the top suggested to Holly that it hadn't been opened in a fair while, and she experienced a tremor of foreboding. Just like the day that she'd discovered that message from Rupert on her phone, she felt convinced that she was about to see something that perhaps she'd rather not. The first postcard on the pile confirmed her fears.

Friday, 30 June 2000
Sandra,

I'm writing to tell you that this will be the last time. It's been so long since I left the island and I have never heard a word from you. I did what I promised – I left and I never came back. I kept what happened a secret, like you asked. I haven't even told Holly, even though it breaks my heart to keep things from her. She's fifteen today – can you believe it? She's a better teenager than I ever was. I was out drinking by the time I was her age (some habits never die), but all she's interested in is her sewing kit. She's much more like you than me. You should see Holly, even if you won't see me. Think about it. As for you and me – I think it's time to stop begging. My heart is black with self-loathing. I will never forgive myself for losing you. Goodbye, Sandy.

Your twin,
Jenny x

So, her mum had tried to stay in touch with Sandra. Ever since she arrived on the island, Holly had assumed that the blame for the estrangement lay firmly with her mother. Despite what Sandra had written in her letter about being unworthy of forgiveness, Holly knew that her mum had been flaky. It was how she'd always been as Holly was growing up – flighty, disorganised, impatient and eventually utterly disconnected, not just where Holly herself was concerned, but from life in general. She'd watched as her mum had given up on living, so it wasn't far-reaching to think she'd given up on her own twin sister too.

The truth, though, which was becoming ever more apparent as Holly skim-read the pile of postcards, was that her mum *had* tried to build bridges. So many times she read the words in her mother's familiar handwriting, asking Sandra if she could come back to visit, begging that they could put the past behind them – but it appeared that her pleas had landed on deaf ears.

After the final postcard from June 2000, in which Jenny had sworn she would not write again, there were no more messages from her mother, but there were more postcards addressed to Sandra, carefully written in her mum's hand. She'd simply sent blank postcards every few months, right up until – Holly peered at the date next to the stamp – six months before she died.

They must have meant something to Sandra, or why would she have kept them boxed up like this?

There were more photos in the box too, some of Sandra and Jenny on the island, tanned and grinning, and lots of them as children. Someone had written on the back of a few in spindly blue pen: *Jenny in Athens aged six. J&S, Zakynthos, 1970.* They all looked so happy.

Holly stacked the postcards into date order and began

reading them again, this time taking in every word. Some of the stuff she read made her smile:

Do you remember the time it snowed on the island and we ran starkers down the beach to Porto Koukla? . . . I thought we would die laughing.

While other bits struck a deeper chord:

Holly would have loved to see you. I won't let her forget her Auntie Sandra, I promise.

As she read, Holly realised with a shiver of understanding that her suspicions about being on the island before had been correct. She clearly had been here in Zakynthos, and she'd even met Sandra, although she had no memory of it. There was something there, beyond all the darkness that she'd bricked up so carefully, a spark of something bright and full of joy. Could it be her memories of the time she'd spent here as a child?

Writing to you seemed like a better idea than opening a bottle of vodka, although neither one makes me feel any better.

Holly continued reading in the hope that she'd stumble across a mention of what had happened, but all there seemed to be were pleas from her mother to be forgiven. One postcard talked about the sale of Jenny and Sandra's childhood home in Kent, with her mum lamenting the fact that Sandra had instructed a solicitor to throw away all her belongings. Jenny had decided against keeping any of the furniture in the end, as she and Holly were still living in rented accommodation at the time and it was all a bit much for her to deal with. She'd written to Sandra thanking her for organising it all and told her that she planned to invest her share of the money in her friend's business venture.

Holly had no idea what had happened to all that money, but there certainly hadn't been any left at the end. Given the company her mum had kept throughout her life, though, Holly wasn't surprised the inheritance had been frittered away.

Jenny had told her when she was still very young that her own parents had both been only children, and she'd never met any grandparents that she could remember. How sad, Holly thought now, that her family seemed to be locked into this awful cycle of losing their parents at a young age. Jenny was too young to lose her mum and dad, just as Holly had been too young to lose Jenny – things could have been so different for all of them if fate had only given them a break. When she'd read through all the postcards a third time, Holly lost her battle against the tears.

It's been so long since I left the island and I have never heard a word from you. I did what I promised – I left and I never came back. I kept what happened a secret, like you asked. I haven't even told Holly, even though it breaks my heart to keep things from her.

What had her mother kept from her? What had been so devastating that it engendered so much loss and regret? It dawned on Holly now that this rift with Sandra was probably a lot to do with why her mother had eventually turned to the bottle. Whatever it was had clearly been eating away at her for years, and without Sandra's forgiveness allowing her to move on, the booze had perhaps provided a refuge. Holly sobbed for her mother, imagining how wretched she must have felt. She had long ago reached the point where she'd almost forgotten what it felt like to be loved by her mum, but these postcards proved that she had been.

In the end, when Jenny's alcoholism had stolen her away, she'd become a shell of the person Holly cared so much about. The lines between sweet Jenny and damaged Jenny had become so blurred in Holly's mind that she'd started to think of her as having always been that way. Everything that had come before, which had been so happy, was infected with the harsh reality of how Jenny had ended up. The past was tainted by the present, and Holly's heart had closed itself to the idea of forgiveness. Sitting here now, surrounded by the words of hope and love that her mum had written, Holly knew that she *must* forgive her. For everything. For the drinking, for the neglect, for the lies and for never introducing Holly to this place, this beautiful island. Jenny had wanted nothing more than for Holly to know her aunt and spend time in the place she'd presumably loved so much as a child, but it was Sandra who had stood in their way. She must let go of it all now, she knew that. It was the only way she would ever be able to be happy.

As she shuffled the postcards into a stack and went to return them to the box, Holly noticed a yellow envelope at the bottom that she hadn't spotted before. Turning it over, she felt a jolt as she saw her mother's name written on the front.

Dear Jenny,

I've sat down and written this letter so many times, but I've never been able to send it. I haven't received a postcard from you in over two years now, so I'm trying my best not to think the worst. I always was a coward – you were the brave one. You led and I followed. I often think that my life would have been very dull without you in it, but then I also wish that you hadn't always been quite so headstrong. You always went after what you wanted when I knew you, as I'm sure you still do now, but why did one of those things have to belong to me?

I remember the day I got that postcard from you telling me that you were leaving India and coming here, and I confess that I felt nervous. When Mum and Dad died you turned into such a brittle version of yourself. We'd always been so close, but even I couldn't crack through that protective shell you built up around you. When you left to go travelling, I was devastated, but a small part of me was also relieved. I'd lost my parents too, but I felt like I wasn't allowed to grieve for them like you did. I didn't have the indulgence of misery because I was too busy looking after you.

I came here to get away from all the ghosts back home and when I met Dennis I just felt as if I'd been reborn. I'd always been fearful of falling in love, as you know, but with him it felt so easy. I know you could tell how I felt about him as soon as you arrived, but I can distinctly remember seeing a look on your face, perhaps it was just for a brief second, but it was a look that told me I belonged to you, not to him.

I know Dennis was just another man to you, but he was everything to me. He was the reason I wanted to open my eyes in the morning and the reason why I never wanted to close them at night. He taught me what love really was and for a time I'd even started to love myself too. You never had that trouble. How is it, do you think, that we can be twins but be so different? Perhaps if I was more carefree like you, I would have been able to forgive you for what happened, but I can't, even after all these years. I have tried, I promise, but these black feelings just won't go away. They've poisoned my life, perhaps even my soul, and it's been so long now that they've just become part of who I am. Asking me to give them up would be like asking for a piece of my heart.

Sometimes I think that if you'd told me in the beginning, before Holly was born, that I may have been able to find a way to forgive you – but to wait all those years? You let me love that little girl when all along you knew what she was, who her real father was. That was cruel of you, Jenny. You should have let me decide who I wanted to love, but you knew I'd love that little girl more than life.

Dennis became someone different to me overnight. All that love I felt for him just sucked right out of me, and it left this gaping hole of rage and bitterness. I know you told me that it only happened one time, that you were both drunk and that it was you who made the first move, but his eyes told me different. Of course, he denied knowing that Holly was his, but how could I believe him? I've tortured myself imagining the three of you taking secret trips out together on the boat. Sharing some family bonding while I waited at home, none the wiser. It makes me so angry that I want to grab the two of you by the hair and shake you. I know Holly is the innocent one, but the thought of looking into those big brown eyes of hers again – his eyes – well, that just breaks my

*heart all over again. He was mine, but you took a part of him
that could never, ever be mine. How can I forgive you for that?*

*Perhaps I will send this letter to you one day, but I don't think
I'll ever have the guts. You were always the brave one, Jenny. I
wish I had been stronger, but I wasn't.*

*Not a day passes that I don't think about you and wish things
could be different, but I don't believe they ever will. I gave up on
love a very long time ago.*

Sandra

So, there it was. Dennis, the man in that photo she'd
found, the same man who Kostas had informed her was
'with Sandra'. He was her father.

For a long time, Holly just sat on the rug, the letter in
her hands, her tears causing the ink to run into untidy
streaks down the page. There was so much to take in.
Jenny had slept with her own twin sister's boyfriend
and she, Holly, had been the result. She was the reason
they had stopped speaking to each other. This was what
her mum must have meant when she told Holly that
she should have given her up. And the worst thing of all –
Holly had followed in her mum's footsteps and done
exactly the same thing. She'd become a cheat. All these
years she'd been promising herself that she would be
nothing like her mum, and she'd gone and turned into her
without even noticing. What Sandra had written about
Jenny putting up a protective shield around herself had
made Holly wince with recognition. And she knew what
it was to be crippled by grief too – but was it reason
enough to behave the way Jenny had?

She forced herself to remember what she'd been like in the weeks and months after Jenny's death. She'd be doing her best to go about her business as usual, then she'd suddenly be hit by a tidal wave of hopelessness and anger. Sometimes the pain was so acute that it left her gasping for breath at the side of the road. She could very easily believe that grief on that level could make a person do anything. Certainly do anything they could to escape the agony. Poor Jenny, and poor Sandra too. Once that sadness had got under their skin, they were both lost.

The truth that she had an actual, real, presumably still-living father was slowly working its way through Holly's senses. The shock of the revelation was still resonating, but she could sense a surge of emotion brewing in her chest. She'd looked at that photo so many times and never made the connection – never even questioned it. She'd always held on to a fairy-tale belief that she'd know her dad the second she saw him. She'd imagined walking past him in the street or sitting opposite him on the tube. Now all she felt was confused, upset, and very, very angry.

She read her Aunt Sandra's letter again, sniffing away her tears and wiping them angrily from her cheeks. It was implied that her dad had known about her, but he too had chosen not to pursue any sort of relationship with her. Even if her mum had fled Greece, he could have tried. Or perhaps he had. Maybe he had come all the way to their door only to be turned away. It seemed unlikely, but then so did the idea of finding out you had a father in a dusty old box of postcards. At this moment in time, Holly believed that literally anything could be possible. What she needed was answers. She needed to find Dennis and ask him what happened that summer. Ask him why he'd abandoned her. But where the hell was she even meant to start?

When the knocking started downstairs, it made Holly jump so violently that she cracked her elbow on the bed-frame. It was loud and insistent, but she didn't move. Whoever it was, she didn't want to see them.

'HOLLY!' Aidan's voice was muffled, but he sounded upset. So what? He could sod off.

'HOLLY! You really need to let me in!'

She didn't move. The sunlight shining in through the window was illuminating the cloud of dust she'd disturbed by unearthing the box, and she watched as the particles danced and dived around each other.

'HOLLY, PLEASE!'

Bloody hell, what was his problem?

Holly stayed put, even when she heard a key in the lock and the sound of running feet on the stairs. Aidan appeared in the bedroom doorway a second later, his cheeks flushed and a bunch of keys in his hand. A quick scan of the room caused him to look momentarily confused, and then he beckoned to her.

'Come on, we need to go.'

'Go where?'

Aidan sighed and crouched down on his haunches.

'To the hospital.'

'What? Why?' She was doing her best to remain calm, but the intensity in his eyes was scaring her.

'It's . . .' He paused. For a few seconds he stared down at the floor, at the pile of postcards, and then he looked right at her.

'It's your dad. He's had a heart attack. You need to come now.'

He was already up on his feet again, but Holly found she couldn't move.

'What the hell do you mean?' she snapped, finding her voice. 'I only found out who my dad was myself a few minutes ago.'

'Holly.' Aidan gripped the door handle. 'Trust me, we have to go. There's no time for a discussion about it.'

When she didn't move, he reached down and grabbed her by the wrist, pulling her up on to her feet.

'Come on, I'll drive you.'

'Get off!' She yanked her hand away as if he'd branded it. 'I'm not going anywhere with you.' The urge to cry again was almost overwhelming, but she was determined not to let Aidan see her weak side ever again.

He took a deep breath and glared at her. She was still holding the letter Sandra had written and her face was a mess of red blotches and smudged mascara.

'Holly,' he said again, moving as close to her as he dared. 'You have to come and see Dennis. I don't want it to be too late.'

Dennis? So, Aidan knew who her dad was. Too stunned by this information to reply and too exhausted to put up any more of a fight, Holly let him lead her down the stairs and out to his jeep.

26

Aidan drove dangerously fast all the way to the hospital, narrowly avoiding clusters of tourists and parked cars. Holly sat mutely beside him, wincing every now and then at the near misses but refusing to say a word – she didn't trust herself to say anything, such was her confusion and anger. The same thought was repeating itself over and over in her mind: *My father is Sandra's ex, Dennis. He is in hospital. Aidan knows who he is.*

But *how* did Aidan know? Had he found the letter before her and worked it out? Had he known all along? And if so, why the hell hadn't he told her?

Even after the arrival of Clara and the horrible way he'd been behaving towards her ever since, Holly still refused to believe that he was capable of keeping such a big secret from her. She trusted him. He was one of the only people she'd ever really trusted. He couldn't and wouldn't have done that to her, would he?

Zakynthos hospital turned out to be a large rectangular building, with a yellow and terracotta paint job that did little to detract from its bulky, blocky ugliness. Holly's first thought as Aidan screeched to a halt across two parking spaces was relief that he hadn't actually crashed the jeep on the way. This didn't look like the sort of place where you'd want to end up after an accident.

While the inside was clean enough, the grey plastic

chairs in the downstairs waiting room looked faded and the green walls dull, as if the sunlight had long ago robbed them of any vibrancy. Aidan was babbling away in Greek to the woman behind the reception desk, and soon he was leading Holly towards a wide bank of stairs.

He'd barely looked at her since they left the house, but Holly could tell that he was concerned. A muscle twitched continually in his cheek and his hair was sticking up in all directions where he kept running an agitated hand through it. Dark patches had also formed under his arms and in the groove of his back, lending an almost tie-dye effect to his goat-eaten T-shirt. Holly noticed all this, but couldn't really process it. The notion that she might soon see her real father in the flesh for the first time had stolen away all rational thinking and replaced it with an intense dread.

'Aidan.'

A dark-haired woman was rushing down the corridor towards them, fresh tears all over her face. She immediately began speaking in Greek, only pausing to look over his shoulder to where Holly was cowering, unsure of what to do. The woman was clearly distraught, and Aidan put his arms around her and forced her into a reluctant embrace.

'He's out of immediate danger,' he said in English, turning to Holly. 'They got here in time.'

She nodded, still mute. The woman pulled her face away from Aidan's chest and stole another look at her. There was something in her eyes that Holly couldn't quite place. Not mistrust, exactly, more like curiosity. After eyeing Holly up and down, she stepped back and beckoned to her and Aidan that they should follow her back along the green passageway. As they neared an open doorway, Holly noticed a young girl sitting on another sad-looking chair that had been left outside. She had a sullen expression on her face and was swinging her legs underneath the seat. As she looked up, Holly was hit with a punch of recognition. She'd seen this little face before, at the taverna above the beautiful cove in Porto Limnionas, but the first time it had been smiling and happy and covered in smears of chocolate ice cream.

'This is Paloma,' Aidan said, motioning towards the older woman. Holly remembered the name – Paloma was the lady who worked with him in the clinic. Up close, she looked a lot younger than her clothes and grey-streaked hair had led Holly to believe. She looked so much like the little girl sitting in the chair that she could only be her mother.

'*Yassou,*' she muttered, trying her best to smile.

Paloma looked her up and down again and sniffed, before saying something in Greek to Aidan. The little girl stopped swinging her legs and leaned around her mother to peer at Holly, her deep-set eyes wide beneath her dark fringe. Holly wondered if she too remembered that they had already met one another.

'Paloma only found out about you a few weeks ago,' Aidan said now. He still wasn't quite meeting her eyes.

'Well, tell her that I only found out about *her* a few moments ago,' she snapped, finally finding her voice. 'And that I don't even know who *she* is, despite everyone else apparently knowing everything about me.' She'd meant that last part to sting him, and it worked. Aidan flinched as if she'd slapped him.

'I know this is hard for you,' he started, but she held up her hand.

'You don't know me at all,' she stated. 'Don't you *dare* presume to know how I'm feeling. Not now, not ever.'

'Paloma is Dennis' wife,' he told her, ignoring the outburst. 'And this is their daughter, Maria.'

The little girl, who was apparently her half-sister, braved a smile and Holly felt her anger subside a fraction. It was then that she realised, with an increasingly frantic hammering of her heart, that she had probably seen her dad before too – she'd seen him more than once. She couldn't blame Aidan for the first of those encounters at Porto Limnionas, when Dennis had stared at her across the banks of tables and she'd assumed, ridiculously, that he was checking her out. But the second, when the two men had stood by the fishing boat in Mikro Nissi and watched her, was all on him. Just what the hell had he been playing at?

A doctor appeared just as the silence was becoming uncomfortable and ushered Paloma and Aidan inside, shutting the door behind them and leaving Holly in the putrid green corridor with Maria. For a few seconds, they just looked at each other, and then Maria began to cry. Her sobs were so loud and so heart-wrenching that Holly found herself kneeling down and taking her hands. Maria looked at her beseechingly and sobbed a few jumbled words at her in Greek. Her nose was running and there were two streaks of clean skin where her tears had made a path through the dirt on each of her cheeks. At a loss as to how to tell her that everything would be okay, Holly merely reached up and stroked the wet hair off her half-sister's face. She had the same dark, slightly almond-shaped eyes as Holly.

Despite the fact that they were total strangers, Maria clutched Holly against her as if she was the most precious person in the world, and Holly hugged her right back just as tight. For a few minutes, as she knelt there on the cold floor, Holly stopped worrying about what was to come next. All that mattered was Maria, her very own sister. Now that she had her, Holly felt as if she was invincible. She was not alone in the world after all, and the realisation was both startling and magical. It was as if she'd made a wish and had it granted, without even knowing that she'd made one in the first place.

'Holly?'

It was Aidan, his touch gentle on her shoulder.

'Dennis is stable and you can see him if you want to.'

Maria had finally stopped crying, but Holly took her time disentangling herself from the little girl's clinging arms. Aidan's eyes were shining and he looked to Holly as if he'd aged five years in the last half an hour. His freckly skin bore a grey tinge and his shoulders were uncharacteristically hunched.

'You look wretched,' she told him matter-of-factly, giving Maria's little hand a final squeeze before letting it drop. Paloma had joined them and was staring unashamedly at Holly again, her blatant curiosity as clear as the cloudless sky outside.

'Shall we get this over with then?' Holly said, addressing both of them.

'Are you sure you're ready?' Aidan asked.

Was he insane?

'No. I'm not sure,' she replied, growing angry again. 'But given as how you stormed into my house and ordered me down here, I don't think I have a choice in the matter now, do I?'

He nodded, looking sheepish. Holly sneaked a last look down at Maria, and then followed Aidan into the room and towards the figure under the blankets.

27

When Holly was still a child and prone to making up all kinds of stories in her head, her favourite of all these make-believe tales was the one she'd conjured up about her father. In her fantasy, he was always tall and far more handsome than any of the other dads she'd met, with twinkly eyes, a huge cheesy grin and the best cuddles in the world. She would imagine him knocking on the front door after years spent in the foreign places that her mum had told her about, and she would answer it and gaze up at him in wonder. Then he would smile in his wonderful way and reach down to pick her up, telling her over and over again how much he'd missed her and how proud he was. It was a silly story, but Holly thought about it often as she grew up, willing it to be true even though she knew there was no likelihood of that. Her mum moved them around so much that even if her dad did want to track her down, he'd never be able to find them. She'd raised this point a few times when she was still young, but her mum had simply shaken her head and smiled. 'He'll find us if he wants to,' she would say, leaving Holly to wonder why on earth he wouldn't.

Perhaps it was this romanticised childhood fantasy that made Holly's legs tremble with expectation when she finally saw her father, or maybe it was just the shock of everything that had come to light in the past few hours – but it was certainly nothing like she'd ever imagined. Dennis wasn't smiling, for a start. His eyes were open and he was looking directly at her, but his face was contorted with misery and what looked to Holly like fear. She noticed the tears all over his face just as her own began to fall.

Dennis opened his mouth to speak, but he seemed too weak to manage it. He looked tormented, and Holly instinctively reached out to take his hand. It felt cold, and she shivered as he gave her fingers a gentle squeeze. He tried to speak again, but still she couldn't make out what he was saying because his voice was so hoarse. The machine monitoring his heart rate was bleeping with reassuring regularity, and Holly found herself staring at a tiny red light that was flashing on and off.

'He says that he is sorry,' Paloma whispered beside her. She'd left her spot next to the door to join Holly by the bed, and was now gesturing that she should bend forward in order to hear what Dennis was saying. Aidan had moved to the window and had his back to them, his hand shaking ever so slightly as he brought it up to move the curtain aside. Holly closed her eyes as she leaned over towards Dennis. She wanted to block out Aidan. If she couldn't see him, then she could pretend he wasn't there at all. If she was being honest, she resented him for being there in the room with them, intruding into her life during such a moment.

'Sorry,' breathed Dennis again. It was barely a whisper.

Holly moved her hand up just in time to stop her tears from falling all over him, and a sob erupted from somewhere in the depths of her chest. Paloma put a hand in the small of her back and rubbed a warm circle. It was such an instinctively maternal thing to do that Holly was reminded horribly of her own mother again, and this set off a whole new flood of tears.

'I'm sorry too,' she managed at last, finally opening her eyes and looking down at the man on the pillows. 'I'm so sorry.'

And she was sorry. Sorry that she was crying when he was the one in the hospital bed; sorry that she couldn't articulate to him how she was feeling, about how happy she was to have found him; and sorry that they had met each other this way, so very long after they should have.

As her juddering sobs slowed and the room fell silent again, Paloma pushed her gently into the chair by the bed and backed quietly away. Holly felt rather than saw Aidan leave the room too, and for a long time after they left she just rested her forehead against the edge of the mattress, Dennis' cold fingers stroking a timid pattern across her hand.

She wasn't alone any more.

After spending an entire thirty-six hours at the hospital, a good portion of them in the grotty plastic chair outside Dennis' room, Holly was finally persuaded by a concerned nurse to go home and get some sleep. But after four hours spent staring morosely at the ceiling, she admitted defeat at the hands of her old friend the Insomnia Troll and slipped noiselessly out through the front door, pushing her moped down the hill before she started the engine. She didn't think Aidan would dare to show his face, but she didn't want to risk bumping into him.

She still couldn't believe he'd paraded Dennis in front of her and told her nothing. He'd listened while she poured her heart out about her mum, about how she'd spent so many years on her own, and still he'd said nothing. There was no possible way that she would be able to see him without saying something really awful, something that would undoubtedly sever the bond between them for ever. Despite his crimes, the thought of losing Aidan permanently still made Holly feel queasy. She knew she should hate him, but she had been reluctantly comforted during the hours he'd stayed with her at the hospital. But it was still all so hopeless. How could they ever go back to the way things had been just a few days ago? How could she ever trust him? It had taken her so many years to find someone she felt comfortable enough with to let her guard down, and that person had turned out to be lying to her all along. It just wasn't fair.

She drove without really thinking and ended up heading towards Kalamaki, parking the bike by the beach and walking up to the viewing platform she'd noticed on her very first visit. It felt like a lifetime ago now. The sun was yet to rise, but a trail of blue-grey light was just visible on the horizon. Holly took her time climbing up the stony path towards the top of the cliff, where she was greeted by the full splendour of the moon. It seemed so much larger and brighter than it did back in London, but Holly found that she couldn't fully appreciate its beauty. Her head was throbbing with fatigue and her back was sore from all the hours spent sitting on the hard plastic chair. After standing for a few minutes to absorb the view, she sat down on the dusty ground and dangled her feet over the side.

She had a father.

Everyone had a father, of course, but Holly had never had a living, breathing one before. Simon had been a kind of stepdad for the few years that he and Jenny had stayed together, but her mum had never encouraged her to refer to him as 'Dad', and certainly not to think of him as such. She was adamant that Holly's dad was a hero, someone who had dedicated his life to trying to make the world a better place. Of course, the reality was that Holly's real father was neither a hero nor a random drifter: he was just a man much like any other. A man who had made mistakes that had cost him dearly.

Holly peered down past her toes to where the waves were snaking their way up and across the sand.

'I have a dad,' she said aloud, waiting to feel absurd. It was all too real, though – too horribly, yet brilliantly, but still mind-screwingly real to laugh about. There was a knot in her stomach like a tightly wound ball of barbed wire. She could feel it now – it felt like it was slowly tearing her insides to pieces.

How could Aidan have just stood there that day at the beach when he knew her father was merely metres away?

Holly stopped staring at the ground and looked up in time to see a thick wedge of sunlight slide across the surface of the sea. For a while, she simply sat and stared at the twinkling crests of the waves through half-closed eyes.

Dennis had been fairly groggy for the first few hours that she spent in his room, but he'd still found the strength to take her hand in his. She'd watched, as if in a daze, as he'd squeezed it gently with his own, his thumb rotating against her wrist. It was as if he was trying to say in a gesture what he was unable to put into words. Holly had just stared at him mutely, trying her very best not to cry again. When she finally found the courage to meet his eyes, he had smiled, and she had felt some of the pain fall away. There were so many questions she wanted him to answer, but she understood that for now they could wait.

The truth, her truth, the one that she'd been searching for since she arrived in Zakynthos, suddenly scared her. Holly wasn't sure if she was ready to hear the full story of exactly what had happened all those years ago – especially if it meant she would end up back where she'd started: hating her mum. Was there even more left for her to forgive? Holly felt sure that there was, and she didn't have the strength to face it.

'Penny for them?'

She was lost so deep in her own thoughts that she hadn't heard Aidan coming up the cliff behind her and she swung round in alarm, sending a shoal of stones over the ledge.

Aidan lunged forward to grab her, but she slapped his hands away.

'Don't touch me.'

'Holly . . .' he began, but stopped when he saw the look on her face. 'Can I sit down?'

She shrugged.

It was difficult for someone of Aidan's size to shrink into a small, unobtrusive ball, but somehow he managed it as he slid down and sat hunched on the platform. He had a large scab on his knee and she could see marks on his ankles from the socks he must have recently discarded.

He was careful not to go within touching distance of Holly, which was wise, given that she was seriously contemplating hurling him over the side on to the wet sand below.

'How did you know where I was?' she asked him after a time. She'd been so careful to leave the house without making a sound.

'I followed you.' He risked a half-smile. 'I was sitting at my window waiting for you to get up. I figured you wouldn't stay cooped up in the house for very long.'

'What makes you think I want you here?' she asked, not bothering to keep the venom out of her voice. She wasn't about to make this easy for him.

'I didn't think you would. I just thought someone should keep an eye on you. You've had a big shock.'

'No thanks to you.'

'Yes, no thanks to me. Maybe that's why I feel responsible.'

There was a long pause as Holly seethed and Aidan gazed out towards the dark shapes of the mountains. He looked genuinely upset, but this only made her even angrier.

'This doesn't change anything,' she told him. 'I'm still going to sell the house.'

Aidan raised his shoulders and let them drop again. Holly knew he was only pretending not to care – there was a bead of sweat working its way down the side of his face.

His silence was starting to grate.

'Don't you have anything to say to me?' she demanded. Her bottom was going rapidly numb on the hard, stony ground and she shifted irritably.

Aidan looked up at her, waiting until she finally met his eyes before he replied. 'I had no choice. I made a promise. Sandy made me prom—'

'Promise what? To sneak me off to see my dad and then not even tell me who he was? To stand by and say nothing when I poured my bloody heart out to you? To stare at a photo of my father and pretend you had no idea who he was?'

Aidan shrugged again and Holly picked up one of the small stones and threw it at him.

'Don't just sit there and shrug your shoulders at me! I trusted you.' Her voice cracked as she yelled at him. She had trusted him – she hadn't trusted anyone for so many years and she'd let her guard down with him – and he'd thrown it all back in her face.

'Holly, please,' Aidan looked as though he might actually cry. 'Try to understand—'

'No, Aidan. I don't want to understand how someone could do what you've done to me. How someone could lie and cheat and—' She stopped, realising with a fresh stab of guilt that she too had lied and cheated. She was no better than him.

'I never set out to hurt you,' Aidan said. Holly felt as if someone had taken an ice-cream scoop to her insides and scraped them all out.

'Sandra was dying. She was my friend and I owed her – how could I say no? I thought it would just be hiding a few things round the house for you to find and pointing you in the right directions . . .'

'What did you just say?' Holly glared at him. 'You hid things in my house?'

'The map,' Aidan shrugged uncomfortably. 'Sandra gave it to me not long before . . . Well, you know.'

Holly clenched her fists and said nothing. She had felt such a surge of excitement when she found that tatty old bit of paper containing so many amazing secrets. It had felt like fate. But no, it had just been Aidan, playing a game with her all along.

'What else?' she demanded, watching as he visibly shrivelled under the weight of her stare.

'The photo,' he said quietly. 'The one of Dennis and Sandra and Socrates and your mum and—'

'I know who's in it,' she interrupted, ignoring his wince of discomfort.

'Listen, Holly, I had no idea all this was going to happen. I didn't know how much you'd already been through with your mum dying the way she did. And then I started falling for you and it just became even more difficult to tell you the truth. I was a coward. I wanted that bubble we were in to stay intact. I knew if I told you what I'd done then I would lose you.'

'Shut up! Just shut up!' She glared at him. 'Don't you *dare* say that to me. Don't you dare try to mask what you've done with some flimsy excuse for real feelings. If you cared about me even the tiniest bit, then you never would have let this happen.'

Aidan held up a hand. 'You know I care about you,' he told her. 'You're the one who ditched me the minute your boyfriend turned up.'

'Don't bring him into it,' Holly snapped. 'He's a million times the man you'll ever be.'

'Clearly.' Aidan was getting riled now. There was a vein

pulsing on his temple and his face had turned an ugly shade of puce.

'And you can talk about going off with other people,' she added, thinking excruciatingly of the long-limbed and Titian-haired Clara.

Aidan opened his mouth to retort and then shut it again. They sat in silence for a few seconds, both distracted by the rising sun that had sneaked up behind them. Despite her temper, Holly felt her eyes widen to drink in the view.

'Sandy thought it would all be too much for you, if you turned up and were confronted by a father on the very first day,' Aidan told her. 'She asked me to wait until the time was right. But then Dennis had the heart attack and . . . well, everything just got so confused.'

'Confused?' Holly laughed shortly. 'What was there to be confused about? You knew who my dad was and you didn't tell me. Seems pretty clear to me. What if the heart attack had killed him? Would you just never have told me about him?'

'Of course not.' Aidan put his head in his hands. 'But nobody could have predicted what happened to Dennis.'

'Exactly!' Holly was yelling again. 'That's exactly my point. It could have happened at any time. You should have told me about him as soon as I got here, you know you should.'

'I was just trying to do the right thing by everyone.' Aidan's voice had become very small. 'By you, and Dennis and Sandy. Dennis was never sure that you were even his daughter until he saw you that day at his restaurant.'

'What do you mean? Oh, he owns the place at Porto Limnionas?'

Aidan nodded. 'He moved back here not long after my mother left. Paloma started working with me at the clinic and we all became friends. It was only when I happened to mention him to Sandra one day that it all came out. She was petrified at the idea of seeing him. She made me promise never to tell him that she was still on the island, and now I have to live with that too.'

Holly let this new information sink in. Dennis had been here at the same time as Sandra, but the two had never seen each other. It was heartbreaking and so, so, stupid.

'So, Dennis didn't know until recently that you even knew Sandra?' Holly asked him now. Her mind was whirling all these new nuggets of information round like a gooey cake mixture as she tried to make sense of what she was hearing.

'No,' Aidan shook his head. There was a slant of sunlight across his face and Holly could see grey hairs intermingled with the black in his sideburns. 'I didn't know the full extent of what had happened between them until . . . Well, until Sandra was very frail. After she died, I asked Dennis to meet me and I told him everything – I warned him that you could arrive at any time,' he added. 'Sandra only told me about you right at the end.'

Holly stayed silent and waited for him to continue.

'As soon as you arrived on the island, I drove straight over to Porto Limnionas and told Dennis you were here, and that I would bring you to see him when the time was right. But then you went and found your own way there. He recognised you straight away, of course. You look so much like him.'

'Why didn't he say something?' Holly wasn't even sure

if Aidan knew the answer to that question, but saying it out loud made her feel better.

'I don't know.' Aidan picked up a pebble and turned it over in his big hands. 'I guess he was just freaked out. It would have scared you if he had, anyway. Some random hairy Greek man bowling over and telling you he was your long-lost daddy.'

This was probably true, but Holly glared at him all the same.

'And why are you such an expert of when the time is right all of a sudden?' she asked quietly. 'Who made you God?'

At this, Aidan sighed. Holly could tell he was losing his temper with her, but she had no intention of backing down. The rage she'd struggled to control for the past decade was dangerously close to the surface.

'Holly,' he went to reach across and touch her but then thought better of it. 'You told me how confused you were. I knew you were still hurting so badly about your mum's death. I didn't think you were strong enough to have everything else dumped in your lap. Finding out about Sandra was shocking enough, let alone suddenly gaining a dad.'

He trailed off as he saw her expression.

'You arrogant arse. You had no right to decide when I should find out about my father. I don't need some scruffy Irish idiot making my decisions for me. I'm not some damaged little puppy that needs rescuing.'

'That's exactly what you are,' Aidan interrupted, his tone decidedly cold. 'Be honest, Holly. You couldn't wait to tell me your sob story. You wanted me to look after you. You just reel people in, then push them away. You let me believe that we had a real connection – something I haven't felt about anyone for a very long time – but then you went running back to your boyfriend. It was like I didn't exist any more.'

He had stung her now, and Holly felt a mixture of anger and horrible misery bubbling like acid in the back of her throat. Why was he trying to make her feel bad about Rupert when all he'd done was run back to Clara? Her head was hurting with the effort of trying to piece everything together and she felt on the brink of letting her emotions flood out of her in a torrent. It was just too much. It was all too much.

'I trusted you,' she said, getting to her feet.

She looked down at Aidan for the final time. 'You were the first person I trusted in a very long time,' she said. 'I thought I'd found someone who really understood me, but I was being ridiculous and stupid – I see that now.'

'Don't run away.' Aidan had taken her hand. There was an edge of panic to his voice as he clutched her. 'Your family is here. You belong here.'

'How could I ever belong in a place where you are?' she asked, removing her fingers from his grip one by one. 'I don't belong anywhere. I never have and I probably never will. It's time for me to stop thinking that the grass is greener, because it isn't. It really isn't.'

He didn't try to follow her as she made her way back down the path and along the beach. Up ahead, she could see the taverna shutters swinging open and the first keen sunbathers laying their towels out across the sand. She kept waiting for the tears to fall, but none came. She knew what she had to do now, and she had to do it today.

28

Two months later . . .

After an unseasonably wet May, the sunshine had arrived in London. The grey clouds had furled apart like spring blossom and gradually shed the last of their rain, and by July the earth in the parks was hard and cracked. To the north of the city, in Camden, the surface of the canal was a deep, impenetrable blue – a perfect reflection of the clear canvas directly above – and the local geese bobbed gently on the surface, their warning squawks silenced by the calm of another flawless morning.

Holly picked her way over the discarded kebab wrappers and beer bottles on the canal path, smiling a greeting to the street cleaner as she passed. He had attached a portable radio to the side of his cart, alongside the brooms and spare rubbish sacks, and was humming along to a Bob Marley song as he went about his business. As she reached the bridge by the main set of locks, Holly felt her pumps slip slightly on the wet decking. The ground was sprayed clean every morning before the market traders set up their stalls, and there was a curtain of condensation floating in the air above the sodden cobbles.

This was Holly's favourite time of day at the market, and she found herself rising earlier each morning in her eagerness to get here. As long as she registered by 8.15 a.m. at the latest and paid her daily fee, she had a guaranteed stall spot until 7 p.m. She and Ivy had agreed to take it in turns to set up their stall, but Holly preferred to be here in plenty of time. There was something soothingly methodical about getting everything ready, and as she worked she would feel her brain begin to wake, layer by layer. A few metres from her own stall, there was a little place selling Greek coffee, and she liked to order a frappé and take it up on the narrow cobbled bridge over the canal to drink, watching the light on the water and letting herself settle into the day. Once the market started to fill up, which it tended to very quickly, the time seemed to fly past, and these few morning hours had become all the more precious as a result.

Holly was particularly excited on this bright Saturday morning because she had a big case of new stock that she'd finished off last night. Annie had stuck to her word and was still sending Holly large parcels of local Zakynthian lace, refusing to take anything except expenses from her friend back in the UK. It would have made Sandra happy, she told Holly, to see her niece creating such lovely things in the same way that she had once done. Holly had responded by spending every spare minute creating the garments that she planned to sell.

Once the stall was up and running, it hadn't taken long for word of her unique and delicately beautiful clothing to spread, and her five rails of creations were now selling out as fast as she could replenish them. Rupert's flat resembled a material bomb site most evenings, but he didn't seem to mind. On the rare evenings that he didn't have after-work drinks to attend, Holly would pack everything away into boxes and cook them dinner. Rupert adored being spoilt by her and coming home to a meal waiting on the table, and she was willing to do anything to make him happy.

Resigning from her job at Flash had been much easier than she'd thought. Her boss, Fiona the Dragon, had been surprisingly understanding and non-dragon-like, shortening her six-week notice period to two weeks, and had even promised to put Holly in touch with some of the designers that featured small collections on the website. Aliana, on the other hand, had been less delighted to see her desk buddy leave, but was somewhat comforted by Holly's promise that she would be setting up down the road in Camden Market, meaning the pair could still spend every lunch time together as they always had. Holly found herself looking forward to the middle part of each weekday, when her friend would push her way through the market crowds and entertain her with office gossip and ongoing tales of her current dating disasters.

Three weeks after starting out on her own, Holly met Ivy, who'd set up a jewellery stand on the stall right next to her. They hit it off straight away, with the slightly older Ivy going into ecstasies over Holly's stunning lace creations. Her own stuff was a mixture of handmade and vintage, and they soon discovered that Holly's clothing and Ivy's jewellery looked even better together than they did as stand-alone pieces. The next step was so obvious and so simple that they barely even discussed it. Holly & Ivy had been born shortly afterwards, and they hadn't looked back since.

Just like Holly's mum, Ivy had done a lot of travelling in her time, and Holly was reminded of how Jenny used to be in the years before her drinking took over. Now that she'd managed to let go of some of the bitterness she'd carried around with her for so long, Holly found that she could remember much more about her mum – and that it wasn't all tinged with sadness or resentment. The darkness that had hung like stained tarpaulin over her memories had lifted, and when she thought about her mum now, it wasn't followed by an automatic stab of pain or anger. For the first time since Jenny's death and those awful, dark months that followed, Holly was allowing herself to smile at those memories and feel affection towards her mother. It was a big step.

As she stood staring down into the canal, a lone drake paddled out from underneath the bridge below her, his green plumage emerald bright in the sunshine. Holly took a deep breath and swigged the last of her frappé. Sometimes the enormity of how much her life had transformed took her breath away. Just a couple of months ago, she had been lost, and now she felt as if she was on a path she'd chosen for herself. London didn't stir her senses and make her heart sing in the same way as Zakynthos, but she kept stubbornly reminding herself that she had everything she needed here in London. *Well*, whispered a voice from somewhere deep inside her, *almost everything*.

Ivy was doing a roaring trade this morning, mostly thanks to the haul of jewellery and trinkets that she'd picked up at an antique fair in the South of France the previous weekend.

'Who is this?' Holly asked when they finally reached a lull, picking up a pendant. The oval-shaped photo hanging off it was of a young man, the sepia tint and mildly ludicrous facial hair he was sporting hinting at age.

'I have no idea,' Ivy shrugged. 'I bought a whole batch of them. The *Madame* told me that they were made from an old photo of a French rugby team.'

'I think we should name them!' Holly declared, peering in turn at the ten or so other necklaces from the same set. 'This one can be Philippe.'

'And I'm going to name this one Bernard,' Ivy laughed, selecting by far the most handsome of the bunch.

'Oi! Are you ogling other men behind my back?'

It was Rupert, his hair wet from the gym and a sports bag slung across his shoulder. Ever since he'd lost Holly to her stall at weekends, her boyfriend had become a regular at the posh squash club in nearby Primrose Hill. He looked rugged, flushed and handsome, and Holly told him so, accepting his offer of coffee and cake with a grin.

'Your boyfriend is such a darling,' Ivy said, watching as Rupert made his way through the melee of tourists clustered around the food stalls.

'He is.' Holly nodded.

Things between the two of them had been good since she'd returned from Zakynthos, but she still carried around a residue of guilt about what she'd got up to behind his back. She told herself that she'd been a different person then, and that her dalliance with Aidan had happened during a moment of madness when her world felt as if it was caving in around her. Nothing good could come from him finding out – and anyway, she reminded herself, Aidan was as much ancient history as the French rugby players swinging off the end of Ivy's pendants.

She'd made a promise to herself that final morning on the island that she was going to make a go of things with

Rupert. She knew what her future would be like with him – it would be safe and predictable and she would never end up like her mother had: alone, depressed and riddled with regrets. Once she'd shoved any lingering thoughts about Zakynthos to the back of her mind, Holly had thrown herself into the Rupert project with an enthusiasm that even he seemed to find surprising. Within the first few days of returning to London, she'd given notice on her flat, and two weeks later she arrived on his doorstep with her modest possessions all packed into boxes and bags. Her only extravagance had been a brand-new sewing machine, although she still found herself missing the creaky old one she'd been forced to leave behind on the island.

Living together was a new experience for both of them, but Holly was eager enough to make it work to overlook things like wet towels on the bed, stinking trainers kicking out a hum in the hallway, or the toilet seat being left up every single morning. Rupert retreated into himself a bit during the first few weeks, even becoming slightly shy around her, but he'd relaxed as that initial time passed without mishap. Holly was so preoccupied with the stall and creating stock to sell that she didn't have much time to dwell on the state of their relationship, and Rupert too was out of the flat more than he was in it. The situation suited them both perfectly.

'Here,' Rupert pushed a moist slice of banana cake into her hand and put a takeaway coffee down beside her. 'I know you don't get time to eat when it's this busy.' He'd bought cake and coffee for Ivy too, and she beamed at him with undisguised adoration. In the beginning, Holly had been concerned that her new co-worker's dread-locked hair, swirly ethnic clothing and numerous tattoos wouldn't go down that well with her more conventional boyfriend, but the two of them had hit it off right from the start. She watched now in amusement as Ivy broke off pieces of her own cake and fed them into Rupert's open mouth.

'What are you up to this afternoon?' Holly asked, wiping crumbs from around her lips with a paper napkin.

'Oh, you know, hanging around at home, missing you,' he winked. 'Are we still on for dinner later?'

At Holly's insistence, they'd ended up staying in on the night of her thirtieth birthday at the end of June. She just hadn't felt up to celebrating at the time, and it seemed like a huge waste of resources to pay for a big party when she had a business to start. Rupert, however, had not forgotten that the occasion had as yet gone unmarked, and he was determined to treat her to a fancy night out whether she liked it or not.

'We better not be going anywhere too expensive,' she chided. Rupert merely raised an eyebrow, then leaned forward and whispered something into Ivy's ear.

'OH MY GOD!' she shrieked. 'That's the best place *ever*!'

'Only the best for my girl,' Rupert grinned, grabbing his bag from the ground and slinging it back over his shoulder. 'I'm off to tart myself up – see you tonight, gorgeous.'

The two women watched as he snaked his way through the crowds and disappeared from view, and Holly laughed as Ivy let out a deep sigh.

'What did you ever do to deserve him?' she breathed.

Holly made herself smile in response, but all she could think was: *I don't deserve him. I don't deserve him at all.*

When it reached six, Ivy shooed Holly away from the stall, insisting she go home early and get ready for her big night.

'I can pack everything up,' she told her. 'You've sold pretty much all your stock, anyway.'

It was true – Holly had made a killing. She hugged her friend farewell and headed off through the market, but instead of taking a left and heading for the station, she ducked right and made her way along the canal path towards Regent's Park. The sun was beginning to dip but the water still shone with the heat of the day. The pathway was littered with empty food wrappers, and tourists sat huddled in the few remaining patches of sunlight, their knees pulled up to avoid banging their toes on the river-boats that were moored, bow to stern, most of the way along. Holly breathed in the smell of the wood burners and admired the boxes of brightly coloured flowers that the more discerning boat owners had arranged along the rooftops of their vessels.

She left the pathway just after passing the famous London Zoo aviary, pulling a face at a peacock that was peering at her through the bars. On the opposite bank, hunting dogs padded up and down the edge of their waterside enclosure. Holly always felt it was an added cruelty to house them right next-door to the warthogs – the smell of those snuffling little creatures must drive the poor things mad with longing.

Regent's Park was alive with the hustle and bustle of

summer. Holly passed groups of friends playing volley-ball and Frisbee, families sharing picnics and just about every breed of dog imaginable nosing their way individu-ally through the longer grass by the boating lake. Phelan would love it here, she thought, before quickly pushing the image of the silly red setter out of her mind. There was an ancient willow tree lazily trailing its branches into the water, and Holly found a shady spot on the grass nearby. For a few minutes, she sat and watched as the sun-light danced through the tangle of leaves and warmed the round bellies of the daisies, which were spread out in a chaotic mess by her feet. Nowadays, all she seemed to do was try her best not to think about Zakynthos, but it was always there, sitting like a smudge of light in the corner of her subconscious – there didn't seem to be any way of ignoring it. Shaking her head to break the trance, Holly took out her mobile phone.

The first time she and Dennis had spoken on the phone, the awkwardness between them had been palp-able. A lifetime spent serving British tourists had provided her father with very good English, so that wasn't an issue; it was more that they talked around what they really wanted to say. Holly had persevered, though, determined that she and Dennis would manage to maintain some sort of relationship, even if it was going to take a lot of time and effort.

She'd made the first call just a few days after arriving back from Zakynthos, and now made sure they spoke to one another at least once a week. Dennis always answered, and increasingly he sounded delighted to hear from her. He was only just back at work now after the heart attack,

and complained to Holly at length about how much business he'd missed out on by being ill during the peak
summer months. It wasn't true, of course, as his wife Paloma was now working all hours at the restaurant in Porto
Limnionas instead of at the clinic, but it was the Greek way
to have a nice old moan – a fact that Holly had picked up
on pretty quickly since she started making her weekly calls.

They discussed his childhood, his work and, most
often, Maria. Holly missed her half-sister with a surprising yearning that she felt might break her apart at times,
so it was a huge comfort to hear what she'd been up to.
According to Dennis, she was just like he had been as a
child – cheeky, spoilt and liable to get into trouble on a
daily basis. It made Holly love her all the more.

The only subjects Holly and her father did not discuss
were anything to do with how she was conceived, and
Aidan. Holly had no idea what Dennis did or didn't know
about the situation, but he seemed to respect the fact that
the subject of Aidan was off limits. She suspected that this
was due to the man himself warning Dennis not to mention him, but whatever the reason she was relieved. She
didn't want to think about Aidan, let alone talk about him.

It took a while for Dennis to answer today, and when
he did the line sounded scratchy.

'I am on my boat!' he told Holly proudly, and she giggled at the mental image.

'I am happy for you,' she told him, and they slipped
easily into chit-chat about the weather over in Greece and
how many fish he'd caught that day.

'I want to cook my fish for you,' he said after a time. 'It
is the best fish in the whole of Greece.'

Holly laughed again. There was nothing quite like a Greek man's humility.

'When are you come?' he demanded.

There was an awkward silence and Holly chewed her bottom lip.

'Soon,' she murmured. 'I promise very soon.'

Dennis took a deep breath and Holly thought she could hear the sounds of water lapping against the sides of his boat. 'I have things to say,' he began, clearly struggling. 'I need to say these in person. I do not want to say them on the phone. You understand?'

Holly did understand, because she felt exactly the same way. She knew that he wanted to tell her about her mother, about what had happened all those years ago, but the idea of it still scared her. She was content at the moment, and the prospect of rocking the proverbial boat did not appeal. She wanted to feel like she knew this man better before he told her things about her mother.

'Holly?'

She had been nodding into the phone without speaking, and now she hurriedly said yes, first in English and then in Greek.

'I am very busy with work,' she added. 'But I will come and see you all. I promise.'

This seemed to do the trick, and Dennis let the subject drop, launching instead into a long rant about how one of his older sisters was fussing around him like his mother and trying to make him sell his boat.

'It is the most important thing that I love,' he said, before laughing and adding, 'after my daughters. And my wife!'

Holly laughed nervously. Dennis was her father and she'd managed to come to terms with that in her head, but it still felt beyond weird to hear him refer to her as his daughter.

'What you do tonight?' he asked her now. She realised that it must already be past 8.30 p.m. in Zakynthos, and asked him when he was planning to head for dry land.

'You are as bad as my sister,' he bellowed with laughter. 'I am a big boy. I am happier on the water than on the land, like Caretta caretta turtle.'

Holly didn't want to tell him that she had a romantic evening planned with Rupert, who they never really talked about either, so instead she muttered something vague about getting an early night. This earned her another playful rebuke from the other end of the line. According to Dennis, a young thing such as her should be out having fun, not sitting on the sofa staring at the TV. 'It will rot your mind,' he warned, with more guffaws. 'Maria is only watching one hour in the morning of television, then she is at the restaurant or going for swimming.'

It sounded like an idyllic way to spend your time.

'I should go,' she told Dennis, not bothering to elaborate. One of the nice things about the Greeks, she'd learnt, was that they didn't require excuses. If she needed to get off the phone, then that was that. Dennis thanked her warmly for calling and made her promise to ring again the following week. For a long time after he'd hung up, she sat still in the same spot, trying to picture him as he pulled up the anchor and turned the boat back towards the shore. Zakynthos was still so alive in her mind that she could conjure up even the smell of the ocean if she really concentrated. She'd fallen in love with the place, and getting over it was proving much more difficult than she'd anticipated.

Her phone rang again as she made her way back through the park, but this time it was Aliana.

'You won't bloody believe what that Andy arsehole has done now!' was how she started the conversation.

Holly grinned. Aliana and her disastrous love life was just the distraction she needed.

29

'Did I mention you look gorgeous tonight?'

'Only about twenty times.' Holly reached across and took Rupert's hand. He had insisted that they splash out on a taxi to take them to the mystery dinner destination and Holly could see the neon lights of the West End glaring in through the windows.

'Where are we going?' she pleaded.

'You'll see,' was all he would say.

When they pulled up outside a wall of stained-glass windows a few minutes later, Holly laughed with pleasure. No wonder Ivy had been so impressed – it was her restaurant namesake.

'The Ivy?' she beamed at him. 'I've never been here before.'

Rupert took her arm as the restaurant doorman stepped forward to open the cab door for them. 'I know,' he grinned. 'I thought it was about time you did.' He was looking very handsome this evening, in a navy shirt that made his eyes light up and grey trousers that fitted so snugly across the bottom that they made Holly's eyes light up too.

They were ushered straight through a small cloakroom area and across to their table, which seemed to be the only one left empty in the busy dining room. Despite the fact that the restaurant was full to capacity and the waiting staff were buzzing around like bluebottles, The Ivy still managed to afford its guests a real sense of intimacy. The overhead lighting was muted, and a candle in the centre of their table was lit almost as soon as they sat down. Holly spotted Jonathan Ross sitting in a far corner and pointed him out to a grinning Rupert.

'Play it cool, yeah?' he joked, laughing at the look on her face. She supposed he dined in places like this all the time with work, but Holly had never seen a real celebrity in the flesh before. She was glad she'd worn the dress that Rupert had bought her on their very first date – she had the feeling one of her own creations may not have fitted the setting quite as well.

'Champagne, please!' Rupert told their waiter, who had already brought them water and bread and taken their coats away to be properly stored.

'This place is amazing.' Holly sipped her water and smiled at him. 'Thank you so much for bringing me here.'

'Like I said, you deserve it.' He crinkled his eyes across the table. He looked so excited and happy – it was infectious.

They took their time ordering, with Holly eventually agreeing to try the oysters as long as she was allowed a glass of red wine afterwards. Rupert rather predictably chose the steak for his main, while Holly opted for skate wings with a brown shrimp and butter sauce. She'd been craving fish ever since her conversation with Dennis, remembering how amazing the fresh fish had tasted every time she'd ordered it back on the island.

Rupert told her about a new client he was working with who had started up a women's lingerie business from scratch. Apparently this woman was Italian and only twenty-five. Holly whistled in appreciation, thinking what Aliana would say if she was here. Something along the lines of, 'Aren't you jealous that your boyfriend is spending all his time with a hot young Italian bird?' But Holly didn't think that Rupert would ever stoop so low as to cheat. He was a better person than her.

The conversation moved on to her business, and Holly told him how well she'd done that day on the market.

'You should think about expanding,' he urged. 'I'm sure Flavia would meet us for lunch and give you some pointers.'

'Maybe one day,' she smiled. 'But I'm quite happy with how everything's going at the moment. I don't want to rush into anything.'

'Well, whatever you think is best.' He clinked his Champagne flute against hers. 'I think you're set to be a huge success.'

The first bottle was gone in no time and Rupert ordered a second, telling Holly to hurry up and drink her large glass of red so they could have another toast. It wasn't long before her eyelids started to feel heavy and her speech began to slur.

'I think I'm pished,' she informed Rupert happily. By comparison, he seemed completely fine.

'My little lightweight,' he joked, stroking her wrist.

Rupert hadn't seemed very surprised when Holly arrived back from Zakynthos and told him, through a flood of tears, that she'd discovered her biological father. After the shock news of what had really happened to her mother, it appeared that nothing could shake him – not even a long-lost Greek father turning up close to death in a hospital bed. She hadn't told him about her weekly phone conversations with Dennis, though, and she wasn't really sure why. She wondered briefly if her dad talked to anyone about their chats over in Greece – and if so, who.

When Rupert accepted dessert menus, Holly shook her head. 'I'm full,' she wailed. 'Don't make me!'

'Don't be such a wimp.' Rupert topped up her glass. The bottom of the Champagne bottle was wet and the freezing droplets fell on to her bare knees.

'We'll have two chocolate fondants,' he told the waiter, who had magically appeared next to them.

'Very good, sir.'

'I thought we could go and visit my parents next weekend,' Rupert said now, causing Holly to choke on her bubbly.

'What about the stall?' she spluttered.

'Ivy will cover for you.' He pulled a face like an injured puppy. 'They really want to meet you again, and my brother is coming too – I haven't seen him for months.'

'I just don't know if it's . . .' She paused as two chocolate fondants were put down in front of them with a flourish, ' . . . a good idea at the moment.'

'I think you'll change your mind.' He sounded very confident. Holly picked up her spoon and put it down again. There was something about his manner tonight, a certain smugness, that was beginning to grate. She told herself very sternly to stop being such a reactionary drunk. They could talk about this visit tomorrow, when she hadn't consumed two bottles of Champagne and a pint of red wine.

'This is absolutely delicious,' Rupert informed her, licking the gooey inside of his dessert off the sides of his spoon.

She really was full, but perhaps this pudding would help her to sober up a bit. Taking hold of her spoon again, Holly struck it deep into the heart of the fondant, only to encounter something hard and unyielding in the middle.

'There's something in my pud—' she began, but then stopped short as she turned to where Rupert was now kneeling beside her.

'Oh my God!' she gasped, her hands flying up to her mouth.

'Fish it out then.' Rupert's voice was shaking slightly.

Very carefully, Holly used her spoon to ease what she could now see was a diamond ring out from the depths of chocolate goo. Even covered in sauce, it glittered beautifully in the candlelight.

'Holly Wright . . .' Rupert began. He'd taken her hand now and people were peering discreetly at them from neighbouring tables. The waiter, who was standing off to one side, looked as though he might start cartwheeling across the carpet with joy. Holly stared into the remains of her fondant and concentrated very hard on not throwing up her oysters, skate wings and gallons of booze.

'Please look at me.' Rupert had leaned forward until his chest was pressed against her leg. She could feel his hand turning clammy in her own and sniffed loudly to stop the tears from falling.

'Please sit down,' she pleaded quietly. 'We can't do this here.'

'Holly, for God's sake, I'm trying to propose to you.'

He said it through gritted teeth, but several people turned to look at them again. If ever there was a time for the floor to open up and swallow her, Holly thought, now was it. Rupert clearly wasn't going to get up off his knee, and now he was reaching across with a napkin to pick up the ring.

'Please stop,' she whispered. The tears that she'd been trying so hard to hold back were starting to fall, taking her carefully applied mascara with them. The waiter let out a small, uncomfortable cough and backed away, while a large middle-aged woman two tables away actually shook her head in dismay.

'Holly, I know you're scared. But I really love you and I think you really love me. I want to make you happy for the rest of your life.'

This should be the happiest moment of my life, Holly thought, at the same time wondering seriously if she could make a dash for the front door and flag down a taxi in the time it took Rupert to get up off the carpet and chase after her.

'You're the most amazing person I know,' he went on. 'I want you to be my wife.'

He'd dipped the corner of his napkin into his water glass and cleaned the ring, which he was now holding up right under her nose. The diamond was obscenely large and Holly saw that he'd had today's date engraved on the inside of the gold band. Her heart should be bursting with joy, but instead she could feel it shattering into pieces.

'You're being silly,' she tried instead, shaking her head to stop the tears.

'I'm not being silly, Hols. I've never felt less silly in my life,' he said, pulling a slightly sheepish expression. He was on his knees on the floor of The Ivy, after all, and still seemed absolutely in denial about the fact that she was stalling.

'I think we should talk about this later,' she whispered. 'This isn't the right place to have this conversation.'

Rupert's loving gaze dropped a fraction as he took this in, and Holly was sure she felt her heart actually break. There was a time when she used to imagine this moment happening, and in the fantasy she would always be thrilled. She would fall into his arms and they would live happily ever after. But a fantasy was exactly what it had always been. She had been trying to love him for so long, she hadn't even noticed that she never did.

'We don't need to have a conversation,' he told her now. 'All you have to say is yes. We can sort out all the details later, when we're alone, but right now I just really want you to say yes, Holly. I need you to say yes so I can get up off the floor and kiss you.'

'Please,' she started to cry again. She didn't want to have to tell him the truth here, when he was in such a vulnerable position. Not with all these people staring at them, willing her to put the poor man out of his misery.

'Holly, come on now.' Rupert was starting to get irritated. The apples of his cheeks had turned an angry pink and there was a hardness in his eyes that hadn't been there before. 'You can't leave me down here all night. I know you love me. You do love me, right?'

Holly swallowed.

'Answer me, Holly.'

She shook her head and tried to reach for his hand to pull him up, but he jerked backwards.

345

'There's something you're not telling me,' he guessed, all traces of affection now gone from his face.

She nodded her head. 'I do have something to tell you,' she said in a small voice. 'But I really think we should go home first.'

'*I* really think you should just tell me right here, right now,' he demanded. His face was a mixture of anger and fear, and Holly shut her eyes again to block it all out. She thought of Aidan, of how he had run his big hands into her hair, pulled her face towards his own and kissed her with a ferocity that made her chest burn.

'Holly, I mean it. You bloody well tell me right now!'

For a few seconds, they just stared at one another, Rupert challenging and Holly defeated, and then she gave in.

'I cheated on you.'

The ring quivered in his hand.

'What?'

'I slept with someone else.'

Rupert finally stopped leaning towards her and sat back on his heels. The ring was still in his hand, but he let it fall slowly into his lap. He looked utterly deflated and Holly felt self-loathing flood over her.

'Who?'

'Please can we just talk about this at home?'

'WHO?' His shout caused several diners to jump in their seats. The waiter scuttled towards them looking concerned, but Rupert held up a hand to stop him.

'This really isn't the place,' she persisted again. 'Let's just go hom—'

'No. I want you to tell me the bastard's name right NOW.'

346

How can he not know? Holly thought, remembering how awkward she'd been that day in the garden, when Aidan and Clara had appeared and invited them out to lunch.

'It was Aidan.' She said it as quietly as she dared, and Rupert snapped his head towards her irritably.

'Who? Stop whispering and speak up, will you? I'm sure everyone here is just dying to know.'

'Stop it.' Holly was properly crying now. Everyone in the restaurant must be disgusted with her, but none of them could hate her as much as she hated herself.

'Aidan,' she said again. 'Aidan from Zakynthos. My neighbour.'

There was an awful silence as Rupert glared at her. She knew he was picturing Aidan in his mind, picturing the two of them together, and slotting all the pieces into place.

'So, that's why you were so cold towards me when I arrived in Greece?' he said slowly, a look of horrible rea-lisation crossing his face. 'It was because you'd been shagging your neighbour the whole time.'

'It wasn't the whole time,' she said at once, realising a fraction too late that it was definitely not the right thing to say.

'Oh, well, that makes it all right then.' Rupert laughed, but it was a nasty, hard sound.

'Of course it doesn't.' Holly dared herself to look at him. 'I'm sorry I never told you, but I was scared and—'

'You were *scared*?' he scoffed, and took an aggressive swig of her wine. 'You were so scared that you rolled over on to your back as soon as my back was turned. Yeah, that sounds exactly right.'

There was barely a sound in the dining room now. A few less scrupulous guests had even turned their chairs so that they could enjoy a proper view. Holly hated all of them, but she hated herself more.

'It didn't mean anything,' she lied. 'It was just a moment of madness. I'd been drinking and there was a storm and—'

'Wow,' Rupert interrupted, staring at her as though she was a total stranger. 'You really are your mother's daughter, aren't you? Didn't she cheat with her own twin sister's boyfriend?'

Holly felt like she'd been slapped, but what could she say? He was absolutely right – she had done exactly what her mum had done. She was no better than Jenny Wright had been at her very worst. She was a lost cause, an evil person and a waste of everyone's time.

'I'm so sorry,' she said. Rupert was too angry with her to be upset yet, but she knew he would give in to the tears later. She couldn't bear to think of him being in pain. *You should have thought about that before*, she scolded herself. It was no good being sorry for it now, all these weeks later.

'I'm sorry too.' He finally sat back down in his chair. 'I'm sorry that I ever met you in the first place. I'm sorry that I believed you were special, and I'm sorry that I ever fell in love with you. I'm sorry that I planned this night and bought you that ring. I'm sorry that I called my parents today and told them that I was going to propose to the woman of my dreams.' At this, his voice cracked. The woman two tables away sobbed loudly into her napkin and there was an assorted chorus of tuts from every corner of the room. Even Jonathan Ross hated her.

'Aidan means nothing to me,' she continued, wincing internally at the lie. 'I was going mad over there. All that stuff about my auntie and my mum, and inheriting that house – it just made me crazy. I know it's not an excuse, but I want you to know that I never set out to hurt or deceive you.'

It seemed bizarre to Holly now that she'd even entertained the idea that she was falling in love with Aidan. There had been moments, of course, when the intensity between them had reached a peak and she'd thought what she was feeling was real, but then he'd betrayed her with his lies and all she'd felt was angry and ridiculous. Her dear, sweet Rupert was so much better than Aidan in so many ways, and here she was, throwing him away. What was the matter with her?

'I would never cheat on you, Holly,' he said. 'You said you loved me, but how could you do this to a person you love? To me?'

'I don't know.' She shook her head and rubbed the tears off her cheeks. 'But I can't lie to you any more. I don't want to be like my mother – what she did caused so many people so much pain, I can't make the same mistakes.'

'You already did,' Rupert reminded her, but he'd stopped shouting. Holly wasn't sure this defeated and broken version of him was any better than the angry one. This Rupert scared her.

'I'm so sorry,' she whispered, hating the emptiness in her voice. She heard the nearby woman let out a disbelieving snort.

'You know what?' Rupert raised weary eyes to her. 'I could probably try to forgive you for cheating on me with that weird Irish bloke, but only if I believed for a second that you actually loved me.'

She wanted to fall at his feet and tell him that she did love him, that the whole thing had been a mistake and that it was him she wanted to grow old with, but it just wasn't the truth.

'You really don't love me at all, do you? For the first year we were together, you weren't even being yourself around me. I trusted you all that time, but you never trusted me – not even enough to be honest about your past or anything. It's like you told yourself not to fall for me, so you didn't.'

He'd got it so spot on that for a moment Holly was rendered speechless.

'I didn't tell myself,' she whispered. 'I just didn't know that I could love you. It sounds mad, I know, but it's the truth.'

'How can I believe anything you say now?' He sounded almost regretful. Holly could feel him slipping away from her and she felt the panic mounting in her chest. 'Please don't do this,' she begged, no longer caring that everyone in The Ivy was staring at them. 'I can't bear for it to end like this. I can change.'

Rupert sighed and sat back in his chair. 'That's just it, Holly. I don't want you to change – I've never wanted that. All I wanted was the real you. Why do you think you have to become someone else?'

'I didn't. I don't,' she lied, stumbling over her words.

Rupert just stared at her, shaking his head. The sadness in his eyes was unbearable, and Holly started furiously twisting the napkin that was still lying in her lap.

She heard him stand up and watched, helplessly, as he pushed the chair back under the table. For a few seconds they just looked at each other, then he turned to go.

'Do you have somewhere you can stay tonight?' he asked, almost as an afterthought. Holly simply nodded, then watched in silence as he weaved his way around the tables, through the curtain into the cloakroom, and out of her life.

30

'The hottest summer since records began!' screamed the tabloids.

'Half-price offers on all barbecues!' yelled the voice-over man on the Argos TV adverts.

London was sweltering. When a balmy June eased rain-lessly into a humid July, the initial joy of the capital's inhabitants descended rapidly into a mild panic. It was too hot now, everyone moaned. Commuters were passing out on the underground and the Camden drunks were peaking earlier every day, having been woken by the relentless heat and then been tempted by the thirst-quenching qualities of a cold can of cider. Down on Lockside, Holly and Ivy perched soundlessly in the shade of their stall, any conversation they may have had bull-dozed out of them by the rocketing temperatures. Holly could only think how much nicer it would be if she was back in Zakynthos, where this sort of weather was catered for far more efficiently. She had yet to hear anything about a potential buyer for Sandra's house.

'I'm going to get some more water,' she croaked at Ivy, who merely fanned her face in reply. While the weather certainly brought the crowds to the market, nobody seemed to be spending money on anything other than hats, ice lollies and sun lotion. It had been a very slow day.

Holly took her drink to her favourite spot up on the

bridge. The sky was the colour of a blue Slush Puppie and there was a clump of clouds nestled fatly in the west.

She took out her phone and scrolled again to the last message she'd received from Rupert. It was nothing groundbreaking, just a thank you for leaving the keys at the reception of his work followed by a 'take care'. Holly kept waiting to fall apart, for the realisation to sink in and drag her under, but it had never come. After that first awful night, when Rupert had walked out and left her in The Ivy and Holly had wandered around Soho in a daze, tears all over her face, until she plucked up enough courage to call Ivy and beg for a bed for the night, she hadn't felt anything other than a kind of numbness and – something she hadn't admitted to anyone – a small amount of relief. She wasn't sure whether it was finally letting go of her secret about what had happened in Zakynthos or if it was being released from a relationship that she knew in her heart wasn't right, but she did feel lighter somehow, as if she could spread metaphorical wings and take off in flight to anywhere she liked.

She hadn't, though – she'd stayed put. It would have been easy to pack up and run away, but she didn't want to abandon her business, or Ivy. And where would she go, anyway? There was only one place her head ever took her, and she didn't feel ready to face what was waiting for her there yet. She sensed that her journey, as she loathed describing it – even to herself – had led her to where she was now for a reason. She was beginning to think of fate in a similar way to Hope the fairy, or her nasty little Insomnia Troll, as a tricky, mischievous little creature throwing obstacles in her path wherever she went. She couldn't really be angry with it, though, or even afraid. There was no battling the inevitable.

Her phone started ringing in her hand, startling her so much that she almost dropped it into the canal below.

'We still on for tonight?' Aliana always got straight to the point.

'Yes,' Holly forced herself to sound more enthusiastic than she felt.

'I'll come and get you from the stall,' she was informed. 'And I'm broke, so the first two rounds are on you, right?'

'I guess so,' Holly replied. 'You know I can never say no to you.'

'Too right,' Aliana chirped, and Holly had to laugh.

'Do you think I should get an epilator?'

Aliana had stretched her bare legs out across the bench seat and was picking at an ingrown hair in disgust. They had pitched up in the Pembroke pub, not far from Primrose Hill, and the beer garden was full to overflowing with rowdy groups of mildly inebriated locals.

Holly reached across and picked a stray eyelash off Aliana's cheek, blowing it swiftly into the air. 'There,' she said. 'I've made a wish that you'll never grow hair on your legs again.'

'If you say it out loud, it'll never come true,' Aliana shrieked, but she was laughing.

Holly stared into the bottom of her glass. She had something to tell her friend, but she needed to wait for the right moment. If she knew Aliana, the reaction was going to be a very loud one.

'Aren't you going to ask me?' Aliana said suddenly, nudging Holly under the table with her sandalled foot.

'Ask you what?' Holly was genuinely at a loss.

'I saw Rupert last night.'

'How would I have known that?' she asked. 'Is he well? That's all I want to know.'

'Why do you even care?' Aliana was aghast. 'He walked out and left you alone in the bloody Ivy. I'd say that's unforgivable!'

'I deserved it.' Holly reached for another of the triple-cooked chips they'd ordered. They were greasy and going cold, but she swallowed it anyway before continuing. 'He still paid the bill before he left, even though I'd just gone and broken his heart. I'd say that makes him probably the most decent man alive.'

Aliana pulled a face. 'I'm glad you feel that way,' she said.

'What is it?' Holly pressed, noticing her friend's slightly sheepish expression.

'He's started seeing someone.'

She'd expected to feel a stab of pain at the news when it inevitably came, but now that it had happened Holly realised that she felt fine. In fact, she almost felt happy – now she could finally let go of some of the suffocating guilt that she'd been lugging around with her like a bag of wet cement.

'I'm happy for him,' she said.

'She's a total airhead,' Aliana went on. 'Hangs off his every word, so of course he's smitten. Not that he wasn't with you,' she added quickly.

Holly laughed and took a swig of her drink. Aliana was still looking mutinous, although Holly suspected it might have more to do with the fact that Rupert had moved on with someone that wasn't her. She had always known that Aliana had a huge crush on him, even if they had never openly discussed it.

'Are you missing Zakynthos?' Aliana asked now, shocking Holly with such a rare flash of insight.

'So much,' Holly blurted, slapping a hand over her mouth when she realised what she'd said.

Aliana laughed and wagged a finger. 'You're allowed to miss the place, you know? You can even go and live there if you miss it that much. Why the hell would you want to live here anyway, when you have a house in Zante?'

For a brief second, Holly felt her heart fill up with pleasure at the thought of it, but then she shook her head.

'Something actually happened today that means I really have to stay here,' she teased, laughing as Aliana's eyes widened with intrigue.

'Well . . .' Her friend was literally bouncing on the spot.

Holly waited for her to stop jogging the table. 'This guy came to the stall earlier and told me he works as a scout for an upcoming designer. He'd had a meeting with Fiona, of all people.'

Aliana's eyebrows went up so far they were in danger of colliding with a passing plane.

'I know! She actually showed him a few items of mine that she had photos of on her iPad and told him to come and seek me out. I feel guilty for ever bad-mouthing her now. Anyway, I talked to this bloke for a while and then he wandered off again and came back ten minutes later with his boss in tow. He then took a look at my stuff and, well, he wants me to make some garments for a show he's got coming up and—'

'THAT'S AMAZING!' Aliana yelled, leaping up from her seat and spilling a good portion of Holly's drink in the process.

'I know!' Holly laughed. 'I only have three weeks to create five outfits completely from scratch, so I'm going to be very busy – but I think it could be really good for me, and for the business. Apparently he dedicates a portion of each of his shows to unknown designers and, well, people like me. I don't really think of myself as a designer, but I suppose I am.'

'What's his name, this bloke?' Aliana asked, sitting back down.

'Anton Bazanov. He's Russian.'

'Not *the* Anton Bazanov, of AB Couture?' Aliana was practically frothing at the mouth. 'He's only, like, the biggest up-and-coming designer on the planet!'

'I thought the name sounded familiar,' Holly grinned.

'I can't believe Anton Bazanov has asked *you* to be part of his show.' Aliana sounded almost disgusted. 'And he's bloody gorgeous! If I didn't love you so much then I'd be insane with jealousy. In fact, sod that – I *am* insane with jealousy. And I hate you very much,' she added, making them both laugh.

The summer heatwave strode confidently from July into August, causing newsreaders to talk fervently about hose-pipe bans and the risk of forest fires. Holly woke up most mornings to discover that her mum's world map had fallen off the wall in her tiny studio flat because the Blu-Tack had melted during the night. She'd added her own, different-coloured pin to the tiny green dot of Zakynthos, and spent a lot of time just lying on her narrow bed gazing up at the map, as she knew Jenny must have done once upon a time, dreaming of all the places she could explore.

Her fingers were blistered from all the extra hours' sewing she'd put in to get everything ready for the AB Couture show, which was taking place that evening at a very trendy pop-up venue in Hoxton, East London. Anton had popped to the stall in person just a few days ago to check that she was on track and pass on all the details.

The Russian had told Holly that she must arrive at the venue no later than 4 p.m., because she needed time to set up and meet the models who would be wearing her 'collection', as he referred to it.

'I can recognise zee talent ven I see it,' he explained, his glorious Russian growl making the hairs on her arms stand up. 'I vant to offer chance to all zee talented people I meet.' And what a chance it was.

Hoxton Gallery was situated in a disused railway arch at the Old Street end of Kingsland Road, which connected the borough of Hackney to the City. Aside from clearing out all the fixtures and rubble, the space had been left largely unchanged, with exposed brickwork curving up from floor to half-moon ceiling. As well as fitting in perfectly with the hip simplicity so adored by the capital's fashionistas, the linear design also provided a desirable blank canvas to whoever rented it out for the evening.

Anton Bazanov, Holly had learnt after many a late-night

Googling session, was a big fan of simple and understated designs when it came to his clothing (save for the extravagant hats he liked to wear), and this had translated into the layout of tonight's show too. Rather than hang up fairy-light bunting and erect speakers the size of small cars, he'd opted for a plain black runway with one large screen at the far end, and a few age-stained mirrors propped up between the rows of chairs. An industrial-sized fan was standing at the end of the catwalk waiting to be switched on, and everywhere Holly looked, Anton's army of staff were all busy scurrying about with clothing bags, cases of make-up and complicated-looking hairdryers. There was a buzz of excited expectation in the air, and Holly felt the telltale bubbles of nervousness start to work their way up from her belly to her throat.

'Who are you?' barked a bored-sounding voice.

Holly jumped guiltily. 'I'm, er, Holly. Holly Wright.'

The woman frowned and ran a slim finger down the clipboard she was holding. Her nails had been filed into sharp points and were painted black to match the polished catwalk.

'Oh, you're *that* Holly – the designer. You should have said. Follow me.'

Holly followed, thinking privately that she bloody well *had* said, but guessing that it was probably best to remain mute. Her head was spinning as she took in the scenes of organised chaos unfolding around her. Clipboard woman led her past the catwalk and lifted the edge of a black curtain to let Holly pass underneath. The back of the room had been obscured on both sides and separated by clothing rails into rectangular sections of varying sizes. It was into one of the smaller areas that Holly was told to set up and wait for her models. Clipboard handed her a schedule, pointed vaguely to where the toilets were and scurried away again, narrowly missing a man with bright green hair who was balancing precariously on a stepladder.

'I know what you're thinking, and you're right – we are all bonkers.'

Holly turned to find a man standing in her little alcove. He was neck-achingly tall and his hair was bleached the colour of lemon curd.

'Are you one of my models?' Holly guessed.

He nodded, extending a long, thin hand in her direction. 'I'm Bernie,' he told her, 'but everyone calls me B. And I don't mind at all, because that's what all Beyoncé's friends call her, and she's the queen of the bloody world.'

They shook hands and Holly told him who she was, which turned out to be completely unnecessary.

'I've done my homework on you already,' Bernie grinned, waving his finger at her like a conductor's baton. 'You used to work at Flash, but now you have your own stall in Camden, right?'

Holly hated the idea of anyone doing 'homework' on her, but she supposed in this instance it was better to appear flattered.

'I know – I'm a total stalker!' Bernie laughed again, running his hand through his spiky thatch of hair.

'I had no idea that anyone knew who I was,' Holly told him honestly.

'Babe, you're AB's darling. One of his star acts! To get a slot in his London show is just, you know, a very special honour.'

'I very much doubt I'm a star act,' she said, turning away to hide her blushes and beginning to hang up her modest collection of garments. Even after all these months, the smell and texture of the Zakynthian lace made the hairs on the back of her neck stand up.

'Seriously!' Bernie squealed, peering at her through narrowed eyes. 'Word on the catwalk is that you're his latest big discovery.' As he said the last part, he brought his long fingers up and mimed inverted commas. Holly felt her earlier nerves swiftly intensifying.

'Oh wow, babe, now I see what all the fuss is about.' Bernie was holding up a silk blouse with intricate lace panels. 'These really are something special. I can't wait to feel this lace against my skin.'

'Thank you,' Holly smiled at him. 'This is the first time I've done something like this, and I'm just a bit . . .' She trailed off, shrugging at his bemused expression.

'Come on, babe!' he told her, grabbing her clammy hand. 'I'm going to give you the grand tour.'

After Holly had been introduced to at least twenty other models, a handful of make-up artists and two very harassed-looking stylists, Bernie led her right to the back of the room where a makeshift bar had been set up.

'Nonsense, darling,' he scolded when she refused the miniature bottle of Champagne he thrust at her. It was the norm to be absolutely hammered at these things, he assured her, sticking a pink straw in the neck of her bottle.

According to the schedule, her collection would be showcased after the main event, along with three other designers that Anton had deemed worthy. One of these fortunate souls arrived not long after Holly and was led into the alcove right next to hers. She guessed from his appearance and accent that he was Russian too, and his speciality was hats. Holly could see at once why Anton had fallen for his outlandish designs.

The room was steadily filling up and the models were wandering around in various states of undress, each one with a straw clamped firmly to their bottom lip. Bernie was right: there was an awful lot of drinking going on. When Anton himself emerged through the curtain to loud cheers, he had his own bottle of Champagne clutched firmly in one hand. Holly tried to catch his eye as he passed, then chided herself for thinking that he'd have time to exchange pleasantries. She had hung up all her clothes in the correct order and everything was neatly labelled. Clipboard had been back round with a wad of Post-it notes bearing names and stuck them clumsily on each of the hangers. One of the models was called Clara, Holly noticed, immediately curling her lip in disgust. She knew it was grossly unfair of her to hate the woman that Aidan loved, but it made her feel better all the same. She'd been haunted for months by memories of the stunning girl he'd dangled in front of her face, more often than not when she was examining her own far curvier and less statuesque figure in the mirror.

At that moment a voice broke through her reverie. 'Holly, is that you?'

That faint Irish accent . . .

Those endless legs . . .

That hair . . .

It couldn't be.

31

'It *is* you!' Clara clapped her hands together.

Holly was doing a very good impression of a goldfish. How could Clara be here? *The* Clara. The very same ridiculously attractive woman who tortured her memories of her time in Zakynthos. How could this actually be happening?

'You look very pale,' Clara said kindly, stepping forward and putting a slender arm around Holly's shoulders. 'Are you feeling okay?'

'Yes.' It came out as a squeak.

Holly coughed loudly. 'Yes,' she said again. 'I'm fine. Just very surprised to see you, that's all.'

Clara furrowed her blemish-free brow as she stood back. 'Not that much of a shock, I hope?' she laughed. 'I am a model, after all.'

'Of course you are.' It took every ounce of self-control Holly possessed not to let any sarcasm creep into her voice. Putting her miniature bottle of plonk down, she pinched herself hard on the arm. Nope, she wasn't in the middle of a nightmare.

'These are gorgeous.' Clara was now rifling through the clothes on the rail. 'Did you make all of them? You're so clever, like.'

Why did she have to be so bloody nice?

Anton suddenly emerged in an eye-watering cloud of spicy aftershave and Champagne fumes.

'You have met each ozzer!' he crowed, clearly delighted. 'Zee muse and zee talent. You are my ladies of zee night!'

He made a big show of hugging them both, almost causing his hat – which today was exceedingly tall and wrapped in purple lace – to fall off his head.

'Isn't he the best?' Clara crooned as Anton swept away. 'I met him in Paris last year and he's demanded that I do every single one of his shows ever since.'

'That's great,' replied Holly, thinking that it was anything but. If, by any chance, Anton wanted her to continue working with him after today, would that mean she'd have to face Clara at every turn? She'd done a pretty decent job of not thinking about Aidan so far, but this was too much. It occurred to her then with a wave of accompanying nausea that he might even be here, in this very room, ready to cheer his girlfriend on as she strutted down the catwalk. Holly sucked her Champagne straw extra hard.

'This lace is from Zakynthos,' Clara stated. She was holding a pair of embroidered shorts labelled with her name and was rubbing the delicate fabric between her fingers.

Holly felt a coldness creeping through her; she didn't want to talk about Zakynthos with this girl. It was *her* place.

'Are you going back anytime soon?' Clara asked. She was either completely oblivious to Holly's blatant discomfort or choosing to ignore it.

'Maybe.'

'I'm sure Aidan would like to see you again.'

'I'm sure he wouldn't,' Holly snapped back, far louder than she'd intended. Clara looked round at her in alarm.

'What's the matter? I thought you two were pretty close?'

'Not as close as you two are,' Holly was appalled to hear herself sneer.

Clara looked incredulous. 'Well, I suppose not, but then he is my brother. We're pretty close, as siblings go, but then we didn't even meet each other until . . . Holly? Are you okay?'

Holly had sat down abruptly on the floor and Clara crouched down next to her. She was wearing a minuscule navy blue playsuit with a pattern of little white bunnies all over it. Holly swallowed bile.

'You're Aidan's sister?' she managed at last.

'Yeah, his half-sister.' Clara sat back on her heels. Even when her legs were bent underneath her, her thighs were still about a third of the size of Holly's. 'But you already know that.'

Holly shook her head. 'I didn't know. I thought you and him were . . . Well, you know. I thought you were his ex-girlfriend.'

At this, Clara actually started laughing. It was a deep and filthy laugh too, as if Sid James from the *Carry On* films was nestling secretly in the back of her throat. 'You thought I was shagging my own brother?' she bellowed, tears of mirth streaking her immaculate make-up.

'Sorry,' she spluttered, catching sight of the look on Holly's face. 'But that's the funniest thing I've heard in ages, like.'

'I feel stupid,' Holly admitted. She was still sitting on the floor and Clara took both her hands and went to haul her up again.

'Come on, Missy – let's be having you up on your feet. No more bubbly for you.' She waggled a finger at Holly, her face mock stern.

'I can't believe he didn't tell me,' Holly said in reply, more to herself than to Clara. She thought back now to the moment she'd first set eyes on the leggy redhead, to what had happened between herself and Aidan just hours before. Had he said anything about having a half-sister? No, she was pretty sure he never had.

'Aidan can be very secretive,' Clara informed her happily. She was watching Holly with undisguised fascination. 'But he was so excited to have met you. I mean, I partly popped over for a visit because I'd spoken to him on the phone and he'd talked about nothing else. I was in Athens for a shoot, anyway like, so it seemed like the perfect opportunity. It was a bit of a shock to turn up and find you next door with a boyfriend in tow, but Aidan refused to talk to me about it. He just said that it was complicated. But then you barely spoke to him, or to me, so I thought he must have just got it all wrong and was too embarrassed to admit it.'

She looked over for confirmation, but Holly's head was spinning. Why hadn't he just told her the truth? Why had he let her believe that Clara was his ex-girlfriend?

'I think he was horribly jealous of your man,' Clara continued, as if reading her mind. 'What's his name again?'

'Rupert.'

'Yes, that guy. He's very handsome, if you don't mind me saying. A bit short for me, like, but I like blonde hair on a man. Aidan had such a face on him around that guy.'

'We broke up,' Holly told her. 'I told him what had happened between your brother and me. He didn't like it very much.'

Clara let out a long, low whistle. 'I'm not surprised. So, why haven't you been in touch with my big brother? Clearly you were close at one time?'

Holly looked up at her in surprise. 'Has he not told you what happened after you left? About Dennis?'

'Which Dennis?' Clara folded her arms. 'Paloma's husband, that guy from the restaurant? That Dennis?'

'He's my dad.' Holly was amazed how easily it was all flooding out. This morning, the girl in front of her had been an enemy, and now she was telling her things she hadn't even told her so-called best friends. Clearly this girl and Aidan had something about them that made people open up.

Clara let out another whistle. 'I had no idea,' she said. 'Did Aidan know?'

Holly merely nodded, thinking about that awful moment when he'd found her on the floor in her aunt's house, surrounded by heaps of unearthed secrets that had been buried for decades.

'He told me that Sandra made him promise to keep it a secret. She gave him stuff to hide in the house for me to find, like a map and this photo of my dad with my mum and my aunt, and it was him who told Dennis who I really was – the two of them were watching me. But then Dennis had a heart attack and Aidan made me rush to the hospital and . . .' She had to stop before the tears started, and Clara put a comforting hand on her shoulder.

'No wonder you're pissed off with him, like,' she said,

shaking her head with apparent disgust. 'It must have been a bit of a shock.'

'Just a bit.' Holly forced herself to smile. 'But he's okay – Dennis, I mean. We talk on the phone all the time.'

'Sorry, but I'm confused,' Clara said. 'Who is your mum?'

'Her name was Jenny,' Holly explained. 'Dennis was with her sister, my Aunt Sandra, but then they, um, you know . . .'

Clara's green eyes widened. 'Wow – what a complicated mess of a thing.' She let out a deep breath. 'I wonder why he did that?'

'I have no idea,' Holly admitted. 'We haven't ever discussed it. It's the only thing we don't talk about, in fact. I suppose I don't feel like I can ask.'

'Nonsense!' Clara threw up her hand. 'You have every right to know everything about where you came from. Did you know that Aidan's mum buggered off and left him back in Belfast when he was just a boy?'

'Did she?' Holly was intrigued.

'She met Aidan's dad, who's also my dad, by the way, at art college when they were both barely teenagers. Next thing you know, she's pregnant and the family don't want Jerry – that's my dad – they don't want him involved. Savannah kept Aidan, but she had a time with it all. In the end she went off to Greece and left his granny to raise him. He didn't even meet his dad until he was sixteen.'

Holly shook her head. 'He never told me all this, he just said that things with his mum were difficult.'

'I told you.' Clara sniffed dismissively. 'He's secretive, that one. He's his own worst enemy half the time.'

'He's bloody arrogant,' Holly muttered, ignoring Clara's

frown of displeasure. 'He had no right to decide when I should meet my own father – it wasn't his call to make. He lied to me and manipulated me and made me look like an idiot.'

'You fell for him, didn't you?' Clara guessed, frowning again as Holly shook her head violently from side to side. 'Falling for someone doesn't make you an idiot, you know. He wasn't one hundred per cent honest with you, which is bad of him, but I think his intentions must have been good. I know my brother, and his main fault is that he feels the need to look after everyone – especially us girls.'

'I'm not an injured puppy,' Holly grumbled, rubbing her eyes. She was suddenly overwhelmed with fatigue. She felt like she could lie down on the dirty concrete floor and sleep for a month.

'I'm not saying you should forgive him,' Clara said. 'But you should know that he does care about you. His feelings were genuine – he thinks the world of you.'

Holly was about to reply, but at that moment Clipboard reappeared and barked at Clara to get a move on and finish up in hair and make-up. The show was starting in less than an hour. Throwing her an apologetic grimace and promising that they'd catch up later, Clara scurried away.

32

The moment Holly stepped out of the air-conditioned cabin and into the warm, early morning air, she knew she'd made the right decision. The heat slipped around her like a welcoming embrace as she made her way down the metal staircase and on to the toasted tarmac below, and she skipped rather than walked over to the waiting shuttle bus. She could feel her senses exploding into life as she breathed in the dusty air and gazed at the distant mountains. There was something so reassuring about the solid, dependable way they were still here, just as she remembered them. She picked up a citrus scent in the air and closed her eyes with pleasure: it was the smell of home.

She had assumed that everyone in London would be baffled at her decision to leave behind the life she'd so painstakingly spent the last few months putting into place, but she couldn't have been more wrong. Ivy had taken her hand and told her to go for it, while Aliana had simply said it was 'about time, you silly cow'. Holly told them both the same thing: that she could have stayed in London and made her life work, but that she had realised something was missing. Zakynthos had wormed its way under her skin, and she knew the yearning in her heart wouldn't settle unless she came back here.

This was where her family lived, and she wanted to have a life with a dad and a sister, and perhaps even a slightly reluctant stepmother in time. She wanted to see them every day, watch little Maria grow up and teach her how to sew. She wanted to wake up to that view from the back garden and breathe in the warm, fig-scented air; she wanted to look at herself in the mirror and actually like what she saw. Zakynthos was the only place she had ever been able to do that. And, of course, she did want to make peace with Aidan.

She belonged here, it was as simple as that, and the realisation of that fact, as she stood waiting for her case to trundle out inside the airport, was nothing short of miraculous.

Instead of getting a taxi to her house in Lithakia, Holly asked her chatty Greek driver to head into Zakynthos Town. She was meeting Dennis in the Square for coffee, breakfast and, as he had cryptically texted in clumsy English, a 'speshall saprise'. As they passed hotels, souvenir shops, restaurants and scrubby fields dotted with olive trees, Holly felt the last of her London tension evaporating. She even laughed out loud when they stopped at a set of traffic lights to let an untethered goat trot haphazardly across the road.

She had thought the prospect of seeing her father again would be a bit daunting, but as they neared the town, all she could sense within herself was excitement. Now that she had arrived, Holly wondered why she'd waited so long. What had she really been so afraid of? Okay, so she was probably about to hear more things about her mother that might cause her some upset, but it was nothing she couldn't handle. Being back here in Zakynthos made her feel stronger, as if the mountains on the horizon were her personal guardians, and the turtles down on the beach her very own little army of soldiers.

Solomos Square was tucked just one street in from the coast, with a cluster of gardens at one end and a large museum at the other. A statue of the Greek poet Solomos looked down on passers-by from his impressive plinth in the centre, and a number of small coffee vendors were dotted along each edge.

The last time Holly had seen her father he'd been propped up in a hospital bed looking drawn and deathly pale. He'd seemed incredibly small and frail to her then, so it was a nice surprise when he stepped out from the dappled pool of shade underneath one of the square's many trees and enveloped her in a strong embrace.

'My girl,' he smiled as he stepped back. 'You are here.' There was a smudge of colour on each of his cheeks as he beamed at her, and Holly noticed the telltale nicks of a recent shave across his jaw. He was wearing a dark blue shirt tucked into canvas shorts, and was clutching a bottle of water. There was a short pause as neither one of them said anything, both awed into silence by the sheer pleasure of seeing each other again. Holly found herself overcome with shyness, as if their long and boisterous chats over the phone hadn't been happening over the past few months. She knew how to talk to this man, but to be confronted with him now, standing strong and tall and proud in front of her, felt quite overwhelming.

Dennis was looking at her with a mixture of what looked to Holly like admiration and trepidation, and she wondered how much of her mother he could recognise in her. It was something that she'd struggled with when she was young – how little she looked like Jenny. Where she was softy rounded and olive-skinned, her mother was angular and pale. When she was still a small child and before her mother's life nose-dived into alcoholism, Holly had thought of her as the most beautiful woman in the entire world, and it would upset her greatly that she didn't look just the same. Being here, though, in front of Dennis, it was very clear to Holly exactly whose attributes had been the most dominant. Nobody could deny that she was his daughter.

'Are you ready for your surprise?' he asked her now, still beaming.

'That depends.' She cocked a playful eyebrow. 'What is it?'

Dennis boomed with laughter and pointed towards the harbour behind them. 'We are going on my boat,' he declared. 'I want to tell you a story, and there is no better place to listen than on the water.'

Holly looked into his eyes, so like her own, and detected a sparkle.

'Lead the way.'

Dennis Maniatis had always loved women. With a doting mother and five older sisters, he'd grown up surrounded by an abundance of bosoms to be clasped against and relished his position as the golden boy of the family.

Dennis senior, not keen on how precocious and self-involved his teenage son was becoming, started taking him out on the fishing boat every weekend, working him until his hands bled and sweat ran in rivulets down his cheeks. Angry that he was missing the opportunity to hang around at the beach with his friends, but far too proud to ever let on, the young Dennis gritted his teeth and got on with what he was asked.

In time, he even began to look forward to those long hours out on the water. He and his dad grew closer, and Dennis was absolutely devastated when his father died suddenly from a rare virus that affected his heart.

Despite nearing seventy, his lithe dad had always been fit and healthy, with only a sprinkling of grey over his head and through his beard. He'd always seemed invincible, and his death threw Dennis into a dark depression. It hurt him to see his mother so upset too. She was far younger than her late husband, but Maria Maniatis continued to shroud herself in the traditional black and seemed to almost turn herself inside out with grief. Dennis watched, with increasing despair, as his once vibrant and lively mother seemed to shrink and fade in front of him. His sisters did their best to rally round, but Dennis was the man of the family now and he took that position very seriously indeed.

As his friends drank beer on the beach and romanced holidaymakers over the summer, the nineteen-year-old Dennis borrowed enough money from his mother's two brothers to buy a small plot of land in Laganas and built a small restaurant. His friends mocked him, his mother fretted about him and the other bar owners in the area openly laughed at his modern ideas, but by the end of his first season, Dennis had paid back almost half of the capital his uncles had lent him.

He was a fair boss and he worked tirelessly at his little beachside taverna, arriving at 7 a.m. to rake the sand and set out the loungers and leaving long after midnight every night. On Sundays, he left his oldest sister in charge for the day and took his father's boat out just as the sun was rising. There he would sit, listening to the waves lapping gently against the keel and smoking cigarette after cigarette – his only real vice alongside the odd glass of whisky. During the winter months, when the island was free of tourists and the rain lashed against the mountains, Dennis would allow himself time off. He and his friends went on hunting trips and played poker through until the early hours. He also loved to read, and would spend whole days lost in another world. His English was steadily improving thanks to summers spent in the company of holidaymakers, and he pushed his level of understanding up a notch by picking up novels written in English. There was always an abundance of them left in hotels over the summer months, so he never ran out of options.

Dennis' love and admiration for women had never left him, but he often found himself quickly disillusioned when it came to relationships. Greek girls wanted to marry him and English girls wanted to use him to satisfy their own curiosity. He had no problem with being someone's holiday romance, but after a few years even the consistent stream of meaningless sex began to bore him. He wanted to fall in love with someone as deeply as his parents had fallen for one another, and eventually promised himself that if he couldn't have that, then he would have nothing.

The first time he'd set eyes on Sandra Wright had been on a nondescript Tuesday afternoon in April 1984. He was at the restaurant, balanced at the very top of a rather rickety wooden ladder, repainting the sign in preparation for the start of the season in a few weeks' time. There was barely a soul in sight, so he'd spotted her coming from quite a way off. He found himself drawn to the way she moved with such fluidity, her long hair blowing round her shoulders and a wide smile on her face. She appeared to Dennis to be simply smiling at the view, and she stopped every now and again to pick things up off the sand by her bare feet. By the time she neared the bottom of his ladder, he was utterly entranced by her.

'*Yassou*,' she said, coming to a halt behind his hairy calves.

'You speak Greek?' he asked, turning to face her. She was wearing a rather tatty-looking white vest and a red sarong was knotted at her waist.

'Oh God, no!' She laughed at him, flashing small, neat teeth. 'Just the basics, really. I'm hoping to learn.'

The Dennis of old, who had female tourists eating out of his hand in mere minutes, would have shimmied slowly down the ladder and offered to teach her himself, but something about this girl made him feel uncharacteristically nervous.

'Is this your first time in Zakynthos?' he asked instead, putting his still-wet paintbrush carefully on the edge of the open pot.

She shook her head, causing those brown shiny locks to fall excitingly round her shoulders. Dennis fought an overwhelming urge to step down and run his hands through them.

'I came here with my mum and dad when I was a little girl,' she told him, fiddling absent-mindedly with a shell that she'd picked up. 'We came every summer for many years.'

'Are they here with you now?' he said, thinking privately that if he had a daughter who looked like her there would be no way on earth that he'd ever let her out of his sight.

She shook her head again. 'They died.'

Dennis clambered down the ladder so he could look her in the eye. 'I'm so sorry,' he told her sincerely. 'My own father died, so I know how it is to feel such pain.' For a few uncomfortable seconds he had to blink away unexpected tears, and when he looked up again she was smiling at him, a misty glow of pity detectable in her eyes.

They chatted for a while about their remaining families – his mother and sisters and her twin sister, who she told him was called Jenny and who was travelling in the Far East – and he told her about his business and his love for fishing.

'I used to love going fishing!' she exclaimed, suddenly animated. 'I used to go with my dad.'

'It is the same for me,' he smiled, thinking to himself right then that Fate himself must be alive and well, because surely he had led this angel here to him.

'I can take you fishing,' he offered. 'Every Sunday I go. I have a boat.'

This seemed to thrill her and she nodded her head enthusiastically, rushing out lots of 'are you sure's and 'only if it's not too much trouble's. By the time she finally headed off in the direction of Kalamaki with a promise to meet him back at this spot at 6 a.m. on Sunday, Dennis was pretty convinced that he'd just fallen in love at first sight. He thought about little else than his mysterious English angel for the rest of the week.

When Sunday morning arrived, he drove to the beach via the bakery and picked them up some breakfast, his hands shaking slightly as he wrapped up the pastries in paper and set them carefully in a picnic basket he'd found at his sister's house. The sun was rising as he strolled along the sand to find Sandra waiting there, a straw hat shielding her eyes from the sunlight and a bag of similar breakfast goods clasped in her hand. From that shared moment of laughter, the day passed in a blur of fun, happiness and excitement, and Dennis found himself falling harder and harder for her. She was so easy to be with, so full of kindness and so sweet in nature: it was as if his subconscious had created the perfect girl and now she'd come to life, brighter and better and more beautiful than he would ever have believed possible. By the time the sun was heading south and they were sitting with their bare feet up on the edge of his boat, a bottle of slightly warm beer in each of their hands and a bucket of fish between their chairs, Dennis was telling Sandra that he hadn't felt this happy since before his dad died – and it was the absolute truth.

For Sandra, who was just nineteen and yet to feel the flush of true love, it was, she told him, the most fun she'd ever had away from Jenny. She'd been so apprehensive about letting her precious twin go off travelling without her, but now the yearning she'd felt to come back to Zakynthos alone was all starting to make sense – she was destined to be here now, at this time, and meet this wonderful man. For the first time since her own parents had died, Sandra thought she might just have a shot at real happiness after all – and for the first time in her entire life, it wasn't Jenny that was the one instigating it all.

Over the next few weeks, they barely spent a day apart, and Dennis quickly introduced her to all his sisters and even his mother, telling everyone he knew that he had met his future wife. While the Greek women remained outwardly reserved, they were actually secretly thrilled to see their baby brother smiling again. It wasn't ideal that he'd fallen for an English girl, but it was better that he was with her than moping around on his own.

Dennis found Sandra a lovely little apartment not far from his own house in Lithakia and a week after their first date she started working as a waitress in his beachside restaurant. Her Greek was getting better every day, and she spent every minute that she wasn't serving customers teaching the rest of his staff English. Dennis wanted her by his side constantly, and the two of them could increasingly be found kissing and giggling in corners or gazing at each other across the banks of tables. They were adorable without a hint of corniness, and Dennis became a better boss and – he told Sandra – a better man as the weeks passed. Everything was as perfect as he'd ever dared to hope it would be.

Then Jenny arrived.

From the moment Sandra's twin sister burst colourfully on to Zakynthos that summer in 1984, Dennis noticed a change in his beloved girlfriend. Where she had been happy and carefree, she now seemed preoccupied and wary, almost as if she was waiting for something awful to happen. As far as Dennis was concerned, Jenny was loud, selfish and unnecessarily demanding of his girl-friend's time. In fact, it seemed to him that Jenny did everything in her power to come between him and Sandra. She invited herself to dinner when it was just supposed to be the two of them, brought tourists she'd hooked up with back to their house for the night without even bothering to close the bedroom door most of the time, and then threw almighty tantrums whenever Sandra attempted a gentle reprimand.

After a month of disturbed sleep and a crackling tension that hung around the house, Dennis was starting to find excuses to go home – he simply couldn't relax when Jenny was in situ and, even when she wasn't, he was afraid of what state she'd be in when she did crawl back.

Sandra was the sweetest, kindest girl he'd ever known – it was a large part of the reason why he'd fallen so deeply in love with her – but her inability to recognise that her twin sister's behaviour was out of control started to frustrate and then infuriate him. Sandra would argue that Jenny had taken the death of their parents harder than she had, and that she just needed time to settle down and feel like herself again, but Dennis thought privately that this precocious little thing knew exactly what she was doing when she deliberately pressed both his and Sandra's buttons.

It was August on the island and the busiest time of the year for his restaurant, but Dennis was finding it increasingly difficult to focus on work. Jenny would turn up at the beach just after she woke up around lunchtime and beg and plead with Sandra to take the rest of the day off and spend it with her. Although he never knew for sure,

Dennis heard that the two girls were getting up to all sorts of trouble around the island – streaking naked down the hill from his house, skinny dipping, drinking beer all day then driving back on their mopeds with no helmets. He couldn't allow himself to believe that the rumours were true, but the island community was a small one and the gossip spread fast. Dennis' own sisters were beginning to question the suitability of the English girl who had charmed them just a few months before. They started to suggest to him that he would be much better off with a quiet, respectful Greek girl, one who wouldn't embarrass him or the family. When he eventually cracked and told Sandra what they'd said, she tearfully told Jenny and the fiery twin drew battle lines between the two sets of sisters.

Dennis, who was stranded hopelessly in the middle, simply took himself out on more fishing trips and started to stay at the restaurant until the early hours, working his methodic way through a bottle of whisky while he watched the moon cross the sky. The crack that had opened up between him and Sandra when Jenny first arrived soon began to feel like an enormous chasm, and he was starting to worry that they would never find their way back to each other.

The thing that kept him going through it all was how much he loved Sandra. He had fallen hard and he wasn't ready to give her up without a fight. And it was this, in the end, which convinced him to do something that would change all their lives for ever.

33

Holly had been gazing out across the sea as she listened to Dennis talk. His deep, accented voice had an almost hypnotic quality and she liked the way he paused every now and then to search his mind for the correct English word. He seemed to like telling stories, and Holly wondered if he had ever sat and read to her when she was a child.

Now that he'd reached the part in the tale that was presumably the most difficult, however, his measured and gentle tone had ground to an uncomfortable halt. Holly saw that he was tapping his fingers on his broad, hairy thigh, the other hand stroking its way through his hair.

'Are you okay?' she asked tentatively, not wanting to ruin the calm mood that had settled between them.

'My hands, they are bored. I have to give up the cigarettes and the beer.' He shrugged, motioning to his chest. 'It is hard, because my hands, they remember more than my head.'

Holly could relate to what he was saying – now that she spent so much time sewing, her hands felt hugely redundant when they were sitting still in her lap as they were now. Getting up from the deckchair and clutching the rail on the edge of the boat for support, she walked steadily over to the cooler box and pulled out two bottles of water.

'Here,' she handed one over. 'Not very exciting, but it might help.'

'This story is very hard for me to tell,' he said now, not taking his eyes off the horizon. 'I have only told two people before – you are the third.'

'Was Sandra one of them?' Holly guessed, unscrewing the lid of her bottle as she sat back down.

He nodded. 'And Paloma, my wife. She also knows.'

A few minutes passed while neither of them spoke, but Holly didn't feel uncomfortable. On the contrary, ever since she'd landed back on the island, she'd felt an over-whelming sense of comfort. Being here now, on the boat with her father, made her chest swell with a happiness she couldn't quite put a label on yet. They weren't very far from the shore, but the white-stone beach behind them was deserted. Dennis had driven them up to the north-west corner of the island, where his boat was moored, in almost total silence, watching the road carefully and occasionally glancing over at Holly as if she was a precious cargo that he was afraid might crack on the bumpy roads.

'Jennifer, your mother, she came to see me one night at the restaurant.' He paused again, clearly struggling, but this time Holly remained silent.

'She was crying and she told me that Sandra would not come away with her. She wanted to travel the world with her sister, but Sandra said she would not leave me. Jennifer wanted me to talk to her, to make her change her mind. She wanted me to admit that I did not really love Sandra and to let her go. She did not seem to believe that what we felt for each other was real. But I do not know why she was like this.'

Upon hearing his words, Holly experienced feelings of both anger and pity towards her mother. She knew that

Jenny had it in her to be selfish – she'd witnessed as much during her years of drinking – but she also remembered a woman with a kind heart. Why would her mum have wanted Sandra to be unhappy? She must have been so broken by the death of her parents that it infected her like a disease. Her fear of losing her sister, the only person she really had left that she cared about, must have been palpable. For the first time, Holly thought she might understand what motivated Jenny to destroy what Sandra and Dennis had found with each other. It wasn't because she wanted Dennis, it was because she wanted to keep Sandra all to herself.

'She was very jealous of what we were together, you understand?' Dennis went on. 'She found it very easy to meet men everywhere she went, but they would never stay. I think she felt, how you say it, worthless? She wanted to be loved like her sister was loved.'

How sad, Holly thought now, that aside from a few years with Simon, her mother had never really been in a loving relationship. There had always been men, of course, but nobody who respected or cared for her. Perhaps because she didn't really believe she deserved to be loved after what had happened that summer in Greece. With a pang Holly thought fleetingly of Rupert and all the love he'd wrapped her up in before she'd ruined everything.

'At that time, I did not want Jennifer to stay in Zakynthos,' Dennis continued. 'We both wanted Sandra to ourselves, and I am sorry but I did not want to share. But I lied to Jennifer – I told her that I would talk to her sister and I told her that I would be happy if they went for holidays together.'

'But you never did?' Holly guessed.

'No. I did tell Sandra what Jennifer had said, and it made her very angry. I had never seen her get so angry before, but I thought it was something she needed to know. Jennifer had been, how you say, walking with her boots all over her. I am sorry, but I thought that if they had a fight, Jenny would go away again and I would get my beautiful girl back.'

Holly, who knew very well that this was not what had transpired, took her eyes off the view and let them rest on her father's face. She'd been slyly examining him all day, the shape of his mouth and the curve of his jaw, looking all the time for the genetic clues that linked them.

'They did have a very big fight,' he said, his voice growing quiet as he dug up the memory. 'I think every person in the whole of Lithakia heard them. Jennifer shouted that Sandra had chosen me over her and there were many tears. I hated to see my girl so upset. I wanted her to be happy again, and I think it was all making me mad.'

Holly could sense that he had reached a pivotal point in the story, because he shifted in his chair and took several, hurried glugs of water.

'I was at the restaurant, like always,' he said, keeping his voice steady. 'Jennifer came again and waited until everyone was gone.'

A stray cloud had been drifting across the sky and chose that exact moment to briefly obscure the sun. The deck plunged into shadow and Holly shivered violently, immediately clasping her hands around her upper body. Dennis didn't even seem to notice, lost as he was in a memory he rarely ventured into.

'I was drunk, like I always was in those days,' he said. 'Jennifer was also drinking. She told me she was jealous of Sandra. She told me that she wanted me to love her as much as I loved Sandra. She didn't understand why I did not feel this way.'

Holly swallowed.

'She followed me inside,' he said, wincing slightly at the words. 'I pushed her away but she came again and put her hands on me. She whispered to me that she wanted me and I . . .'

There were tears on his cheeks now. Holly didn't even trust herself to breathe.

'I said to her that she could have me, just for one time, but she had to leave Zakynthos. She had to promise to go and leave Sandra behind. She promised that she would do as I asked, and even as she said it she was taking off her clothes. I was too weak to stop her. I should have . . . I do not know what I was thinking, you understand?'

'What happened afterwards?' Holly asked, trying to imagine how her mum must have felt when the alcohol and anger wore off and she had to face up to what she'd done. It must have been horrendous. She had to have regretted it with every fibre of her being, but once it had happened there was no going back.

Dennis lifted his head from where it had been resting in his hands and looked across at Holly. For a minute he looked horribly distraught, but then he smiled.

'For so many years, I wished that I could turn the

clock back to change what I did on that night. But now I see you, and you are . . .' he searched for the word, 'magnificent.'

Holly actually laughed at this, feeling the tension crumble a little.

'It happened and the next day she went away. I thought she had left the island, as she promised, but she had not – she went to stay in the north with a man she had met and then she went to the mainland. Sandra was so worried, but I couldn't say anything to make her feel better. It was a horrible time.'

'When did she come back?' Holly asked.

'At Christmas time.' He sighed deeply. 'She had only just found out about . . . about you. She was very scared and she wanted her sister.'

'Did she know?'

'She did, I think.' He nodded to himself. 'She did not say anything to me. Of course, I knew that it could be me, but I told myself that it would be another man.'

'Did she ever talk about, you know, giving me away for adoption?' Holly asked now, remembering again the hurtful words Jenny had mumbled at her in their grotty kitchen that day.

'Never.' Dennis held her gaze. 'She was scared, yes, but she wanted you as soon as she found out. I think you gave her a purpose in life. She was lost, and now she had a role to fulfill – she was going to be a mother.'

Holly was ten years older now than her mum had been when she had her, and she couldn't imagine being brave enough to have a baby. She felt another wave of sympathy for the young Jenny.

'Being pregnant changed her totally,' Dennis went on. 'When she stopped with all the drinking and all the men, she was easier. She was quiet.'

Holly liked the idea of having been created and nurtured on this beautiful island. Could it be possible that her body and her mind somehow knew that she was back where she was made? Was that the reason she felt so at peace here, even after everything that had happened?

'It was a nice time to be waiting for a baby. Springtime here can be very wet, with very much rain, but it is better than the heat of the summer. She was at her very best at that time, Jennifer, and after you came she was even better.'

Dennis smiled briefly at some private memory. It was odd to think that he had seen her as a newborn baby, and that he must have held her and talked to her. The fact that he could look at her and see a past she could not recollect made her feel suddenly vulnerable.

'I think she was born to be a mother,' he continued, causing Holly to gasp out loud in disagreement.

'She was a natural,' he assured her. 'I know that things became difficult, but in the beginning she loved you so much. It was – how do you say – a fierce kind of love? Is that correct? She would hold on to you so tight that I was afraid she would break you.'

Tears snaked down Holly's cheeks and she wiped them away furiously.

'Sandra loved you almost as much as Jennifer did. It was not long before she told me that she wanted to have a baby too. It was fast,' he admitted, 'but I was very happy that she saw her future with me and relieved that my secret was still hidden. I let myself believe that it had all been a bad dream and that I could forget it ever happened. We started to try right away, and the summer arrived and passed by.'

Holly, who had read Sandra's letter to her mother so many times that she could now recite it by heart, already knew how this part of the story ended. Dennis and Sandra had spent many years trying to start their own family, but fate had cruelly stepped in and drawn a line through their plans. She was at last beginning to understand exactly why Sandra had been unable to forgive Jenny in the end. How hard it must have been to fail over and over at the one thing that had come so easily to your twin sister, and then to discover that the one man you wanted that baby with was the very same one who had given it to her. Despite the warmth of the afternoon, Holly shivered with discomfort.

'When did she tell you?' she asked, staring not at Dennis but at a spot of peeling blue paint on the deck. This part was going to be difficult for both of them.

'It was the day you were going to turn five,' he began, rubbing a nervous hand through his greying hair. 'Sandra was trying to be happy, but she was so tired of the disappointment of not having a child. I was sure that it would happen one day, but she was starting to give up. The sparkle that she had in her eyes was starting to fade. She wanted you to know your father, she said to Jennifer that it was important, that their own father had been important.'

'Did they fight?' Holly guessed, but Dennis shook his head.

'Not at the start. Jennifer had become more patient and quiet since you were born, and she was just shaking her head and laughing. We had guessed that your father must be Greek because of the way you looked, but your mother always said that she did not know for sure. I should have known. Maybe I did, but I did not want to admit it to myself.

'Later that day, after you had your party at the beach and had gone to bed, Sandra was drinking. She never drank very much, but this night it was a lot. She started to cry and get angry with me. Jennifer, she came to see if everything was okay.'

Holly tried to picture the three of them, all so young and hiding their various secrets from one another. She knew then that her mother had never planned for the truth to come out – she had wanted to keep Holly all to herself and stay in Greece.

'Sandra, she started shouting at me that I was not a real man, that if I was, then I would have given her a baby. I felt that her words were true and we were both crying and shouting.'

He was wincing at the words and Holly stretched over a timid arm and squeezed his wrist. 'It's okay,' she told him. 'You can tell me.'

'She started hitting me on my chest,' he grunted, touching his chest with both hands as if to demonstrate. 'She was so angry with me. I am ashamed to say this, but I was angry with her too. I was angry that she would accuse me of not being a real man.'

He paused again to regain his composure, and Holly

made herself concentrate on a point in the middle distance.

'It was a very bad fight. When Jenny came, she tried to get in the middle, but there was a lot of screaming. It got very hot and then your mother . . . She shouted that it wasn't my fault, that I was not the problem with the baby.'

Putting himself back in that horrible scene had clearly made Dennis feel uncomfortable, because he was now hugging himself tightly with both hands, his upper body slumped forward in his seat and deep frown lines appearing like freshly dug trenches on his forehead.

'Sandra stopped screaming afterwards, but I remember that the quiet was much more frightening. She wanted to know how her sister knew this about me. She knew what the answer was going to be, but she still made Jennifer say the words. Even when I heard her say that I was your father, forgive me, but I could not believe it. I was sure she was playing a trick on her sister, that it was just a plan to punish her, as she had done before in the past.'

'Did you love my mother?' Holly blurted. The question had come from nowhere and she immediately tried to take it back, but Dennis held up his hand to silence her.

'As a sister, at times yes – she was not a bad person – but never as I did Sandra. I did not want to be with Jenny. I was perhaps still young and selfish – I wanted to have a family with the woman that I loved, not her sister. I'm sorry,' he added, 'but I want to tell you the truth of how it was.'

'I wonder if she loved you,' Holly said, but Dennis was shaking his head again.

'I do not think she did. You were the only person that she really loved. She never even looked at her own sister like she looked at you. I saw the love in her eyes, and it was beautiful.' He smiled at Holly. 'Whatever happened to your mother in the end, when demons stole her away from you, she did love you more than the world itself. This is the truth.'

A few months ago, Holly would have scoffed at his comments and snapped that her mum hadn't cared a dot about her, but now she simply nodded. She had been loved. That love had been lost along the way somehow, but it had been there, and it had been the real thing.

'Then what happened?' she asked, bracing herself for what she knew was a murky end.

'Sandra told me to go and she told Jennifer to go. I kept going back every day, but she would not see me. Even when she looked at me, it was as if I was not there. She looked through me like I was made of glass. In the end,' he shrugged, 'it became very difficult for me. I told her that she could have the house and I sold my restaurant. My sister had married a man from Kefalonia and he was keen to start a new business. I left at the end of the summer.'

'And my mum?' Holly prompted.

Dennis lifted up his hands. 'She was gone the day after the fight. She took all her stuff in one bag and she took you and she left. I told myself that it was for the best, but I should have tried to find you. I did not want to believe it. I am sorry for that now.'

His eyes were moist and he looked grey with fatigue. Holly had never been comfortable with affection, but something made her kneel down in front of him on the deck and wrap her arms around his shoulders. He felt reassuringly solid and warm, and she closed her eyes for a few seconds to enjoy the sensation of him.

'It is all in the past,' she said at last, pulling back and looking into his eyes, the same eyes she gazed at every time she looked in the mirror. 'We cannot change what has happened, nobody can.'

'I am glad that I have found you now,' he told her, bringing a weathered hand up to touch her cheek.

'It was Sandra that found me,' she reminded him. 'I think she thought that if we were reunited then it would mend some of the wrongs. I know she wanted to forgive my mother and see me, but she loved you so much that she never could. She must have died with such sadness inside her.'

As she said it, Holly thought painfully of Aidan, who'd been trusted with Sandra's secrets and been made to promise that he would ensure Holly and Dennis were brought back together. It must have been a difficult choice to make, she realised, and wondered then if she wouldn't have made exactly the same decision as he had. What was it he'd said to her on that final morning above the beach in Kalamaki? That he hadn't planned to fall for her? Just like Dennis hadn't planned to cheat on Sandra, and Jenny hadn't planned to have a child, and Sandra hadn't known that she was going to lose everyone she had ever loved. What a mess they had all made, but none of it with malice.

'I think she would be happy for us today,' Holly said, turning away from him to gaze once again at the ocean. 'I think my mother would be happy today too.'

Dennis did not reply, but instead placed a warm hand on her shoulder. For a long time, they sat watching the waves, the fisherman and his daughter, content just to be with one another in a place that they loved.

34

The wind had picked up during the afternoon and stirred the sea into a swirling lather of activity. The waves crashed noisily against the shoreline, their white frothy tips racing heedless across the sand.

Holly watched from her spot behind the wooden fence along the cliff edge, momentarily mesmerised by the majestic display of nature that was unfolding in front of her. Back in May, the sea had been so much calmer and flatter, but there was something about the unashamed wildness of it now that she liked. The sea, she mused, like so much about herself, could not be tamed. She thought about this as the waves continued to thrash and scurry below her.

The graveyard was situated not far from Volimes, the very same place that Aidan had brought her for breakfast the first day they spent together. Clearly it had been a place that meant a lot to Sandra, as not only was it marked firmly on the hand-drawn map in Holly's hand, but it was also where she'd wanted to be buried. Annie had told her about it on the drive up here, taking her hand off the taped-up gearstick every now and then to grasp Holly's fingers. Nobody had mentioned Sandra's grave when she had first come to the island back in May, and she hadn't wanted to ask. At that stage her aunt had still felt very much like a stranger, and Holly would have felt awkward bringing flowers up here. Now, however, her aunt was almost as alive in her mind as her mother. Holly felt she understood the two of them so much better, and so it was finally the right time to pay her respects.

Annie had dropped Holly off at the gates and taken herself off into Volimes for coffee, not wanting to intrude on the moment. She'd been such a support over the past few weeks, ever since Holly had called her from London and told her everything – the truth about her parents and Sandra, about the house and, in not such explicit terms, Aidan and Rupert. It was finally getting an offer on the house that had done it. As soon as she'd opened that email from the estate agent informing her that someone wanted to buy Sandra's house, her house, she knew in her gut and in her heart that she could never sell it. It was her home. The home of her family.

So much had happened in such a short time – this place had changed her, made her realise who she was, what she loved and what really mattered. She finally understood why Sandra had chosen to stay here, despite everything that had gone wrong and all the lingering heartbreak that she'd endured. It was this place that she really loved, in the end. It was this island that had turned out to be her soulmate. Holly only knew this now because her own heart had shifted – she was as hopelessly in love with Zakynthos as she ever had been with anything, and being here made her feel as if she might even start to love herself one day too.

For all those weeks in London, the thought of coming back to the island had filled her with trepidation. There was so much here that she hadn't felt ready to face, but as she stood here now, the busy pattern of the waves lulling her into a contented trance, she couldn't believe she had stayed away so long.

Reaching into her bag just as a brisk gust of wind whipped her hair across her face, Holly pulled out the letter she'd written on the flight over. She had planned to just prop it up against Sandra's headstone and leave, but now that she was here, it didn't seem like enough of a gesture. She wanted the words to take flight on the wind, so they could scurry and somersault their way to wherever Sandra and Jenny were now. Holly knew that if they each had a choice, then those words would not have far to travel.

Glancing around one final time to make sure she was alone, Holly sat cross-legged on the earth beside the stone bearing the name 'Sandra Mary Wright' and started to read aloud.

'Dear Sandra and Jenny,' she began, her voice already cracking slightly as she said her mum's name. 'I wanted to write you both a letter to say thank you. Thank you for finding this place and for falling in love with it, and for leading me back here all these years later.'

There was a pause as Holly pulled herself together and a small brown bird landed on the top bar of the fence above her head. Peering down at her, it cocked its tiny head to one side as if to say, 'Do continue.'

'I know that you both did things to hurt each other,' she went on. 'And I wish more than anything that you had been able to overcome those issues before it was too late. But I've also learnt that you can't live your life looking backwards – the only way to move on is to accept the past and take the lesson it offers, not spend years dwelling over what could have been.'

The next part was going to be tough, and Holly failed to stop her voice from collapsing into sobs.

'Mum. I forgive you. I'm sorry it took me so long . . .'

The bird flew down and sat on the top of the head-stone, clearly bewildered by this strange English girl sitting crying in the dirt. There was something very comforting about the way it was watching her, as if it knew she needed some company and a bit of support to get through this. Holly struggled on.

'I want you to know that I miss you every day. I always have, even if I pretended not to. And I love you, so very much. I'm sorry that you went through such heartache.' And she was sorry, so very sorry. Now that she was getting the chance at a better life, it felt even more unfair that Jenny had never had it.

'Sandra,' she began. 'I forgive you too. I figured that someone needed to forgive both of you, because you never forgave each other. Well, perhaps you did, but you never forgave yourselves. A good friend of mine told me off once for being too hard on myself, and I know where I get that from. I want to make a promise to you both now that I will try not to be so tough on myself any more. The three of us, we are all only human and we made mistakes. I'll probably make lots more, but I will never let them devour me in the way that you did. I promise you that.'

The bird had now hopped down to the ground and was so close to Holly that she could see the delicate pattern on its wings. As she wiped her eyes on the back of her hand, it let out a shrill and impatient chirp.

'I hope that you're together now,' Holly said, no longer reading from the letter but staring out towards the sea. 'I hope you both found your way home, to each other. It feels to me as if you did, and I want you to know that it comforts me. We are all here together now, on this island. It's where we belong.'

Dusting herself off as she stood up, Holly turned just as a wide shaft of sunlight slipped out from the clouds and shone directly across Sandra's grave. The flowers Holly had laid there were the same ones Aidan had left for her before they'd even met – pink and bright and unashamedly happy – and they looked vibrant in the light. Reaching over, she placed her small hand on the warm stone, smiled, and then turned and made her way back down towards the gates.

The little bird waited until she was out of sight before opening its wings and taking flight. It hovered above the grave for a few seconds, as it did every single day, then took off into the blue.

The house was in darkness as Holly made her way quietly along the path. She'd left the place in a hurry back in May, but had still remembered to leave the spare key underneath the pot. She had deliberately avoided looking over to where Aidan's house lurked in the fading light, but she knew he wasn't there because his jeep was missing from its usual place on the road.

There were no flowers in a vase on the table this time, and a thin layer of dust was clinging to the wooden arms of the sofa. The fridge offered nothing more exciting than a half-empty bottle of water and some very questionable cheese, but Holly immediately felt at ease. It was such a contrast to how she'd felt the first time she'd crossed the threshold, when the house presented itself as a sad mausoleum of unwanted trinkets and hidden secrets.

Now that she knew she'd spent years playing here as a child, Holly examined the downstairs space through new eyes, searching the walls and floors for anything that might trigger a memory or a feeling. She remembered how crazed she'd been on her first visit, how she'd turned the place upside down, rifling through drawers and into the back of cupboards. Of course, it had all been fruitless in the beginning, because Aidan was in possession of most of the physical clues to her past. He couldn't have known then that it was her instincts, in the end, which led her in the right directions. Those feelings of déjà vu that she could never quite shrug off, the way that her real self came boldly to the surface when she'd buried it so deeply and so painstakingly. There was no escaping what was true and what was right.

After investigating the upstairs rooms and finding nothing altered, Holly poured herself a glass of the village wine she'd picked up from Kostas on her way up the hill – along with a hug so tight she was afraid her ribs might crack – and plonked herself down on the sofa.

'What the hell?' Wine splattered out of her mouth and landed on the floor.

There *was* something different in the house – something that made the glass Holly was holding shake as she took it in.

As she stood up on unsteady legs to take a better look, there was a knock at the front door.

35

Holly and Aidan stared at each other. The summer months had added a coppery tinge to his black curls, which seemed to glow under the overhead light. There was an untidy spread of stubble across his jaw and a tangle of faint lines laced their way from the corner of his eyes out towards his temples. As she stood, rooted to the spot, Holly was aware of his scent assailing her senses. It was a strange yet still alluring mixture of man-sweat, dog hair and coconut sun lotion.

'Hi.'

As he said it, Holly realised that she'd been staring at his mouth, and quickly looked away. The silence hung in the air between them like a wet shower curtain, and she was horribly conscious of her heart smashing away inside her chest.

'Hello,' she replied, coughing to mask the squeak that came out.

'It's nice to see you,' he tried, a half-smile starting to lift one corner of his mouth. 'You look well.'

She didn't return the compliment, but lifted a hand to bat his away. She may not smell of BO and dog, but she did have dried patches of dust all over her legs and she was pretty sure her hair looked like something you'd find in an English country field the day after a good harvest.

'I spoke to Clara,' he continued, leaning against the

doorframe as it became apparent she wasn't going to invite him inside. 'She told me what you've been up to, with your clothes designing and all that – it sounds great.'

She must have pulled a face at this, because he frowned at her.

'Okay, so it's better than great. It's fecking brilliant. I thought my heart was going to burst with pride when I heard and—'

'Enough.' Holly held a hand up again. She was finding it very hard to meet his eyes.

'How's the puppy?' she asked, steering the conversation on to safer ground.

'Lexi?' Aidan seemed momentarily surprised. 'She's well. Spends most of her time down at Annie's – she loves it down in the bar. She's become a regular little tourist attraction, the flirty wee madam.'

Holly thought of the little dog's lopsided ears and patchwork coat.

'I can imagine,' she said, smiling for the first time.

'I left Phelan at home,' Aidan told her. 'Thought it would be easier to talk if you didn't have a dog's nose stuffed in your crotch.'

Holly blushed at his casual mention of her crotch. Feeling suddenly exposed under his relentless gaze, she squirmed uncomfortably, unable to stop thinking about what she'd just seen on the wall behind them.

'Why did you bother to knock?' she asked him now. 'Clearly you still have a key.'

Aidan shook his head. 'No. I used the one you left under the pot.'

Feeling stupid, Holly finally dropped her arm and took

a step back into the house. Aidan, taking this as his cue to follow her, stepped over the threshold carefully, as if there were smouldering embers on the cold floor tiles.

'I've missed you,' he said, his words hitting Holly in the back like a thump. She ignored him, crossing instead to the sofa and retrieving her glass of wine. She didn't offer him any.

'When did you make it?' she asked, taking a gulp to mask the tremble in her voice.

'Not long after you left,' he replied. He had stepped across to join her and the two of them stood side by side, looking at the large, framed map on the wall. It was a cheap foldout one of the island, the kind which Kostas sold for two euros down in the shop, but this one had been annotated with notes and covered with drawings. Aidan had labelled the area where they'd gone to drink coffee in Volimes and the path down to Jenny and Sandra's secret beach. He'd scribbled a note about the market stall where she'd bought her first swathe of lace and doodled church bells next to it. The bakery where they'd picked up the delicious spanakopita was there too, along with lots of very bad drawings of goats all over the place. Up in the north of the island, he'd crudely drawn bottles of beer next to Mikro Nissi and there was a large happy face at Navagio, where he'd shown her the infamous Shipwreck Cove.

As Holly let her eyes stray round to Lithakia, she saw that Aidan had added a photo of her house alongside one of himself and her Aunt Sandra that she'd never seen before. At the highest point of the island, he'd cheekily stuck a photo of Big Ben, and round at the Blue Caves he'd sketched a large sea turtle. Holly blushed as her eyes found Keri – Aidan had stuck on a handful of those glow-in-the-dark stars and simply scribbled beside them the words 'when I knew'.

Holly stepped forward and gestured to the photo of Aidan and Sandra. Similarly to the one she'd pinched from Annie's bar, the two of them looked as if they had just been laughing.

'Phelan was getting chased by a bee,' Aidan said. Holly didn't turn to look at him, but she could hear the smile in his voice. 'He was spinning round in circles like a mad thing. Annie took the photo,' he added. 'It turned out to be Sandy's last summer.'

'She looks happy,' Holly said, ignoring the faint prickle of tears. 'I'm glad she was happy in the end, after everything that happened.'

'She always had a sadness about her,' he admitted. 'Sometimes when she laughed – like, really, really laughed – I'd notice her catch herself and then she'd act all guilty, as if laughter wasn't something she deserved. When she told me about what had happened with you and with her sister, it all made sense. But yes, I think she was as happy as she allowed herself to be. I think in the end, you can't let the grief take over, you have to move it to one side before it eats you up and spits you out.'

Holly nodded. She was still staring at the map – on the label next to the secret beach where they'd discovered Sandra and Jenny's engraving in the cave, which Aidan had defiantly named 'our beach', he'd drawn a big red heart in biro. Unable to quite take in what she was seeing, Holly sat back down on the sofa and reached again for her glass. Aidan remained standing, staring resolutely at his feet as he continued talking.

'After you left,' he said, 'I felt as if someone was watching me. I felt a presence with me all the time. I thought I was being haunted there for a while.'

Holly looked up at him to see if he was winding her up, but he was still looking down.

'I realised that it was my conscience,' he said. 'Everything that you'd been through, losing your mam and then finding your dad only to almost lose him again, it shook me up.'

Holly wanted to tell him that he wasn't the only one, but she sensed the need to remain silent.

'I never really told you the whole truth about my own mam,' he said now, daring to glance at her. 'She left me when I was just a boy and I felt as if I spent my whole life just trying to be loved by her, trying to be enough. Honestly, Holly, I was a man obsessed. I was so desperate for her approval that I let her get away with anything. My ex pointed this out to me, of course, but I wouldn't hear a word against my mam. In the end, she had enough and she left – and that was when it all went wrong.'

'Did you blame your mum for the break-up?' Holly asked, so quietly that she wasn't sure if he'd heard her at first.

'Yes.' He turned to her again and this time their eyes met. 'For a long time I was eaten up with anger towards her, but meeting you made me realise what a stupid eejit I'd been.'

He took a deep breath and looked at her again. 'After you went back to London in May, I went over to

Kefalonia to see her. To see my mam, I mean. I wanted to try and make up for the past few years. But most of all I went because of you, because of what you'd taught me.'

'Me?' Holly was shocked.

'You made me realise that I was wasting my time being mad at her. You don't even have a mother and there I was being a stubborn arse and refusing to speak to mine. All of a sudden, I just let go of all that resentment. And I tell you what, it felt fecking amazing.'

Holly couldn't help herself, she beamed at him.

'But then I came back here,' Aidan's tone was serious again. 'And I still felt as if something was haunting me. It took me a while, but then I realised that it was Love. The pesky fecker was sat up on my shoulder waggling his fing—'

'Oh, come on!' Holly interrupted him with a loud snort of laughter. 'Love living up on your shoulder? Are you on something?'

Aidan looked shocked, then he too started to chuckle.

'You're right,' he said, running a hand through his untidy stack of curls. 'I've contracted a right case of the soppies. Here, take my keys and drive me to the hospital immediately.'

At the mention of the hospital, Holly's momentary good cheer evaporated.

'I still can't believe you hid the truth from me,' she whispered. 'Dennis could so easily have died that day, and I would never have known him.'

'But he didn't,' he said, almost pleading with her. 'I know what I did was wrong, but I am a fecking eejit. I always have been. I made the wrong decision and then my feelings for you confused everything. I was selfish and arrogant, I know that now, but what went on between us . . . Holly, that was all real.'

'I understand why you did it,' Holly said, glancing at him then looking back up towards the map. 'I'm just not sure I can trust you again.'

He appeared stung by this and stood again, pacing up and down in the small space as Holly sat watching him.

'In the beginning, you were just another girl who needed to be looked after,' he said. 'I'd been looking after women my entire life, so I think I took on that role willingly. I didn't even stop to question whether or not you wanted looking after. That was wrong of me, because looking at you now, and all that you've achieved with your work, I can see that you don't need anyone to look after you.'

'You're wrong,' Holly interrupted him. 'I do need to be looked after – but it's me who has to do it. Not you, not Rupert, not even my dad. If I can't look after myself and make myself happy, then what chance have I got of ever being happy with someone else?'

'But what if someone else *wanted* to make you happy? What if that someone wanted it to be their job?' He was edging towards her now and Holly flashed him a warning look.

'I would say that it shouldn't be a job,' she replied. 'I'm not a stray puppy that you have to nurse back to health – and I'm not going to let what happened to my mum and Sandra happen to me.'

He went to interrupt but she hurried on, talking over his words.

'The thing is, I don't think people ever really change, they just become a better or worse version of who they've always been, depending on what happens to them. But I do believe now that, at a certain point, you get to make a choice: to follow a darker, easier path, or cut your way through the undergrowth to find a better one. I think I've been taking the easy path for far too long now, and it's about time I grew a pair and changed my life for the better.'

'I think you already have,' Aidan said. He was smiling at her now and had stopped pacing, coming to a halt in front of the map he'd created for her. 'What you've been doing, with your work and the catwalk shows and all that – it's so amazing. I know I haven't known you long, but I can honestly say I've never been prouder of a single soul in my entire life.'

Holly looked up again to see if she could detect anything in his face that hinted at humour, but he looked deadly serious. She'd spent all this time despising him for what he'd done to her, but being here now, with his eyes boring holes in her skull with their sheer intensity, she saw how short-sighted she'd been.

'I think you know me well enough,' she said. 'You knew I'd love that map, for example.'

Aidan glanced over his shoulder and Holly was surprised to see a slight blush creep across his cheeks.

'I wasn't even sure if you'd ever see it.' He shrugged. 'I wanted to make it anyway, just in case. It's my map of you, Holly – my map of how I fell in love with you.'

A solitary tear slid down Holly's cheek and landed with a splash in her wine glass.

'I was scared to come back,' she admitted. 'I knew I

would have to at some point, to see Dennis and Maria, but I kept telling myself to wait a bit longer.'

'What made you change your mind?' he asked.

'Someone made an offer on this place.' She swung an arm round. 'I couldn't bear the idea of losing it and it made me realise that I wasn't in the right place, that this is my home, not London, and . . .' She trailed off as she took in the smirk on his face. 'What?'

'I might have a small confession to make,' he said, trying and failing to keep the corners of his mouth downturned.

'Another one?' She raised an eyebrow. 'What the hell have you done now?'

He laughed at that, and it was a glorious sound. 'I'm the one who made the offer, you daft mare,' he grinned. 'It turns out that I couldn't bear the idea of you never seeing the place again either. I figured if it belonged to me, then you could always see it again if you ever came back – and of course I hoped that you would.'

'You must have really loved my Auntie Sandra,' Holly realised. 'You knew she'd never want this house to leave the family.'

'That's probably true,' he agreed. 'But my motivations were all linked directly to you, I'm afraid. I'm not quite as heroic as you might have thought.'

'Hang on.' Holly snapped her head round to look at him. 'Was it you who put mud in my washing machine?'

Aidan said nothing, but his face had turned an interesting shade of maroon.

'It bloody was, wasn't it? You sneaked in and sabotaged the place!'

'In my defence,' he laughed, blocking the blows Holly

was now raining down on him, 'I thought it would be harder to sell if everything was falling apart.'

'I had a lump on my head for a bloody week from that cupboard door!' she scolded.

'Shit – I'm sorry.' He was still laughing. 'Your poor little head. I didn't mean to hurt you. You shouldn't go slamming doors, though, really.'

'The funny thing is,' Holly told him now, a sweet warmth spreading through her chest, 'this house actually belongs to Dennis. After the truth came out and my mum left with me, he told Sandra that she could have it. He felt so guilty about what he'd done to her that he handed it over without asking for a single penny.'

'Steady now!' Aidan laughed. 'That dad of yours will be stealing my good-guy crown in a minute.'

For a few minutes, they were both laughing too much to speak, more with pure relief than because anything was particularly funny. It felt good to let go of some of the tension that had been crackling between them ever since Aidan knocked on the door.

'Don't go home,' he said now, suddenly serious. 'Stay here. I'll give you a job. You can be my receptionist or something.'

'There you go again, trying to rescue me,' Holly scolded him gently, with a light slap to the back of his hand. 'That man who hired me to make stuff for his show, he wants me to do lots more, and I can work from wherever in the world that I want. And I still have my stall back in London. I'm going to be sending clothes back there as well. So, I've got a perfectly good job, thanks very much – and it's one I happen to love.'

'Sorry.' He looked downcast and wrapped his fingers around her wrists. 'I just thought . . .'

'What? That you could look after me? That I would move here and work in your little clinic and we'd live happily ever after?'

'Is that such a bad thing?'

'If you must know,' she told him, removing her hands carefully from his, 'I have decided to stay. I've made all the arrangements already.'

'You're kidding?' Aidan looked like he was about to leap out of his seat and punch the air. 'That's . . . Well, that's great news. The best!'

'You just told me not to go home,' she explained. 'But the thing is, I already *am* home. This is the only place that's ever felt remotely like a home. I can be myself here.'

'You know, my mam said the exact same thing to me in Kefalonia,' Aidan said, his eyes bright with reluctant tears. 'And now I can't imagine living anywhere else in the world but here, on this stupidly gorgeous island with all these stupidly brilliant people.'

'I think me being here would make my mum happy,' Holly told him, putting her empty glass down on the table. The two of them had settled next to one another on the sofa now, both looking up at the map rather than at each other. 'She asked Sandra to forgive her so many times, over so many years. I think she always wanted to come back here.'

'So many people have made so many mistakes,' Aidan said, shifting slightly. 'And I include myself in that.'

Holly turned to face him and put a timid hand on his shoulder. 'I don't want to talk about the past any more. I

411

want to focus on the future. I'm sick of carrying so many ghosts around with me all the time.'

'Does that mean you forgive me?' he whispered, letting his head fall to the side so that his hair brushed the back of her hand. Holly felt a stirring deep inside herself and moved her hand quickly back into her lap.

'I think so,' she told him honestly. 'I'm no angel myself, you know. What I did to poor Rupert was inexcusable. You told me that I just wanted to be looked after, that I reeled people in then pushed them away – and you were right.'

'I shouldn't have said that.'

'But you did. And it hurt, it really did, but I needed to hear it. I told myself that I wasn't in my right mind when I slept with you – I even moved in with Rupert when I got back to London, for God's sake.'

Aidan flinched.

'But I never forgave myself. I always felt like he deserved better, and it was true. I never loved him, not really, it just took me a while to pluck up enough courage to admit it. I hadn't really had any stability in my life since my mum died, then I met Rupert and he was so . . . I don't know. So capable. I think I was so tired of looking after myself at that point that I relished the chance to let someone else take over for a while. Admitting that I was wrong about that and choosing to be alone again has been a very big step for me.'

'I was so jealous,' Aidan told her. 'I was a complete arse to you, but I didn't appreciate how tough it must have been, him turning up like that.'

'It wasn't the best timing,' Holly agreed, laughing now at the ridiculousness of it all.

Aidan looked sheepish. 'I followed you down to Laganas that night,' he confessed, earning himself a stare of disbelief. 'What? I did! I sat in my bloody jeep all the time you were dancing in that bar, then I watched you and that posh boy walk up the road together arm in arm, like some scorned hero in a slushy romance film.'

'Well, that's just embarrassing,' Holly laughed. She couldn't believe she was hearing all this.

'It is. I'm pathetic,' he sighed dramatically, pulling what Holly could only presume was his best scorned-hero-in-a-slushy-romance-film face.

For a few minutes, as she looked into his eyes and traced the haphazard freckles down to his big, smiling mouth, Holly could picture herself falling into his arms. She imagined what it would feel like to have him kiss her again, remembering how her body had responded to him before with such an urgent need that it left her breathless. It would be so easy to give in to what he wanted.

Aidan, as if reading her mind, leaned towards her and slipped one big hand gently into her hair. His lips were only centimetres from her own when she abruptly pulled away.

'What's the matter?' He looked more confused than hurt.

Holly took a deep breath, forcing her spinning insides to slow down a few gears. 'It's not you . . .' she began, stopping before she finished it with 'it's me'. Aidan was looking at her with a mixture of lust and bemusement.

'I don't want to be with you,' she managed at last.

The smile vanished from his face and he stared at her, bewildered.

'Right now, I mean. I do have feelings for you,' she assured him. 'It's just that I need some time on my own. I need to have a relationship with myself for a while – does that even make sense?'

He nodded, trying to smile.

'Before you met me, I'd hated myself for a very long time. I don't think I'd given myself a break since I was a teenager – certainly not since my mum died. I did my best to pretend that I was a confident person, that I knew what I wanted, but really I was a mess. When I got the letter from Sandra and came over here, I was terrified. I'd grown so used to hating myself and my mum and everything about my past, I was afraid that I'd be made to face up to all that if I came here – and I was right.'

'But . . . ?' he asked, letting his hand rest casually against her leg.

'But the longer I spent here, the more I realised that I needed to forgive my mum – and forgive myself too. I blamed myself for what happened to her, and even now I still feel partly responsible. If I'd never been born, she would probably have stayed here with Sandra and every-thing would have worked out.'

'You can't think like that,' he said.

'I know. Dennis made me realise that today.' She smiled at the memory of her trip out on the fishing boat that afternoon. 'I think meeting me has helped him forgive himself too.'

'That makes sense.' Aidan was smiling at her again with what looked like real affection. 'You're quite some-thing, you know. Of course your old man's proud of you.'

'But it's taking some getting used to, this whole liking

myself thing,' she continued. 'I just think that if I start something with you then I might never know what it feels like to just be with myself for a while – the version of me that I actually like, that is. I need to be comfortable in my own skin before I let you get underneath it.'

She thought he would come back at her with an argument, or plead with her to change her mind, but instead Aidan just leaned forward and pulled her into a hug, pressing her cheek against his chest and resting his stubbly chin on the top of her head. The feel of him, so firm and warm beneath his T-shirt, almost caused Holly's resolve to crumble like a broken biscuit, but she forced herself not to lift her head. If her mouth happened to find itself anywhere near his in that moment, she was pretty sure that there would be little if anything she would be able to do to stop it taking charge of the situation.

Aidan said something, but it was muffled by her hair. Holly pulled back and looked up at him questioningly.

'Under your skin?' he grinned. 'You make me sound like I'm Hannibal Lecter or something, woman.' Then, suddenly more serious, 'Do you think there will ever be a me and you?'

Holly looked at his tatty clothes, at the dark smear of grease on his shin and the scab on his knee. There were patches of peeling sunburnt skin in the crooks of his arms and an angry-looking pimple had started to emerge from the soft area around his nose. He looked so beautiful to her that she thought she might cry, so she made herself look away, up at the map he'd made for her – his map of her – and let her eyes find the little red heart he'd scribbled in biro.

'Oh, you know, maybe one day,' she said at last, grinning sideways at him and reaching for her empty glass. 'But for the time being, why don't we start with a glass of this very excellent wine?'

Holly and Aidan sat together in the little house on the hill in Zakynthos, oblivious to the late September sun slipping down behind the mountains and the moon rising up to take its place. The white-stone walls around them turned indigo as night fell and the stars took it in turns to twinkle, each one competing to shine the brightest.

If they'd stepped outside and looked up at the sparkling tapestry laid out above them, they would have been able to trace a map between the burning points, running their fingers north, east, south and west, discovering new ways to navigate from one star to the next. But there was no need. After a lifetime of searching, they had each found their way home.

Epilogue

The little girl fanned her dress out behind her carefully before sitting down on the sand. She'd picked a spot far enough back not to be in range of the waves, but she still let out an excited scream as a particularly big one stopped just short of her bare toes.

She'd usually be out on Granddad's boat at this time on a Sunday. They all went to his restaurant for a big lunch and then afterwards he would take her out on a little trip. Last week he'd taken her right round into the Blue Caves, where the water glowed from underneath the surface as if a secret fairyland existed just out of sight below the rocks. She hadn't told anyone about the fairies, of course. If you talk about fairies they stop being real, everyone knows that.

She picked up a stick that had been washed on shore and wrote her name in the damp sand. The sun chose that moment to pop out from where he'd been hiding behind a cloud and the light streaked through the lace overlay of her dress, dropping yellow speckles across her legs and arms. Mummy had made this dress for her. She made most of her clothes, in fact, but this dress was extra special. Granddad had given Mummy some lace that had belonged to his own mother to make it, so it must be very special indeed.

Looking out across the water, her eyes settled as they always did on her favourite place: Turtle Island. Sometimes she pretended she was the queen of that island; that it belonged to her and she got to pick who was allowed to visit. Mummy and Daddy, of course, would have to be first on her list, but she also wanted Maria to come as well, and Granny and Granddad and Auntie Clara. Auntie Aliana was also on the list, but she would have to leave behind whatever horrible man she'd brought with her. The last one who came with her had bad breath and snored even louder than Phelan. She'd probably let Kostas come, if he could get a day off from the shop, and Annie could come too — but only if she brought Lexi so that Phelan had someone to play with. Then all her friends from school, not to mention Nikos and that funny man Alix — it would end up being quite crowded, but she didn't want to leave anyone behind.

She could hear her mum calling her from the front steps of the taverna and reluctantly dragged her eyes away from her turtle-shaped kingdom. It would still be here tomorrow, after all, and it wasn't every day that she got to be a bridesmaid.

As she ran up the beach with the skirt of her dress flapping and her dark curls lifting in the light summer breeze, a wave made it right up to the tiny dent she'd left in the sand and washed over the words she'd left there. It only took a few seconds for 'Jennifer Savannah Flynn' to vanish, but, like so many before her who had left their mark on the island, a little piece of her would always be there.

Acknowledgements

Oh my gawd – I wrote a book and it got published and everything! Thank you so much for reading it, dearest reader. I really hope you enjoyed it. Please do come and chat to me about it on Twitter @Isabelle_Broom – I would love that.

I must start by saying an absolutely huge thank you to the brilliant and beautiful Hannah Ferguson, who has been making all my dreams come true from the moment she became my agent. She and the team at Hardman & Swainson and the Marsh Agency have been so professional, supportive and legendary since Day One, and I have nothing but love and admiration for all of them.

To Kimberley Atkins, my extraordinarily talented and utterly brilliant editor at Penguin Michael Joseph, if I could get the entire cast of Disneyland to stand in a line and sing you a huge thank you, then I would. This is a poor second, but I hope you know how much I love and respect you. Thank you for taking this book and turning it into something I can be truly proud of – you are a marvel. To the great Maxine Hitchcock, the awe-inspiring Francesca Russell, the fabulous Sarah Bance, the dazzling Emma Brown and the entire team over at Penguin Michael Joseph, you are all superstars. Thank you so much. And a big fist-pump to Jess Hart, who designed the eye-wateringly beautiful cover of this book – you are a genius of unparalleled brilliance.

My journey into the publishing world really began to gather steam over two years ago, when I won a competition with a short story entitled 'The Wedding Speech'. During that time I was lucky enough to get some amazing advice from Clare Hey, Sara-Jane Virtue, Lizzy Kremer and Milly Johnson, who are all so talented and so lovely. Your kind words helped me take the leap into proper novel writing, and this book would not be here without you.

It's no myth that writing folk are the very best of people, and I'd like to send out very special love and thanks to Hannah Beckerman, Lucy Robinson, Giovanna Fletcher, Paige Toon, Ali Harris, Stella Newman, Katie Marsh, Lindsey Kelk, Cecelia Ahern, Jane Fallon, Jo Thomas, Kirsty Greenwood, Cesca Major, Harriet Evans, Cressida McLaughlin, Nikki Owen, Eleanor Moran, Adele Parks, Tasmina Perry, David Whitehouse, Jo Carnegie, Jennifer Barclay, Lisa Dickenson, Peter James, Ben Willis, Sam Eades, Nina Pottell, Georgina Moore, Fran Gough, Lizzie Masters, Elaine Egan, Sophie Ransom and Tess Henderson. Thank you for all the laughs, advice and support, you gorgeous bunch.

To the team at *heat* magazine – you guys have always had my back and I love you all very much. Thanks for making me laugh every single day without fail.

I'm very lucky to be friends with some of the most awesome people on the planet. Massive thanks to Sadie Davies, Ian Lawton, Ewan Bishop, Tom Harding, Corrie Heale, Jamie Green, Alex Holbrook, Becky Bachelor, Dominic Morgan, Vicky Zimmerman, Rosie Walsh, Tamsin Carroll, Ranjit Dhillon, Gemma Courage, Sarah Beddingfield, Chad Higgins, Colette Berry, Jim Morris, Sue Pigott, Kostas Kapsaskis and Molly Haynes for all your words of wisdom, continuing love and eagerness to drink booze with me. Thanks to John Richardson for your support and encouragement when I was writing this book, and mega-thanks to my Running Club buddies Mark Tamsett and Lindsay Perkins – you keep me sane through the madness. Hard to believe, but true. And to my Zakynthos family – you are all nutters, but I love you. I hope you agree that I've done our little rock proud.

To my family, you are all nutters too – especially the dog contingent – but I wouldn't have you any other way. Thank you for all the love and support, and for catching me every time I fall. Mum, I could list all the very best words in the world here, but they'd never be enough to tell you how amazing you are. Thank you for everything – I love you. Always.

Look out for the new novel
by Isabelle Broom
– *arriving November 2016*

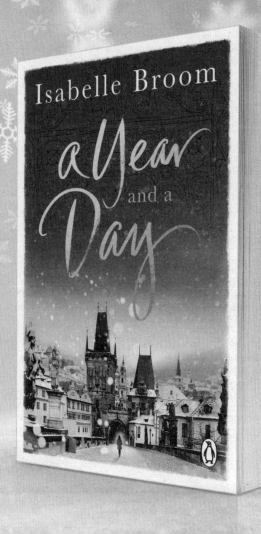

He just wanted a decent book to read ...

Not too much to ask, is it? It was in 1935 when Allen Lane, Managing Director of Bodley Head Publishers, stood on a platform at Exeter railway station looking for something good to read on his journey back to London. His choice was limited to popular magazines and poor-quality paperbacks – the same choice faced every day by the vast majority of readers, few of whom could afford hardbacks. Lane's disappointment and subsequent anger at the range of books generally available led him to found a company – and change the world.

'We believed in the existence in this country of a vast reading public for intelligent books at a low price, and staked everything on it'
Sir Allen Lane, 1902–1970, founder of Penguin Books

The quality paperback had arrived – and not just in bookshops. Lane was adamant that his Penguins should appear in chain stores and tobacconists, and should cost no more than a packet of cigarettes.

Reading habits (and cigarette prices) have changed since 1935, but Penguin still believes in publishing the best books for everybody to enjoy. We still believe that good design costs no more than bad design, and we still believe that quality books published passionately and responsibly make the world a better place.

So wherever you see the little bird – whether it's on a piece of prize-winning literary fiction or a celebrity autobiography, political tour de force or historical masterpiece, a serial-killer thriller, reference book, world classic or a piece of pure escapism – you can bet that it represents the very best that the genre has to offer.

Whatever you like to read – trust Penguin.